MY DAD
WROTE A

This book contains adult content and is not suitable for those under the age of 18

First published in Great Britain in 2016 by

Quercus Editions Ltd
Carmelite House
50 Victoria Embankment
London EC4Y 0DZ

An Hachette UK company

A CIP catalogue record for this book is available
from the British Library

HB ISBN 9781786483478
TPB ISBN 9781786483485
Ebook ISBN 9781786483492

10 9 8 7 6 5 4 3 2 1

Design by Carrdesignstudio.com
Illustrations by Amber Anderson

Printed and bound in Great Britain by Clays Ltd. St Ives plc

MY DAD WROTE A *Porno*

THE FULLY ANNOTATED EDITION OF
Belinda Blinked 1

JAMIE MORTON, JAMES COOPER,
ALICE LEVINE AND
ROCKY FLINTSTONE

Quercus

Thanks to the Belinkers for making this happen.
Thanks to Mum for letting this happen.

Foreword

Fathers and sons. It's a complicated relationship. Oedipus and Laius. Darth Vader and Luke Skywalker. Jesus and God.

But those guys don't have shit on me.

When my own sixty-year-old father, with a devilish sparkle in his eye, informed me he'd written his first novel, little did I know my life would change forever. In my naivety I was encouraging, supportive, even proud.

What an idiot.

From the moment my eyes scanned the first sentence it became instantly clear this was no swashbuckling tale of pirates on the high seas, no espionage spy series with gadgets and cars.

This was porn.

Well, erotica to be fair to him. But the sexual fantasies of the man who took you fishing and shares a bed with your mother isn't something you want to engage in. Ever. I slammed the laptop shut, unsure if I could ever un-see the first chapter.

My childhood died that day. Death by dad-porn. My world was in freefall and it wasn't long before the five stages of grief visited me in turn:

DENIAL

It couldn't be true. *Belinda Blinked 1* had to be a joke. The man's a retired builder from Northern Ireland for God's sake. He has as much knowledge of porn as Mary Berry. Just because he's heard of *Fifty Colours of Grey* (as he calls it) doesn't mean he's the heir to E. L. James. I've been to Wimbledon; it doesn't make me Rafael Nadal.

ANGER

How could he do this to me? To my sisters. To my mum. Granted, he'd adopted a creative pen name. But how far could Rocky Flintstone really protect us from the ridicule of the world? A pseudonym does little to numb the pain of having a porn baron for a father, believe me.

BARGAINING

It's not too late – I can reason with him. As fun as this undoubtedly was, he must realize the damage his randy ramblings could do – divorce rates are soaring as it is. But perhaps a more pressing concern is why the pots and pans industry?! Is that really the best setting for a steamy tale of sex and 'dripping passion'? Vom.

DEPRESSION

He's self-published it on Amazon. Great. It's real now. And anyone can find it courtesy of the three Google tags he's employed: erotica, lesbian, and business & leadership. So it's both a carnal caper and business studies manual?! Hysterical in one breath, tragic in the other. I just can't shake the deep-rooted despair churning my stomach daily. Why? Just why?

ACCEPTANCE

OK, so he's written a porno. So what? Man up, Jamie – you should read the bloody thing before you judge it. It might be good? It might be . . . sexy.

But I can't read it alone. No, that would be just too weird. There's safety in numbers and so in a vague attempt at retaining my sanity I roped in my mates James and Alice to share the burden with me. We braced ourselves, we bulk-bought beer and together we tentatively dipped our toes into the devilish mind of my, ever so slightly, perverted father.

And what a mind.

From the word go, as you're about to discover, we knew we had stumbled upon a gold mine of literary shambolics. This was no Jilly Cooper. This was better. The grammar, the lexicon, the boldness with which Flintstone pushes the boundaries of conventional syntax is revolutionary.

And the sex. This is imagery the likes of which you've never heard. And for good reason. Honestly, if I didn't exist I'd question whether my dad had ever even had sex.

And what of our protagonist? The titular character herself, Belinda Blumenthal. She's a results-driven businesswoman with a penchant for unorthodox tactics with which to secure her 'deals'. She'll literally do anything to sign a client. Imagine a woman with the determination of Hillary Clinton, the business acumen of Karen Brady and the sexual appetite of Jenna Jameson.

That's our Belinda. One of the greatest heroines in English literature.

I bet you can hardly contain your excitement. And a good thing too, because we've reached the moment. It's time. Strap yourself in, charge your glasses and prepare to enter the world of *Belinda Blinked 1*, my dad's smutty work of genius. Enjoy.*

Jamie

*If that's in any way possible.

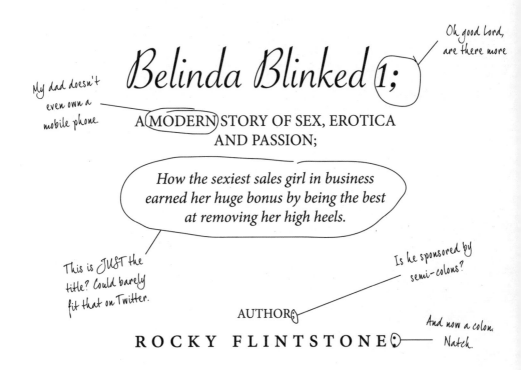

Belinda Blinked 1;

Oh good lord, are there more

My dad doesn't even own a mobile phone.

A MODERN STORY OF SEX, EROTICA
AND PASSION;

How the sexiest sales girl in business
earned her huge bonus by being the best
at removing her high heels.

This is JUST the title? Could barely fit that on Twitter.

Is he sponsored by semi-colons?

AUTHOR

ROCKY FLINTSTONE

And now a colon. Natch.

Chapters;

Language Alert!

Dreams are a popular motif in literature, from *The Iliad* to *Wuthering Heights*.

However, here Flintstone explicitly reveals this was not a dream. Therefore negating any such allusion to Bronte or Homer.

Brassiere (n) Early 20th century: from French brassière, literally 'bodice or child's vest'.

Basically he wants her in a posh bra.

This is classic dad - he's obsessed with inanimate objects when he's trying to turn people on.
Who cares about the coat racks?

Chapter 1;

The Job Interview;

Drink! (See page 207 for the official drinking game rules)

(Belinda blinked,) it wasn't a dream, the job interviewer had just asked her to remove her jacket and silk blouse. The Managing Director across the desk who had innocently brought her through from reception smiled and nodded at her. Slowly with the hint of a tease, Belinda removed the two garments. Her black brassiere was doing (overtime) to contain her full breasts, she had worn this one for today as it was tight fitting on purpose… she never thought it would be exposed in such a simple way.

Even her tits are business minded

The MD got up and took her blouse and jacket. He hung them onto one of (two elegant wooden coat racks) in the corner and sat back down. What next Belinda thought?

The interviewer resumed his questioning of her CV and after about five minutes, asked her to remove her knee length skirt. Belinda stood up, removed the offending garment and passed it with some (surprise) to the MD.

Surprise? Why, she's removed everything else!

Can I please take this opportunity to apologise. To everyone.

Cultural Context

The word is considered vulgar slang and often derogatory. Use of the word 'pussy' was brought to mainstream prominence in the seminal works of 1990s rappers, whose oeuvres Flintstone is clearly referencing.

Because her socks have gone.

So, she's as surprised at getting the job as she is when she's asked to remove her skirt?

Cultural Context

In 2016 the average salary for an International Sales Director was £43,962 per annum. The role at Steele's is inexplicably double that figure. Together with a company car, Belinda has sewn up a six figure salary.

Dad, little tip – no woman wants their breasts to nosedive to their knees.

Clearly — anyone who gets naked in a job interview is pure class.

Underneath she was wearing a skimpy black thong and sexy black stockings which she didn't apologize for; after all she was an upmarket woman. She sat down again and crossed her long legs. She knew they looked good, but she really felt she wanted to keep her private pussy area hidden. Belinda leaned back on the white leather seat and started to gently sweat.

Erotic. There's nothing sexier than a sweaty lady.

After a further ten minutes of questioning the MD got up and walked round to Belinda, he gently pulled her stockings down to her ankles. He removed her bright red high heels and stuffed the stockings inside them. They were placed under the coat rack by the interviewer. Belinda was now feeling exposed, with only a bra and thong left, she thought total nakedness was not far away, and then what?

— Her skin?!

The MD then surprised her by saying they wanted to offer her the job as their Sales Director today on completion of a few further details. Belinda was surprised as the job was worth £85,000 a year plus car and all the travel perks, so she nodded her head. With her agreement given the MD walked behind her and unhooked the tight black bra in a rapid movement, Belinda's breasts plunged to freedom and her nipples immediately stood to attention.

Wait, she agreed to the job not stripping.

The MD sat down and appraised her, whilst the interviewer calmly asked her to stand up and remove her thong. Her shaven pussy was revealed with just a delicate runway of dark pubic hair guiding any viewer to the top of her vagina.

If you need guiding there you've already gone wrong.

I've never thought of a vagina as a Tupperware box.

Language Alert!

Runnel (n) late 16th century (denoting a brook or rill), variant of dialect 'rindle', influenced by the verb 'run'. *Or could just be a typo . . .*

How is HR in the room? Starting the petition to get Bill fired immediately.

Talking point

Notice that this is the first time in the novel that Belinda speaks. What does Flintstone's choice of dialogue say about her character?

How is Bill not fired yet?

Oh. Holy. Jesus.

'Now sit down and relax Miss Blumenthal.' said the interviewer. 'In fact, just spread your legs wide so we can get a good look at your internal attributes.'

Belinda lay back in the leather chair and spread her legs wide as requested. Her vaginal lids popped open and her labial pinkness was there for them to assess. She quickly became moist and a runnel of liquid trickled down her left lower thigh.

What a great time for introductions! She's starkers and now he reveals his name.

The MD then said, 'My name is Tony, and you will report directly to me. Bill here is our Human Resources Director and he's available to you at all times. You might need him as you have a direct staff of 28, some of whom may need fucking off!

Belinda nodded and asked, which, was to her the obvious question, 'When are you guys going to fuck me?' Tony quickly replied, 'Well, Bill here never will as it's not in his area of responsibility and I might, depending on how hard you work for me. But let's get to the point Belinda, the reason we've put you through this scenario is to ensure your positive reaction to certain members of our customer base who will definitely try you out. So I have to ask you here and now, does this give you any problems?'

Belinda blinked, shook her head and said, 'As long as I have your and the companies backing I will do whatever is necessary to make the sales happen.'

Why do I have a feeling this won't just be her working weekends and taking some paperwork home?

Cultural Context

Etiquette between colleagues varies vastly from culture to culture. The French favour *faire la bise,* or exchanging kisses on both cheeks. The Japanese exercise *eshaku,* a fifteen-degree 'greeting' bow.

Giselle and Belinda have forgone convention and opted for the exchanging of fluids. Do you think this a portent for future relations?

I see Dad's misspent youth in the Scouts is rearing its head – be prepared

Language Alert

Here is another example of the Flintstonean vernacular. His penchant for the word 'deft' only draws into sharper focus his ungainly approach to writing.

'Well done Belinda.' said Tony as a large smile crossed his rugged features.

Yay, Bill's finally fucked off.

Tony then dismissed Bill and said to him as he left the room,

Literally NO ONE in pots and pans is called Giselle.

'Send in Giselle with the contract.'

Most awkward small talk ever – a few minutes?!

After a few minutes a 26 year old, stunningly attractive, blonde haired girl joined them with notebook and sheaf of papers in hand.

'Put the paperwork down Giselle and meet Belinda our new Sales Director.'

Giselle's not been brought up right.

Belinda stood up, still totally naked and shook Giselle's hand. In response Giselle held Belinda's face in her hand and kissed her fully square on her lips, Belinda instinctively opened her mouth and Giselle's tongue snaked in and they both shared the touching of ecstasy.

In no way sexy. All I see is Voldemort.

At that magical moment Giselle started to strip off. It didn't take long as she wasn't wearing any underwear and Belinda thought, this girl does this too often for it to be a once in a lifetime event. However Giselle was a magnificent creature, tits that were to die for and an ass that was so tight, even Belinda felt tested, though she was equal in every respect and in all truth felt she had better shaped boobs. With soft deft actions, she soon had Belinda gasping. Belinda could only respond by sucking Giselle's breasts and teething her nipples vigorously. Not a bad final interview for the job of her dreams.

Just enjoy the kiss. Why compare and contrast?

Stop body-shaming, Belinda.

CHARACTER PROFILE: Belinda Blumenthal

Belinda is the female lead: an open-minded woman who is quietly ambitious and meets her targets but uses unorthodox methods to get there. Her career is her main drive.

The world of Steele's Pots and Pans is delivered to us through her blinking eyes.

We meet the eponymous heroine at the apex of her hunt for a new job.

The reader is led to question her reason for seeking new employment.

Belinda's first appearance establishes her as passive, as well as snappily dressed. Though she seems demure and innocent in the initial paragraphs she is soon to be found revealing her 'vaginal lids'.

Though these submissive themes recur there are active verbs associated with Belinda, such as 'blinking', 'nodding' and 'removing [clothing]'. Dialogue is minimal for Blumenthal, her first line not appearing for nine paragraphs ('When are you guys going to fuck me?').

Belinda is refreshingly body confident; she 'doesn't apologize' for her sensuality and regards her figure as superior in many ways. Many people have hailed her as the ultimate modern woman.

She is clearly highly qualified as she has made it to the final round of interviews in a competitive market, and then manages to secure the 'job of her dreams'.

• **Physical Attribute:** Superior breasts to almost everyone

• **Dominant Character Trait:** Passivity and drive in equal measure

• **Unusual Skill:** Her sexual arsenal - which always seals the deal

• **Fun Fact:** She has no friends

KEY THEME: Pots and Pans

Through the fictional creation of Steele's, Flintstone has lifted the lid on an otherwise unexplored corporate world. As the first novel set in the pots and pans industry, *Belinda Blinked 1* grants us unprecedented access into the dark underbelly of kitchenware. Natural comparisons have been drawn between Jordan Belfort (*The Wolf of Wall Street*) and John Niven (*Kill Your Friends*) for their similar revelatory accounts of the trading and music industries.

KEY MOTIF: Blinking

Winking is traditionally the more provocative and sensual of the eye-closing actions. However, Rocky only realized this once *Belinda Blinked 1* was completed and he could not spare the time to amend every mention (he has since learned of the ctrl + f command). Thankfully he also quite liked the alliteration.

It is not the first time blinking has been misappropriated in literature. There is a theory that the first recorded appearance of the phrase 'in the blink of an eye', in the King James Bible, was originally intended to read 'in the twinkling of an eye'.

Blinking was also attractive to Flintstone as it can be interpreted in many ways. It can be a coquettish advance, a shocked wince or a confident acknowledgement of a done deal. Blinking also ensures a refreshed water supply to the eyes, protecting them from irritants.

Rocky uses Belinda's blinks to punctuate happenings as a very successful literary device. Her eyes almost take on their own persona, although their colour is never revealed.

✏ AUTHOR'S NOTE

Why did you choose the pots and pans industry as the business setting for your debut novel?

I've always respected the pots and pans trade. In my youth they went from house to house selling their wares . . . effectively tinkers. Door-to-door selling is a hard job and I respect that. In essence I wanted to pay homage to the pots and pans sector for the important but very much overlooked contribution they make to our society. If I'm completely honest, I am drawing on all my business experience; the series of novels are all based on events I happened across in my steamy sales world. Of course this is over a period of forty years; don't get the impression this sort of thing was happening to me every day . . . perhaps every other day.

As for Belinda, physically she's based on my hero Angie Harmon who plays Jane Rizzoli in the smash hit USA TV series *Rizzoli & Isles*. Belinda herself is truly fictional, but when I was a Ready Mixed Concrete Manager many years ago, we had some very attractive ladies call at the depot selling cleaning materials; they would show a bit of leg . . . and get the order. That was a while ago of course and I'm sure this practice doesn't happen today.

Stephen King, my writing inspiration, has always maintained 'write what you know about . . . and make the rest up'. Business, and especially the sales environment, was my best bet. That's why everything revolves around the world of business.

Rocky x

ACTIVITY – Using Synonyms

Rocky plays with interesting and colourful phraseology for the female anatomy.

Try to use one of the synonyms below in a sentence today.

E.g. 'Excuse me, can you stop staring at my _____. That's it. I'm calling the police.'

private pussy area	**vaginal lids**
internal attributes	**labial pinkness**

📖 Reading group discussion points

- Is Belinda a feminist?

- Discuss the strengths and weaknesses of Belinda's interview technique.

- How does Flintstone use the minutiae, e.g. "elegant wooden coat racks", to distract the reader from the less palatable aspects of the novel?

- Find 5 examples of breaches of HR protocol.

- Despite his only brief appearance in the chapter, most readers loathe Bill: discuss your thoughts.

- Which character holds the power in this scene?

- Giselle appears before the close of the chapter, what have we learned about her?

Language Alert

Pathetic fallacy is a commonly used literary device whereby the author attributes human emotion to nature, in this case weather.

Here Flintstone equates the ever aroused Belinda's nether regions to the rainy climate of Britain.

Cultural Context:

Tennis, croquet, and crown green bowls are among the most traditional upper-class pastimes in English society. Here Flintstone paints a picture of the chairman's event as a high-class affair, perfect for seducing prospective clients.

Not outraged? Not running to
Bill in HR? Not that he'd care.
God I hate Bill.

CHAPTER 2;

The Leather Room;

Thank goodness for the clarification that Friday is the day after Thursday.

Three weeks later Belinda had settled into most of the administration parts of the job, but was still to get to grips with the large customer base and her new sales force. It was a typical wet dismal Thursday afternoon at the office and tomorrow, Friday was her first Regional sales meeting where she would discuss sales with her four regional managers. The town hall clock had just chimed three when Giselle called her to Tony's office.

What weird French village is their office in?

'Afternoon Belinda.' said Tony, 'There's a very senior company event on Sunday at our chairman's country house, BBQ and all that. Wear tennis gear... very casual, no and I repeat no undergarments such as thongs or bra.'

Belinda looked up now intrigued. Tony smiled and said... 'You'll understand when you get there! I'll get Giselle to book you a room for Sunday night at the local hotel. It's called the Horse and Jockey. OK? It's probably best if you check in before you get to the old man's place.'

If she's actually going to play tennis I fear for her eyes.

With a secret door I see Dad's love of
James Bond is shining through… ———————

Belinda's always thinking
of the bottom line. ———————

It's the classic tale:
boy interviews girl.
Boy strips girl.
Girl gets job.
Boy ignores girl. ———————

Talking Point:

Professionalism is a running virtue in *Belinda Blinked 1*.
Note how often Flintstone uses proficiency in business as
a representation of a character's worth.

Belinda nodded, 'I can certainly rearrange my shopping trip to Saturday. Oh and I'll not bother purchasing any thongs or bras!' She smiled sweetly and Tony laughed.

Doesn't she own any already?

'Good, go through to my leather room whilst I get Giselle'. Tony opened what looked like a normal cupboard door in the corner of his office and switched on some delicate lighting. Belinda went in and the door shut behind her.

How can lighting be delicate?

'Wow!' she thought, Tony wasn't joking, this was her first visit to this part of the offices and the entire room including the floor was covered in exquisite leather tiles, they must have cost a fortune. There was no other furniture except an extremely sophisticated and expensive drinks cabinet in the corner.

I love that a drinks cabinet is more sophisticated than Belinda.

'What does he get up to in here?' she thought.

Sex, Belinda.

Belinda realized that she might find out sooner than she bargained for. Anyway, what did it matter, she had been surprised that he hadn't come onto her since that final interview. After all he was a good looking single guy and was very professional in his approach to the business. With his astute guidance she had successfully installed herself as Sales Director and was now preparing her strategy on some major accounts, again with his help.

Hang on, Giselle was twenty-six last chapter – this is like some shit GCSE maths problem. If Hardeep has twenty-four sweets in a bag and four of them are orange, and Jenny eats two of them, how old is Giselle?

Talking Point

Playwright Michael Shurtleff famously said 'conflict is what creates drama'. Here Flintstone stops any potential intrigue in its tracks. What does this do to raise or lower the stakes of the novel?

How are Giselle's nicotine-stained, grubby talons scratching at Belinda's breasts sexy?

Belinda thought about Giselle, she was probably Tony's preferred taste in women, five years younger than herself at 24, Giselle was blonde not dark like Belinda, She was Tony's PA and right hand man, foreign, of Dutch nationality, and probably the successor to Tony as MD in four or five years when Tony moved up in the company hierarchy. Belinda was not interested in becoming MD so no conflict would ever exist between her and Giselle. This was probably a good thing for her longevity with the outfit.

Like a budget Marilyn Monroe.

How small is this company? PA to MD in five years? That's quite the meteoric rise.

Belinda's thoughts were interrupted when the door opened and Giselle walked in.

Really? Plural?

'Hi Belinda, what do you think of his "fucking leather room"?'

Belinda smiled and said, 'I could do with a drink....'

Tell me about it.

Giselle walked over to the drinks cabinet, poured two stiff Gin and Tonics and started to stroke Belinda's tits with her long fingernails. Belinda felt herself respond and took a swift drink while she still could. Unasked she put her tongue into Giselle's mouth.

Unasked? Does Giselle require written permission?

'That tastes good' said Giselle as she removed Belinda's jacket and skirt. Belinda slipped the straps of Giselle's dress down her arms and in a swift movement removed the whole dress.

Dad's always been inspired by the 1980s tablecloth trick.

Cultural Context:

Occupations where undressing is integral to job efficiency include:

• Theatre dressers

• Triathletes

• Prostitutes

Sales Directors are not usually required to be adept in the removal of clothing at pace.

Language Alert:

Deft (a) Neatly skilful and quick in one's movements.

A Flintstone favourite. Keep a tally of every reference to this word throughout *Belinda Blinked 1*.

Cultural Contex:

Gwyneth Paltrow's popular lifestyle website Goop suggests women should indulge in a v-steam where a 'combination of infrared and mugwort steam cleanses your uterus, et al. It is an energetic release that balances female hormone levels.'

UP?! Where? Is she wearing her bra as shoulder pads?

'Very professional Belinda.' said Giselle as she again turned her attention to Belinda's tits. It only took Giselle a second to remove Belinda's satin blouse and push up her bra cups. Belinda's nipples started to swell in anticipation before Giselle's lips and teeth started to punish them.

Sounds like her nipples have gone into anaphylactic shock.

It took about as much time for Belinda to unhook Giselle's bra and then slip her knickers to the floor. Giselle deftly stepped out of them and kicked her heels to the side of the room.

'Lie down on the floor Belinda, and enjoy all that leather.' said the now completely naked Giselle.

Belinda did as she was told as well as pulling off her bra. Now stretched out on the floor with only her thong in place Belinda was game for anything… besides what else would she be doing on a wet Thursday afternoon, twelve hours before her first Regional Sales meeting?

God forbid her job.

claws

Giselle's ~~hands~~ soon made light work of Belinda's thong. The two girls started to excite each other and soon their respective vaginas were wet and steaming. They took it in turns to lick each other's clits and when Tony entered the room they were both ready for a bit of male interaction.

That phrase has never been written down EVER.

There's a joke to be made about discussing Tony's lunch box while Belinda tucks into her lunch box, but I'll leave that kind of thing to Dad ————————

How can a thong be wonky? Unless you've got a crooked arse crack of course. ————

Language Alert:

Typos are another key trait of the Flintstonean lexicon.

However, it can be argued that Flintstone's choice of spelling is deliberate, with it embodying the dizzy disorientation Belinda is experiencing in the moment.

Talking Point:

Belinda's breasts have been scratched, scraped and scored. Now red raw, an appropriate treatment would be the application of calamine lotion. Often prescribed for sunburn, insect stings and poison ivy contact it would protect Belinda's chest area from infection. Particularly if she develops weeping or oozing blisters.

Does that mean he was being enthusiastic or that he'd disappeared up there?!

However Tony had other ideas and just brushed Belinda's body with his hands feeling her responsive breasts and ass. His real objective was Giselle and pretty soon he was deeply into licking her pussy. Meanwhile Giselle was doing the same to Belinda so all in all everyone was getting satisfaction. After about fifteen minutes of this intense activity Belinda excused herself, gathered together her discarded clothes and let herself out of the leather room. Giselle and Tony stayed on for an extra session which Giselle would no doubt enlighten Belinda about at Friday lunch.

It's not a family meal. 'Please can I leave the table, Mum?'

Does anyone do ANY work?

Whilst starting to dress in Tony's office the main receptionist Bella walked in and caught Belinda naked adjusting her thong. 'Here, let me do that for you,' said Bella, 'I know how important it is to achieve a straight line with a thong'... look at mine.' Bella hitched up her dress and revealed an even more skimpy thong than Belinda was wearing. Belinda stroked Bella's ass in appreciation and thought the obvious... not another one! What is this office running on... high powered sexual adrenelin?

A handshake would suffice.

Bella turned round and caressed Belinda's substantial tits which were still suffering from Giselle's attentions. Belinda responded by putting her hand between Bella's legs, pushing Bella's thong to one side so she could finger her clit. Bella groaned and started kissing Belinda's mouth.

I can't believe my dad has written 'finger her clit'.

'Help me dress' gasped Belinda, not wanting to be discovered by Tony and Giselle exiting the leather room, which Bella had probably no idea existed.

That's the second time she's pissed on the parade today.

How dumb is Bella if she doesn't?

Lest we forget, they
don't even know each
other's names.

It's just been available twice. And she didn't
'take it in good stead' either time.

I love that going home is her
favourite part of the job.

22

Bella took the hint and calmed down, taking inordinate pleasure in placing Belinda's bra and stockings onto her smooth body.

'Let's do this again and in private.' said Belinda. Bella nodded whilst straightening Belinda's thong for the last time and picked up the *It's not a tie.* correspondence she had gone to Tony's office to collect for the last post.

Finally a worker bee.

'I'll hold you to that Belinda,' said Bella, 'My place next Friday evening, say 9.00pm.'

'It's a date!' Belinda replied, wondering how she'd have the sexual strength to get through the next week, but instinctively she knew if sex was made available then she'd take it all in good stead.

Belinda went to her office and picked up her briefcase. On the desk was an agenda with client attendance details of the Sunday bash at the Chairman's house. It would make interesting reading that night when she got back to her apartment as well as the final preparations for her Regional Sales Manager meeting in the morning. Outside in the car park Belinda jumped into her two week old Mercedes coupe. Swish and expensive, Belinda so loved this part of the job. She gunned the engine and drove the twenty minutes to her new central London apartment.

Clearly just for show.

Probably more interesting than this chapter.

WHERE THE HELL IS THIS?

CHARACTER PROFILE: Giselle

Giselle is the PA of Steele's Pots and Pans and Tony's right-hand man in more ways than one. Indeed she is embroiled in an ambiguous affair with her boss, though they are yet to formally label their relationship.

Stunningly attractive with hair as yellow as the sun and an ass so tight it tests even the lithest of colleagues, Giselle is a Dutch beauty. Young at only twenty-six or twenty-four, she is keen to avoid being tied down and is game for anything.

Despite her demure appearance, she harbours a steely determination befitting the namesake of her parent company. Her ambition knows no bounds and her sparkling blue eyes are firmly set on becoming Tony's successor in a mere five years' time. She infuses every action with purpose and drive as razor-sharp as her impossibly long fingernails.

Paradoxically she is never happier than when she is shunning her workload and engaging in illicit sexual liaisons, be it in broad view of the wider office or in a shrouded 'fucking leather room'. She'll relish any opportunity to show off her very tight posterior and attractive breasts, though they're inferior to Belinda's in shape.

• **Physical Attribute:** Long finger nails

• **Dominant Character Trait:** Ferociously ambitious

• **Unusual Skill:** Getting marks out of leather

• **Fun Fact:** She's sleeping with the boss

KEY THEME:
Interior Design, the Role of Leather

For centuries leather has been entrenched in the erotic milieu. From the whips and bondage collars of BDSM, to the jackets donned by the T-Birds in *Grease*, cowhide has aroused generations.

However, its prominence in interior design is less celebrated. Leather has featured in many buildings, often serving as the bridge between class and smut. The House of Commons, the lower house of the UK Parliament, boasts 427 green-leather seats on either side of the chamber and the Batcave enjoyed a padded leather wardrobe in the 1997 bomb *Batman and Robin*. The leather room in *Belinda Blinked 1* is widely believed to be the first and only depiction of an entirely leather-lined room.

Leather experienced a sexual renaissance in the 1970s when the LGBT community embraced the fabric. The inaugural Easter Fetish Week in Berlin served as Europe's biggest gay fetish event and today leather culture is most prominent in and associated with gay communities. It is unclear if Flintstone is conversant with this particular subculture.

AUTHOR'S NOTE

Why did you decide to create a leather room in the Steele's office?

I've always loved leather: beautiful to touch, divine to smell. Someday someone's going to make a lovely female thong out of it with Belinda Blinked printed on it. Besides, it's great on car steering wheels . . . gives fantastic grip, so golfers adore it. It's also waterproof, which makes it ideal for sexual play, such as dildos.

Rocky x

ACTIVITY

Elect three people to engage in a fictitious threesome.

Designate one as 'the dominant force', one as 'the scratcher' and one as 'the most likely to excuse themselves before reaching climax'.

📖 Reading group discussion points

- What are the potential risks of an askew thong?

- Steele's Pots and Pans is based near a town hall clock twenty minutes from central London. Can you pinpoint the location of the office?

- It is suggested that Belinda is a little threatened by Giselle in this chapter. Do you think her anxieties are justified?

- As a group discuss what scenarios could result from a steaming vagina.

- Is Belinda a lesbian? Debate arguments for and against.

Probably?? It either is or it isn't, Dad. You're the author – you tell us...

Can ANYONE understand this sentence? Answers on a postcard

Talking Point:

Many well-known businessmen and women have famous mantras that define them. One of Richard Branson's favourite phrases is 'Screw It, Let's Do It'. 'Done is better than perfect' is the mantra of Facebook COO Sheryl Sandberg, and Coco Chanel is well known for her motto 'Keep your heels, head and your standards high'. Interestingly, all of these could be applied to Belinda's approach to her sex life.

CHAPTER 3

The Regional Sales Meeting;

Belinda had an early breakfast and was in the office for 07.30am. This was probably a pretty important day for her as it would be the first time she would meet her UK senior sales management, in other words the people who reported to her in business terms. She had no particular views… just lots of third party information about the performance and caliber of these four managers. There were also twenty or so salesmen who reported to them on the ground and she had fairly, or unfairly, pessimistic thoughts about how the whole sales organization was performing.

No surprise there. She's the most passive woman in the pots and pans industry.

But in sales you can always be surprised, especially when you talked to people in confidence and got them on board… to accept your way of doing things. Belinda was good at this, and Tony knew it… this was probably one of the many reasons he had hired her. There was no major desire in Tony's business plan to sack all the sales force and bring in new people… develop what we have was his mantra.

And the fact she got butt naked in the job interview might have tipped the balance…

Laughed heartily at 'cost centre'?!
Gotta get the laughs where you can
find them, I suppose.

Basically if they've got a pulse, they can keep their job.

Belinda had already thrashed out a strategy with Tony in her first three weeks of induction to the company... it was simple, if the salesmen and sales managers show any (sign of performance then keep them.) If not, bite the bullet and dispose. Belinda was tough but not mercenary and she would use all her talents to make the existing sales team work. She just wondered how far she would have to go to get them onside.— *Very, very far.*

Can't get a taxi from Heathrow?! You should be fired.

Nine-o-clock came and Bella rang her from reception to say the two northerly Regional managers wanted a lift from Heathrow as they (couldn't get a taxi to take them to the offices.) Classic, Belinda thought, the company locates near Heathrow and you can't get a taxi between the two places as the taxi fare is too low! Belinda picked up the phone to her Sales administration manager, Jim Thompson... her Mr. Fix It in the sales organization. 'Hi Jim, Belinda here, can you rescue my two Regional Sales Managers from the Airport?'

Belinda is the pool car of the pots and pans industry.

'Be delighted to Belinda, can I take the pool car?' replied Jim.

'Sure,' Belinda replied, 'Just put the cost centre to both of them!'

Jim (laughed heartily) and said, 'Will do!'

Anyone else think Dave Wilcox
cries during sex? —————————

Stop using his full name, Belinda
Blumenthal. —————————

Translation: Are you ready to get naked . . . with
your team . . . and your customers . . . for me? —————————

A knock on Belinda's door saw her London and Home Counties Regional Sales Manager stick his head around the door. 'Pardon the intrusion Ms. Blumenthal, but I'm Des Martin… you know, your London man.'

Belinda got up, 'Des! Great to meet you, grab a seat, we're just picking two of the guys up from Heathrow, which only leaves our man from the West to appear.'

'Ah, you mean Dave Wilcox from Bristol.' said Des.

'I certainly do.' replied Belinda as she sat down behind her desk. 'Oh by the way, call me Belinda from now on.'

'Will do Belinda.' replied Des confidently as he eyed her shapely legs and ass.

Belinda thought, 'I like you Des Martin, confident, sophisticated, good looking, but why the terrible sales performance?' She sighed and leaned back in her chair pushing forward her breasts. 'So Des are you prepared for today? Are you ready to expose yourself, your team and your client base to the new lady and master?'

She's sat down. How can he see her ass?

'Belinda,' said Des, 'If I'm honest it will be the first time anyone in this company has taken an interest in us salesmen instead of bypassing us with corporate deals done from head office over a bottle of whisky.'

Get the violins out, Des! Ever thought that YOU might be the problem?

This is the most Belinda has ever spoken and it's clunky at best. Is English her first language? I preferred it when she was mute.

LITERALLY. NO ONE. CARES.

We're halfway through the chapter and the meeting still hasn't started.

Talking Point – How To Do Business:

It is common knowledge that Flintstone intended this book to be both titillating and educational. He wanted it to be a manual on best practice in business. A key piece of advice he delivers is that impressive rooms for meetings are a must. However, as will become clear later, he goes on to suggest that the best way to negotiate large deals is to have sexual intercourse with potential customers. His methods are yet to be endorsed by the wider business world.

Cultural Context:

God's Own Country was initially used to describe the Wicklow Mountains in Ireland. It has also been used to refer to places in Surrey, Australia, United States, New Zealand, Kerala (India) . . . It is occasionally used to describe Yorkshire.

Belinda looked shocked, "Tell me you're joking… is this the real story I'm about to find out about today?"

'Put it this way,' said Des, 'you can't say I didn't warn you!' He also thought what a magnificent pair of tits, how long will it take me to get them into my hands and is my job worth it?

A second knock at her office door saw the Western Regional Sales Manager, Dave Wilcox, pop his head around. 'Hope I'm not late, but the traffic on the M4 was desperate!'

'Come on in Dave, I'm Belinda and very nice to meet you!'

Minutes later Jim Thompson rang and told Belinda the two other Regional Sales Managers would be in the car park in three minutes. 'Thanks Jim, get them up to the conference room ASAP and we'll get started for 10.00am.'

The conference room was upmarket, Tony liked to impress those customers who visited the offices and one of the best ways was decent meeting spaces. Jim quickly introduced Patrick O'Hamlin, the Scottish and Ireland Regional Sales Manager and Ken Dewsbury, Regional Sales manager for Central and North England. Both were like chalk and cheese… Patrick was a fast talking Irishman, originally born in Dublin, whilst Ken was from God's own country, South Yorkshire, and sported an accent to match.

Dad is already running out of clichés.

WHY. AM. I. STILL. READING???

Not sure why Dad's so obsessed with leather. I don't want to know.

This sounds like a rubbish wet T-shirt competition.

About as subtle as a brick through a window.

'My God,' thought Belinda, 'What a varied team, surely we can do something with this lot.'

Belinda called the meeting to a halt at noon. Patrick and Dave had each given their hourly presentation, though Belinda could have asked enough questions to extend their presentations to three hours each. However she knew she needed an overview, and the detail could come later in the field when she spent time with each manager individually. Lunch was a quick pint and sandwich in the local pub... The Bull in the Rushes, and as time was of the essence she felt she could only work a little bit of her female magic.

In the ladies toilets, Belinda removed her jacket, blouse and bra, she ran the cold tap and dabbed the water onto her nipples, making them stand to attention. 'That'll have to do for now she thought as she shoved her bra into her leather handbag. She put her blouse back on leaving three of the five buttons undone. She was now showing her cleavage big time and threw her jacket casually over her shoulder. The silken blouse quickly became transparent due to the water and clung longingly to her stunning breasts.

The blouse seems pretty pointless at this stage.

She walked back into the drinking area and observed the effect she had on her new sales team. Only two of her Managers immediately observed her subtle change of attire, and Belinda soon noticed some astute elbowing going around the team, accompanied with wry smiles from the Northerners. Jim was chuckling to himself as he was office based and had

Totally contradicts himself. I
thought Des had a terrible sales
performance? Classic Dad. ⎯⎯⎯⎯

Four hours, two locations
and no progress later, this
is STILL the meeting!

Bloody freeloaders ...

This company needs to inforce a confidentiality agreement.

heard the rumours put around by Bella and Giselle. Now he could believe them.

The afternoon sessions were equally as professional and Belinda was particularly impressed by Ken Dewsbury, the man showed wit, style and competence in that order. Des Martin was however a true pro, his London bearing and obvious sales talents indicated to Belinda that he was probably her first avenue to finding out how the individual members of the regional sales team ticked.

By the end of the meeting Belinda's blouse had dried out, but her lack of bra and hardened nipples chaffing continually against her tight blouse were still being noticed. Good she thought, let's see who has the guts to make the first move. In her short closing comments which wound down the business side of things, Belinda suggested they all adjourn to the Pentra Hotel which was beside Heathrow airport. That meant the two managers who were on evening flights to Leeds and Glasgow could get off easily and the rest of them could drive home after the rush hour traffic. *Is anyone still reading this??*

Belinda also decided to throw in a couple of wild cards so she asked Giselle and Bella if they would join her team for a couple of drinks on their way home. Both were as keen as mustard when they found out it was all on Belinda's expenses. Jim Thompson drove the three girls over to the Pentra where they met the Regional Sales Managers in the "Long bar" which

WTF does that phrase mean?

Is it school uniform? Why has everyone got a blazer on? And on a separate note, why will no one wear a bra?

Talking Point:

In groups try to make the sound of a 'quiet gasp of admiration'.

It's really not appropriate to wap your baps out in a hotel bar in the early evening.

overlooked the runway. It was now six o clock and the bar was filling up. Jim found seats at a table tucked away in the far corner of the room.

Belinda started the proceedings by taking off her jacket and downing her G&T in one. Bella followed and Giselle "accidently" spilt some of her drink over her blouse, which meant she had to go to the restroom to dry off. In fact, all that came off was her bra and like Belinda earlier that day, she was ready for action with a translucent white blouse and to die for nipples. Jim was on the ball and by the time Giselle had returned he had two replacement G&T's on the table. Bella by now had gathered the "drift" of the drinks session and decided to do her bit for team building. As she wasn't wearing a bra that day she coyly unbuttoned the top three of her blouse buttons and slowly removed her jacket.

Her cleavage was revealed and a quiet gasp of admiration went around the table. Giselle flicked some tonic water at Bella's nipples and soon achieved the desired result. 'Take it off Bella.' Des Martin whispered…'the tonic will stain your blouse… look at Belinda's and Giselle's already!'

Bella smiled and thought, 'Will I be the first? Surely Belinda can't as these guys report to her. Then in a quick movement Bella unbuttoned the rest of her blouse and let her magnificent breasts hang out for all to see.

Handwritten annotations:
At the same time? That's quite a party trick

Has Dad suddenly turned American?

No nipples are worth a human life.

Oh yeah, the TRANSPARENT tonic will stain her blouse.

41

Fell loose?! She's meant
to be twenty-nine!

Finally, he's decided
to abbreviate it.

Ken Dewsbury <u>choked over his pint of bitter</u> whilst the other three Regional Managers chanted quietly, 'Who's next! Who's next!' Belinda looked at Giselle who nodded and in a leisurely fashion with a big hint of tease unbuttoned the rest of her blouse. Her tits hung freely like pomegranates and she gently massaged them with her hands. 'Come on Belinda!' whispered Ken, ''Don't let the sales team down now!'

Dad clearly thought melons was too obvious and went for something a bit more . . . exotic.

Belinda smiled, and replied, 'I'll want a 10% increase in your sales next month Ken!'

'Done!' he replied.

Belinda slowly opened the remaining two buttons of her blouse, her tits fell loose, she took a drink and started to <u>massage her nipples with her fingertips</u>. The RSM's all clapped in admiration. Never had they had a sales meeting culminate like this one, things were looking up, and with three pairs of stunning breasts on show, they could do anything.

What, like browsing an old iPod?

A standing ovation seems a little OTT.

Jim Thompson went to get more drinks and the girls started to finger and discuss the merits of each other's nipples.

'Don't make us more jealous girls.' said Patrick O'Hamlin, 'but I've got a plane to catch!'

Feels like that
ship has sailed

Think this is one of the worst
sentences of the whole novel. One
of the characters isn't in the
book AND the pun is shit.

Talking Point – Who Is Donna?

Readers have always been confused by the sudden, unexplained
introduction of a new character here. It raises numerous
questions. Who is Donna? What makes her tick? Where has she
come from? Did Rocky just accidentally rename Bella briefly?

What a poetic turn of phrase.

'Me too!' said Ken Dewsbury. They both got up, shook everyone's hands and departed with much looking over their shoulders at the line up of tit available at the table. How they wished they both had the guts to finger those breasts. *Fingering? Like poking a jelly to see if it's set?*

The bar was now getting more crowded and Belinda thought it was sensible to button up their blouses, as they didn't want to get accused of being prostitutes. Des Martin and Dave Wilcox drank up, sadly said their goodbyes and disappeared out of the bar.

'Thanks Donna and Giselle you really helped me make a breast of it!' said Belinda laughing. 'One more drink and Jim will get us back to the office.' Jim went back to the bar ordered the drinks and paid the tab. The girls drank up slowly, reliving the looks on each of the Regional Managers faces when they showed them their breasts.

'That was interesting Belinda,' said Donna, 'Any more events like that for us?'

'Let's wait and see,' replied Belinda, 'Let's wait and see!'

I can hardly contain my excitement.

CHARACTER PROFILE:
The Regional Sales Managers

The Regional Sales Managers (or RSMs as Flintstone inconsistently refers to them) are Belinda's four-man team, overseeing the work of approximately twenty salesmen. As we meet the RSMs, sales at Steele's Pots and Pans are in dire straits. It's clear that these men have become far too safe and comfortable in their jobs, making them complacent and inefficient. Their inability to perform basic tasks like booking a taxi from the airport and arrive punctually for a meeting demonstrates this.

Belinda's key task is to reinvigorate the team and give them a new direction and strategy. Her approach seems flawed: keep the people who show 'any sign of performance'. Simply put, if they can send an email, they can keep their job.

Flintstone's choice of pedestrian names for the RSMs (Des, Dave, Ken, Patrick) reflects the mundanity of their jobs and everyday lives. This is further demonstrated in their almost primitive reaction to the 'line up of tit' at the Pentra – they clap and chant like cavemen.

The way Flintstone has drawn the dividing lines of each sales manager's area shows no regard for regional borders and there are some discrepancies between the size of each character's purview. For example, Des Martin is responsible for London and the Home Counties, while Patrick O'Hamlin oversees two entire nations, Scotland and Ireland.

📖 Reading group discussion points

- Have you ever struggled to get a taxi and why?

- Discuss Belinda's morale-boosting techniques. Is getting her breasts out an effective strategy to get the best from her team?

- Find the person with the most boring name in your group. How does it match their personality?

- Which RSM do you identify with most and why?

- Has anyone ever got your name wrong in the same way that Flintstone mistakes Bella for 'Donna'? How did it make you feel?

Le Creuset are clearly shitting themselves.

Language Alert:

The practice of sporting no undergarments or 'inner clothing' [sic] is referred to as 'going commando'.

Certain types of clothes, such as cycling shorts and kilts, are traditionally worn without underpants.

CHAPTER 4;

The Maze;

Not for me. This has taken forever.
Is it really only Chapter 4??

Saturday morning came all too quickly and was bright and breezy, but dry, ideal for a quick game of tennis and then later a spot of shopping and browsing through the cook shops of London's Oxford Street. Belinda thought it was important to not only know her own brand but also those of the opposition. That evening she planned to do an internet search on the guest list for tomorrow's function where she would be unable to wear bra or thong… definitely a strange request.

OK, Nana.

Sunday morning was warm so Belinda put the soft top down and motored over to Windsor. True to her instructions she checked into the Horse and Jockey and removed her inner clothing. Now dressed in only her tennis gear she drove to the Chairman's house. She parked next to Tony's car and jumped into his passenger seat.

Mercedes Coupes don't have soft tops… so…

Why does everyone inspect everything? What is he checking for? That they're good? That there's two?

Cultural Context:

Trellis (n) A framework of light wooden or metal bars used to support fruit trees or creepers.

Those of a larger girth could viably accommodate a Sales Director.

Cultural Context:

Police handcuffs are sometimes used in sexual play or BDSM. Use in this context is potentially unwise as they are not specifically designed for this purpose and wearers can suffer from nerve injury or 'handcuff neuropathy'.

Flintstone pre-empts readers' concerns by clarifying their toy classification.

'Good morning Tony.' Her tennis skirt had risen up to show the top of her thighs. Tony pulled it up at the front and studied her pussy. He then pulled up her tennis shirt and inspected her tits.

'Hi Belinda, good to see you're good to go, so lets quickly go through the guest list and discuss our targets with their potential. After we've done this we'll get some lunch and take up our positions.

Less sass from you, Blumenthal.   — *Drink!*

'So I can readjust my clothing Tony?' Belinda blinked. 'Or do you want me to parade to lunch like this?'

Forty minutes later after some food and two strong gin and tonics, Tony took her to a medium sized garden maze located at the rear of the property. They entered the tall undergrowth and Tony led her through it without a pause. Belinda was glad someone knew their way through the myriad of paths and openings. After three minutes they entered a glade which was obviously the central point of the maze. He pushed Belinda's back onto a flimsy wooden trellis, gave her a quick kiss and attached her arms to the trellis with a set of red plastic handcuffs attached to a length of parcel string. Belinda was now thoroughly intrigued and a little excited at what was about to happen and laughed out loud, 'Tony, how did you know my favourite handcuff colour was red? Seriously though, I've not seen a pair of these since my days in Kindergarten!'

She's being trussed up like a spatchcock hen!

Who has a favourite handcuff colour?

When does anyone ever play with handcuffs at nursery?!

Is this the same as 'whetting her appetite'?

It's parcel string and plastic - my ninety-year-old grandma could break free.

Talking Point:

Whistling can connote many moods, from ominous in the iconic scene from *Kill Bill* to defiant pride in *The Bridge Over the River Kwai*. What mood is Alfonse's whistling intended to create?

Cultural Context:

The glades of fairytales are magical places filled with mythical creatures, from pixies and fawns to centaurs and unicorns.

As a jagged anticlimax, Rocky Flintstone places only Belinda Blumenthal in his.

So creepy.

Tony smiled as he backed away from Belinda.

'Tony… what's going on?' said Belinda now seriously trying to control her amusement.

'Trust me Belinda, treat your clients well and let's see the business roll in. I'll return and "release" you in under two hours. Keep your chin up and let your tits and clit do the talking!' With these erotic words ringing in her ears, Tony walked off. *FUCKING. HELL.*

The grass underfoot felt wet and Belinda could hear a sprinkler nearby which kept wetting her ankles, the area of wet grass would soon become a mud patch she thought… how disgusting. She hated mud at the best of times, but tied to this garden fence meant she couldn't move around… much, it would soon get really muddy and quickly.

Those tennis whites are gonna need to go on a hot wash for more than one reason.

Her thoughts were interrupted by the sound of cheerful whistling coming down the maze. Ahh, here's my first client she thought.

Not so much a name as a collection of letters.

Alfonse Stirbacker from Belgium strolled into the glade and studied Belinda's position with obvious interest. From Tony's outline and her internet research, Belinda recognized him and his potential immediately… over 300 supermarket outlets throughout Belgium, Northern France and Southern Holland and they were soon to push into the UK.

'A good start.' she thought.

CHARACTER PROFILE: Tony

Tony is MD at Steele's Pots and Pans and one of the first characters we meet. His rugged features make him the focus of much sexual attention from the ladies of the office.

His number-one key to success is premium meeting spaces, and at great cost to the company he installed a room decked out entirely in leather tiles. He uses this much like a prayer room at an airport – for moments of deep contemplation and seducing his PA.

The stripping of Belinda, his interviewee in Chapter 1, can only lead us to believe that he has scant respect for HR directives. Put simply, he's a renegade with a powerful penchant for breasts and vaginas which he often indulges.

• **Physical Attribute:** Rugged features

• **Dominant Character Trait:** Risk-taker

• **Unusual Skill:** Ability to manage Belinda Blumenthal

• **Fun Fact:** Only has sex on leather

ACTIVITY

In this chapter Belinda is liberated by her lack of underwear. Put yourself in her shoes and remove your 'inner clothing' for the rest of the day. How does this lack of bra and/or thong make you feel? What are the limitations and benefits?

🔑 KEY THEME: Horticulture, the Greatest Mazes of the World

The maze can be read as a metaphor for Belinda's labyrinthine sex life – a series of dead ends, wrong turns and bad decisions. Flintstone himself has gone on record to state he found inspiration in the oldest hedge maze in Britain: Hampton Court Maze. Built in 1689 during the time of William of Orange, several other works of literature over the generations have incorporated its corridors and passages.

However, the world's longest maze is at the Dole Plantation on Oahu, Hawaii, and is made up of nearly 12,000 tropical native plants. Dole has not only created the largest maze on earth; the company also offers a virtual version so you can try your navigation skills from the comfort of your laptop.

Flintstone had the opportunity in this work of fiction to compete and create a magical never-ending warren of walkways. Instead he opted for an unremarkable 'medium-sized maze'.

✏️ AUTHOR'S NOTE

Why did you choose to dress Belinda in tennis wear?

All white tennis wear on a woman is a total turn-on, perhaps that's why I like Wimbledon so much. A crisp white short-sleeved shirt with short shorts is close to a uniform but still not quite that. It makes a statement shouting 'Watch me, I'm professional – give me the respect I deserve.'

Rocky x

This chapter finds Belinda tied to a trellis in a medium-sized maze.
Help each of the three potential clients find their route to our
horny heroine and her handcuffs.

✎ LANGUAGE ALERT
Vaginal Personification

The 'talking vagina' is a significant tradition in literature and art, perhaps most prominent as the central trope of *The Vagina Monologues*. In the 'let your tits and clit do the talking' passage of *Belinda Blinked 1* Flintstone's fascination with this theme is brought to the fore. Belinda herself is essentially a mute, but her clitoris is highly talkative. Another tradition is a vagina that acquires the power of speech to play the role of informant, revealing a lover's previous sexual history. We assume the author has avoided this incarnation as in the case of Belinda it would require a much longer novel.

📖 Reading group discussion points

- In what setting is it appropriate to study your colleague's pussy?

- Discuss the best ways to track your route through a maze.

- What does your favourite handcuff colour say about you?

- There are several health and beauty benefits to mud. List three.

- Have you ever been attached to a piece of garden equipment? What were the emotions connected to the event?

Talking Point:

We have seen Belinda impressing in the business environment – acing her initial interview and asserting herself with the RSMs – but this is a turning point in the book. We finally get to see Belinda in her natural habitat: using her substantial arsenal to woo clients.

Is she saying this to Alfonse? What's dialogue and what's not? This is chaos.

Language Alert:

The reader may have noticed discrepancies in the spelling of the company name. Sometimes with an 's', a possessive 's' or sometimes with no 's' at all.

This is symptomatic of the writer's quick and loose form.

She is the least enigmatic character ever written.

CHAPTER 5

The First Client; Alfonse Stirbacker

How old is Alfonse?

'Good afternoon young lady, and who do I have the pleasure of meeting, albeit in this strange situation?'

Thank fuck someone is addressing the elephant in the room.

'Hi Mr Stirbacker, my name is Belinda Blumenthal and I'm the Sales Director of Steele Pots and Pans. She always felt she should apologise for the terrible company name, but she also knew it was so awful that very few people ever forgot it.

I wish I could forget this book.

Stirbacker replied, 'Excellent, you look like my type of girl… young, dark and mysterious! As you know my name you will also know I am the purchasing director of my company. Let's get to know each other, we have only 20 minutes contact, and I intend to make full use of them.

It's not a prison visit.

Cultural Context:

The author is known to have met an 'Alfonse' in South America who was from the Belgian Congo. He had lots of money, was really good company and was a pretty good cook. He never met his wife.

Speculation is rife that he informed the character of Alfonse Stirbacker who we meet here in Chapter 5.

Language Alert:

Alfonse uses 'lady' and 'girl' to address Belinda; she uses 'gentleman' for him – what does this tell us about their relationship?

Cultural Context:

Here Flintstone harks back to the popular 'Pool Rules' posters of the 1970s and 1980s, which outlined the sanctions on swimming etiquette.

Controversially, running, ducking, bombing and shouting were all banned during this era, but it was the clamping down on 'heavy petting' that Flintstone never forgot.

Language Alert:

People often confuse the vulva with the vagina. The vagina, also known as the birth canal, is internal. The vulva, however, consists of the external genital organs of a woman. It is quite possible Flintstone believes these terms can be used interchangeably.

Alfonse immediately got to work by removing his one garment of a black thong and taking off Belinda's shoes and socks. Completely naked he pushed up her white shirt partially uncovering her breasts. He then pulled her tennis skirt down to her knees and backed off. How strange Belinda thought… he's just a voyeur… he doesn't want any close contact. Maybe he's happily married?

How HAPPILY married are you if you're willing to fuck a stranger in a maze?

I think what's about to happen is disgusting - let's not blame the environment.

Alfonse then said to Belinda, 'Would you visit me in my offices in Brussels and let me see your body again? Perhaps I could see more of it, and possibly in a less disgusting environment. Belinda immediately understood, Alfonse needed order and homely comforts in order to progress his male desires, though his cock had quickly become completely erect. She replied, 'Absolutely Mr Stirbacker I'm so glad I fit your expectations, and I would really like to do a lot of business with you.

Why do I think this has nothing to do with pots and pans?

Her tits are at a bus stop.

Stirbacker grinned and said, 'That is assured my lovely Belinda, and he fondled her waiting tits with relish. Belinda groaned softly, one of his hands slipped down to her vagina and started to gently caress it. In return she stroked his penis with both hands.

I just can't get the idea of him slathering her with piccalilli out of my head.

Hang on, her hands are tied to the trellis. Is she Debbie McGee?

'A gentleman from Brussels thought Belinda, what a great start to the afternoon!' After a further ten minutes of extremely heavy fondling, Belinda was becoming very wet, Alfonse had now gotten to her tits big time with his teeth and his very long cock had penetrated her vulva. He was obviously

I notice he hasn't put 'big'; he's chosen 'long'. Is it like a Peperami?

61

That is the weirdest
euphemism for an orgasm I've
ever heard.

Never have I been
so relieved to hear
any sound ever in my
whole life.

How would anyone know if she
has her thong on or not?! It's
UNDER her clothes.

Is she ever living in the moment? CONCENTRATE.

enjoying her tits and clit as Tony had put it so aptly just fifteen minutes earlier, and she had her first major client breakthrough. She mentally penciled in a visit to Brussels in ten days time. No sense in not striking whilst the iron was hot... so to speak!

Like a wounded animal.

A far off whistle sounded and Alfonse backed off... 'Time for me to go Belinda, I thoroughly enjoyed your lack of bra and thong... very thoughtful, but don't forget them when you visit me in Brussels very soon. We will have dinner at my very exclusive gentleman's club and all our ladies are expected to be properly dressed... at least when they arrive!

Belinda replied, 'Don't worry Mr Stirbacker I'll be in touch very soon!

You can't shut her up in this chapter.

I beg to differ. It's really thoughtful to send flowers or a thank-you card, not to whip off your knickers.

CHARACTER PROFILE: Alfonse Stirbacker

Alfonse Stirbacker, of Brussels, is impressive to Belinda thanks to his 300-strong fleet of supermarket outlets throughout Belgium, northern France and southern Holland. She likes that he is a powerful businessman who clearly understands the market. But it's not just his corporate acumen that she's attracted to; he has a very long cock – almost two hands' worth.

Alfonse is a mover and a shaker in the world of pots and pans – an award-winning entrepreneur, he enjoys the finer things in life. To give us an idea of his status, Flintstone lets us know that he is a member of a very exclusive gentlemen's club.

Belinda and Alfonse are somewhat kindred spirits in terms of approach, mixing business and pleasure effortlessly. Though sometimes mistaken for just a voyeur, Stirbacker can be seen chatting through meeting arrangements mid-intercourse. He is not afraid to wear his sexuality on his sleeve, happily sporting a black thong.

- **Physical Attribute:** Has never been seen without a black thong

- **Dominant Character Trait:** Belgian

- **Unusual Skill:** Voyeurism

- **Fun Fact:** Responds adversely to whistles

ACTIVITY

Belinda and Alfonse only had '20 minutes contact'. In pairs see how much you can learn about each other in the same amount of time, using only your hands and faces.

🔑 KEY THEME: Belgium

Stirbacker originating from Belgium is no arbitrary detail. The country was chosen for its rich and varied history. It's not just the land of waffles and praline, but a hub of creativity and business know-how. Famously, Belgian physicist and mathematician Ingrid Daubechies developed the model used by the FBI to record fingerprints. But perhaps more notably Belgians are the most avid users of discount coupons in the world.

✏️ AUTHOR'S NOTE

Why did you choose thongs for the men?

Brazil, where I spend half the year, is just full of men in thongs. Never mind the ladies, you even see ninety-year-old grannies wearing them. I think men look good in thongs; you avoid that tiresome white tan mark around your backside, and they do look sexy. It can be a liberating experience wearing a thong but not every male will dare to do it.

Rocky x

📖 Reading group discussion points

- In a group discuss how disgusting it is to see a man wearing a thong. What adjectives could describe your repulsion?

- Have you ever visited Belgium? Discuss the worst elements of the trip.

- What are the pros and cons of securing a business deal through sex?

What? Smooth like
an Action Man? ———

If you don't see it straight away
there's a concern.

CHAPTER 6

The Second Client; Jim Stirling

Is it a t. rex?

A few minutes after Alfonse had gone Belinda heard her second visitor stomping through the maze. He appeared a few seconds later, again dressed only in a black thong. It was becoming a type of uniform she thought. From the guest list info Belinda recognized Jim Stirling, a Yankee from the USA. His operation had 1257 outlets and was also growing fast in Mexico and Brazil. He was a big guy but short, and upon seeing Belinda's plight quickly threw his somewhat stained thong to the ground.

Drink!

Belinda blinked;   *WHAT IS IT STAINED WITH????!!!*

For the first time that day she was caught unawares… there was nothing there, but then she saw it underneath covered in pubic hairs lay a very   — *GAG.* small and in Belinda terms, somewhat pathetic penis. Belinda gasped, what was she expected to do with this?

Why, is it curled up in its nest like a small woodland creature?

It's a vole. His penis is a vole.

No one is turned on by the word 'squatted'.

Jim's penis is an apparition and it's haunting Belinda's vagina.

We need back-up - get the thumbs!

'Hi, my name's Stirling, from the US. Let's get these garments out of the way!'

With one powerful movement he ripped Belinda's tennis shirt completely from her body, and seconds later had done the same to her skirt. He flung them to the ground where they now lay ruined in the mud. *Poor bastard he's got huge everything, but a tiny dick*

'Hope you don't mind Missy as I likes 'em bare!' Jim didn't hang around and immediately took her tits in his massive hands. His large thumbs tentatively rubbed her nipple tips, making them rise and harden. This fast reaction from Belinda seemed to please him and he started to push his cock into her vagina. *You have to ask yourself some big questions when your thumbs are the most erotic thing about you.*

Belinda squatted slightly as Jim was shorter than her, pulling her legs apart to allow him easier access. Jim grunted and Belinda thought she felt something entering her pussy. He started to fuck her hard, Belinda breathed deeply, did the man know he was only tickling her? This was going to take all her concentration, Stirling's was a massive account and if she did well today, who knew what might develop from it. He started to press her harder and harder against the trellis, he had found his rhythm but Belinda couldn't feel anything and whilst she had the appetite for it she knew she would have to fake it and Belinda never faked anything. To make matters worse the ground was now really boggy and her torn garments were well and truly stained.

Why is there a rogue comma? Is that Jim's penis? To scale?

Ironic

This sounds like a cable TV legal advert. 'Have YOU got the friction you need to complete your ejaculation? If not, why not? Call 0800 GET WOOD to make a claim.'

The only work she's done in this entire book.

Cultural Context:

Notable aphrodisiacs include oysters, chocolate and Flintstone's favourite fruit, the pomegranate.

Runny, barely cooked eggs are a food less commonly associated with sex.

Great time for introductions, Jim. Priorities.

Basically anything but this.

Belinda thought of (delicious sexual scenarios) and succeeded in making her vagina become wetter and wetter. She started to slowly contract her cervical muscles to ensure Jim got the friction he needed to complete his ejaculation. After ten minutes of (hard work) he came and then started to lick her tits. He obviously had little regard for women as he then pushed her head down to his cock ensuring Belinda's long black hair fell nearly to the by now muddy ground, her ample (breasts followed) and Stirling pushed his penis into her mouth. Belinda smiled to herself, she could have eaten two of these for breakfast, never mind the scrambled eggs. *Are they on a time delay?*

Just then she heard the whistle and she knew she had (done her best). Stirling reluctantly let go of her tits and put his thong back on… it was now even more stained than when he had entered the maze and Belinda wondered where all the (semen had come from) Perhaps she had underestimated his resources? *Mighty cum from little acorns gush.* *A for effort.*

'Hey babe, (what's your name?)' said Stirling.

'Belinda Blumenthal, I'm the Sales Director of Steele Pots and Pans.'

'Good work Belinda, come and see me in (Texas in a couple of weeks)… I need a new cookery utensil supplier and I guess you fit the bill!

'Why Jim, I'd love to… let's say in three weeks time? *I imagine Belinda dressed up as a cowgirl, doing the cowgirl sex position. *Shudder**

Talking Point:

It is not uncommon for Sales Directors to receive commission based on their job performance.

How much do you think Belinda will earn from securing the Jim Stirling deal?

'Yup… let's do it… and I promise to replace your soiled garments with something a little bit more sexy!'

People in stained thongs shouldn't throw stones.

With that he stumped off leaving Belinda completely naked, very muddy and still tied to the trellis around the maze. She massaged her wrists where the red plastic handcuffs had managed to keep her attached to the trellis and thought of the bonus money she would personally make when she tied up the deal with Jim Stirling. She also thought she should take a crash course in Yoga, or some sort of exercises which developed the cervix muscles. If Jim couldn't rise to the job then she would have to ensure he was completely satisfied… the things she did to make her fortune!

I think I'd rather be on the breadline.

Jesus, ANOTHER one?!

But wait, she could hear another client approaching through the maze. 'Oh no,' she thought, 'I hope this one's a bit better hung, I can't take much more of these small appendages.' But she had to… the handcuffs and parcel string ensured it!

Amen.

Oh yeah, the kids' toy and some twine. It's a proper Fort Knox.

CHARACTER PROFILE: Jim Stirling

Jim Stirling is an Austin-based Dallas-born American who is proficient in business, who oversees a massive account of 1,257 cookware outlets. His entrepreneurial flare is so strong that his organization is growing fast in the markets of Mexico and Brazil, despite both nations being in recession (at the time of publication).

Not a man known for his good looks, Jim is blessed with size in every area except one. Fat and with massive hands but a tiny penis, he would have plenty of cause to shy away from intimate relations with the opposite sex. However, Jim is as body confident as a man twice his height and double his girth.

Despite his 'pathetic' penis being dubbed 'the vole' in popular culture, his incessant grunting during intercourse and being the subject of the revisionist nursery rhyme – 'I'm Jim Stirling short and stout, here's my handle, where's my spout?' – Stirling is a content crooner and the perfect foil for Belinda.

• **Physical Attribute:** Huge thumbs

• **Dominant Character Trait:** Brash

• **Unusual Skill:** His penis can pass as a vole in a hole

• **Fun Fact:** From the same state as Beyoncé

(Ⓟ) **KEY THEME: The Male Body**

Jim Stirling appears to possess what has long been believed to be a mythical organ dubbed 'the chode'.

A chode is purported to be a penis that is wider than it is long. Debate rages as to whether such a thing exists in reality, though the plight of the 'micropenis' was examined on popular daytime talk show *This Morning* in January 2016.

The desirable size of the male human's penis has shifted throughout history. Kenneth Dover's landmark study *Greek Homosexuality* concluded that in ancient Greece a small penis was culturally seen as desirable.

However, in subsequent centuries a large penis has been viewed as a symbol of strength and power. It is therefore notable that Flintstone has chosen to depict Stirling with a 'very small' and 'somewhat pathetic' endowment.

ACTIVITY

Take it in turns to perform your best 'fake orgasm'.

Reading group discussion points

- Debate whether Rocky is making a social comment against the 'bigger is better' adage in relation to the male sexual organ.

- Belinda is nothing if not determined and goes to extraordinary lengths to secure a business deal. What is the most extreme thing you have done to get what you want?

- What substance do you think Jim's thong is stained with? What clues does the text provide?

Cultural Context – Bowing:

Bowing is most prominent in Asian cultures or typical of nobility and aristocracy in Europe. Peter is neither Asian nor an aristocrat.

CHAPTER 7

The Third Client; Peter Rouse

Not easy in that quagmire.

Belinda stood her ground hoping this one would be so much better, she had had enough titillation, she wanted, no, needed a good fuck. A tall blonde haired man, with an impressive physique strolled into view. Belinda quickly recognised Peter Rouse, his operation was located in Holland with 357 retail outlets, and again was growing strongly throughout the Scandinavian countries. An evasive entrepreneur, Peter could not be overlooked as he had recently expanded to Spain and Portugal. On seeing Belinda he quickly removed his thong and threw it to the ground whilst approaching her.

The spiritual home of pots and pans.

Imagine having that effect on someone. As soon as they see you, they whip their pants off.
'My name is Peter,' he said and quickly bowed, 'I believe you are Belinda, the Sales Director of this fantastic customer bash your superiors are putting on here today!'

What year is Peter from? Has this become a Jane Austen novel?

He's gone for the fail-safe neck, boobs, bum manoeuvre.

Two uses of 'body'. We know you have a thesaurus, Dad, no excuses.

You get a lot of vagina to the pound in this book. At least it's value for money.

Now she blushes …

'Why yes I am Mr. Rouse.' said Belinda, blushing at her naked appearance in front of this, so far, delightfully hung man. After all, he was the first to know who she was. *He knows your name?! If that's not a reason to shag someone, I don't know what is.*

'Please, please call me Peter,' he replied, 'especially as we are to become more intimately acquainted in the next 25 minutes.' He took Belinda's hands and said, 'What a delightful body you have, may I handle it?' *It's not a fragile item.*

Belinda replied, 'Why yes of course… I would love to feel you touch me, feel as free as you wish.'

'Now that's an offer I cannot refuse,' Peter replied and immediately started to massage her neck slowly spreading to her breasts and buttocks. Belinda immediately started to relax and responded by gently massaging Peter's penis. *Kinda sounds like she's kneading it like dough, like an uncooked baguette.*

He had a fantastic body and his muscles were very well toned, Belinda started to caress his body and in return he moved his massage to her vaginal area. He stroked her small runway of pubic black hair leading to her vaginal lips, and soon he was inside her with his fingers Belinda had rarely experienced anything as delicate as this and soon began to moan softly. In return she still had the sense of presence to massage his now extremely hard and large penis. She somehow knew she was going to enjoy this man. *How many fingers? What's he doing in there? Playing rock paper scissors? Cat's cradle?*

Does not sound delicate.

I think Belinda
might die in this
chapter.

Via the mouth?!
With his penis??!

What's wrong with just saying 'They had sex'? ——

Is she exfoliating him? —

She's as mad as a box of frogs! ——

After a few moments Peter pushed Belinda onto her knees, into the soft mud and gently guided her head to his penis. Belinda opened her mouth and slowly pushed her lips over his foreskin, pulling it back before slightly gagging as she swallowed his entire cock down her throat. 'You are very skilful Belinda, would you let me teach you more techniques?'

Aaaaaand vomit.

'Why yes Peter I always love to learn new things.'

How's she answering? Her mouth is definitely full.

He then lifted her from the ground and slowly penetrated her vagina with his now throbbing cock. Belinda again moaned softly…his penetration was so fluid she felt in ecstasy. He started to move inside her, she responded by contracting and releasing her vaginal muscles in time to his thrusts. They were now completely intertwined, Belinda had never experienced anything like this before, she was floating on air and Peter was penetrating deeper and deeper. Belinda started to gasp in short spasms, she needed more and more oxygen just to feed the gigantic orgasm she was about to encounter. For the first time in her life she was not in control, but she was enjoying it to death.

What? Actual normal sex? With a nice polite man?

Peter started to sweat profusely, Belinda started to rub his skin more vigorously and he approached his climax. Of course Belinda was now wild with delirium, she was completely out of her head, all her actions were mechanical, Peter kept thrusting, Belinda kept flexing her vaginal muscles, until they both came in a violent explosion of ecstasy together.

Give it a minute, Belinda! That
was barely a pit stop.

TEETH!?!?!?!

Wasn't her first thought 'girlfriend'
rather than 'sex slave'?

How big are her lobes that he
can draw on them?

I'm picturing him plopping out of the end of the flume at the local swimming pool.

Are they actually sinking now?

Peter fell out of her, Belinda collapsed onto her knees in the mud… the plastic handcuffs around her wrists saving her from being completely immersed. Now on her knees she was spattered all over with the horrible slime, and there was nothing she could do about it… except linger in the fantastic orgasm she had just experienced.

But Peter's cock remained erect and Belinda was so impressed with his skills, she knew she could learn much more from him. So she crawled back to him and put her mouth over his penis and continued to screw him with her lips, teeth, tongue and throat… she secretly knew she was ready to become his sex slave if he would ask her. She would scream for more until he agreed she thought.

That wouldn't be annoying at all.

But Peter Rouse was no normal individual and he knew when a girl was under his sexual spell as Belinda now was, so he let her screw his penis in her mouth and began using the mud to mark Belinda's tits, ass, mouth, and ears with symbolic signs. She was still kneeling on the ground so he took the opportunity to write more symbols on her back which would bind her to him sexually for the next year.

Is he Spider-Man?

His cock then started to ejaculate semen which he quickly caught in his hands. He then covered her hair with it, twisting it all into a ponytail, Belinda's long black hair mixed with translucent sperm… the most powerful sexual symbol he knew. Belinda, though she didn't know it, was now well

I'm never borrowing my dad's Brylcreem again…

Said no one ever. ————————————

Weirdest wedding vows I've ever heard ————————————

and truly ensnared, though truth be told it was what Belinda would have
wanted.

Is the maze a time machine?

Definitely clear up the mud before the cum.

The whistle brought them both back to the present day, Peter hurriedly
put on his thong whilst Belinda tried to get rid of some of the mud she was
now covered in. Belinda gasped, 'When can I see you next Peter…. please.'
she said desperately. 'Hush my beautiful Belinda, I will see you tonight at
11.30pm in the Horse and Jockey pub, where I know you have a room we
can use.' Belinda smiled her gratitude to him and said, 'It will be so good… I
promise you… ask anything you want… I somehow feel enslaved to you.'

'You are Belinda, as I am to you.' replied Peter. 'Until tonight!'

⊙ CHARACTER PROFILE: Peter Rouse

Peter Rouse is a tall blond man from Amsterdam, Holland. He currently manages 357 retail outlets and that number is growing quickly throughout Scandinavia. Peter is notoriously hard to pin down for a meeting so to have him in the maze is a real career coup for Belinda. With a toned, sculpted physique, a confident demeanour and a large penis (uncircumcised), Peter is clearly a hit with the ladies and Belinda is instantly drawn to him. He appears to be a very experienced lover. Early speculation suggests Peter is the first real romantic interest for Belinda.

Sexually Peter observes some unusual customs; he bows to greet people, he draws symbols in mud all over Belinda's body and he rubs his semen all over her hair. The sources of these affectations are never explained.

• **Physical Attribute:** Golden haired

• **Dominant Character Trait:** Overly formal - bows on greeting

• **Unusual Skill:** Fluent in ancient languages

• **Fun Fact:** He's happily married

KEY THEME: Ancient Iconography

Peter's interest in symbolism is revealed early on. Flintstone has stated that Peter is a very religious man and a member of a secret sect who only worship at midnight. What is clear is that they use a series of markings to tie future sacrifices to them mentally; whether this is a romantic gesture or misogynistic territory-marking is open to interpretation.

AUTHOR'S NOTE

It feels like there's a burgeoning romance between Peter and Belinda. Was this intentional?

Belinda was in a rebound period after Jim Stirling. This left her open to a deeper emotional connection. Basically she was feeling a bit let down and then Peter arrived in the maze. It was inevitable sparks would fly. Whatever happens romantically Belinda has locked in a key player in the European pots and pans distribution field. Put it this way, the future is bright for both of these characters.

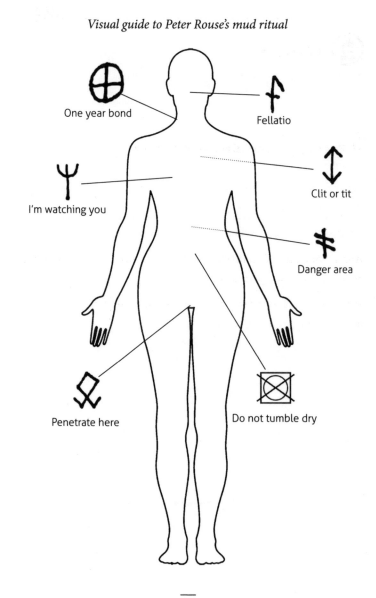

Visual guide to Peter Rouse's mud ritual

One year bond

Fellatio

I'm watching you

Clit or tit

Danger area

Penetrate here

Do not tumble dry

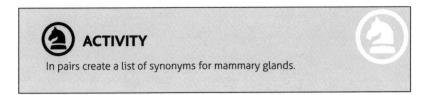

ACTIVITY

In pairs create a list of synonyms for mammary glands.

Reading group discussion points

- What do you think of Belinda and Peter's relationship? Could you see them getting married?

- Discuss the weirdest sexual encounter you've ever had.

- Apart from penis size, in what ways is Peter Rouse different to Jim Stirling, Belinda's previous maze encounter?

- We are now at the halfway point of the book. How much of your life do you feel like you have wasted?

It's starting to sound a bit like a David Attenborough programme. 'The male approaches the female with a black thong.'

How strong is Belinda?
She's the female Hulk.

CHAPTER 8

The Tombola;

*Harsh...
but fair. Two
and a vole.*

Belinda was now both exhausted and exhilarated, she had been fucked by three males.. well let's be honest.. two and a half in the last two hours and had been totally mesmerized by one of them. She also had a sixth sense that she could never opt out of the special relationship Peter Rouse and herself had developed in their short meeting. But for all that she was completely up for it, Peter was a successful, dominating character... and come to think of it, so was she.

*He's Blair
and she's
Bush. So to
speak*

Quite the spa weekend.

Now relaxing against the trellis she pulled the parcel string sharply and it fell to the muddy ground. She slowly twisted the plastic handcuffs, they <u>fell apart</u> and she bent down to pick up her tennis outfit. It was a real mess, but for decency's sake she put what was left of the shirt and dress back on. She knew Tony would be here any minute to bring her <u>back to the BBQ area</u> and then she could get back to her <u>lovely bath at her room in the Horse and Jockey.</u>

*There'll only
be a cold
sausage left
by now.*

*She might need two dips. (One
medicated).*

Can we just see the job spec one more time?

Soon she heard footsteps coming through the maze and thankfully it was
Tony, he had a large smile on his face.

Entertained? She didn't make them balloon animals.

'You're a star Belinda, those three guys you just entertained are over the
moon with you… and the other girls have done good as well.'

'What do you mean other girls?'

'Didn't you know? Giselle and Bella are here as well, it's not just you… it's
your glee team as well!'

Even his own characters are confused.

'Tony! What do you mean by "glee team" we're all just girls out for a good
time and I need a bath!'

Yes we know.

As it's mainly his fault, probably best to keep schtum.

Tony looked at her and decided not to comment on her condition…he had
never seen so much mud stick to a person and what were those symbolic
marks on her <u>face and thighs</u>? *And ears. Don't forget the ears.*

They soon reached the BBQ area which had been transformed into a
Roman style amphitheater with over 40 people sitting around on chairs.
They were mostly clients with their wives who had up to this point no
knowledge of the sexual adventures which a few of their number had been
allowed access to. Belinda sat down on a chair which Tony had found for
her. She looked around and tried to locate Giselle and Bella.

Sooooo many people are getting divorced tomorrow.

Where did they get all these safety pins from? Is there a haberdashery in the maze?

Does this feel like an appropriate time to be playing games from a school fete?

Belinda gasped when she recognised Giselle, her beautiful blonde hair had been, to say the best, remodeled, by perhaps a maniac with a twist for the dramatic??? Her dress had seen as much wear as Belinda's tennis outfit and was being held together by a few safety pins. Giselle looked up and saw Belinda staring at her, she smiled and stared back at Belinda's equally disgusting condition and torn clothing. Belinda thought perhaps she had gotten off lightly, but why was Tony so happy, Giselle was his girl and she seemed to be in a bit of a state. Belinda gave Giselle the thumbs up and looked around for Bella.

Giselle's like 'bitch stole my look'.

She soon spotted her and to be honest Bella didn't look that much better than Giselle, though her hair was intact, her outfit was sporting half a dozen safety pins. Bella's face was however covered in red lipstick as though another maniac had tried to apply it. They had definitely succeeded in making her look like a tart. Belinda caught Bella's eye and smiled at her. Bella gave her the thumbs up and smiled back.

Is Giselle bald????

Who invited all the maniacs?

Will everyone stop doing this - they're clearly not OK

Belinda thought, 'This is very strange, what's going to happen next?' *We're literally five steps ahead of you.*

A couple of minutes later a tall chap stood up and addressed the gathering.

'Welcome everyone to our annual Tombola where our prizes are the same as previous years I also want to personally thank Sir James Godwin for letting us have this opportunity to raise some much needed money for our local

Yeah, Dad. But as this is fictitious can you just tell us?

This guy's going to be gold.

What some hand lotion and a bath bomb?

You win a human being??

No name. Why waste time on detail?

Cultural Context:

With his 'there is also only one rule [of the tombola]' speech, Flintstone is making a shrewd reference to David Fincher's cult film, *Fight Club*:

'The first rule of Fight Club is: you do not talk about Fight Club. The second rule of Fight Club is: you DO NOT talk about Fight Club!

I imagine this said very quickly like the small print on a radio ad.

THIMBLE THIMBLE THIMBLE
THIMBLE THIMBLE THIMBLE
THIMBLE THIMBLE.

What sort of charity is endorsing this form of fundraising?

What kind of asses are we talking here?

'Charity, The Asses & Donkeys Trust. Now, please remember as your prize is a real person you will only get your servant for the time period of 12 hours. The highest bidder from this audience for each individual prize gets to take them home!' The audience clapped enthusiastically.

Feel like this might be the longest half-day of all our lives.

The tall man continued, 'There is also only one rule, and that is we have a safe word, which when uttered means the owner stops the directed task right away and the servant is released from their 12 hour duty. The down side of that is, the servant has to match the donation paid by the bidder to our charity! We all win! OK! Yes, now please remember girls and potential owners the safe word is THIMBLE, yes thimble... easy to remember, it stops you from getting pricked!! Ha ha!' The crowd groaned and started clapping.

Bravo! Lovely joke from the Tall Man.

Tough crowd.

Drink!

Belinda blinked; she was intrigued, this sounds like great fun. She quickly thought, 'Who would I pick as my prize... Tony?... Bella?... no, Sir James Godwin and boy would I enjoy that scenario.'

Really?!

Based on nothing.

'Today we have three servants on offer and to find out who they are, and take note it could be any one of you here, I want you all to look under your chairs and see the number attached to it.' The sound of hurriedly scraping chairs filled the air whilst the now hushed audience checked their numbers. Belinda's was 13, Unlucky for some, she thought.

Spoiler; and you.

Even the wives who thought they were off to Ascot?

Surprise fucking surprise #1. _____

Surprise fucking surprise #2.

Cultural Context:

There is a great importance and relevance to the numbers selected in the tombola: 22, 37 and finally 13.

Traditional tarot decks have twenty-two cards, the number thirty-seven is used four times in the Bible and Thirteen is the nickname of Dr Remy Hadley in medical drama *House*.

*Can you have a receding pubic hairline /
a pubic widow's peak / a pubic cowlick?* _____

I've been to a lot of tombolas in my time. And no one has ever said that.

'Ok,' the tall man shouted, 'let's tumble the tombola and see what the three "lucky" numbers are.' The tombola went round and round, Belinda felt a sense of adventure take over her persona, she somehow felt she knew she would be a prize, but she didn't know who would be her owner.

What's the number again?

'The first number is 22, I repeat 22, would the person sitting on chair number 22 please stand up.' Belinda looked around to see who the lucky person was. It was Giselle and as she stood up a safety pin fell out revealing a beautiful right breast to the crowd. An appreciative murmur came from the men, which saw many of their wives elbowing them in the ribs. Did they dare bid for her after that Belinda thought?

If they're getting pissed off now wait till the bidding starts.

'The second number is 37, I repeat 37.'

Bella stood up, her safety pins held and Belinda started to smell a rat.

'The third number is, unlucky for some, 13, I repeat number 13.'

Belinda jumped to her feet, ready to go, wondering who she would be a servant to for the next twelve hours. Her torn shirt fell wide apart revealing her breasts and her tennis skirt flapped wide in the mounting breeze revealing her pubic hairline to the assembled body, but she didn't care, she was Belinda and she was going to make sure a big butch man took her home!

THIMBLE

Why's she talking in the third person?

Best of luck, chuck

Gutted. Talk about short
straw. Literally.

What's wrong with a sponsored bike ride?

'Now,' said the tall man, 'This is where we make some money for our charity as the rest of you can bid for their services, but firstly, do I have the agreement of these three very fine ladies to be coerced into these important roles?'

Belinda thought, 'What the fuck, this might be fun… it's probably just doing a bit of cleaning and lawn mowing on a Sunday evening.'

OF COURSE IT'S NOT.

She shouted out, 'Yes I'm game!' whilst covering up her private parts with her hands and arms.

Never have been, never will be, private.

The other two girls followed suit and happily agreed, the tall man bowed to them.

Is the Tall Man Japanese?

'Thank you for your noble assistance, our charity The Asses & Donkeys Trust is much indebted to you.' he said.

The bidding quickly started with Bella and she soon went for £350 to the American Jim Stirling who Belinda thought could do with a cock transplant, and very soon at that. Giselle went next for £300 from Tony of all people, definitely a case of protecting his own. Then it was Belinda's turn. The bids started slowly, and Belinda couldn't believe her body was that bad… perhaps it was all the mud… where was her butch man? Finally

FIX!!!!

This is why the rest of the country is
having a hosepipe ban!

I would say how undignified but I
think we all know it's completely
necessary.

To get into all those
nooks and crannies.

Cultural Context:

WW1's frugality drive was embodied by the mantra 'waste not, want not',
which featured on public advice propaganda posters, educating citizens on
how to be more resourceful.

The Duchess likely remembers these from her early teens and lives her life by
this philosophy today.

It's the man from Del Monte!

A cool £16 an hour.

she went for £200 from a lady dressed in a white linen trouser suit and a panama hat called only the Duchess.

With Belinda sold, the tombola was over and the three girls were taken away to start their twelve hours of duty. The now devastated Belinda was immediately led to a hosepipe near the stables where the Duchess striped her of her torn skirt and tennis shirt and hosed her down. She roughly fondled Belinda's tits and ass in the washing process with a long handled brush and then pushed her, still naked, into a horsebox. With the rear tail gate down it was obvious that it all had been planned in advance, instead of straw and manure there was a sofa and drinks, albeit chilled, tinned Gin and Tonics.

Why because she went for the least cash?

Now there's a curveball.

Money can't buy you manners.

The Duchess rudely pushed Belinda onto the sofa and offered her a drink. Belinda nervously poured the can down her by now parched throat, she was still feeling horny and didn't think her new owner could give her what she still craved even after the afternoons events. Quite a lot of the can didn't get down Belinda's throat and she made sure the liquid trickled down her neck onto her breasts and then into her tummy button where it pooled, overflowed and ran down her track of black pubic hair into her vagina.

Why not?

Vagina & tonic!!!

Much to Belinda's surprise the Duchess murmured, 'Waste not, want not,' and promptly licked the gin off Belinda's tits, stomach and clitoris.

Again with the manners. At least use a straw. ⎯⎯

Probably best. ⎯⎯⎯⎯⎯⎯

Belinda would love that – can she trade in the Duchess?

Number three already!
She's going to be wasted.

Cultural Context:

A motel is a hotel designed for motorists, which came to prominence in the 1920s as long-distance road journeys became more common.

They are traditionally an inexpensive and 'no frills' alternative to hotels, which poses questions as to why a woman of the Duchess's means would frequent such an establishment.

As is her trademark.

Belinda thought "Result!' but said nothing and let the Duchess enjoy her
slurping hoping this was setting the tone for the rest of the evening. She
asked for another G&T and this time the Duchess decided to pour it down
Belinda's throat herself. It was obvious the Duchess was enjoying this
relationship, as she cupped her free hand around Belinda's left breast whilst
carelessly slopping the drink into her mouth.

A niche choice.

'Had enough servant?' said the Duchess, 'as we have to move on or Sir James
will be joining our little party!' The Duchess efficiently closed the tail door
of the horse trailer to the chagrin of the quickly assembled party of stable
lads, leaving Belinda reclining on the sofa and helping herself to another
Gin and Tonic in comfort. It was just as well she could stretch out because
the Duchess was not a competent driver of the large four wheel drive vehicle
plus trailer. Belinda lost count of the cut corners and sudden halts as they
drove through the country lanes to an exclusive Motel which had some
private chalets in the grounds. Belinda wickedly hoped the Duchess was
better at fucking than driving... or had a companion who could do both.

Wouldn't be difficult from the sound of it.

(Ω) KEY THEME: Philanthropy

Collaboration with a wealthy benefactor can make or break a charity's future. Like the Asses and Donkeys Trust, most charitable organizations have a public patron, such as Sir James Godwin. The hope is that they will raise awareness with their profile and potentially die and bequeath their fortune.

This can be a precarious approach as often figureheads fall for a particular animal and leave their money not to the organization but instead to their favoured pet. Animals can reap huge rewards if just they bide their time. For example, publishing mogul Miles Blackwell left £10 million to his hen when he died, whereas it is reported that the Queen Mum left a cool £3 million to some cows and sheep.

(✎) AUTHOR'S NOTE

What is the personal significance of the tombola?

I used to do a lot for charity when the kids were at junior school, and I invariably ended up running the tombola stall. This was great fun; I loved spinning the ticket container so it was a no-brainer to add this experience into a gloriously English occasion and to add three beautiful girls as willing prizes.

Having the wives at the tombola comes directly from my experiences in selling stuff to customers. I personally don't subscribe to the 'day on the golf course' technique where only males attend. I, like Tony and Sir James, much prefer to have a day out with the wife or partner. It also makes good business sense; you get to know the clients' other halves and what pushes their buttons.

Rocky x

CULTURAL CONTEXT

History of Gin and Tonic

Gin and tonics are the favoured tipple of the cast of characters of *Belinda Blinked 1*. According to some reports tonic water was first enjoyed in 1825 when British officers in the Indian army improved their bitter anti-malaria medicine – Peruvian quinine extract – by mixing it with soda and sugar. At some point during this time the daily dose of protective quinine tonic was combined with a shot of gin ration, adding lime to fend off scurvy. Winston Churchill is reputed to have said, 'The gin and tonic has saved more Englishmen's lives, and minds, than all the doctors in the Empire.' Rocky Flintstone has been known to enjoy one or two while he writes in his pavilion, though he prefers new world wines.

Asses and Donkeys Trust (ADT)

Our mission: to transform the quality of life for donkeys and asses across the globe and to ensure their contribution to humankind is fully valued.

Our dream: a world where donkeys and asses live free from cruelty and suffering.

Case study: *Alan the Ass was left abandoned by the side of the M25 with*

no food or shelter. His owner said he'd be 'right back' but never returned. Alan didn't trust humans and was very nervous when we first met him, but now he averages thirty rides a day on Skegness beach.

Sponsor Alan today and receive a signed photograph, monthly correspondence and a knitted toy that looks just like him.*

*scaled down

Registered charity no. 7312861864814821547 61481

ACTIVITY

Using only household balms and creams style a friend's hair into a 'maniac' updo. Wear the look out of the house and document the reactions you receive.

Reading group discussion points

- How important is female friendship in this chapter?

- What would someone feel like after having sex with two and a half men?

- What are the main adversities facing modern day asses and donkeys?

- How much would it cost to convert a traditional horsebox into a modern sex cart?

- How bad are women drivers? Why?

Cultural Context – Horsebox:

It is illegal to have a human being in a horsebox without a seat belt. Furthermore, it is illegal to drive under the influence of alcohol. Cumulatively the Duchess could face six months in prison, a driving ban and thousands of pounds in fines.

Cultural Context – Jilly Cooper:

A key influence for Flintstone seems to romantic novelist Jilly Cooper and her best know work *Riders*, set in the competitive world of show jumping. There are comparisons to be made between Flintstone and Cooper. Both authors draw heavily on their own point of view and experiences. Cooper's love of dogs and horses features prominently in her work, whereas Flintstone's passion for breasts and gin and tonic are key themes of his writing.

Is this like the Leather Room?

Chapter 9

The Chalet;

Bless! It's like when you leave a dog in the car. Make sure you crack a window for Belinda!

Belinda felt the horse box reversing accompanied with the grinding of gears and then the engine of the four by four went dead. There was a silence for at least thirty minutes and Belinda started to feel abandoned. Then suddenly the tail gate opened and the Duchess climbed up the ramp. She was dressed in full horse riding gear, a red jacket, white jodhpurs, black boots, black jumping hat and crop with a scarlet tag on the end. Belinda blinked fearing the worst.

The Duchess grabbed Belinda's ass and pulled her up to a standing position. She then pushed her down the ramp and pulled her by her left tit into a chalet style building. The Duchess made for a doorway at the end of the lounge which led to a large wet room. She stood Belinda under the shower and turned it on. Slowly the Duchess started to strip off her riding gear in front of Belinda. Like Belinda the Duchess was well endowed, but her ass was showing signs of her 50 something years, and childbirth had not been kind to her stomach muscles. However she was still in good shape and the

Does the Duchess have a dick?

How do you guess someone's age from their ass? Is it like the rings on a tree trunk?

Is that a triple or quadruple negative? Either way, it makes no sense.

That's such a Dad thing to say. She used her Christmas smellies . . .

Language Alert – 'My Lady':

The Duchess's insistence that Belinda call her 'My Lady' could be interpreted as an homage to Milady de Winter from *The Three Musketeers*. Milady is Cardinal Richelieu's chief spy and assassin, amoral and dangerous. Does this suggest the Duchess is not to be trusted and may not be all she appears?

Does she think Belinda's tits are a soap dispenser?

riding clothes had made the most of her attributes. Belinda could not help
but hope she would not be in worse shape when she reached the same age,
albeit some twenty years away!

Now totally naked the Duchess started to wash Belinda and herself down
with shampoo and smelly natural oils. Belinda whispered a word of thanks
for this thoughtful act, even though the Duchess's hands were all over her
vagina, ass and breasts. The Duchess immediately frowned and stepped out
of the shower area to pick up her crop which was laid close to hand across
the wash hand basin.

I'm guessing that word of thanks was 'thanks'.

'Address me as "My Lady" and nothing else!' and to emphasize this she
flicked the crop onto the cheek of Belinda's right ass. The crop's impact
made Belinda jump and left a nasty bright red mark on her skin. Belinda
grimaced and replied quickly,

Has Belinda got two asses?

'Thank you My Lady.'

'That's better servant.' said the Duchess.

Oh God, it's getting a bit BDSM now.

The Duchess set the crop aside and continued to wash down Belinda, again
applying plenty of hand squeezing to her tits. After five minutes of this the
Duchess changed her tactics and concentrated on her vagina and clitoris.
Belinda's nipples started to respond, she was after all, that type of girl and

Is that the most words
Belinda has used in a row
so far?

Has Belinda got varicose veins
she needs treating?

couldn't help it. However, the Duchess started to smile and said, 'That's very good servant.'

'Thank you My Lady.' replied Belinda.

How long are they?

With her nipples now (fully extended) and her vagina starting to become wet, the Duchess decided to dry down Belinda and move her to the bedroom. Belinda was told to lie down, open her legs wide and masturbate herself in front of the Duchess.

'Masturbate' is one of those words you think and hope your parents would never know or use.

'My Lady, please fuck me as you wish, I know I am your servant, so please use me for your pleasure.' said Belinda.

The Duchess smiled and said, 'Yes servant, I do believe you mean it, and I will test you soon, don't you worry!' — *The Duchess seems a little creepy.*

The Duchess left the room and Belinda looked around her. It was a classic motel bedroom, there was nothing to look at which would give her a clue as to where she was. She would just have to wait until the Duchess wanted to have sex with her and perhaps tell her where she was. The Duchess soon returned with two glasses of Gin and Tonic in her hands. She set them down, and started to massage Belinda's long legs. She stretched them out and quickly shackled her ankles to the bottom of the bed with a similar pair of handcuffs Tony had used on her that afternoon in the Maze. This

This doesn't sound sexy. It sounds like physiotherapy.

What? Like a tablecloth? They sound paper thin.

She's got napkin-thin breasts with bolts on the end, scratching her dry skin. How is this supposed to be erotic?

Cultural Context – Equestrian Erotica:

There have been a number of romantic/erotic novels written over the years involving horses. Titles include *Tame Horses Wild Hearts*, *Unbridled Love: A Romance With Horse Sense*, *Texas Rein*, *One Wild Cowboy* and, of course, *There's Something About Horses*. Why? Perhaps it's the kinky nature of the clothing and accoutrements (whips, long leather boots etc.) of horse riding and showjumping. Or maybe it's the nature of the relationship between human and horse that reflects the dominant and submissive roles of BDSM.

Has she somehow read Belinda Blinked? Because I've never read about this before.

*How strong is her tongue?
Sounds like she's giving her a
deep-tissue massage*

time they were coloured yellow, Belinda wondered idly where they were purchasing them from... Toys Ur Us?

The Duchess started to massage Belinda's arms, it felt so good and she half expected them to be tied to the bedhead but this didn't happen and Belinda soon found out why. They finished their drinks, the Duchess who was also still totally naked, started to massage Belinda's body with her tongue. The Duchess's breasts draped over Belinda's body as she licked her from head to toe. Belinda found it strangely erotic, especially when the Duchess's nipples, now as hard as rivets scraped her soft skin. Belinda responded by rubbing her hand up and down the Duchess's vagina and eventually picked up enough courage to massage her clit.

Rave reviews. Sounds like a wild session.

After some very satisfactory moments according to the loud moans emanating from the Duchess, she stood up and left the room. Belinda started to wonder what she had done wrong, but the Duchess returned with her riding crop in hand. Belinda immediately thought that this was where it was going to get nasty. But being the servant of the Duchess didn't necessarily mean you were going to be whipped into a sexual frenzy. Instead the crop handle was to become a substitute penis. The Duchess smiled at Belinda and said 'Are you ready for this, servant?'

Belinda nodded her head slowly in disbelief, she had read about this type of sexual fantasy, but had never, ever experienced it.

Understatement of the century. ———

Only the best for Belinda. ———

This book feels like an eternity. ———

Wasn't that about an hour ago? ———

Some sales job this was turning out to be! The Duchess wasted no more time and pressed the crop handle into Belinda's vagina. Belinda jumped as she hadn't had really enough foreplay to make her wet enough to receive this size of object. However she grinned and said,

'Thanks My Lady.' She also wickedly thought, 'I must send Jim Stirling one of these.'

Great comedy timing from Belinda. Poor Jim!

Belinda started to grind onto the leather crop handle, in actual real life experiences the handle was smaller than a lot of the cocks she had encountered. The Duchess held it in position and let Belinda enjoy the experience while she sucked her breasts and ate her nipples. The Duchess became more vigorous with the leather crop and Belinda became very wet, orgasming at least three times in quick succession. After some ten minutes the crop was withdrawn and the Duchess licked it all over.

The Duchess thinks she's at a buffet.

Satisfied, she then walked over to the wardrobe and brought out a strap on penis again made of finest leather. She put it on and entered Belinda in a single thrust. This time Belinda knew she was in for a real hammering and took what felt like an eternity of heavy thrusting, it was truly the best ride she had experienced since the Dutchman Peter Rouse. The Duchess then unlocked Belinda's ankles from their plastic shackles and expertly flipped her onto her front. She started to massage Belinda's back and buttocks.

All four of them??

What's with all the health
and safety checks? It's not
a roller coaster. ———————

And not a second more! ———————

Because manners are still important
when you're pounding someone with a
strap-on. ———————

Like a pair of curtains? ———————

Because there's nothing sexier
than a friction burn. ———————

She's in and out like a fiddler's elbow! ———————

After a fairly short time the Duchess said to Belinda, 'OK servant it's your turn'. Belinda couldn't believe what she was hearing and watched warily whilst the Duchess removed the straps and put the penis onto Belinda. The Duchess made sure everything was tight and in the right place and slapped Belinda's ass as a gesture of good to go. *Like a horse?*

There's a phrase I didn't think I'd read

Belinda walked around the bedroom with her monster prick out in front of her. She could hardly believe it and happily got to work on the Duchess, first in a standing position, giving it as hard as she had had it all that day. After about seven minutes of pounding the Duchess's vagina and cervix, Belinda asked her to get onto her knees, still remembering to call her 'My Lady'.

'Now hold your tits apart using your nipples My Lady'. Belinda then slid the leather penis up and down between the Duchess's breasts making sure there was a lot of friction taking place. After about five minutes of this technique the Duchess's skin became red and chaffed. 'True justice for keeping me in those plastic handcuffs.' thought Belinda.

And cervix? Vagina's fine – no need to go any deeper.

Bit harsh! Poor Duchess.

In fairness Belinda thought the old bird was not doing too badly, but she didn't let up on the pressure. She had always felt that the British aristocracy needed pain to make any sexual experience worthwhile. She also knew if she didn't give her mistress what she wanted, she would end up back in the cuffs tied to the bed. Belinda entered her vagina again and took her for another five minutes. The Duchess groaned and held her long legs wide for more.

Who's timing this? Someone got a stopwatch?

Is the Duchess's vagina
a revolving door? ————

Like crumpled bits of paper. ————

Why's everyone using breasts as handles?

That's not entirely unusual. Belinda arrives
most places totally naked.

Take cover – she's gonna blow!

'OK' thought Belinda, 'it's time for a couple of volcanic orgasms and she entered her mistress's vagina again. The dildo penetrated her cervix whilst stimulating her clitoris and the Duchess quickly orgasmed for her first time.

Belinda kept up the stimulation and soon the Duchess had orgasmed four times. She stammered 'Thank you servant, that was utterly fantastic.' Belinda came out of her and looked at the Duchess's face, she looked totally shattered, her make up was ruined and her immaculate hair was all over the place. Belinda then held her tits hard in her hands and pulled her into an upright position. The Duchess flopped back onto the bed, No stamina. thought Belinda. Then to Belinda's surprise her mistress immediately fell asleep. Belinda had obviously worn her out and suddenly thought what do I do now? She was free to leave, or was she?

I know how she feels.

Give the woman a break – she's in her fifties!

Has she got narcolepsy?

Belinda thought for a few moments and an idea entered her head. She took the discarded yellow handcuffs and put them on the Duchess's ankles. The Duchess didn't stir throughout this procedure and was now sleeping very deeply.

Something's actually happening. Is this going to become a story?

'Perfect.' thought Belinda, 'she should stay this way for at least four or five hours which will take me past my twelve hour servant contract'.

The second part of Belinda's plan was simple. As she had arrived at the chalet totally naked she had no clothing and needed something to get

No surprise there. She very
rarely wears underwear.

Belinda, give it a rest for two
seconds. She's sex mad!

You don't need to accessorize!
Just get dressed!

The Duchess is totally conked out.

Belinda's sexy weekend in a caravan has to
be a spin-off book, surely?

back to the Horse and Jockey for her late evening appointment with Peter Rouse. Calmly Belinda went to the wet room and picked up the Duchess's discarded riding clothes and boots. They would fit her just fine and she didn't need to wear the underwear. She quickly pulled on the jodhpurs and riding boots. Standing up she looked at herself in the large mirror… 'Not bad' she thought, 'Indeed they look very sexy' the black boots suited her colouring and the elasticated jodhpurs took the shape of her perfect ass extremely well. She pulled on the white blouse and attached the black cravat around the collar. Lastly she put on the red riding jacket, it indeed was a beauty and must have cost a small fortune. A last look in the mirror told Belinda what she already instinctively knew… she looked a million dollars.

She looks like a discount from a bargain bin at best.

She checked on the now snoring Duchess, grabbed the back riding cap and crop, switched off the lights and left the chalet. As she had hoped the Duchess had left the keys in the ignition. Belinda had no need for the horsebox so she unhooked it and mentally thanked one of her past male flings for teaching her how to caravan. She jumped into the driving seat, started up the engine, put on the headlights and headed for the main road. All she needed now was a signpost to the local town where she could orientate herself, find the Horse and Jockey and keep her appointment with Peter.

🧑 CHARACTER PROFILE: The Duchess

It is universally acknowledged that the British aristocracy are generally eccentric and the Duchess is no exception. This is immediately brought to the reader's attention through her flamboyant fashion sense. When we meet her she is wearing a white linen trouser suit and a panama hat, much like the man from the famous Del Monte adverts of the 1980s. Not much later she changes into full horse-riding gear, hinting at her keen interest in all things equestrian.

A woman in her fifties (or an 'old bird' as Flintstone unflatteringly describes her), the Duchess is also a mother, although it is not revealed how many children she has. She is a mysterious presence at the tombola and her motives behind bidding for Belinda are unclear. However, what does quickly become clear is that the Duchess is a kinky lover, favouring toys and whips in her sexual encounters and insisting Belinda calls her 'My Lady'.

She is also a terrible driver, although this could have something to do with the fact she has had a gin and tonic (her tipple of choice) before getting behind the wheel of her four-by-four.

• **Physical Attribute:** Two-ply tits

• **Dominant Character Trait:** Regal bisexual

• **Unusual Skill:** Adept with a dildo

• **Fun Fact:** Enjoys shagging, sobbing and sleeping

KEY THEME: Dildos

The earliest dildos are believed to date back to Upper Paleolithic times, nearly 30,000 years ago. Early dildos were made of stone, tar, wood and other firm materials that could be shaped as penises. Ancient Greeks even used a dildo made of bread.

Dildos were referenced in literature as early as the 1590s, when English playwright Thomas Nashe wrote a poem known as 'The Merrie Ballad of Nashe his Dildo'. Shakespeare also makes reference to them in Act IV, Scene IV of *The Winter's Tale*.

Modern dildos are made from many different materials, including glass, chrome-plated steel (popular in the BDSM scene) and silicone rubber. Silicone rubber dildos are the most inexpensive, making them the perfect choice for a first-time user.

The possession and sale of dildos is illegal in some jurisdictions, including India. Interestingly the American state of Alabama prohibits the sale of sex toys to this day. Furthermore, in Japan, many dildos are created to resemble animals or cartoon characters, so that they may be sold as toys, thus avoiding obscenity laws.

ACTIVITY

Find a local caravan and practise hooking it to a car using the following instructions:

1. Ensure the caravan handbrake is on.

2. Use the jockey wheel to raise the caravan hitch height until it is above the car tow ball.

3. Reverse the car, bringing the tow ball underneath the caravan hitch. Put the car's handbrake on.

4. Raise the hitch lever and lower the hitch on to the tow ball by winding up the jockey wheel.

5. Keep winding the jockey wheel up until the hitch fits over the tow ball, and the hitch-safety mechanism pops out, showing green, or in older types until the handle clicks back into place.

6. To check you have locked on properly, wind down the jockey wheel until the rear of the car starts to lift.

AUTHOR'S NOTE

Where does the equestrian influence in your writing come from?

I actually grew up in the countryside and while horses weren't a part of my everyday life they were around. Anyone who was fairly well off would own a horse and take it out fox hunting or racing at the annual tombola. The horse to me represents money, affluence and an aristocratic bearing. They're lovely animals and are the ideal way for Belinda to develop her social network, which will bring in even huger bonuses. There is also an awful lot of British life and fashion revolving around the horse and this gives me the opportunity to develop her friends, such as the Duchess, in various plot directions.

Rocky x

Reading group discussion points

- Compare and contrast the sexual approaches of Belinda and the Duchess. What does it say about their attitudes to life?

- The Duchess has flamboyant fashion sense. List celebrities who dress flamboyantly and discuss what this reflects about their personality.

- Are you pro- or anti-aristocracy? Debate the reasons for your stance.

- Reflect on the plot of *Belinda Blinked 1* at this stage. What has/hasn't happened? Where do you expect the story to go? Do you care?

Language Alert:

The spelling of Rocky Flintstone is an unyielding treasure trove of inconsistencies.

This is an important element of his oeuvre, displaying his maverick approach to writing and disregard for proofreading or copy-editing.

How vague. It's your novel, give him an age!

It's 8 p.m. What restaurant stops serving at 8:20?! That's prime time.

Language Alert:

Astute readers will have noted the erratic misuse of quotation marks in *Belinda Blinked 1*.

Here we witness the punctuation placed in the wrong direction. Rationale for such usage is unclear.

CHAPTER 10

The Horse and Jockey;

Of course they are. Being 'true to their word' is their only function.

The signposts were (true to their word) and Belinda soon found her way to the Horse and Jockey. She maneuvered the large car into one of the parking spaces, cut the engine and (found her way) to reception. It was now 8pm and she asked the youngish man on duty if dinner was still serving.

Ten points to Belinda.

'There's still (twenty more minutes left for orders madam) and might I add how extremely attractive you are looking this evening'. Belinda grinned and wondered if he had recognized the clothes or was just fishing for a bit of <u>sex later on that night</u>, whatever, she didn't want to disappoint so she replied,

Belinda is so arrogant – she construes even a kindly word as a sexual advance.

'Why thank you, how very gentlemanly of you to say so, especially as I'm dining alone!'

He smiled in return and nodded slowly as if confirming he might be available that evening.

I feel like I'm living on the edge. This time frame is SO tight.
Don't make a reservation, JUST SIT DOWN.
T-minus seventeen minutes till kitchen closes.

The stolen clothes of an old-aged pensioner? Yeah,
it'll be on the catwalks of Milan in no time.

Finally some urgency.
T-minus nine minutes.

Wine's the bar's jurisdiction!!!!
Order a fucking starter!!!
T-minus two minutes.

There are certain things a father should
never show his child. Not that I'm exactly in
a position to judge.

'She doesn't have time to 'eat at
her leisure'. Unless her food's been
blended and served intravenously,
that is.

'Please book me in for dinner, I'll be down in ten minutes.'

'Certainly Madam.'

She better be bloody quick. T-minus thirteen minutes.

Belinda asked for her key and went immediately to her room, she quickly spruced herself up and viewed the mirror. Yes she agreed, I do look extremely attractive in a very raw sexy way in this riding gear. I think this is a must new style for me, hopefully Peter Rouse will feel the same.

Pride before a fall, Belinda.

However there was no time to lose, she was famished, she hadn't eaten since that very quick lunchtime BBQ and she needed strength for the rest of what was going to be a very active evening. She ran down to the dining room, got shown her table and immediately ordered a bottle of Chardonnay, Chilean of course. Belinda prided herself on knowing her wines, her father after all was a sales manager for one of the big wine cellars in central London and he had spent many evenings training her in one of the best sales techniques for getting clients to buy without remorse. Drinking very good wine… and lots of it!

T-minus four minutes.

I knew Dad would worm his favourite tipple in here somewhere, the old soak.

Belinda dined at her leisure and for the first time that day she felt she wasn't under pressure, though her strange clothing didn't fit all that well and made her feel quite hot. She couldn't wait to start removing some of it she thought wickedly. Her meal finished Belinda took the rest of her wine to her room in an ice bucket where she sipped it slowly.

It's possible the Duchess didn't anticipate you robbing her blind so didn't take the time to have it tailored for you, Belinda.

She's been drinking white wine alone for 2 hours and 40 minutes. I'm no mathematician but that equals a hot mess.

Yes, because she's the only one there.

Yeah, that would be a mood killer. 'Straight after I had sex with you I went to the Duchess's house and she stuck a riding crop up me.'

And a couple of other things: 'I've stolen her car and left her unconscious at her motel. But how's your day been?'

Language Alert:

To 'pique your interest' is a common phrase in the English-speaking world. Here Flintstone has cleverly flipped the expression to reference the 'tweaking' of 'nipple tips' [sic] and other such sexual activities depicted in the novel.

Maybe just one glass of water?

It was now (11.00pm) and it was time for Peter to make an appearance. Belinda went down to the lobby where she ordered <u>another bottle of</u> <u>Chardonnay</u>, popped it into the replenished ice bucket and waited for Peter. Spot on at 11.30 he walked through the lobby door and <u>saw Belinda</u> <u>immediately</u>. He opened his hands and kissed her on the cheek, both sides…not unusual for a sophisticated European.

I think people would reserve that phrase for their mum's best friend's daughter's husband. Not someone who did them a topknot using their sperm.

'Would you like a drink Mr. Rouse?

'Oh please keep calling me Peter, after all we are (very much acquainted) after this afternoons events. Have I told you, you have a wonderful body my dear, and much, much better without the mud!'

At. What?

(They both laughed) and Peter said,

'I do like your current outfit Belinda… (very much in tune with this hotel'.)

Their small talk's run dry already.

Belinda gently blushed, she couldn't tell him how she had <u>acquired the</u> <u>clothing</u>, and she really (did enjoy wearing it)

'I do like wearing adventurous garments Peter and I hoped these would tweak your interest!'

'Top marks! Is that what they say in the show (jumping circles?) *No*

What, in the lobby? Literally get a room.

So he put his order in BEFORE he put his 'order' in? Awkward.

Belinda replied quickly,

'I'm more of a fox chasing type of person myself!'

Alert me when that begins.

'Ha ha ha… very good Belinda, I do enjoy your style of humour… now let's have some of that delicious wine.'

And a black coffee for the lady.

Belinda poured Peter a glass and leant back on the leather settee. Peter sat beside her and gently fondled her left thigh. Belinda decided to get round to business quickly, before she lost her tentative female advantage.

The classic TFA???!!! Whatever that is.

'Peter, could we position some of our pots and pans range in your supermarkets?'

Oh, for the first time she actually meant business. Finally.

'Absolutely', Peter replied, 'In fact this afternoon we've just ordered 3000 units of your Oxy Brillo range to get you started, and my purchasing team are looking at other products of yours which will fit into our present range of kitchen utensils.

'Wow!' Belinda gasped and opened her legs slightly.

Peter quickly took advantage and moved his hand higher up her thigh. Belinda undid her cravat and slowly unbuttoned the top four of her shirt buttons. Her delicious cleavage was now on view. Peter quickly moved his

That would be the entire blouse then.

Is it like a game of Twister? 'Left hand to upper thigh. Right hand to left breast.'

While cradling a boob is no time to criticize your price point.

Belinda has scheduled visits to Brussels, Texas and now Amsterdam, all in the next three weeks. She's just thinking of the air miles.

other hand to fondle her left breast and rubbed the nipple showing through the white linen.

The opposite of their Sales Director.

'No problem Belinda, after all your company's products are top class, if a little expensive and I'm sure we can overcome that little problem between us.'

You think you've got a relationship and then they invoice you.

'Yes!' Belinda gasped, her senses working overtime between Peter's massaging her very upper thigh and breast.

Vagina?

'I have access to some marketing incentives which will help.'

Seriously. Just shut up.

'Shhh, Belinda, just relax,' said Peter, 'we can discuss this all at the office next week in Amsterdam when you come to visit me.'

'Am I?' replied Belinda, 'Oh yes of course, I really can't wait!'

'Well let's make it Thursday, OK?'

Her diary's pretty full actually, Peter. Get in the queue.

'Yes, yes, I'll be there.'

'But now,' said Peter, let's get down to some real business.'

It should read: 'He slowly walked her out
of the lobby and up to her bedroom.' _____

Like a couple of rugby balls. _____

Drink! Why not. Belinda is. _____

Her mind thought? SHE thought. _____

Cultural Context:

The turn of the millennium and democratization of media
through smartphones and the Internet led to a surge in the
'celebrity sex tape' culture. With this plot twist Belinda is
joining the esteemed company of Kim Kardashian, Paris
Hilton and Pamela Anderson.

Dressing and undressing her simultaneously. That's like taking down her trousers while tying her shoes.

He slowly unbuttoned the remaining buttons on Belinda's shirt and let her full oval breasts fall out. In one fluid movement he tucked her shirt into the back of her jodhpurs and started kissing her. Belinda groaned, she could never resist the soft male touch of a mouth on her nipples, and Peter was exquisite in his sensuality.

Belinda would be GOLD in the Big Brother house.

Above his head in the corner of the lobby Belinda noticed a red light blinking... it was a security camera, no doubt recording what was going on. Her mind thought of the young man-ish behind the desk when she checked in... yes that was it, he was building his profile of her for his personal use. A wicked thought entered her mind, she would give him a session to record, and Peter Rouse a very good time into the bargain.

No, it's to protect the patrons against thieves. I'm looking at you, Miss Blumenthal.

The Horse & Jockey ££ ★☆☆☆

This converted outhouse situated in the picturesque rolling hills of Oxfordshire is a stone's throw from the ancestral family home of the Godwin dynasty.

Old-fashioned and in need of renovation, rooms are fully equipped with sumptuous beds, en-suites and 24-hour room service.

Top tip: don't be caught out by the unorthodox dinner serving times. Also, patrons are advised to keep an eye on their belongings as thieves frequent the establishment, though there is a higher than average security presence.

🔑 KEY THEME: Hospitality and Catering

British culture has long been synonymous with terrible food, and this was never more pertinent than with public houses. Traditionally pubs were drinking establishments and if they served meals at all they were simple cold dishes, such as cockles, a ploughman's lunch or pickled eggs. The invention of gastropubs in the 1990s revived the British pub scene and countless rural eateries have thrived in the twenty-first century. These restaurants tend to specialize in old English favourites, such as fish and chips, steak and ale pie and turkey sandwiches.

✏️ AUTHOR'S NOTE

Why is wine, specifically Chilean Chardonnay, Belinda's drink of choice?

Personally I love wine and in a previous life have even been a sommelier. That's why wine is used to lubricate Belinda's social intercourse with her clients. It's an important facet of modern-day life and one I wholeheartedly prescribe to. My favourite is Chardonnay, especially heavily oaked, which is not so much in vogue today. With Belinda I want to revive it and get it away from the tarty footballer image it sort of has.

I adore English B & Bs. I actually eschew the corporate hotel scene in place of bed and breakfasts/small hotels. I remember once subscribing to a great little book called *Staying off the Beaten Track*; it was simply splendid.

Rocky x

KEY SETTING: The Horse and Jockey Pub

Unlike Thomas Hardy, Flintstone rarely describes locations for their own sake. The description of the interview room in Chapter 1, for example, concentrates solely on the 'elegant wooden coat racks'. However, the reader is afforded one notable exception to this trend when, as Dickensian London or *Sex and the City*'s New York, the Horse and Jockey pub becomes a character in its own right.

In 2015 Flintstone cited Hampstead public house the Spaniards Inn as an influence for the setting of Belinda and Peter's late-night liaison. This is notable given the literary history of the north London watering hole; the pub is mentioned in Dickens's *The Pickwick Papers*, Bram Stoker's *Dracula* and legend states that John Keats wrote his ballad 'Ode to a Nightingale' in the beer garden.

With *Belinda Blinked 1* the Spaniards Inn has inspired another legendary author to create a truly iconic setting.

ACTIVITY

Do an Internet search to find the nearest Horse and Jockey pub to your current location. Take a visit and order a Chilean Chardonnay. Tag your adventure on Instagram: @mydadwrotea

Reading group discussion points

- In pairs discuss whether Belinda and Peter's relationship is healthy for business.

- Hollywood star Elijah Wood has actively lobbied for the role of the Youngish Man in the big-screen adaptation of *Belinda Blinked 1*. Who would you cast as Belinda?

- A hotel lobby is the setting for a sexual tryst this chapter. Have you ever been intimate in a public place?

- Flintstone presents two different sides to Belinda in Chapter 10. How do you view Belinda at this stage of the novel?

- Explore the theme of intimacy through the different perspectives held by Belinda and Peter.

Language Alert:

The first recorded use of 'randy' with the meaning 'lewd, lustful' was in 1847. *first and last time anyone's ever used it*

Can anyone be passionate and just throw stuff on the floor? We don't need a full laundry service.

Have we all forgotten about the camera??

Chapter 11

Sunday Night 11.55pm;

Belinda groaned more loudly,

'Peter, that's so good, would you mind removing my riding jacket and shirt?'

Most proper novels have spelling mistakes, right?

Peter was already feeling randy and he promptly striped Belinda of her upper garments. He folded them neatly, and placed the already discarded cravat on top of them on a nearby table. The lobby was very quiet, Sunday night at just about midnight meant the clients had all retired to bed, he felt he had a free rein to do what he needed to do.   *It's not a necessity.*

I suppose Belinda's breasts go through similar toils to an Olympian's muscles. They should probably have an ice bath.

'Massage me.' continued Belinda My tits so need a good massage. Peter acquiesced and concentrated his hands on her upper body. It was a firm body with lots of good muscle and superb rock hard nipples he thought to himself, she'll need these nipples if she's going to make the sales she wants.

As opposed to the jobs where you don't need nipples?

He'll chip a crown in a minute!

I beg your pardon???????????

Imagine checking in late and seeing THAT.

Literally Pandora's box.

Belinda's vagina is like Home Alone 2 –
everyone has seen it.

Treat it like a newly sown lawn.
Always keep it irrigated.

Belinda groaned more loudly and watched the movement of the camera and its blinking red light out of the corner of her eye.

'Peter, strip me, I so need to feel your hand on my clitoris, handle my cervix hard.' Again Peter acquiesced and gently pulled down the jodhpurs to the top of Belinda's black leather riding boots.

'No,' Belinda gasped, 'everything… take off the riding boots.' Peter took his hands off her jodhpurs and pulled first at her left boot and then her right boot. With both successfully removed it only took a second to pull the jodhpurs off Belinda's body. *Like a sexy hokey cokey*

At last he had her completely naked lying in front of him on the hotel lobby leather sofa. Belinda slowly moved her legs apart showing him her seductive vagina and all the mysteries he was about to again discover. *Like the hands on a Swiss watch.*

'Pass me my glass of Chardonnay.' Belinda drank it all in one go and calmly poured the remaining few drops over her vagina. She rubbed the golden liquid into her soft tanned flesh and beckoned Peter to taste it. Behind his head Belinda observed the camera recording the event. *Why wouldn't she be calm?*

Peter Rouse was no mean artist when it came to sexual activity, but never before had he been so completely entranced by such a beautiful female. He had no doubt in his own mind that he had come here to seduce her but this

What even is that?

151

So he thought, we really should go to the room, but in the meantime ... cunnilingus, Belinda?!

How do we break it to Peter? It's not her first orgasm of the night.

He's finally run out of synonyms, so he's started making them up.

Realized?! What is it? Adam and Eve?

one was different, could he have met his equal in his sexual symbolic world?
He shook his head, there was no way this girl was not his equal, she was
better than all the others, he had to stick to his plan and attempt to make
himself dominant over her. But he couldn't do it in a public hotel lobby,
he needed a private room away from prying people and no doubt hidden
security cameras.

Finally we can agree on something.

They're not prying; they're just trying to check in.

After five or six minutes of massaging Belinda's clitoris with his tongue he
tasted the first orgasm Belinda had that night. It was so sweet, yet bitter. As
an aphrodisiac he needed nothing else… except complete privacy. Belinda
was now moaning consistently and Peter, still fully clothed, continued to
massage her vagina and breast nipples. Each in their turn… and making
sure to never let the sexual pressure he had now so carefully built decline.

At last he had had enough.

That's weird. I had by line 3, Chapter 1.

Isn't that a flavour of Nik Naks!? Oh, wait, no, that's Nice 'n' Spicy. False alarm.

'Belinda, I want you, I want all your body with my body and we need to
retire to your room.'

Are these wedding vows?

'Peter, I thought you'd never ask.' replied Belinda winking at the silent
camera.

Some things you can just take for granted.

They both slowly stood up and realized Belinda was completely naked and
Peter was completely dressed.

153

Talking Point:

Belinda and Peter seem to share a unique sense of humour, both laughing at comments from the other when the audience has detected nothing of remote amusement. What is Flintstone saying here?

What would they
look like exactly?

Nice repetition of 'completely' to absolutely no effect.

SUNDAY NIGHT 11.55PM;

Yeah, for God's sake don't let anyone see your shoulders; leave the vagina out on show.

'We must look completely stupid.' Peter exclaimed.

Another corker from Peter.

Belinda burst out laughing and said, 'Pass me my riding jacket and boots'. She put on the jacket which neatly covered up her breasts and then pulled on both leather riding boots which hid nothing except her lower legs and toes. *So, boots then.*

'Very daring!' said Peter with a laugh and collected the unfinished wine in its ice bucket.

Walking past the reception area, Peter asked Belinda if she would like a nightcap as well as another bottle of wine. They both decided on brandy and the youngish man behind reception poured the golden liquid into two impeccable glasses. He said he would bring up the wine to Belinda's room as soon as he located some more ice. Peter now carrying both glasses of the swirling golden brown liquid followed Belinda's seductively swaying ass up the main staircase to her room.

Has he been there the whole time??

Anyone else picturing a camel?

Once inside, Belinda immediately removed her red jacket and asked Peter to do the honours with her riding boots.

'Have a sip first my dear, it's too good to delay any longer.' Belinda sat down on the edge of the bed and sipped her brandy.

155

Can it be aroused separately from him?

Cultural Context:

There are key differences between a massage for sports injuries and those during sexual play. Namely the former should not initiate sexual arousal and the latter would not necessarily improve a groin strain; in fact, it could severely exacerbate it.

Language Alert:

The pubic bone is a constituent part of the pelvis. It is covered by a fat layer, which is then covered by the rounded mass of fatty tissue known as the mons pubis. *sexy.*

She just asked you to take them off, but whatever.

'Besides, I'd like to fuck you with your boots on... they're extremely sexual in their own way you know!'

Belinda murmured 'If only you knew their origins.' and lay back on the bed anticipating Peter's desire.

Is everything Velcro?

He's going to kill her! That's so far north!

It only took Peter Rouse twenty five seconds to remove his clothes and position himself beside Belinda on the bed, he grabbed her cervix his penis was already well aroused and Belinda knew it would only take a little bit of extra encouragement to make it rock solid. She started to massage his chest, concentrating on his nipples. She then dipped her right forefinger into her brandy glass and rubbed it onto his upper body making a delicate figure of eight in a clockwise motion over his stomach. Peter relaxed, lay on his back and let Belinda's tongue follow the pattern of the brandy.

More symbols!

His cock shuddered and Belinda lifted herself onto it. Slowly, slowly she went down on his hard penis and when she felt it had fully entered her she started to grind her pubic bone against his. Peter started to groan in time to her motion, his voice became more intense as Belinda increased the friction between their two bodies. Within a minute he orgasmed and white semen came trickling out of Belinda's vagina.

Disappointing

Just in case we thought it was that radioactive green stuff from Ghostbusters.

Has he fallen asleep still inside her?? —————

What are you suggesting, Peter? —————

That's completely Belinda's mantra. —————

Belinda immediately caught the escaping liquid with her forefinger and once again traced the figure of eight pattern onto Peter's abdomen. He groaned more deeply and cried out as if in torment,

'More, more, more… Belinda!

Yes, exactly.

(Sshhh,) my darling Peter, you will get as much as you need, trust me!

Belinda continued the deep sexual movement until Peter again orgasmed, this time very deeply. Within seconds he had fallen unconscious, deeply asleep and Belinda withdrew her vagina knowing she had hit the target.

Was that bittersweet taste chloroform?

It took Peter Rouse one complete hour to wake up and when he did he felt as if he had shed twenty years of his life. He felt so energetic, so composed, so fulfilled. He looked around the hotel bedroom until he saw the naked Belinda, sitting on a casual chair watching him wake up.

He's thinking, SHIIIIIIT.

'Belinda, Belinda,' he stammered, 'that was stupendous, I feel so very good, so very alive, what did you do to me?'

''Peter, we just had good old fashioned sex… it was what we both wanted, and when you get what you want, you feel great!'

I did not see that coming; is this . . . a twist in the plot?!

Talking Point:

Belinda and Peter seem to have found a prime love match, when he drops the bombshell about his marital status. The doomed relationship is a theme visited over and over in great works of literature. Tragic couples range from Vronsky and Anna in *Anna Karenina* by Leo Tolstoy to Gatsby and Daisy in *The Great Gatsby* by F. Scott Fitzgerald. But perhaps none are as ill suited as Rouse and Blumenthal.

How much faster could he have been? Twenty-five seconds to get his clothes off, and one minute to get his rocks off!

Peter nodded slowly, as if realizing he had missed something important, but couldn't just quite remember what it was.

'Ok, but thank you, very, very much.'

'Peter, it's all my pleasure and thank you for your business order.'

'Belinda, it's nothing, but could you excuse me, I do need to get back to my wife, we both didn't expect me to be out for so long.'

Belinda smiled and said, 'Peter that's no problem, I'll see you Thursday afternoon in your Amsterdam offices.'

Doesn't give a shit.

'That's a date.' He replied, 'I'm so looking forward to it, but you must experience Amsterdam at night and we'll get you back to London on the late afternoon Friday flight.' —————— *Just a bit of admin before the chapter is through.*

'I'll make the arrangements and bring some evening wear.'

'Not too much, Belinda, not too much.' said Peter as he let himself out of the room.

I don't think Belinda bringing too many clothes is ever a concern

Female reproductive system

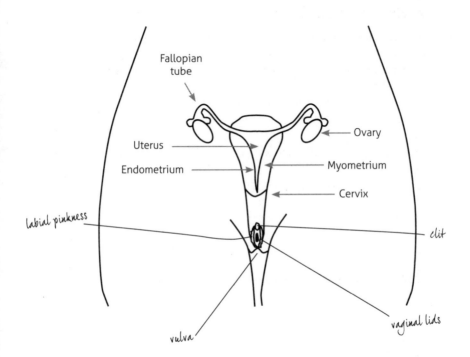

Fallopian tube

Ovary

Uterus

Endometrium

Myometrium

Cervix

labial pinkness

clit

vulva

vaginal lids

✏️ CULTURAL CONTEXT
Cervix (see diagram)

The cervix is the lower part of the uterus, which joins to the top of the vagina. The opening of the cervix allows blood to flow from the vagina during menstruation. In pregnant women it is closed to help keep the foetus in the uterus until the time of birth. Around half the cervix is visible with suitable medical apparatus; the rest lies above the vagina, far from view. Its structural integrity should not be compromised by grabbing, jabbing or stabbing.

The cervix has been documented anatomically since at least the time of Hippocrates, over two millennia ago. So it is not clear why Flintstone has no idea where it is or what function it performs.

🔑 KEY THEME: Foreplay

Peter Rouse is fully aware of the power of foreplay, using the time at the beginning of each sexual encounter to build arousal and excitement for both himself and Belinda. Whether this be through prodding, probing or groping, his approach is clear; in sex, as in business, never a second should be wasted. Not all of these moments of sexual prep are physical, some can also be psychological, and he uses his mental connection with Belinda to great effect.

✎ AUTHOR'S NOTE

How do you create a scene that is passionate?

I take it as a compliment that people think that this chapter is quite hot and heavy. I felt it was important to revisit and to emphasize the sexual nature of this erotic novella. Creating a great sex scene is all about the words; without the right words, such as 'cervix' and 'vulva', a good erotic writer would be nowhere. It's also important to have the characters properly dressed and to undress them without skipping too many of the actions this involves. If you want it racy, undress them faster; if you want it more romantic, then undress them slower. It's as simple as that!

Rocky x

♞ ACTIVITY

Print out a picture of the female reproductive system and stick to the wall. From a separate piece of paper cut out an image of the cervix, attaching a drawing pin to it. Blindfold a member of the gathering, spin them thrice, and see if they can pin the cervix on the vagina.

Reading group discussion points

- How do the styles of sexual play represent the characters' respective personalities?

- Who in the book group do you think is 'no mean artist'?

- How long is too fast to remove all your clothes?

- Who is in control in this chapter?

- How do you think Belinda felt when Peter mentioned his wife?

Cultural Context:

In trying to estimate the Youngish Man's age, it is helpful to refer to the Dating Equation. This rule defines that it is acceptable to be romantically connected to someone half your age plus seven and no lower. As Belinda is twenty-nine, using this formula the Youngish Man could be no younger than twenty-one. ....

Cultural Context:

Flintstone revealed in an interview that another favourite late-night snack is beef on white sliced bread with lashings of English mustard. ....

CHAPTER 12

The Night Receptionist;

Belinda put on her riding jacket, jodhpurs and leather boots, sat down in the corner chair and slowly sipped the rest of her unfinished brandy. Sure enough five minutes later there was a knock on her door.

Isn't it 2 a.m.? It's probably time for bed, Belinda.

'Room service, Madam.'

Pretty sure what she's about to be served isn't on the menu.

'Come in please.'

Will we ever know his name??

The youngish man on reception entered the room with a trolley on which sat the ice bucket with a full bottle of Chilean Chardonnay. Beside it sat two rounds of what looked like turkey sandwiches, one of Belinda's many favourite late night snacks

Dad does love a bit of turkey. On the twenty-fifth of every month, we have a full Christmas dinner.

'My sincere apologies for the lateness of the hour, but the ice machine started to play up Madam.'

Talking Point:

Thirty seconds is a long time in conversation. Try having a discussion in which your partner can't reply for thirty seconds. How does this affect the flow of the chat?

'Language Alert – Similar Vigour':

In phonaesthetics 'similar vigour' is an example of a phrase that is beautiful purely in terms of its sound without regard for meaning. J. R. R. Tolkein once cited 'cellar door' as the most beautiful combination of words in the English language.

This is the FIFTH person Belinda has shagged TODAY.

'I'm sure it did young man, don't apologise, your timing is appropriate, and I hope it's not the first time tonight it will be so!' It took about thirty seconds for the receptionist to understand Belinda's remark and he burst into a wide grin.

THIRTY seconds?!

'I understand Madam, thank you.' With that he shut the door, walked over to Belinda and kissed her on the lips.

Like she's holding a baby?

Belinda took his head in her left hand and returned the kiss with a similar vigour. He put his hands around her waist and pulled her body into his. She could feel his cock throbbing with excitement as they drew closer, but she did feel a tad hungry after her couple of hours with Peter. Slowly she let him go and said,

Is it wriggling around like a cat in a bag?

'It would be a pity to waste such a good wine and these wonderful sandwiches… have you eaten tonight?'

'In actual fact I haven't.' he replied, 'I tend to satisfy my sexual appetite first and then eat.'

She should be careful – sex is like swimming. You have to wait for two hours after food.

'Well in that case I think we'll break the rules just a little, here and now.' Belinda reached over and took a sandwich, at the same time she unbuttoned the only single button on her riding jacket. Her breasts once again fell out

A glass of wine and a turkey sandwich in the worst hotel in England – the Youngish Man has such small dreams.

She only asked for the trousers.

Where else would they go?

and stayed on show whilst she finished the sandwich. The youngish man took one as well and poured them both a glass of wine.

He sat on the edge of the bed and announced,

'You can't beat the high life!' Belinda laughed and toasted him with her half empty glass. One sandwich was enough for Belinda and she removed her riding jacket. She watched the instantaneous response in the youngish man's trousers and asked him to remove them. He obliged, but also took off his shirt, pants, shoes and socks. Now standing naked before her, she called him over. Belinda took his erect penis and gently rubbed cold chardonnay onto it. In fairness to the youngish man he didn't flinch and Belinda put his cock between her breasts. Using her two hands she squeezed both breasts together tightly and started to masturbate his penis.

Was it a footlong?

BOING

She's obsessed with using alcohol as lube.

It only took half a minute for him to start groaning. His hands fondled her long black hair bringing it up to the top of her head and letting it fall time after time. However to Belinda's surprise he didn't ejaculate and she guessed she'd have to work a bit harder to get that result.

Same amount of time it takes him to get a joke.

Give the guy a chance!

Good job she had that turkey sandwich for energy.

'Would you mind removing my riding boots… it enables me to pull down my jodhpurs you see.' He nodded understanding immediately and helped pull them off Belinda's legs and feet. By now Belinda had lost count of the

Oh THAT he gets straight away.

Weathered, worn and tatty – I suppose she
is getting like a pair of old boots.

It's grown so large it's now been described as
a region rather than an area. Belinda's vagina
has its own postcode.

His tongue is Sputnik and Belinda's
vagina is the Final Frontier.

She's not the only one.

times she had pulled on or pulled off these riding boots in the past ten hours, but she thought they were getting more supple each time. Perhaps like her own body she mused.

'Ravish me!' she commanded the youngish man, and he immediately removed her jodhpurs. Now naked he followed the black line of pubic hair to Belinda's vaginal region. He got down on his knees, pushed her legs apart and gently started probing her clitoris with his tongue. Belinda once again that evening groaned softly at the foreign invasion of her pubic area. But this time it was different she thought, this unexpected pleasure was for her and her only… a perfect way to end a busy working day. No business deals, no reputations to be lost or offended, just a plain simple fucking session.

What a weird metaphor. Sounds like a game of Risk.

Is that Dad's version of a fairytale 'happily ever after'?

173

⊙ CHARACTER PROFILE: the Youngish Man

The Youngish Man is employed at the Horse and Jockey Hotel in Windsor. He appears to work every available shift on the reception desk, although he is best known for his work as the Night Receptionist. We are left to speculate about his age and Flintstone's definition of 'youngish', prompting readers to guess at anything between eighteen and fifty-seven years old.

His only story arc is the turbulent time he has trying to repair the hotel's only ice machine. He manages to fix the problem but the source of the issue is never revealed. The Youngish Man is the only person Belinda sleeps with that day whom she has nothing to gain from. He offers respite from a seemingly endless day with potential business clients. It is, as Flintstone describes, 'just a plain simple fucking session' and perhaps an attempt to fill the book's word count.

- **Physical Attribute:** Looks between 18 and 57

- **Dominant Character Trait:** A desire to serve

- **Unusual Skill:** Fixing mechanical equipment

- **Fun Fact:** His name's Sam

AUTHOR'S NOTE

Belinda has sex with five people in one day. Were you worried that was too many?

When you're an author it's great to be lost in your own web of intrigue, plot development and unique simile assessment. So you can see how simple it is to lose track of time and sexual activity. I hadn't actually realized I'd written that Belinda had had sex with five people in a day by the end of this chapter.

Belinda was getting a little bit hacked off with corporate life. I mean, she'd just had three chaps who were all worth a few million quid, why not enjoy a fling with a youngish chap who was obviously starting out in life? He could have his own hotel within three years . . . why wouldn't you???

Rocky x

♞ ACTIVITY

Groaning is repeatedly referred to in *Belinda Blinked 1* (as an indication of sexual fulfilment as opposed to representing displeasure at a bad joke).

With a partner (sexual or platonic) practise your nuanced groaning – try to express a variety of emotions only through guttural moaning and see if they can guess which you are performing.

Rocky's Turkey Sandwich Recipe

Ingredients:

White sliced bread

Salted butter

Turkey breast in thick slices

Salt

Method:

1. Butter the slices of bread thickly. Gently salt the thickly sliced turkey to taste.

2. Place the turkey thickly over the first slice of buttered bread.

3. Place the second buttered slice of bread over the top. Push down firmly.

4. Cut into three pieces and arrange delicately on a white plate. Serve.

Step 2

Step 3

Step 4

KEY THEME: Alcohol

Alcohol is a recurring motif in *Belinda Blinked 1* and serves a number of literary functions – however, it is rarely used for its actual purpose of drinking. The two beverages that feature most heavily are gin and tonic and Chilean Chardonnay. Not coincidentally, these are two of Flintstone's favourite tipples. Gin and tonic is used flirtatiously by the women to tease their breasts through their wet blouses in Chapter 3. Furthermore, it is used for foreplay when the Duchess drinks tinned gin and tonic out of Belinda's vagina at the tombola. And, of course, it is used as a lubricant in this chapter when our heroine rubs wine over the Youngish Man's penis. Despite alcohol being used in these unusual scenarios, it is interesting to note that all the characters drink responsibly. This is most likely due to the fact that men find it harder to get and maintain an erection after prolonged, heavy drinking.

Reading group discussion points

- Discuss your favourite late-night snacks.

- Does Belinda receive good customer service at the Horse and Jockey?

- As a group, decide what constitutes 'the high life'.

- What's the latest you've ever gone to bed?

- Share any late-night hotel anecdotes with the group.

- Would you feel short-changed by a tit wank with a push-up bra?

Didn't Margaret Thatcher survive on only
four hours of sleep a night? Belinda 4 PM?

A dress is always in one piece. Otherwise it would be a skirt and top.

Oh, unless it's a one-piece because the bra and panties are attached
to the dress like a cheap shirt and T-shirt combo from Primark . . .

Like a caged animal - return her to the wild.

Talking Point:

Morality is a fluctuating concept throughout Flintstone's prose. Belinda is
undoubtedly a thief, yet here she redeems herself by returning the stolen
garments to the Duchess.

What does the inclusion of the word 'reluctantly' tell us about Belinda's ethics?

CHAPTER 13

The Duchess comes clean;

— She must be knackered.

It was six thirty in the morning when Belinda awoke from her deep sleep. The receptionist had left at two thirty giving her a much needed four hours sleep. There was much to do and certainly no time for breakfast, even if it were being served by the very sexually fulfilled night receptionist called Sam.

— FINALLY he gets a name. Just as she fucks off.

This time Belinda dressed in one of her simple one piece, black, work dresses with matching lace bra and panties. Her plan was very simple. She would get back to the motel, release the Duchesses ankles from the yellow handcuffs, take her back to the chairman's house where she could collect her company car and get into work for nine. The Duchess could then collect her trailer from the motel and continue her sex life as she wanted… but without her involvement. Belinda would also reluctantly return the horse riding outfit which had served her extremely well all Sunday evening.

Surely she deserves a day in lieu for all this?

She was all over her a few chapters ago. Fickle Belinda.

She's hard as nails. He's been
inside you; at least say goodbye. _____

Thank God I'd heard horsebox
theft was on the rise. _____

It's like a shit fairytale. Belinda
is now Prince Charming. _____

No, that's not how it works. Plus
she has to be in work for nine. _____

Bull. Shit. She could have taken Belinda to
the motel and made her a nice cup of tea.
The riding crop was not necessary. _____

Yes. Because it's 6:30 in the morning, Belinda.

He'll always be the Youngish Man to me.

The traffic was nonexistent as she left the Horse and Jockey. Sam had obviously gone to kitchen duty so no time was lost in saying farewell. The company was picking up the tab on the overnight room and meals, so she got off to a good start. She quickly motored through the beautiful Oxfordshire countryside to the Motel where she had left the Duchess attached to her bed. The horsebox was still in the parking spot where she had left it and the motel room looked quiet.

But not that vat of wine she guzzled, surely?

Belinda jumped out of the big vehicle and entered the room. In the bedroom she found the Duchess where she had left her, albeit her make up now smeared to hell.

Handcuffs will do that.

Is she the 'maniac with the taste for the dramatic'?

Belinda switched off the bedside light and gently shook the Duchess awake.

Like a rag doll?

'You've come back to release me.' was the first words she murmured.

'Yes.' said Belinda equally as softly, 'But you must understand that as I was your sex servant, so now you are mine.'

A bit late to recap the rules of the tombola.

The Duchess started to sob softly and replied,

Someone give the poor woman a hug and a hankie.

'I always knew it would come to this, I have to tell you, I was a very reluctant player in this erotic game, they left me no choice in the end, and now here I am… a sex servant to you, Miss Belinda.'

Who are 'they'?? Could there be a plot after all?

Well, she was just about to tell you. _____

*In what world are the monikers 'My Lady'
and 'Miss Belinda' equal?* _____

Cultural Context:

Here the theme of feminism shines through. *Belinda Blinked 1* is the only
known erotic novella that passes the Bechdel test.

The Bechdel test is a feminist benchmark developed by Alison Bechdel in
1985 for cinema. It states that there must be a scene in which two or more
named female characters have a conversation about anything besides men.

*Does he mean 'over the hill' or is she
just a really flamboyant lover?* _____

*Run. For. The. Hills.
Keep on the handcuffs and get the hell out of there.*

Drink!

Belinda blinked, was this whole episode a game organized by someone else, was there a master planner behind all of the tombola activities and the ramifications they were producing. It certainly couldn't be coincidence that she, Bella and Giselle were the ones to be made servants. Perhaps the Duchess knew more than she was telling, she needed to proceed softly, she needed the Duchess on her side.

Obviously. She's a few turkeys short of a sandwich, our Belinda.

'If you can call me Miss Belinda then I can happily call you 'My Lady'. Is this a good start to an equal relationship between us?'

'I think so, yes I know so… oh how I do want to be a sexual servant to you Miss Belinda! I just want you to fuck me hard with my beautiful black leather dildo and respect me for what I am… a happy sex servant to you!'

This is a beautiful greetings card. Not.

'Well that's fine I suppose, from your perspective, but what do I get out of the relationship.' replied Belinda.

Sex

The Duchess thought for a moment.

'I know that sexually I'm a bit over the top, age wise that is, but I do assure you I am a fanatical lover, and in my role as your sex servant I will do your every bidding. I am open to all new sex erotica and I promise to never disobey you in the sexual act. I will drink your orgasms, and eat your vagina all day long until you order me to stop.

I'll never eat again.

I order you to stop.

You met her last night. And have barely spoken.

> **Talking Point:**
>
> The theme of class becomes more pronounced as the novel progresses. In Chapter 1 Belinda is described as an 'upmarket woman'. By Chapter 7 she is knee-deep in mud and tied to a trellis. Here Belinda appears to have reached the pinnacle of her perceived sophistication.

Is that what happens when you're suddenly freed? Nelson Mandela's must have been smuggling peanuts.

> **Cultural Context:**
>
> The *Titanic* was a luxury liner that infamously sunk on its maiden voyage in 1912 after hitting an iceberg.
>
> In 1998 two of its wrought-iron rivets were recovered for scientific research. It was discovered that they were riddled with atypically high levels of slag, making them brittle and prone to fracture.

I'm imagining Belinda slamming into her nipples with force.

Belinda quickly interrupted and said,

'I get your intentions, and they are truly what I need of you if you wish to become my sex servant. But surely a person as well connected to the lineage of Britain, I mean you being a Duchess with all what that means could surely open doors I couldn't dream of ever even encountering.'

Why has she turned into Nancy from Oliver!?

'Miss Belinda, I adore you so much, yes, I will be able to introduce you into the highest sexual circles in the land.'

Nothing says sexy like cramp.

Belinda bent over and pulled the plastic handcuffs off the Duchesses ankles. The Duchess stood up and stretched her cramped body. Her nipples hardened with her feeling of freedom and they were now as large as the three inch rivets which had held the hull of the fateful Titanic together. Belinda was drawn to them like a magnet, she needed to touch them, caress them and finally suck them. The Duchess stood still as Belinda fulfilled her desires. *Tighten them with a spanner.*

7.5cm-long nipples?!

After two minutes of caressing and sucking, the Duchess carefully removed Belinda's one piece black work dress. She then slowly removed her black lace bra and after a few moments her panties. Belinda stepped out of her high heels and guided the Duchess back to the bed.

Get a move on - you need to get to work.

Will it never end? Please let it end.

185

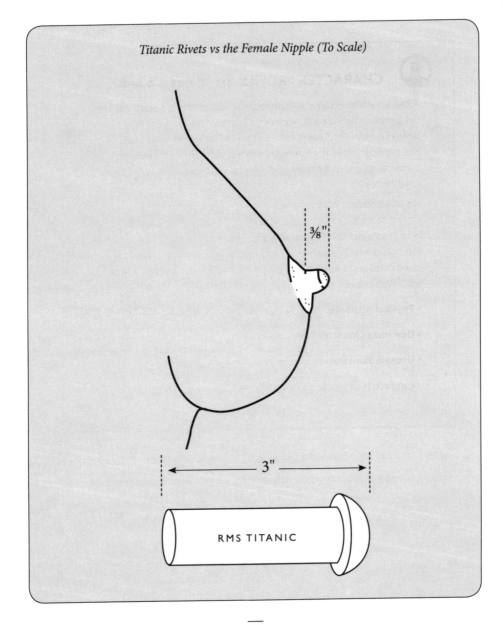

Titanic Rivets vs the Female Nipple (To Scale)

³⁄₈"

3"

RMS TITANIC

CHARACTER PROFILE: Sir James Godwin

A character who is rarely mentioned, but who serves as the mysterious link between Belinda and her 'sexual mistress' the Duchess, is Sir James Godwin. The Chairman and Chief Executive of Steele's Pots and Pans, Sir James is a formidable character. He has high-society connections and as a Knight of the Realm has been known to move in royal circles.

His philanthropic work is substantial and varied, though the cause closest to his heart is that of the Asses and Donkeys Trust of which is he is sole patron. He generously hosts the annual fundraiser and tombola at his Oxfordshire country house, which boasts a medium-sized maze and a Roman style amphitheatre. He also puts on a large BBQ. With chairs.

- **Physical Attribute:** Silver haired and suave

- **Dominant Character Trait:** Well-bred

- **Unusual Skill:** Donkey whisperer

- **Fun Fact:** His maze brings all the boys to the yard

🔓 KEY THEME: Naming Convention in Literature

Rocky Flintstone has a decidedly laissez-faire attitude to naming his characters; it took Belinda to be stripped naked for Tony to introduce himself in Chapter 1, for example. Indeed, throughout the novel the seductive victor of the tombola is known only as the Duchess. This ambiguity is typical of idiosyncratic novels and as such Flintstone is in good writerly company.

Fight Club by Chuck Palahniuk plays on the identity of protagonist Tyler Durden, ultimately rendering him nameless. Similarly in Daphne du Maurier's masterpiece *Rebecca* the narrator remains as ghostly and illusive as the titular character haunting the Manderley estate. It appeared we were destined for another such character in the form of the Youngish Man until this chapter, when he is revealed to be called by the run-of-the-mill name Sam.

✏️ AUTHOR'S NOTE

The Duchess alludes to a conspiracy in this chapter, hinting at a bigger story to unfold. Where do you see Belinda's adventures taking her next?

You have to remember that the Duchess is related to the highest bloodline in the land, and because she holds this sense of duty it is natural that she will never be able to release her deepest secrets. As a commoner Belinda has no option but to pursue her line of questioning in the bedroom.

The future books are an ongoing diary of Belinda's daily job where she meets both international and UK-based characters in her mission to make Steele's the top pots and pans manufacturer in the world. Tony is very much on board with this strategy, but Sir James Godwin will require winning over as he is the one who takes the ultimate monetary risk. This source of tension continues to run through the company and causes unnecessary strife in Belinda's life . . .

Rocky x

ACTIVITY

Go round the group and reveal a secret about yourself. In the style of the Duchess, stop short of actually divulging any of the details.

Reading group discussion points

- Do you see any similarity between the doomed lovers Rose and Jack in Titanic and the Duchess and Belinda in *Belinda Blinked 1*?

- How far would you go to secure an invite to a high-society luncheon?

- Has there been an instance where you left a lover without saying goodbye?

Still wrong. If it's got a red squiggly line under it, don't press print.

Are they like the T&Cs no one EVER reads when you update iTunes?

CHAPTER 14

Monday Morning 7.45am

The last chapter and he's still making typos.

'My Lady, I feel I need to fulfill your strongest desires.'

'Yes, Miss Belinda, please do what you need to me, and then if you so desire please fuck me with the black leather dildo, hard, up my vagina and don't stop... if it pleases you, Miss Belinda.'

As opposed to what? Sideways?

'My Lady, it does please me and I shall fulfill your needs, but then you need to drive me back to my car so I can get to work and end this very strange weekend.'

Understatement of the millennium.

'Yes, I accept your terms, please buckle on the dildo and fuck me slowly...
Miss Belinda.'

Sounds like she's on the waltzers.
Give that dildo a safety check.

Belinda walked over to the closet and took out the dildo. She carefully strapped it on making sure it was tight around her ass. The leather straps

I can't believe I'm learning how to attach a strap-on from my father.

They're the length of a credit card ——————

Love that Dad has given it a capital D.
Is it now a character? ——————

Who knew this would be an occupational hazard
in the pots and pans sector?
_____

Is she fucking her or fracking her? ——————————————

This reads as if Belinda's ——————————
munching on her own.

Not. A. Sensual. Word. ——————

This is sex not keyhole surgery. ——————

Is that the equivalent of straightening her thong? —————

No. It. Didn't. You're going left and right,
you're turning corners. Suddenly she's just one
big pinball machine.

Is she bulging out of it? It's all those turkey sandwiches.

and chrome buckles took (the strain) and the dildo was ready for action. The Duchess smiled and opened her legs wide as she lay back on the bed and let Belinda enter her slowly. Belinda lowered her head, her long black hair fell over the Duchesses breasts, she (found) the still (extended nipples) and started to (chew them gently) as she increased the friction on the Duchess's clitoris.

Like a rat?

Good for a bit of purchase.

A low moan came from the bed, which increased in intensity as the two females maintained their rhythm; the (Dildo) was strapped on so tightly that Belinda felt its surging movement (hit her pubic area) each time she penetrated (further into the Duchess) Meanwhile the Duchess had (found) Belinda's tits and was massaging her nipples as strongly as Belinda was chewing her (own) The Duchess suddenly climaxed, her orgasm was even more (infectious) on Belinda, and she pushed the dildo harder into her cervix. Eventually Belinda came out as gently as she could, realigned the dildo and went in again. The Duchess (steadied herself) and let out a long sigh as the dildo hit her (ovaries) Belinda pushed it further and further into her vagina, she leant forward and sucked the Duchess's tits and again started to ride her, hard.

Why are they having so much trouble locating things? They're not a Picasso painting.

Look behind you. You've gone so far the vagina is merely a dot.

Lest we forget: someone, somewhere, calls her granny.

'Please don't stop Miss Belinda, this is so good! The Duchess cried out in ecstasy.

'Yes My Lady… even I'm enjoying it, and soon it's going to be even better!'

Body in the bedroom. Mind in the office. ————————

Well, they're paper thin so she's
really just scrunching them. ————————

We're all being
punished ————————

Buyer's remorse there, ————————
Belinda.

Oh God, what's in
there? Will Mr Tumnus
be joining them? ————————

Like an old shire horse after a long day toiling the fields.

Belinda had no idea how what she was doing was going to improve, but she was up for it for at least another ten minutes. The Duchess lasted only two minutes when she orgasmed and Belinda felt it was time to change tack. By now she herself was feeling extremely horny and standing up she unbuckled the dildo and threw it onto the floor.

What is this?

"OK My Lady, it's your turn to please me… suck me all over!"

I'd rather have a Calippo.

Maybe just wait for instruction.

Belinda lay down on the bed as the Duchess got onto her knees. Needing no further instruction the Duchess started to lick Belinda's breasts, her tongue snaked down to her pubic hair and followed the trail to her vagina.

Why does she have a hairy chest?

Meanwhile Belinda grabbed her servant's ample tits and started to rub them hard. The Duchess groaned, Belinda groaned as her clit started to be punished by the Duchess's tongue. A few minutes later, Belinda orgasmed, not once but twice, her mind went into turmoil the deep sensations were too much for her. She struggled to regain consciousness and all she could murmur was,

We all groaned.

How would her eulogy read if this was how she popped her clogs?

'Thank you My Lady, thank you My Lady.'

'Thank you Miss Belinda.' Was the only reply she received as the Duchess got up and went to the closet 'It's time we finished this crazy weekend so let's get back to our real lives before we're missed!'

Oh thank God, this is all going to be a bad dream. And we're all going to wake up.

They'll share a dildo but they won't share a loofah. ————

Sounds like she can't
wait to escape. ————

'I agree, but what are you looking for?' replied Belinda.

Awkward

'My riding gear… I know I had it with me but don't worry, I've got my
white linen suit right here… I'll wear that instead, the midday meeting at
the Jockey Club doesn't require any formal wear… unless it's a dinner of
course! She laughed and Belinda joined in, totally unaware of the etiquette
of horse riding circles.

*Totally blagging it. Belinda does
not get the joke. And neither do I.*

Belinda and the Duchess showered separately, then dressed and prepared
themselves for the day. While Belinda hooked up the horse box to the 4x4
the Duchess packed the leather dildo safely into its special zinc coated case,
much like a professional photographer's camera. With the motel room
cleared, the Duchess locked the door, left the keys at reception and started
the engine of the big vehicle. In fairness she only scuffed one corner on the
journey back to the country house where Belinda's Merc was parked.

*It's not
kryptonite.*

*She'll lose her no
claims for that.*

Belinda jumped out of the front passenger seat and said farewell to the
Duchess. They had swopped email addresses and planned a reunion at
a hotel on the Isle of Whyte in three weeks' time. It was a gala ball and
the Duchess had promised to introduce her 'Sexual Mistress' to some
new acquaintances. Belinda took out her car keys and opened the Merc.
It started first time, she waved goodbye to the Duchess, who promptly
accelerated off in a cloud of gravel and dust.

*It's brand new,
you'd hope so.*

Bye then, Mad Max.

How very fitting for the last word to be 'fucked'. ————

Belinda lost no time in following her and was in the office for a very respectable 9.30am. As she sat down at her desk, Belinda could only wonder what the next two weeks would hold for her, if they were anything like the last 24 hours, she would be truly fucked!

BELINDA'S CHARACTER ARC

When we meet Belinda, she is embarking on a new chapter in her life, in an area of business she hasn't experienced before. But, in her inimitable style, she secures the job of her dreams.

Initially trepidatious about the challenge facing her, she quickly grows in confidence and over the course of a few days almost everyone at the office has seen her nipples, if not had sex with her.

At Steele's her skill set is truly tested; she is quite literally dragged through a hedge (maze) backwards, sold as a sex slave to a member of the British upper classes and is carted around in a horsebox. But within weeks she has secured big ticket sales with some major European operators – totalling 5,000 units, and has made some great alliances and contacts for further negotiations.

Personally she has made great bonds too: her relationship with Peter has a promising future (bar his pesky wife) and she has a great e-penpal in the Duchess.

What's next, we don't know, and until he puts pen to paper, perhaps neither does Flintstone.

KEY THEME: The British Aristocracy

Though the role of the British aristocracy has been drastically diminished in the modern era, well-bred members of the establishment still hold great influence and power within society. Unelected peers occupy the Upper Chamber of Parliament and the monarch bi-annually bestows honours on to the most worthy citizens of the land.

Public schools educate the elite of British society, with students often boarding at extortionate termly cost. The alumni of such institutions include past kings and prime ministers and great folklore surrounds them to this day. One particular myth is that of the 'soggy biscuit' game. Participants engage in group masturbation around a biscuit, ejaculating on to it en masse. The final pupil to do so must eat the creamed cookie as punishment.

AUTHOR'S NOTE

What was your writing process while penning *Belinda Blinked 1*?

Without giving away any spoiler alerts I write to a very defined plot line. I call it a timeline and it's basically the skeleton upon which I put on . . . or take off . . . the clothing of the characters and what they get up to each day. It actually means it's super easy to write the books. My timelines come to me when I'm awake in bed around 3:00 a.m. in the morning. Bammm – an idea just hits me and then I can get back to sleep.

Rocky x

ACTIVITY

Trade email addresses with the next stranger you encounter and become penpals. You must exchange correspondence at least three times a year for the next five.

Reading group discussion points

- How has Belinda changed your life?

- Looking at *Belinda Blinked 1* in its literary context, which novels and authors would you compare it to?

- Discuss what you've learned about sex from Rocky Flintstone.

- What passage of *Belinda Blinked 1* can't you forget?

- What are your hopes for Belinda's future?

- Whatever happened to Bill?

When Rocky Flintstone first sold his e-book to the world he crafted a compelling blurb with which to seduce the online market. Below is what made *Belinda Blinked 1* truly stand out in the saturated sea of self-penned erotica.

BLURB:

[handwritten: Least sexy name EVER.]

[handwritten: Great start, Dad; already a typo.]

Belinda Blumenthal gets exciting, sollicited sex regularly, so regularly *[handwritten: Oh that London.]* in fact she makes big bonuses from it. Based in London UK, Belinda works for Steeles Pots and Pans as their world wide Sales Director. Sexually *[handwritten: This has to be the first erotic novel about kitchenware.]* supported by Giselle and Bella her head office colleagues, Belinda always gets the order when it comes down to the bare facts. The client base is large so Belinda has the whole world to fuck and boy does she get stuck *[handwritten: Already dropped the F-bomb. Great.]* into it. This is the first book in the Belinda Blinked series where she gets hired by Tony her Managing Director and then goes on to make some sales *[handwritten: Oh no. Series means at least three.]* headway by bringing on board a large European customer, Peter Rouse, and makes initial inroads to the North American market through Jim Stirling. Read about the sexual conquests these men make and how the mysterious Duchess makes Belinda alive to the sexual fantasies of the hot riding set through supple black riding boots, jodhpurs and leather handled whips....

ROCKY'S PROFILE:

[handwritten: If this was on the back of the book I wouldn't have bought it. So boring.]

Rocky likes to write in the sun and with a glass of wine in his hand. Nothing makes him feel more at home. Based between Brazil and Marbella Spain he gets to grips with his stories, bringing them to print for his loyal readers. *Belinda Blinked 1* is his first novel of the series and Rocky has just completed his second, *Belinda Blinked 2.*

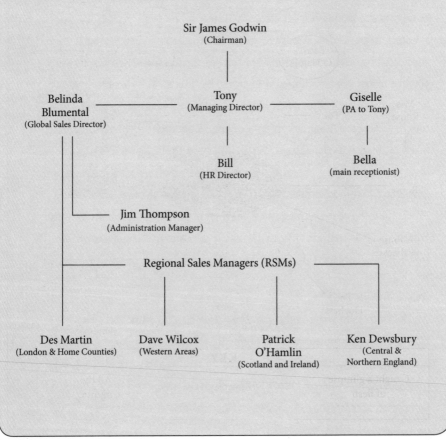

Steele's Pots & Pans
COMPANY STRUCTURE

Steele's is an international conglomerate with a focus on the pots and pans corner of the retail market. The corporation's hierarchy is similar to many sales operations, however uniquely you are able to ascend from PA to MD in 5 years.

Sir James Godwin
(Chairman)

Belinda Blumental
(Global Sales Director)

Tony
(Managing Director)

Giselle
(PA to Tony)

Bill
(HR Director)

Bella
(main receptionist)

Jim Thompson
(Administration Manager)

Regional Sales Managers (RSMs)

Des Martin
(London & Home Counties)

Dave Wilcox
(Western Areas)

Patrick O'Hamlin
(Scotland and Ireland)

Ken Dewsbury
(Central & Northern England)

Fig. 5

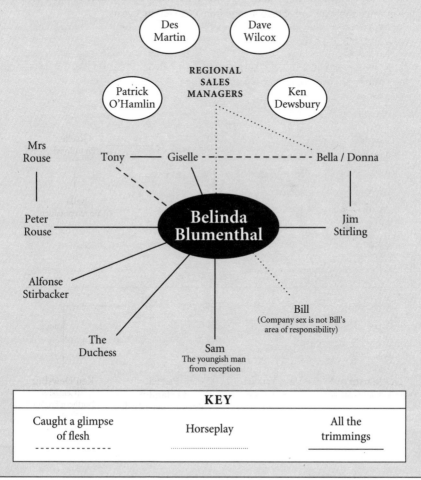

Belinda's Sex Tree

Within the world of *Belinda Blinked 1*, sexuality is fluid and sexual relations are prolific. Here's a handy reference to the carnal connections made throughout the course of the novel.

Des Martin

Dave Wilcox

REGIONAL SALES MANAGERS

Patrick O'Hamlin

Ken Dewsbury

Mrs Rouse

Tony — Giselle - - - - - - - - Bella / Donna

Belinda Blumenthal

Peter Rouse

Jim Stirling

Alfonse Stirbacker

Bill
(Company sex is not Bill's area of responsibility)

The Duchess

Sam
The youngish man from reception

KEY		
Caught a glimpse of flesh	Horseplay	All the trimmings
- - - - - - - - - - -	....	———————

Fig. 6

My Dad Wrote A Porno
THE PORN PEN NAME GENERATOR

Rocky Flintstone's anonymity is maintained with the shrewd use of his pseudonym.

To find your perfect nom de porn, just like Rocky, use our simple Porn Pen Name Generator.

Here's the equation: Month of birth + first initial of the person you'd like to take in the Leather Room = your erotic alias.

FIRST NAME

January	–	Rambo	July	–	Maverick
February	–	Terminator	August	–	Blade
March	–	Robocop	September	–	Cobra
April	–	Apollo	October	–	Chuck
May	–	Jean Claude	November	–	Indiana
June	–	Flash	December	–	Dredd

SURNAME

A	–	Oil	J	–	Boop	S	–	Fudd
B	–	Rubble	K	–	De Vil	T	–	Haddock
C	–	Squarepants	L	–	the Explorer	U	–	Gadget
D	–	Jetson	M	–	Le Pew	V	–	Sneer
E	–	McDuck	N	–	Woodpecker	W	–	Gummi
F	–	Dinkley	O	–	Slaghoople	X	–	Brown
G	–	Dastardly	P	–	Leghorn	Y	–	Griffin
H	–	O'Hare	Q	–	Cartman	Z	–	Simpson
I	–	Pitstop	R	–	Gonzales			

My Dad Wrote A Porno
THE DRINKING GAME

'Fun for all the family' . . . is something that has never been said about *Belinda Blinked 1*. The same is true of this game. Gather your least bashful friends and enjoy a night as thrilling as a lock-in at the Pentra.

The only drinks approved by Belinda are Chilean Chardonnay and gin & tonic but feel free to introduce beverages of your choosing, just ensure that there are enough impeccable glasses for all.

Drinks can be consumed the traditional way (via the mouth) or à la Belinda and the Duchess (via a vagina).

Allocate each player a key *Belinda Blinked 1* theme from the list, then when it arises, bottoms up! All four of them!

For more players, allocate themes in pairs.

THEMES

1. **Nipples** (including rivets or general breast references)
2. **Items of clothing being removed** (double-drink if it's done gently, swiftly or deftly)
3. **Business jargon** (including contractual details and mundane corporate chat)
4. **Genitalia, female** (including vaginal lids, labial pinkness and cervix)
5. **Genitalia, male** (double-drink if you can find Jim Stirling's)
6. **Thongs**
7. **Kissing** (anywhere)
8. **Stroking or sexual touching**
9. **New characters**
10. **When Belinda speaks** (for the lightweight of the group)

Everyone drinks when Belinda blinks!

My Dad Wrote A Porno
THE QUIZ

Belinda didn't get asked a single question in the interview for the job of her dreams, so this test is far more rigorous than her final interview at Steele's. See how well you know the cast of characters, plot points and literary motifs of *Belinda Blinked 1* with this handy revision quiz. When you're done, rate yourself:

1-10 correct = Not even quite as smart as Bella/Donna

11-20 correct = You're as bad as The Duchess is at driving

21-30 correct = A shrewd entrepreneur, you're an Alfonse in the making

31-40 correct = A BTEC in Business for you, like the Youngish Man is currently studying for

Over 40 correct = Genius. Belinda would shag you to congratulate you

1   How many times is the word 'tit' or 'tits' used in the text?

2   What are the first two words of *Belinda Blinked 1*?

3   What colour was Belinda's brassiere in the job interview?

4   What material were the elegant coat hooks made of in the job interview?

5   What colour was the leather seat Belinda was gently sweating on?

6   What job is Belinda interviewing for at Steele's Pots and Pans?

7   What is the job offer on the table?

8   Where does the runnel of vaginal liquid go in the job interview?

9   What is the name of the Human Resources Director who suddenly appears in the job interview?

10   What two ages does Flintstone give to Giselle in the book?

11   What nationality is Giselle?

12   What is Bella's job title at Steele's Pots and Pans?

13 What does Tony tell Belinda to wear for the chairman's country house event?

14 How much time passes between Chapter 1 and 2 of the book?

15 In whose office can the Leather Room be found?

16 What is the only item of furniture in the Leather Room?

17 After their brief dalliance in Chapter 2, when did Bella and Belinda arrange to meet privately for more sex?

18 True or false? Belinda has a briefcase.

19 What make is Belinda's work car?

20 How long does it take Belinda to drive from the office to her central London apartment?

21 Which Regional Sales Manager is responsible for central and northern England?

A: Patrick O'Hamlin
B: Dave Wilcox
C: Des Martin
D: Ken Dewsbury

22 Why can't the Regional Sales Managers get a taxi from Heathrow?

23 What is the name of the pub the RSMs go to for lunch with Belinda?

24 When was the last time Belinda says she saw a pair of red plastic handcuffs?

25 What country is Alfonse Stirbacker from?

26 How many outlets is the Yankee Jim Stirling responsible for?

A: 320
B: 617
C: 1,257
D: 2,184

27 What does Jim Stirling do as soon as he has cum?

28 What state is Jim Stirling from?

29 Name four of Belinda's body parts that Peter draws symbols on (point for each).

30 What hairstyle does Peter craft Belinda's hair into with his semen?

31 Who is in Belinda's 'glee team' (point for each)?

32 What is the Tombola's safeword? (For a bonus point, why is this safeword chosen?)

33 What was Belinda's number on her chair at the Tombola?

34 How much does Bella go for in the Tombola? (For a bonus point, who is the winning bidder?)

35 How does the Duchess demand to be addressed by Belinda?

36 How many times does Belinda make the Duchess orgasm with the leather dildo in the chalet?

37 What does Belinda think she looks like dressed in all the horse riding gear?

38 What time does dinner stop being served at the Horse and Jockey?

39 Which of the following items was NOT made of leather?
A: The settee in the lobby of the Horse and Jockey
B: The Duchess's dildo
C: Jim Stirling's black thong
D: The Duchess's riding boots

40 How many units of the Oxy Brillo range does Peter Rouse order?

41 How long does it take Peter Rouse to remove his clothes at the Horse and Jockey?

42 Belinda draws a figure of eight on Peter's stomach using what alcohol?

43 Complete this saying of Belinda's: 'When you get what you want . . .'

44 What room service does the Youngish Man bring to Belinda's room?

45 What is the name of the Youngish Man?

46 What is the Duchess's dildo case coated with?

47 What time is Belinda aiming to be in work for on Monday morning?

48 What time does Belinda actually arrive at work?

49 Which of these items was NOT black?
A: Alfonse Stirbacker's thong
B: Belinda's one-piece work dress
C: The Duchess's cravat
D: The Duchess's jodhpurs

50 How many times in the text does
Belinda blink?

A: 7

B: 11

C: 14

D: 17

ANSWERS

1: 30

2: Belinda blinked

3: Black

4: Wood

5: White

6: Sales Director

7: £85,000, plus car and all
the travel perks

8: Down Belinda's lower left
thigh

9: Bill

10: 26 and 24

11: Dutch

12: Main Receptionist

13: Tennis gear and no
undergarments, such as
thongs or bra

14: Three weeks

15: Tony's

16: A sophisticated and
expensive drinks cabinet

17: A week on Friday

18: True

19: Mercedes

20: Twenty minutes

21: D, Ken Dewsbury

22: The fare is too low as the
office is too close to the
airport.

23: The Bull in the Rushes

24: Kindergarten

25: Belgium

26: C, 1,257

27: Licks Belinda's tits

28: Texas

29: Tits, ass, mouth and ears

30: Ponytail

31: Bella and Giselle

32: Thimble – it stops you from
getting pricked

33: 13

34: £350 – Jim Stirling

35: My Lady

36: Four

37: A million dollars

38: 8.20 p.m.

39: C, Jim Stirling's black thong

40: 3,000

41: 25 seconds

42: Brandy

43: You feel great.

44: Chilean Chardonnay and
turkey sandwiches

45: Sam

46: Zinc

47: 9 a.m.

48: 9.30 a.m.

49: D, The Duchess's Jodhpurs

50: A, 7

211

'Robert Harris's *Pompeii* is his best yet: as explo   , as addictive as a thriller, as satisfying as great history   g Montefiore, 'Books of the Year', *Daily Telegraph*

'Blazingly exciting . . . Harris evokes   lieu soon to be engulfed by the volcano with confident expertise . . . What makes this novel all but unputdownable, though, is the bravura fictional flair that crackles throughout . . . Harris, as Vesuvius explodes, gives full vent to his genius for thrilling narrative. Fast-paced twists and turns alternate with nightmarish slow-motion scenes. Harris's unleashing of the furnace ferocities of the eruption's terminal phase turns his book's closing sequences into pulse-rate-speeding masterpieces of suffocating suspense and searing action. It is hard to imagine a more thoroughly enjoyable thriller rea   ter Kemp, *The Sunday Times*

'[A] beautifully craf   iller . . . Gripping and illuminating' Nicholas Coleridge, 'Books o   Year', *Evening Standard*

'A stunning novel . .   e subtlety and power of its construction holds our attention to the   Beryl Bainbridge, 'Books of the Year', *The Times*

'*Pompeii* by Robert arris was another triumph . . . put together with the skill of a craftsman' David Robson, 'Books of the Year', *Sunday Telegraph*

'Harris weaves events into a story of intrigue, brutality and even love with mounting excitement' Joan Bakewell, 'Books of the Year', *The Times*

'My favourite read this year has been Robert Harris's *Pompeii* – every bit as good as his earlier historical thrillers' Ian Kershaw, 'Books of the Year', *Mail on Sunday*

'The last days of Pompeii captured amid blazingly exciting drama . . . Dazzling evocation and bravura narrative energy coalesce to make this a masterpiece of suffocating suspense and searing action' Peter Kemp, 'Books of the Year', *The Sunday Times*

'Robert Harris has done the Michael Crichton trick of identifying one of the most basic of human fears and turning it into fiction. There are, however, two big differences between Harris and Crichton. One, *Pompeii* is not a futuristic novel; it is firmly set in the past. And, two, Robert Harris is a good writer . . . Apart from its thriller content — breakneck pace, constant jeopardy and subtle twists of plot — what distinguishes *Pompeii* is its vivid recreation of a former world . . . The depth of the research in the book is staggering . . . *Pompeii* is indeed a blazing blockbuster' Simon Brett, *Daily Mail*

'Harris's skill lies in disturbing the splendidly drawn luxury of Neapolitan life with premonitory intimations of catastrophe . . . Readers must hope that Robert Harris will want to return soon to the classical warm south' Robert McCrum, *Observer*

'Britain's leading thriller writer . . . The key to the tension, which Harris expertly cranks up, is that while the characters in the novel have no idea that Vesuvius is about to blow, the reader does . . . The scenes of violence and doom that Harris portrays with such relish are given added piquancy by the fact that the tourist who has visited Pompeii or Herculaneum will recognise many of them. The long drawn-out death agony of the two cities is brilliantly done. Explosive stuff, indeed — and yes, it goes with a bang' Tom Holland, *Daily Telegraph*

'Harris has done a tremendous job of evoking life in ancient Italy . . . When Vesuvius finally blows its top, you can almost taste the pumice. You can feel the ash in your hair . . . Harris had me imaginatively surrounded. I am lost in admiration at his energy and skill' Boris Johnson, *Mail on Sunday*

'Gripping, topical and dauntingly intelligent' John Carey, *The Sunday Times*

'The ability to disguise the outcome is held to be a vital part of the thriller writer's art. Robert Harris though, has built a major career in open defiance of this rule . . . Harris is equally successful in making us flinch and fear for characters who are going to a doom which we know before them . . . In the post-eruption sequences – chillingly, viscerally described – the novelist makes explicit implied connection with September 11 . . . Readers will be reminded here not of their school history books but of newspaper front pages just two years old' Mark Lawson, *Guardian*

'[Harris] eschews lavish dramatic irony in favour of fast-paced narrative. He judges every element of his craft with perfect professionalism – the page-turning pace, the easy-to-read but informative background-painting . . . Harris's Pompeii seems just around the corner – a Pompeii for our times' Felipe Fernández-Armesto, *The Times*

'The inspired aqueduct angle on events, the lively interaction of characters real and fictional and the time bomb in the shape of Vesuvius places Harris's novel in a distinguished tradition that successfully creates great fiction in an authentically imagined other world' Peter Jones, *Evening Standard*

'The final 100 pages are terrific, as good as anything Harris has done; and the last teasing paragraph, done with the lightest of touches, is masterly. A whole community, buried in volcanic ash 2000 years ago, has been brought to life . . . Stirring and absorbing' David Robson, *Sunday Telegraph*

'Harris has cleverly glossed and expanded on ancient sources, retelling the story very effectively . . . A master craftsman . . . Harris is a writer of integrity who does not seek refuge in postmodern nonsense. There are no temporal dislocations, 'unearthed diaries' or other hocus-pocus. He knows how to tell a story and achieves page-turning readability without effort' Frank McLynn, *Daily Express*

'Genuinely thrilling' *Literary Review*

'Harris triumphs . . . a skilled writer on top form . . . Harris turns the reader's foreknowledge to good effect, creating moments of irony and pathos . . . The pitfalls that come with this territory are skilfully avoided by Harris, who engages with material ancient and modern in a thoughtful way . . . A sophisticated thriller that takes in its stride the conventions of the historical novel, *Pompeii* deserves the place it will undoubtedly have at the top of the bestseller lists' *Times Literary Supplement*

'Vivid and convincing . . . The events are handled with a skill that kept me turning the pages' Jasper Griffin, *Spectator*

'As a writer, Mr Harris is as thought-provoking as he is entertaining. Thanks to his minute attention to detail, his handling of the eruption and his competence as a historian, the novel works both as an engaging thriller and as a believable portrayal of life in ancient Rome, with no small lesson for our own time' *The Economist*

'A gripping novel that carries the reader smoothly along as in a litter borne by several muscular Nubian slaves . . . Harris proves, if proof were needed, that he is a writer who, unfashionably, never loses sight of his obligation towards the reader's welfare and enjoyment . . . this expert piece of storytelling' Philip Kerr, *New Statesman*

'Harris is a knowing capable writer who understands better than anyone how to keep readers gripped. Never less than tremendous fun, *Pompeii* scores highly for quality of research and technical detail' *Time Out*

'Fast, fact filled, and quite fun. A blast, really' *Kirkus Reviews (Starred Review)*

'Harris colourfully evokes the sights and sounds of the ancient world' Christopher Hart, *Independent on Sunday*

'A brilliantly orchestrated thriller-cum-historical recreation that plays outrageous tricks with the reader's expectations . . . As the famous catastrophe approaches, we are pleasurably immersed in the sights, sounds and smells of the Ancient World, each detail conjured with jaw-dropping verisimilitude . . . Few who take this trip into a dangerous past will be able to resist Harris's spellbinding historical saga' Barry Forshaw, *Amazon.co.uk Editorial Review*

'Beautifully crafted . . . gripping and illuminating' Nicholas Coleridge, *Irish Examiner*

'Quite simply a wonderful novel . . . Harris has excelled yet again. His characters leap off the pages . . . It is beautifully written, meticulously researched and comes across as solidly true to the era. But don't take my word, read it and believe' Paul Carson, *Irish News*

'Harris has astounded millions with his ability to tell a captivating tale. Particularly adept at revealing the shocking ties between our past failures and their reverberating effects, this latest promises no less . . . We see the corruption and arrogance of a dying era amid the delicious intrigue and cool precision we expect from Harris' *The Good Book Guide*

'The ultimate page-turner . . . Goodies, baddies and great historical detail' *Good Housekeeping*, 'Top 10 Books of the Year'

'The must-read adventure . . . tremendous pace and verve' *Eve*, 'Books of the Year'

'Deeply researched, faithful to the evidence, and gloriously successful in evoking a plausible picture of what the world of first-century Italy might have been like . . . A gripping taste of the contradictions of a real Roman world' Professor Andrew Wallace-Hadrill, *The Art Newspaper*

'Terrific and prodigiously researched . . . Attilius' scientific curiosity – and knowledge – places him squarely within the tradition of the best literary detectives, such as Sherlock Holmes and Hercule Poirot . . . The author has clearly done a herculean study of Roman civil engineering and waterworks, which *Pompeii* smoothly incorporates without ever feeling pedantic . . . It's a testament to the tightly wound structure and entertaining detail that Harris has built into his idiosyncratic historical-volcanological mystery that, even though you know how his story ends, you still can't put it down as the inevitable comes closer . . . Harris's latest thriller is so cunningly devised that, however unsurprising its denouement is, it still manages to end with a bang' Daniel Mendelsohn, *The New York Times*

'Harris is terrific in describing the grandeur of the aqueducts, inviting the reader inside' *People Magazine*

'Another winner . . . Packed with fascinating historical details, Harris's yarn brings Pompeii to life even as it faces death' *Newsweek*

'Harris vividly brings to life the ancient world on the brink of disaster' *Booklist*

'*Pompeii* proves once again that a talented writer can make anything interesting . . . Vivid atmosphere, rich characterizations and awesome descriptions of nature's fury that show Harris working at the top of his game' *Time Out New York*

POMPEII

ROBERT HARRIS

POMPEII

HUTCHINSON
LONDON

First published in 2003 by Hutchinson

1 3 5 7 9 10 8 6 4 2

Map of Aqua Augusta by Reginald Piggott

Hutchinson
The Random House Group Limited
20 Vauxhall Bridge Road, London SW1V 2SA

Random House Australia (Pty) Limited
20 Alfred Street, Milsons Point, Sydney
New South Wales 2061, Australia

Random House New Zealand Limited
18 Poland Road, Glenfield
Auckland 10, New Zealand

Random House South Africa (Pty) Limited
Endulini, 5A Jubilee Road, Parktown 2193, South Africa

The Random House Group Limited Reg. No. 954009

www.randomhouse.co.uk

A CIP catalogue record for this book
is available from the British Library

Papers used by Random House are
natural, recyclable products made from wood grown in
sustainable forests; the manufacturing processes conform to
the environmental regulations of the country of origin

ISBN 0 09 179493 5

Typeset by Palimpsest Book Production Limited
Polmont, Stirlingshire

Printed and bound in Great Britain by
Clays Ltd, St Ives plc
Bungay, Suffolk

About the Author

Robert Harris was born in Nottingham in 1957 and is a graduate of Cambridge University. He has been a reporter on the BBC's Newsnight and Panorama programmes, Political Editor of the *Observer*, and a columnist on *The Sunday Times* and *Daily Telegraph*. In 2003 he was named Columnist of the Year in the British Press Awards. He is the author of the number one bestsellers *Fatherland*, *Enigma* and *Archangel*, as well as five non-fiction books. He lives in Berkshire with his wife and four children.

To Gill

Author's note

The Romans divided the day into twelve hours. The first, *hora prima*, began at sunrise. The last, *hora duodecima*, ended at sunset.

The night was divided into eight watches – *Vespera*, *Prima fax*, *Concubia* and *Intempesta* before midnight; *Inclinatio*, *Gallicinium*, *Conticinium* and *Diluculum* after it.

The days of the week were Moon, Mars, Mercury, Jupiter, Venus, Saturn and Sun.

Pompeii takes place over four days.

Sunrise on the Bay of Naples in the fourth week of August AD 79 was at approximately 06:20 hours.

'American superiority in all matters of science, economics, industry, politics, business, medicine, engineering, social life, social justice, and of course, the military was total and indisputable. Even Europeans suffering the pangs of wounded chauvinism looked on with awe at the brilliant example the United States had set for the world as the third millennium began.'

Tom Wolfe, *Hooking Up*

'In the whole world, wherever the vault of heaven turns, there is no land so well adorned with all that wins Nature's crown as Italy, the ruler and second mother of the world, with her men and women, her generals and soldiers, her slaves, her pre-eminence in arts and crafts, her wealth of brilliant talent . . .'

Pliny, *Natural History*

'How can we withhold our respect from a water system that, in the first century AD, supplied the city of Rome with substantially more water than was supplied in 1985 to New York City?'

A. Trevor Hodge, author,
Roman Aqueducts & Water Supply

Nola

Abellinum

Vesuvius

AQUA AUGUSTA

R. Sarnus

POMPEII

Stabiae

Salernum

Amalfitana

Aqua Augusta A.D. 79

===== Roads   ▚▚▚▚ Aqueduct

0   5   10 miles

0   5   10   15 km

MARS

22 August

Two days before the eruption

Conticinium

[04:21 hours]

'A strong correlation has been found between the magnitude of eruptions and the length of the preceding interval of repose. Almost all very large, historic eruptions have come from volcanoes that have been dormant for centuries.'

Jacques-Marie Bardintzeff, Alexander R. McBirney,
Volcanology *(second edition)*

They left the aqueduct two hours before dawn, climbing by moonlight into the hills overlooking the port – six men in single file, the engineer leading. He had turfed them out of their beds himself – all stiff limbs and sullen, bleary faces – and now he could hear them complaining about him behind his back, their voices carrying louder than they realised in the warm, still air.

'A fool's errand,' somebody muttered.

'Boys should stick to their books,' said another.

He lengthened his stride.

Let them prattle, he thought.

Already he could feel the heat of the morning beginning to build, the promise of another day without rain. He was younger than most of his work gang, and shorter than any of them: a compact, muscled figure with cropped brown hair. The

3

shafts of the tools he carried slung across his shoulder – a heavy, bronze-headed axe and a wooden shovel – chafed against his sunburnt neck. Still, he forced himself to stretch his bare legs as far as they would reach, mounting swiftly from foothold to foothold, and only when he was high above Misenum, at a place where the track forked, did he set down his burdens and wait for the others to catch up.

He wiped the sweat from his eyes on the sleeve of his tunic. Such shimmering, feverish heavens they had here in the south! Even this close to daybreak, a great hemisphere of stars swept down to the horizon. He could see the horns of Taurus, and the belt and sword of the Hunter; there was Saturn, and also the Bear, and the constellation they called the Vintager, which always rose for Caesar on the twenty-second day of August, following the Festival of Vinalia, and signalled that it was time to harvest the wine. Tomorrow night the moon would be full. He raised his hand to the sky, his blunt-tipped fingers black and sharp against the glittering constellations – spread them, clenched them, spread them again – and for a moment it seemed to him that he was the shadow, the nothing; the light was the substance.

From down in the harbour came the splash of oars as the night watch rowed between the moored triremes. The yellow lanterns of a couple of fishing boats winked across the bay. A dog barked and another answered. And then the voices of the labourers slowly climbing the path beneath him: the harsh local accent of Corax the overseer – *'Look, our new aquarius is waving at the stars!'* – and the slaves and the free men, equals for once in their resentment if nothing else, panting for breath and sniggering.

The engineer dropped his hand. 'At least,' he said, 'with

such a sky, we have no need of torches.' Suddenly he was vigorous again, stooping to collect his tools, hoisting them back on to his shoulder. 'We must keep moving.' He frowned into the darkness. One path would take them westwards, skirting the edge of the naval base. The other led north, towards the seaside resort of Baiae. 'I think this is where we turn.'

'He thinks,' sneered Corax.

The engineer had decided the previous day that the best way to treat the overseer was to ignore him. Without a word he put his back to the sea and the stars, and began ascending the black mass of the hillside. What was leadership, after all, but the blind choice of one route over another and the confident pretence that the decision was based on reason?

The path here was steeper. He had to scramble up it sideways, sometimes using his free hand to pull himself along, his feet skidding, sending showers of loose stones rattling away in the darkness. People stared at these brown hills, scorched by summer brushfires, and thought they were as dry as deserts, but the engineer knew differently. Even so, he felt his earlier assurance beginning to weaken, and he tried to remember how the path had appeared in the glare of yesterday afternoon, when he had first reconnoitred it. The twisting track, barely wide enough for a mule. The swathes of scorched grass. And then, at a place where the ground levelled out, flecks of pale green in the blackness – signs of life that turned out to be shoots of ivy reaching towards a boulder.

After going halfway up an incline and then coming down again, he stopped and turned slowly in a full circle. Either his eyes were getting used to it, or dawn was close now, in which case they were almost out of time. The others had halted behind him. He could hear their heavy breathing. Here was another story for them to take back to Misenum – how their new young aquarius had dragged them from their beds and marched them into the hills in the middle of the night, and all *on a fool's errand*. There was a taste of ash in his mouth.

'Are we lost, pretty boy?'

Corax's mocking voice again.

He made the mistake of rising to the bait: 'I'm looking for a rock.'

This time they did not even try to hide their laughter.

'He's running around like a mouse in a pisspot!'

'I know it's here somewhere. I marked it with chalk.'

More laughter – and at that he wheeled on them: the squat and broad-shouldered Corax; Becco, the long-nose, who was a plasterer; the chubby one, Musa, whose skill was laying bricks; and the two slaves, Polites and Corvinus. Even their indistinct shapes seemed to mock him. 'Laugh. Good. But I promise you this: either we find it before dawn or we shall all be back here tomorrow night. Including you, Gavius Corax. Only next time make sure you're sober.'

Silence. Then Corax spat and took a half-step forward and the engineer braced himself for a fight. They had been building up to this for three days now, ever since he had arrived in Misenum. Not an hour had passed without Corax trying to undermine him in front of the men.

And if we fight, thought the engineer, he will win – it's five against one – and they will throw my body over the cliff and say I slipped in the darkness. But how will that go down in Rome – if a second aquarius of the Aqua Augusta is lost in less than a fortnight?

For a long instant they faced one another, no more than a pace between them, so close that the engineer could smell the

6

stale wine on the older man's breath. But then one of the others – it was Becco – gave an excited shout and pointed.

Just visible behind Corax's shoulder was a rock, marked neatly in its centre by a thick white cross.

A ttilius was the engineer's name – Marcus Attilius Primus, to lay it out in full, but plain Attilius would have satisfied him. A practical man, he had never had much time for all these fancy handles his fellow countrymen went in for. ('Lupus', 'Panthera', 'Pulcher' – 'Wolf', 'Leopard', 'Beauty' – who in hell did they think they were kidding?) Besides, what name was more honourable in the history of his profession than that of the *gens* Attilia, aqueduct engineers for four generations? His great-grandfather had been recruited by Marcus Agrippa from the ballista section of Legion XII 'Fulminata' and set to work building the Aqua Julia. His grandfather had planned the Anio Novus. His father had completed the Aqua Claudia, bringing her into the Esquiline Hill over seven miles of arches, and laying her, on the day of her dedication, like a silver carpet at the feet of the Emperor. Now he, at twenty-seven, had been sent south to Campania and given command of the Aqua Augusta.

A dynasty built on water!

He squinted into the darkness. Oh, but she was a mighty piece of work, the Augusta – one of the greatest feats of engineering ever accomplished. It was going to be an honour to command her. Somewhere far out there, on the opposite side of the bay, high in the pine-forested mountains of the Appenninus, the aqueduct captured the springs of the Serinus and bore the water westwards – channelled it along sinuous underground passages, carried it over ravines on top of tiered arcades, forced it across valleys through massive syphons – all the way down to the plains of Campania, then around the far side of Mount Vesuvius, then south to the coast at Neapolis, and finally along the spine of the Misenum peninsula to the dusty naval town, a distance of some sixty miles, with a mean drop along her entire length of just two inches every one hundred yards. She was the longest aqueduct in the world, longer even than the great aqueducts of Rome and far more complex, for whereas her sisters in the north fed one city only, the Augusta's serpentine conduit – the matrix, as they called it: the motherline – suckled no fewer than nine towns around the Bay of Neapolis: Pompeii first, at the end of a long spur, then Nola, Acerrae, Atella, Neapolis, Puteoli, Cumae, Baiae and finally Misenum.

And this was the problem, in the engineer's opinion. She had to do too much. Rome, after all, had more than half a dozen aqueducts: if one failed the others could make up the deficit. But there was no reserve supply down here, especially not in this drought, now dragging into its third month. Wells that had provided water for generations had turned into tubes of dust. Streams had dried up. River beds had become tracks for farmers to drive their beasts along to market. Even the Augusta was showing signs of exhaustion, the level of her enormous reservoir dropping hourly, and it was this which had brought him out on to the hillside in the time before dawn when he ought to have been in bed.

From the leather pouch on his belt Attilius withdrew a small block of polished cedar with a chin rest carved into one side of it. The grain of the wood had been rubbed smooth and bright by the skin of his ancestors. His great-grandfather was said to have been given it as a talisman by Vitruvius, architect to the Divine Augustus, and the old man had maintained that the spirit of Neptune, god of water, lived within it. Attilius had no time for gods – boys with wings on their feet, women riding dolphins, greybeards hurling bolts of lightning off the tops of mountains in fits of temper – these were stories for children, not men. He placed his faith instead in stones and water, and in the daily miracle that came from mixing two parts of slaked lime to five parts of puteolanum – the local red sand – conjuring up a substance that would set underwater with a consistency harder than rock.

But still – it was a fool who denied the existence of luck, and if this family heirloom could bring him that . . . He ran his finger around its edge. He would try anything once.

He had left his rolls of Vitruvius behind in Rome. Not that it mattered. They had been hammered into him since child-hood, as other boys learnt their Virgil. He could still recite entire passages by heart.

'*These are the growing things to be found which are signs of water: slender rushes, wild willow, alder, chaste berry, ivy, and other things of this sort, which cannot occur on their own without moisture . . .*'

'Corax over there,' ordered Attilius. 'Corvinus there. Becco, take the pole and mark the place I tell you. You two: keep your eyes open.'

Corax gave him a look as he passed.

'Later,' said Attilius. The overseer stank of resentment almost as strongly as he reeked of wine, but there would be time enough to settle their quarrel when they got back to Misenum. For now they would have to hurry.

A grey gauze had filtered out the stars. The moon had dipped. Fifteen miles to the east, at the mid-point of the bay, the forested pyramid of Mount Vesuvius was becoming visible. The sun would rise behind it.

'This is how to test for water: lie face down, before sunrise, in the places where the search is to be made, and with your chin set on the ground and propped, survey these regions. In this way the line of sight will not wander higher than it should, because the chin will be motionless . . .'

Attilius knelt on the singed grass, leant forward, and arranged the block in line with the chalk cross, fifty paces distant. Then he set his chin on the rest and spread his arms. The ground was still warm from yesterday. Particles of ash wafted into his face as he stretched out. No dew. Seventy-eight days without rain. The world was burning up. At the fringe of his eyeline he saw Corax make an obscene gesture, thrusting out his groin – 'Our aquarius has no wife, so he tries to fuck Mother Earth instead!' – and then, away to his right, Vesuvius darkened and light shot from the edge of it. A shaft of heat struck Attilius's cheek. He had to bring up his hand to shield his face from the dazzle as he squinted across the hillside.

'In those places where moisture can be seen curling and rising into the air, dig on the spot, because this sign cannot occur in a dry location . . .'

You saw it quickly, his father used to tell him, or you did not see it at all. He tried to scan the ground rapidly and methodically, shifting his gaze from one section of the land to the next. But it all seemed to run together – parched browns and greys and streaks of reddish earth, already beginning to waver in the sun. His vision blurred. He raised himself on his elbows and wiped each eye with a forefinger and settled his chin again.

There!

As thin as a fishing line it was – not 'curling' or 'rising' as

Vitruvius promised, but snagging, close to the ground, as if a hook were caught on a rock and someone were jerking it. It zig-zagged towards him. And vanished. He yelled and pointed – 'There, Becco, there!' – and the plasterer lumbered towards the spot. 'Back. Yes. There. Mark it.'

He scrambled to his feet and hurried towards them, brushing the red dirt and black ash from the front of his tunic, smiling, holding the magical block of cedar aloft. The three had gathered around the place and Becco was trying to jam the pole into the earth, but the ground was too hard to sink it far enough.

Attilius was triumphant. 'You saw it? You must have seen it. You were closer than I.'

They stared at him blankly.

'It was curious, did you notice? It rose like this.' He made a series of horizontal chops at the air with the flat of his hand. 'Like steam coming off a cauldron that's being shaken.'

He looked from one to another, his smile fixed at first, then shrinking.

Corax shook his head. 'Your eyes are playing tricks on you, pretty boy. There's no spring up here. I told you. I've known these hills for twenty years.'

'And I'm telling you I saw it.'

'Smoke.' Corax stamped his foot on the dry earth, raising a cloud of dust. 'A brush fire can burn underground for days.'

'I know smoke. I know vapour. This was vapour.'

They were shamming blindness. They had to be. Attilius dropped to his knees and patted the dry red earth. Then he started digging with his bare hands, working his fingers under the rocks and tossing them aside, tugging at a long, charred tuber which refused to come away. Something had emerged from here. He was sure of it. Why had the ivy come back to life so quickly if there was no spring?

He said, without turning round, 'Fetch the tools.'

'Aquarius –'

'*Fetch the tools!*'

They dug all morning, as the sun climbed slowly above the blue furnace of the bay, melting from yellow disc to gaseous white star. The ground creaked and tautened in the heat, like the bowstring of one of his great-grandfather's giant siege engines.

Once, a boy passed them, dragging an emaciated goat by a rope halter toward the town. He was the only person they saw. Misenum itself lay hidden from view just beyond the cliff edge. Occasionally its sounds floated up to them – shouts of command from the military school, hammering and sawing from the shipyards.

Attilius, an old straw hat pulled low over his face, worked hardest of all. Even when the others crept off occasionally to sprawl in whatever patches of shade they could find, he continued to swing his axe. The shaft was slippery with his sweat and hard to grip. His palms blistered. His tunic stuck to him like a second skin. But he would not show weakness in front of the men. Even Corax shut up after a while.

The crater they eventually excavated was twice as deep as a man's height, and broad enough for two of them to work in. And there was a spring there, right enough, but it retreated whenever they came close. They would dig. The rusty soil at the bottom of the hole would turn damp. And then it would bake dry again in the sunlight. They would excavate another layer and the same process would recur.

Only at the tenth hour, when the sun had passed its zenith, did Attilius at last acknowledge defeat. He watched a final stain of water dwindle and evaporate, then flung his axe over the lip of the pit and hauled himself after it. He pulled off his hat and fanned his burning cheeks. Corax sat on a rock and watched him. For the first time Attilius noticed he was bare-headed.

He said, 'You'll boil your brains in this heat.' He uncorked his waterskin and tipped a little into his hand, splashed it on to his face and the back of his neck, then drank. It was hot – as unrefreshing as swallowing blood.

'I was born here. Heat doesn't bother me. In Campania we call this cool.' Corax hawked and spat. He tilted his broad chin towards the hole. 'What do we do with this?'

Attilius glanced at it – an ugly gash in the hillside, great mounds of earth heaped all around it. His monument. His folly. 'We'll leave it as it is,' he said. 'Have it covered with planks. When it rains, the spring will rise. You'll see.'

'When it rains, we won't need a spring.'

A fair point, Attilius had to concede.

'We could run a pipe from it,' he said thoughtfully. He was a romantic when it came to water. In his imagination, a whole pastoral idyll suddenly began to take shape. 'We could irrigate this entire hillside. There could be lemon groves up here. Olives. It could be terraced. Vines –'

'Vines!' Corax shook his head. 'So now we're farmers! Listen to me, young expert from Rome. Let me tell you some-thing. The Aqua Augusta hasn't failed in more than a century. And she isn't going to fail now. Not even with you in charge.'

'We hope.' The engineer finished the last of his water. He could feel himself blushing scarlet with humiliation, but the heat hid his shame. He planted his straw hat firmly on his head and pulled down the brim to protect his face. 'All right, Corax, get the men together. We've done here for the day.'

He collected his tools and set off without waiting for the others. They could find their own way back.

He had to watch where he put his feet. Each step sent a scattering of lizards rustling away into the dry undergrowth. It was more Africa than Italy, he thought, and when he reached the coastal path, Misenum appeared beneath him, shimmering in the haze of heat like an oasis town, pulsing – or so it seemed to him – in time with the cicadas.

The headquarters of the western imperial fleet was a triumph of Man over Nature, for by rights no town should exist here. There was no river to support her, few wells or springs. Yet the Divine Augustus had decreed that the Empire needed a port from which to control the Mediterranean, and here she was, the embodiment of Roman power: the glittering silver discs of her inner and outer harbours, the golden beaks and fan-tail sterns of fifty warships glinting in the late afternoon sun, the dusty brown parade ground of the military school, the red-tiled roofs and the whitewashed walls of the civilian town rising above the spiky forest of masts in the shipyard.

Ten thousand sailors and another ten thousand citizens were crammed into a narrow strip of land with no fresh water to speak of. Only the aqueduct had made Misenum possible.

He thought again of the curious motion of the vapour, and the way the spring had seemed to run back into the rock. A strange country, this. He looked ruefully at his blistered hands.

'A fool's errand –'

He shook his head, blinking his eyes to clear them of sweat, and resumed his weary trudge down to the town.

Hora undecima

[17:42 hours]

> *'A question of practical importance to forecasting is how
> much time elapses between an injection of new magma
> and an ensuing eruption. In many volcanoes, this time
> interval may be measured in weeks or months, but in
> others it seems to be much shorter, possibly days or hours.'*
>
> Volcanology *(second edition)*

A t the Villa Hortensia, the great coastal residence on the northern outskirts of Misenum, they were preparing to put a slave to death. They were going to feed him to the eels.

It was not an unknown practice in that part of Italy, where so many of the huge houses around the Bay of Neapolis had their own elaborate fish farms. The new owner of the Villa Hortensia, the millionaire Numerius Popidius Ampliatus, had first heard the story as a boy – of how the Augustan aristocrat, Vedius Pollio, would hurl clumsy servants into his eel pond as a punishment for breaking dishes – and he often referred to it admiringly as the perfect illustration of what it was to have power. Power, and imagination, and wit, and a certain *style*.

So when, many years later, Ampliatus, too, came to possess a fishery – just a few miles down the coast from Vedius Pollio's old place at Pausilypon – and when one of his slaves also destroyed something of rare value, the precedent naturally came back into his mind. Ampliatus had been born a slave himself; this was how he thought an aristocrat ought to behave.

The man was duly stripped to his loincloth, had his hands tied behind his back and was marched down to the edge of the sea. A knife was run down both of his calves, to draw an attractive amount of blood, and he was also doused with vinegar, which was said to drive the eels mad.

It was late afternoon, very hot.

The eels had their own large pen, built well away from the other fish ponds to keep them segregated, reached by a narrow concrete gangway extending out into the bay. These eels were morays, notorious for their aggression, their bodies as long as a man's and as wide as a human trunk, with flat heads, wide snouts and razor teeth. The villa's fishery was a hundred and fifty years old and nobody knew how many lurked in the labyrinth of tunnels and in the shady areas built into the bottom of the pond. Scores, certainly; probably hundreds. The more ancient eels were monsters and several wore jewellery. One, which had a gold earring fitted to its pectoral fin, was said to have been a favourite of the Emperor Nero.

The morays were a particular terror to this slave because – Ampliatus savoured the irony – it had long been his responsibility to feed them, and he was shouting and struggling even before he was forced on to the gangway. He had seen the eels in action every morning when he threw in their meal of fish heads and chicken entrails – the way the surface of the water flickered, then roiled as they sensed the arrival of the blood, and the way they came darting out of their hiding-places to fight over their food, tearing it to pieces.

At the eleventh hour, despite the sweltering heat, Ampliatus himself promenaded down from the villa to watch, attended by his teenaged son, Celsinus, together with his household steward, Scutarius, a few of his business clients (who had followed him from Pompeii and had been hanging around since dawn in the hope of dinner), and a crowd of about a hundred of his other male slaves who he had decided would profit by witnessing the spectacle. His wife and daughter he had ordered to remain indoors: this was not a sight for women. A large chair was set up for him, with smaller ones for his guests. He did not even know the errant slave's name. He had come as part of a job lot with the fish ponds when Ampliatus had bought the villa, for a cool ten million, earlier in the year.

All manner of fish were kept, at vast expense, along the shoreline of the house – sea bass, with their woolly-white flesh; grey mullet, that required high walls around their pond to prevent them leaping to freedom; flatfish and parrot fish and giltheads; lampreys and congers and hake.

But by far the most expensive of Ampliatus's aquatic treasures – he trembled to think how much he had paid for them, and he did not even much like fish – were the red mullet, the delicate and whiskered goatfish, notoriously difficult to keep, whose colours ran from pale pink to orange. And it was these that the slave had killed. Whether by malice or incompetence, Ampliatus did not know, nor care, but there they were: clustered together in death as they had been in life, a multi-hued carpet floating on the surface of their pond, discovered earlier that afternoon. A few had still been alive when Ampliatus was shown the scene, but they had died even as he watched, turning like leaves in the depths of the pool and rising to join the others. Poisoned, every one. They would have fetched six thousand apiece at current market prices – one mullet being worth five times as much as the miserable slave who was supposed to look after them – and now they were fit only for the fire. Ampliatus had pronounced sentence immediately: 'Throw him to the eels!'

The slave was screaming as they dragged and prodded him towards the edge of the pool. It was not his fault, he was shouting. It was not the food. It was the water. They should fetch the aquarius.

The aquarius!

Ampliatus screwed up his eyes against the glare of the sea. It was hard to make out the shapes of the writhing slave and of the two others holding him, or of the fourth, who held a boat-hook like a lance and was jabbing it into the doomed man's back – mere stick-figures, all of them, in the haze of the heat and the sparkling waves. He raised his arm in the manner of an emperor, his fist clenched, his thumb parallel with the ground. He felt godlike in his power, yet full of simple human curiosity. For a moment he waited, tasting the sensation, then abruptly he twisted his wrist and jammed his thumb upward. Let him have it!

The piercing cries of the slave teetering on the edge of the eel-pond carried up from the seafront, across the terraces, over the swimming pool and into the silent house where the women were hiding.

Corelia Ampliata had run to her bedroom, thrown herself down on the mattress, and pulled her pillow over her head, but there was no escaping the sound. Unlike her father, she knew the slave's name – Hipponax, a Greek – and also the name of his mother, Atia, who worked in the kitchens, and whose lamentations, once they started, were even more terrible than his. Unable to bear the screams for more than a few moments, she sprang up again and ran through the deserted villa to find the wailing woman, who had sunk against a column in the cloistered garden.

Seeing Corelia, Atia clutched at her young mistress's hem and began weeping at her slippered feet, repeating over and over that her son was innocent, that he had shouted to her as he was being carried away – it was the water, the water, there was something wrong with the water. Why would nobody listen to him?

Corelia stroked Atia's grey hair and tried to make such soothing noises as she could. There was little else that she could do. Useless to appeal to her father for clemency – she knew that. He listened to nobody, least of all to a woman, and least of all women to his daughter, from whom he expected an unquestioning obedience – an intervention from her would only make the death of the slave doubly certain. To Atia's pleas she could only reply that there was nothing she could do.

At this, the old woman – in truth she was in her forties, but Corelia thought of slave years as being like dog years, and she appeared at least sixty – suddenly broke away and roughly dried her eyes on her arm.

'I must find help.'

'Atia, Atia,' said Corelia gently, 'who will give it?'

'He shouted for the aquarius. Didn't you hear him? I shall fetch the aquarius.'

'And where is he?'

'He may be at the aqueduct down the hill, where the watermen work.'

She was on her feet now, trembling but determined, looking around her wildly. Her eyes were red, her dress and hair disordered. She looked like a madwoman and Corelia saw at once that no one would pay her any attention. They would laugh at her, or drive her off with stones.

'I'll come with you,' she said, and as another terrible scream rose from the waterfront Corelia gathered up her skirts with one hand, grabbed the old woman's wrist with the other and together they fled through the garden, past the empty porter's stool, out of the side door, and into the dazzling heat of the public road.

The terminus of the Aqua Augusta was a vast underground reservoir, a few hundred paces south of the Villa Hortensia, hewn into the slope overlooking the port and known, for as long as anyone could remember, as the Piscina Mirabilis – The Pool of Wonders.

Viewed from the outside, there was nothing particularly wonderful about her and most of the citizens of Misenum passed her without a second glance. She appeared on the surface as a low, flat-roofed building of red brick, festooned with pale-green ivy, a city block long and half a block wide, surrounded by shops and storerooms, bars and apartments, hidden away in the dusty back streets above the naval base.

Only at night, when the noise of the traffic and the shouts of the tradesmen had fallen silent, was it possible to hear the low, subterranean thunder of falling water, and only if you went into the yard, unlocked the narrow wooden door and descended a few steps into the Piscina itself was it possible to appreciate the reservoir's full glory. The vaulted roof was supported by forty-eight pillars, each more than fifty feet high – although most of their length was submerged by the waters of the reservoir – and the echo of the aqueduct hammering into the surface was enough to shake your bones.

The engineer could stand here, listening and lost in thought, for hours. The percussion of the Augusta sounded in his ears not as a dull and continuous roar but as the notes of a gigantic water-organ: the music of civilisation. There were air shafts in the Piscina's roof, and in the afternoons, when the foaming spray leapt in the sunlight and rainbows danced between the pillars – or in the evenings, when he locked up for the night and the flame of his torch shone across the smooth black surface like gold splashed on ebony – in those moments, he felt himself to be not in a reservoir at all, but in a temple dedicated to the only god worth believing in.

Attilius's first impulse on coming down from the hills and into the yard at the end of that afternoon was to check the level of the reservoir. It had become his obsession. But when he tried the door he found it was locked and then he remembered that Corax was carrying the key on his belt. He was so tired that for once he thought no more about it. He could hear the distant rumble of the Augusta – she was running: that was all that counted – and later, when he came to analyse his actions, he decided he could not really reproach himself for any dereliction of duty. There was nothing he could have done. Events would have worked out differently for him personally, that was true – but that hardly mattered in the larger context of the crisis.

So he turned away from the Piscina and glanced around the deserted yard. The previous evening he had ordered that the space be tidied and swept while he was away, and he was pleased to see that this had been done. There was something reassuring to him about a well-ordered yard. The neat stacks of lead sheets, the amphorae of lime, the sacks of puteolanum, the ruddy lengths of terracotta pipe – these were the sights of his childhood. The smells, too – the sharpness of the lime; the dustiness of fired clay left out all day in the sun.

He went into the stores, dropped his tools on the earth floor and rotated his aching shoulder, then wiped his face on the sleeve of his tunic and re-entered the yard just as the others trooped in. They headed straight for the drinking fountain without bothering to acknowledge him, taking turns to gulp the water and splash their heads and bodies – Corax, then Musa, then Becco. The two slaves squatted patiently in the shade, waiting until the free men had finished. Attilius knew he had lost face during the course of the day. But still, he could live with their hostility. He had lived with worse things.

He shouted to Corax that the men could finish work for the day, and was rewarded with a mocking bow, then started to climb the narrow wooden staircase to his living quarters.

The yard was a quadrangle. Its northern side was taken up by the wall of the Piscina Mirabilis. To the west and south were storerooms and the administrative offices of the aqueduct. To the east was the living accommodation: a barracks for the slaves on the ground floor, and an apartment for the aquarius above it. Corax and the other free men lived in the town with their families.

Attilius, who had left his mother and sister behind in Rome, thought that in due course he would probably move them down to Misenum as well and rent a house, which his mother could keep for him. But for the time being he was sleeping in the cramped bachelor accommodation of his predecessor, Exomnius, whose few possessions he had had moved into the small spare room at the end of the passage.

What had happened to Exomnius? Naturally, that had been Attilius's first question when he arrived in the port. But nobody had had an answer, or, if they had, they weren't about to pass it on to him. His enquiries were met by sullen silence. It seemed that old Exomnius, a Sicilian who had run the Augusta for nearly twenty years, had simply walked out one morning more than two weeks ago and had not been heard of since.

Ordinarily, the department of the Curator Aquarum in Rome which administered the aqueducts in regions one and two (Latium and Campania) would have been willing to let matters lie for a while. But given the drought, and the strategic importance of the Augusta, and the fact that the Senate had risen for its summer recess in the third week of July and half its members were at their holiday villas around the bay, it had been thought prudent to dispatch an immediate replacement. Attilius had received the summons on the Ides of August, at dusk, just as he was finishing off some routine maintenance work on the Anio Novus. Conducted into the presence of the Curator Aquarum himself, Acilius Aviola, at his official residence on the Palatine Hill, he had been offered the commission. Attilius was bright, energetic, dedicated – the senator knew how to flatter a man when he wanted something – with no wife or children to detain him in Rome. Could he leave the next day? And, of course, Attilius had accepted at once, for this was a great opportunity to advance his career. He had said farewell to his family and had caught the daily ferry from Ostia.

He had started to write a letter to them. It lay on the nightstand next to the hard wooden bed. He was not very good at letters. Routine information – *I have arrived, the journey was good, the weather is hot* – written out in his schoolboy's hand was the best he could manage. It gave no hint of the turmoil he felt within: the pressing sense of responsibility, his fears about the water shortage, the isolation of his position. But they were women – what did they know? – and besides, he had been taught to live his life according to the Stoic school: to waste no time on nonsense, to do one's job without whining, to be the same in all circumstances – intense pain, bereavement, illness – and to keep one's lifestyle simple: the camp-bed and the cloak.

He sat on the edge of the mattress. His household slave, Phylo, had put out a jug of water and a basin, some fruit, a loaf, a pitcher of wine and a slice of hard white cheese. He washed himself carefully, ate all the food, mixed some wine into the water and drank. Then, too exhausted even to remove his shoes and tunic, he lay down on the bed, closed his eyes and slipped at once into that hinterland between sleeping and waking which his dead wife endlessly roamed, her voice calling out to him – pleading, urgent: 'Aquarius! Aquarius!'

H is wife had been just twenty-two when he watched her body consigned to the flames of her funeral pyre. This woman was younger – eighteen, perhaps. Still, there was enough of the dream that lingered in his mind, and enough of Sabina about the girl in the yard for his heart to jump. The same darkness of hair. The same whiteness of skin. The same voluptuousness of figure. She was standing beneath his window and shouting up.

'Aquarius!'

The sound of raised voices had drawn some of the men from the shadows and by the time he reached the bottom of the stairs they had formed a gawping half-circle around her. She was wearing a loose white tunica, open wide at the neck and sleeves – a dress to be worn in private, which showed a little more of the milky plumpness of her bare white arms and breasts than a respectable lady would have risked in public. He saw now that she was not alone. A slave attended her – a skinny, trembling, elderly woman, whose thin grey hair was half pinned up, half tumbling down her back.

She was breathless, gabbling – something about a pool of red mullet that had died that afternoon in her father's fish ponds, and poison in the water, and a man who was being fed to the eels, and how he must come at once. It was hard to catch all her words.

He held up his hand to interrupt her and asked her name.

'I am Corelia Ampliata, daughter of Numerius Popidius Ampliatus, of the Villa Hortensia.' She announced herself impatiently and, at the mention of her father, Attilius noticed Corax and some of the men exchange looks. 'Are you the aquarius?'

Corax said, 'The aquarius isn't here.'

The engineer waved him away. 'I am in charge of the aqueduct, yes.'

'Then come with me.'

She began walking towards the gate and seemed surprised when Attilius did not immediately follow. The men were starting to laugh at her now. Musa did an impersonation of her swaying hips, tossing his head grandly: '"Oh aquarius, come with me . . . !"'

She turned, with tears of frustration glinting in her eyes.

'Corelia Ampliata,' said Attilius patiently and not unkindly, 'I may not be able to afford to eat red mullet, but I believe them to be sea-water fish. And I have no responsibility for the sea.'

Corax grinned and pointed. 'Do you hear that? She thinks you're Neptune!'

There was more laughter. Attilius told them sharply to be quiet.

'My father is putting a man to death. The slave was screaming for the aquarius. That is all I know. You are his only hope. Will you come or not?'

'Wait,' said Attilius. He nodded towards the older woman, who had her hands pressed to her face and was crying, her head bowed. 'Who is this?'

'She's his mother.'

The men were quiet now.

'Do you see?' Corelia reached out and touched his arm. 'Come,' she said quietly. 'Please.'

'Does your father know where you are?'

'No.'

'Don't interfere,' said Corax. 'That's my advice.'

And wise advice, thought Attilius, for if a man were to take a hand every time he heard of a slave being cruelly treated, he would have no time to eat or sleep. A sea-water pool full of dead mullet? That was nothing to do with him. He looked at Corelia. But then again, if the poor wretch was actually *asking* for him.

Omens, portents, auspices –

Vapour that jerked like a fishing line. Springs that ran backward into the earth. An aquarius who vanished into the hot air. On the pastured lower slopes of Mount Vesuvius, shepherds had reported seeing giants. In Herculaneum, according to the men, a woman had given birth to a baby with fins instead of feet. And now an entire pool of red mullet had died in Misenum, in the space of a single afternoon, of no apparent cause.

A man must make such sense of it as he could.

He scratched his ear. 'How far away is this villa?'

'Please. A few hundred paces. No distance at all.' She tugged at his arm, and he allowed himself to be pulled along. She was not an easy woman to resist, this Corelia Ampliata. Perhaps he ought at least to walk her back to her family? It was hardly safe for a woman of her age and class to be out in the streets of a naval town. He shouted over his shoulder to Corax to follow, but Corax shrugged – 'Don't interfere!' he repeated – and then Attilius, almost before he realised what was happening, was out of the gate and into the street, and the others were lost from sight.

It was that time of day, an hour or so before dusk, when the people of the Mediterranean begin emerging from their houses. Not that the town had lost much of its heat. The stones were like bricks from a kiln. Old women sat on stools beside their porches, fanning themselves, while the men stood at the bars, drinking and talking. Thickly bearded Bessians and Dalmatians, Egyptians with gold rings in their ears, red-headed Germans, olive-skinned Greeks and Cilicians, great muscled Nubians as black as charcoal and with eyes blood-shot by wine – men from every country of the Empire, all of them desperate enough, or ambitious enough, or stupid enough, to be willing to trade twenty-five years of their lives at the oars in return for Roman citizenship. From somewhere down in the town, near the harbour front, came the piping notes of a water organ.

Corelia was mounting the steps quickly, her skirts gathered up in either hand, her slippers soft and soundless on the stone, the slave woman running on ahead. Attilius loped behind them. '"A few hundred paces,"' he muttered to himself, '"no distance at all" – aye, but every foot of the way uphill!' His tunic was glued to his back by sweat.

They came at last to level ground and before them was a long high wall, dun-coloured, with an arched gate set into it, surmounted by two wrought-iron dolphins leaping to exchange a kiss. The women hurried through the unguarded entrance, and Attilius, after a glance around, followed – plunging at once from noisy, dusty reality into a silent world of blue that knocked away his breath. Turquoise, lapis lazuli, indigo, sapphire – every jewelled blue that Mother Nature had ever bestowed – rose in layers before him, from crystal shallows, to deep water, to sharp horizon, to sky. The villa itself sprawled below on a series of terraces, its back to the hillside, its face to the bay, built solely for this sublime panorama. Moored to a jetty was a twenty-oared luxury cruiser, painted crimson and gold, with a carpeted deck to match.

He had little time to register much else, apart from this engulfing blueness, before they were off again, Corelia in front now, leading him down, past statues, fountains, watered lawns, across a mosaic floor inlaid with a design of sea creatures and out on to a terrace with a swimming pool, also blue, framed in marble, projecting towards the sea. An inflatable ball turned gently against the tiled surround, as if abandoned in mid-game. He was suddenly struck by how deserted the great house seemed and when Corelia gestured to the balustrade, and he laid his hands cautiously on the stone parapet and leaned over, he saw why. Most of the household was gathered along the seashore.

It took a while for his mind to assemble all the elements of the scene. The setting was a fishery, as he had expected, but much bigger than he had imagined – and old, by the look of it, presumably built in the decadent last years of the Republic when keeping fish had first become the fashion – a series of concrete walls, extending out from the rocks, enclosing rectangular pools. Dead fish dappled the surface of one. Around the most distant, a group of men was staring at something in the water, an object which one of them was prodding with a boat-hook – Attilius had to shield his eyes to make them out – and as he studied them more closely he felt his stomach hollow. It reminded him of the moment of the kill at the amphitheatre – the stillness of it – the erotic complicity between crowd and victim.

Behind him, the old woman started making a noise – a soft ululation of grief and despair. He took a step backwards and turned towards Corelia, shaking his head. He wanted to escape from this place. He longed to return to the decent, simple practicalities of his profession. There was nothing he could do here.

But she was in his way, standing very close. 'Please,' she said. 'Help her.'

Her eyes were blue, bluer even than Sabina's had been. They seemed to collect the blueness of the bay and fire it back at him. He hesitated, set his jaw, then turned and reluctantly looked out to sea again.

He forced his gaze down from the horizon, deliberately skirting what was happening at the pool, let it travel back towards the shore, tried to appraise the whole thing with a professional eye. He saw wooden sluice-gates. Iron handles to raise them. Metal lattices over some of the ponds to keep the fish from escaping. Gangways. Pipes. *Pipes.*

He paused, then swung round again to squint at the hillside. The rising and falling of the waves would wash through metal grilles, set into the concrete sides of the fish pools, beneath the surface, to prevent the pens becoming stagnant.

That much he knew. But *pipes* – he cocked his head, beginning to understand – the pipes must carry fresh water down from the land, to mix with the sea water, to make it brackish. As in a lagoon. An artificial lagoon. The perfect conditions for rearing fish. And the most sensitive of fish to rear, a delicacy reserved only for the very rich, were red mullet.

He said quietly, 'Where does the aqueduct connect to the house?'

Corelia shook her head. 'I don't know.'

It would have to be big, he thought. *A place this size –*

He knelt beside the swimming pool, scooped up a palmful of the warm water, tasted it, frowning, swilled it round in his mouth like a connoisseur of wine. It was clean, as far as he could judge. But then again, that might mean nothing. He tried to remember when he had last checked the outflow of the aqueduct. Not since the previous evening, before he went to bed.

'At what time did the fish die?'

Corelia glanced at the slave woman, but she was lost to their world. 'I don't know. Perhaps two hours ago?'

Two hours!

He vaulted over the balustrade on to the lower terrace beneath and started to stride towards the shore.

Down at the water's edge, the entertainment had not lived up to its promise. But then nowadays, what did? Ampliatus felt increasingly that he had reached some point – age, was it, or wealth? – when the arousal of anticipation was invariably more exquisite than the emptiness of relief. The voice of the victim cries out, the blood spurts and then – what? Just another death.

The best part had been the beginning: the slow preparation, followed by the long period when the slave had merely floated, his face just above the surface – very quiet now, not wanting to attract any attention from what was beneath him, concentrating, treading water. Amusing. Even so, time had dragged in the heat, and Ampliatus had started to think that this whole business with eels was overrated and that Vedius Pollio was not quite as stylish as he had imagined. But no: you could always rely on the aristocracy! Just as he was preparing to abandon proceedings, the water had begun to twitch and then – plop! – the face had disappeared, like a fisherman's plunging float, only to bob up again for an instant, wearing a look of comical surprise and then vanish altogether. That expression, in retrospect, had been the climax. After that, it had all become rather boring and uncomfortable to watch in the heat of the sinking afternoon sun.

Ampliatus took off his straw hat, fanned his face, looked around at his son. Celsinus at first appeared to be staring straight ahead, but when you looked again you saw his eyes were closed, which was typical of the boy. He always seemed to be doing what you wanted. But then you realised he was only obeying mechanically, with his body: his attention was elsewhere. Ampliatus gave him a poke in the ribs with his finger and Celsinus's eyes jerked open.

What was in his mind? Some Eastern rubbish, presumably. He blamed himself. When the boy was six – this was twelve years ago – Ampliatus had built a temple in Pompeii, at his own expense, dedicated to the cult of Isis. As a former slave, he would not have been encouraged to build a temple to Jupiter, Best and Greatest, or to Mother Venus, or to any of the other most sacred guardian deities. But Isis was Egyptian, a goddess suitable for women, hairdressers, actors, perfume-makers and the like. He had presented the building in Celsinus's name, with the aim of getting the boy on to Pompeii's ruling council. And it had worked. What he had not anticipated was that Celsinus would take it seriously. But he did and that was what he would be brooding about now, no doubt – about Osiris, the Sun God, husband to Isis, who is slain each evening at sundown by his treacherous brother, Set, the bringer of darkness. And how all men, when they die, are judged by the Ruler of the Kingdom of the Dead, and if found worthy are granted eternal life, to rise again in the morning like Horus, heir of Osiris, the avenging new sun, bringer of light. Did Celsinus really believe all this girlish twaddle? Did he really think that this half-eaten slave, for example, might return from his death at sundown to wreak his revenge at dawn?

Ampliatus was turning to ask him exactly that when he was distracted by a shout from behind him. There was a stir among the assembled slaves and Ampliatus shifted further round in his chair. A man whom he did not recognise was striding down the steps from the villa waving his arm above his head and calling out.

The principles of engineering were simple, universal, impersonal – in Rome, in Gaul, in Campania – which was what Attilius liked about them. Even as he ran, he was envisaging what he could not see. The main line of the aqueduct would be up in that hill at the back of the villa, buried a yard beneath the surface, running on an axis north-to-south, from Baiae down to the Piscina Mirabilis. And whoever had owned the villa when the Aqua Augusta was built, more than a century ago, would almost certainly have run two spurs off it. One would disgorge into a big cistern to feed the house, the swimming pool, the garden fountains: if there was contamination on the matrix, it might take as long as a day for it to work through the system, depending on the size of the tank. But the other spur would channel a share of the Augusta's water directly down to the fishery to wash through the various ponds: any problem with the aqueduct and the impact there would be immediate.

Ahead of him, the tableau of the kill was beginning to assume an equally clear shape: the master of the household — Ampliatus, presumably — rising in astonishment from his chair, the spectators now with their backs turned to the pool, all eyes on him as he sprinted down the final flight of steps. He ran on to the concrete ramp of the fishery, slowing as he approached Ampliatus but not stopping.

'Pull him out!' he said as he ran past him.

Ampliatus, his thin face livid, shouted something at his back and Attilius turned, still running, trotting backwards now, holding up his palms: 'Please. Just pull him out.'

Ampliatus's mouth gaped open, but then, still staring intently at Attilius, he slowly raised his hand — an enigmatic gesture, which nevertheless set off a chain of activity, as though everyone had been waiting for exactly such a signal. The steward of the household put two fingers to his mouth and whistled at the slave with the boat-hook, and made an upwards motion with his hand, at which the slave swung round and flung the end of his pole towards the surface of the eel pond, hooked something and began to drag it in.

Attilius was almost at the pipes. Closer to, they were larger than they had looked from the terrace. Terracotta. A pair. More than a foot in diameter. They emerged from the slope, traversed the ramp together, parted company at the edge of the water, then ran in opposite directions along the side of the fishery. A crude inspection plate was set into each – a loose piece of pipe, two feet long, cut crossways – and as he reached them he could see that one had been disturbed and not replaced properly. A chisel lay nearby, as if whoever had been using it had been disturbed.

Attilius knelt and jammed the tool into the gap, working it up and down until it had penetrated most of the way, then twisted it, so that the flat edge gave him enough space to fit his fingers underneath the cover and lever it off. He lifted it away and pushed it over, not caring how heavily it fell. His face was directly over the running water and he smelt it at once. Released from the confined space of the pipe, it was strong enough to make him want to retch. An unmistakable smell of rottenness. Of rotten eggs.

The breath of Hades.

Sulphur.

The slave was dead. That much was obvious, even from a distance. Attilius, crouching beside the open pipe, saw the remains hauled out of the eel pond and covered with a sack. He saw the audience disperse and begin traipsing back up to the villa, at the same time as the grey-haired slave woman threaded her way between them, heading in the opposite direction, down towards the sea. The others avoided looking at her, left a space around her, as if she had some virulent disease. As she reached the dead man she flung up her hands to the sky and began rocking silently from side to side. Ampliatus did not notice her. He was walking purposefully towards Attilius. Corelia was behind him and a young man who looked just like her – her brother, presumably – and a few others. A couple of the men had knives at their belts.

The engineer returned his attention to the water. Was it his imagination or was the pressure slackening? The smell was certainly much less obvious now that the surface was open to the air. He plunged his hands into the flow, frowning, trying to gauge the strength of it, as it twisted and flexed beneath his fingers, like a muscle, like a living thing. Once, when he was a boy, he had seen an elephant killed at the Games – hunted down by archers and by spearmen dressed in leopard skins. But what he remembered chiefly was not the hunt but rather the way the elephant's trainer, who had presumably accompanied the giant beast from Africa, had crouched at its ear as it lay dying in the dust, whispering to it. That was how he felt now. The aqueduct, the immense Aqua Augusta, seemed to be dying in his hands.

A voice said, 'You are on my property.'

He looked up to find Ampliatus staring down at him. The villa's owner was in his middle fifties. Short, but broad-shouldered and powerful. 'My property,' Ampliatus repeated.

'Your property, yes. But the Emperor's water.' Attilius stood, wiping his hands on his tunic. The waste of so much precious liquid, in the middle of a drought, to pamper a rich man's fish, made him angry. 'You need to close the sluices to the aqueduct. There's sulphur in the matrix and red mullet abominate all impurities. *That –*' he emphasised the word '– is what killed your precious fish.'

Ampliatus tilted his head back slightly, sniffing the insult. He had a fine, rather handsome face. His eyes were the same shade of blue as his daughter's. 'And you are who, exactly?'

'Marcus Attilius. Aquarius of the Aqua Augusta.'

'Attilius?' The millionaire frowned. 'What happened to Exomnius?'

'I wish I knew.'

'But surely Exomnius is still the aquarius?'

'No. As I said, I am now the aquarius.' The engineer was in no mood to pay his respects. Contemptible, stupid, cruel – on another occasion, perhaps, he would be delighted to pass on his compliments, but for now he did not have the time. 'I must get back to Misenum. We have an emergency on the aqueduct.'

'What sort of emergency? Is it an omen?'

'You could say that.'

He made to go, but Ampliatus moved swiftly to one side, blocking his way. 'You insult me,' he said. 'On my property. In front of my family. And now you try to leave without offering any apology?' He brought his face so close to Attilius's that the engineer could see the sweat beading above his thinning hairline. He smelled sweetly of crocus oil, the most expensive unguent. 'Who gave you permission to come here?'

'If I have in any way offended you –' began Attilius. But then he remembered the wretched bundle in its shroud of sacking and the apology choked in his throat. 'Get out of my way.'

He tried to push his way past, but Ampliatus grabbed his arm and someone drew a knife. Another instant, he realised – a single thrust – and it would all be over.

'He came because of me, father. I invited him.'

'What?'

Ampliatus wheeled round on Corelia. What he might have

done, whether he would have struck her, Attilius would never know, for at that instant a terrible screaming started. Advancing along the ramp came the grey-headed woman. She had smeared her face, her arms, her dress with her son's blood and her hand was pointing straight ahead, the first and last of her bony brown fingers rigidly extended. She was shouting in a language Attilius did not understand. But then he did not need to: a curse is a curse in any tongue, and this one was directed straight at Ampliatus.

He let go of Attilius's arm and turned to face her, absorbing the full force of it, with an expression of indifference. And then, as the torrent of words began to slacken, he laughed. There was silence for a moment, then the others began to laugh as well. Attilius glanced at Corelia, who gave an almost imperceptible nod and gestured with her eyes to the villa – *I shall be all right*, she seemed to be saying, *go* – and that was the last that he saw or heard, as he turned his back on the scene and started mounting the path up to the house – two steps, three steps at a time – running on legs of lead, like a man escaping in a dream.

Hora duodecima

[18:48 hours]

'Immediately before an eruption, there may be a marked increase in the ratios S/C, SO2/CO2, S/Cl, as well as the total amount of HCl . . . . A marked increase in the proportions of mantle components is often a sign that magma has risen into a dormant volcano and that an eruption may be expected.'

Volcanology *(second edition)*

An aqueduct was a work of Man, but it obeyed the laws of Nature. The engineers might trap a spring and divert it from its intended course, but once it had begun to flow, it ran, ineluctable, remorseless, at an average speed of two and a half miles per hour, and Attilius was powerless to prevent it polluting Misenum's water.

He still carried one faint hope: that somehow the sulphur was confined to the Villa Hortensia; that the leak was in the pipework beneath the house; and that Ampliatus's property was merely an isolated pocket of foulness on the beautiful curve of the bay.

That hope lasted for as long as it took him to sprint down the hill to the Piscina Mirabilis, to roust Corax from the barracks where he was playing a game of bones with Musa and Becco, to explain what had happened, and to wait impatiently while the overseer unlocked the door to the reservoir – at which moment it evaporated completely, wafted away by the same rank smell that he had detected in the pipe at the fishery.

'Dog's breath!' Corax blew out his cheeks in disgust. 'This must have been building up for hours.'

'Two hours.'

'Two hours?' The overseer could not quite disguise his satisfaction. 'When you had us up in the hills on your fool's errand?'

'And if we had been here? What difference could we have made?'

Attilius descended a couple of the steps, the back of his hand pressed to his nose. The light was fading. Out of sight, beyond the pillars, he could hear the aqueduct disgorging into the reservoir, but with nothing like its normal percussive force. It was as he had suspected at the fishery: the pressure was dropping, fast.

He called up to the Greek slave, Polites, who was waiting at the top of the steps, that he wanted a few things fetched – a torch, a plan of the aqueduct's main line and one of the stoppered bottles from the storeroom, which they used for taking water samples. Polites trotted off obediently and Attilius peered into the gloom, glad that the overseer could not see his expression, for a man was his face; the face the man.

'How long have you worked on the Augusta, Corax?'

'Twenty years.'

'Anything like this ever happened before?'

'Never. You've brought us all bad luck.'

Keeping one hand on the wall, Attilius made his way cautiously down the remaining steps to the reservoir's edge. The splash of water falling from the mouth of the Augusta, together with the smell and the melancholy light of the day's last hour, made him feel as if he were descending into hell. There was even a rowing boat moored at his feet: a suitable ferry to carry him across the Styx.

He tried to make a joke of it, to disguise the panic that was fastening hold of him. 'You can be my Charon,' he said to Corax, 'but I don't have a coin to pay you.'

'Well, then – you are doomed to wander in hell for ever.'

That was funny. Attilius tapped his fist against his chest, his habit when thinking, then shouted back up towards the yard, 'Polites! Get a move on!'

'Coming, aquarius!'

The slim outline of the slave appeared in the doorway, holding a taper and a torch. He ran down and handed them to Attilius, who touched the glowing tip to the mass of tow and pitch. It ignited with a *wumph* and a gust of oily heat. Their shadows danced on the concrete walls.

Attilius stepped carefully into the boat, holding the torch aloft, then turned to collect the rolled-up plans and the glass bottle. The boat was light and shallow-bottomed, used for maintenance work in the reservoir, and when Corax climbed aboard it dipped low in the water.

I must fight my panic, thought Attilius. I must be the master.

'If this had happened when Exomnius was here, what would he have done?'

'I don't know. But I tell you one thing. He knew this water better than any man alive. He would have seen this coming.'

'Perhaps he did, and that was why he ran away.'

'Exomnius was no coward. He didn't run anywhere.'

'Then where is he, Corax?'

'I've told you, pretty boy, a hundred times: I don't know.'

The overseer leaned across, untied the rope from its mooring ring and pushed them away from the steps, then turned to sit facing Attilius and took up the oars. His face in the torch-light was swarthy, guileful, older than his forty years. He had a wife and a brood of children crammed into an apartment across the street from the reservoir. Attilius wondered why Corax hated him so much. Was it simply that he had coveted the post of aquarius for himself and resented the arrival of a younger man from Rome? Or was there something more?

He told Corax to row them towards the centre of the Piscina and when they reached it he handed him the torch, uncorked the bottle and rolled up the sleeves of his tunic. How often had he seen his father do this, in the subterranean reservoir of the Claudia and the Anio Novus on the Esquiline Hill? The old man had shown him how each of the matrices had its own flavour, as distinct from another as different vintages of wine. The Aqua Marcia was the sweetest-tasting, drawn from the three clear springs of the River Anio; the Aqua Alsietina the foulest, a gritty lakewater, fit only for irrigating gardens; the Aqua Julia, soft and tepid; and so on. A good aquarius, his father had said, should know more than just the solid laws of architecture and hydraulics – he should have a taste, a nose, a feel for water, and for the rocks and soils through which it had passed on its journey to the surface. Lives might depend on this skill.

An image of his father flashed into his mind. Killed before he was fifty by the lead he had worked with all his life, leaving Attilius, a teenager, as head of the family. There had not been much left of him by the end. Just a thin shroud of white skin stretched taut over sharp bone.

His father would have known what to do.

Holding the bottle so that its top was face down to the water, Attilius stretched over the side and plunged it in as far as he could, then slowly turned it underwater, letting the air escape in a stream of bubbles. He recorked it and withdrew it.

Settled back in the boat, he opened the bottle again and passed it back and forth beneath his nose. He took a mouthful, gargled and swallowed. Bitter, but drinkable, just about. He passed it to Corax who swapped it for the torch and gulped the whole lot down in one go. He wiped his mouth with the back of his hand. 'It'll do,' he said, 'if you mix it with enough wine.'

The boat bumped against a pillar and Attilius noticed the widening line between the dry and damp concrete – sharply defined, already a foot above the surface of the reservoir. She was draining away faster than the Augusta could fill her.

Panic again. *Fight it.*

'What's the capacity of the Piscina?'

'Two hundred and eighty quinariae.'

Attilius raised the torch towards the roof, which disappeared into the shadows about fifteen feet above them. So that meant the water was perhaps thirty-five feet deep, the reservoir two-thirds full. Suppose it now held two hundred quinariae. At Rome, they worked on the basis that one quinaria was roughly the daily requirement of two hundred people. The naval garrison at Misenum was ten thousand strong, plus, say, another ten thousand civilians.

A simple enough calculation.

They had water for two days. Assuming they could ration the flow to perhaps an hour at dawn and another at dusk. And assuming the concentration of sulphur at the bottom of the

Piscina was as weak as it was at the top. He tried to think. Sulphur in a natural spring was warm, and therefore rose to the surface. But sulphur when it had cooled to the same temperature as the surrounding water – what did that do? Did it disperse? Or float? Or sink?

Attilius glanced towards the northern end of the reservoir, where the Augusta emerged. 'We should check the pressure.'

Corax began to row with powerful strokes, steering them expertly around the labyrinth of pillars towards the falling water. Attilius held the torch in one hand and with the other he unrolled the plans, flattening them out across his knees with his forearm.

The whole of the western end of the bay, from Neapolis to Cumae, was sulphurous – he knew that much. Green translucent lumps of sulphur were dug from the mines in the Leucogaei Hills, two miles north of the aqueduct's main line. Then there were the hot sulphur springs around Baiae, to which convalescents came from across the Empire. There was a pool called Posidian, named after a freedman of Claudius, that was hot enough to cook meat. Even the sea at Baiae occasionally steamed with sulphur, the sick wallowing in its shallows in the hope of relief. It must be somewhere in this smouldering region – where the Sibyl had her cave and the burning holes gave access to the Underworld – that the Augusta had become polluted.

They had reached the aqueduct's tunnel. Corax let the boat glide for a moment, then rowed a few deft strokes in the opposite direction, bringing them to halt precisely beside a pillar. Attilius laid aside the plans and raised the torch. It flashed on an emerald sheen of green mould, then lit the giant head of Neptune, carved in stone, from whose mouth the Augusta normally gushed in a jet-black torrent. But even in the time it had taken to row from the steps the flow had dwindled. It was scarcely more than a trickle.

Corax gave a soft whistle. 'I never thought I'd live to see the Augusta dry. You were right to be worried, pretty boy.' He looked at Attilius and for the first time there was a flash of fear across his face. 'So what stars were you born under, that you've brought this down on us?'

The engineer was finding it difficult to breathe. He pressed his hand to his nose again and moved the torch above the surface of the reservoir. The reflection of the light on the still black water suggested a fire in the depths.

It was not possible, he thought. Aqueducts did not just fail – not like this, not in a matter of hours. The matrices were walled with brick, rendered with waterproof cement, and surrounded by a concrete casing a foot and a half thick. The usual problems – structural flaws, leaks, lime deposits that narrowed the channel – all these needed months, even years to develop. It had taken the Claudia a full decade gradually to close down.

He was interrupted by a shout from the slave, Polites: 'Aquarius!'

He half turned his head. He could not see the steps for the pillars, which seemed to rise like petrified oaks from some dark and foul-smelling swamp. 'What is it?'

'There's a rider in the yard, aquarius! He has a message that the aqueduct has failed!'

Corax muttered, 'We can see that for ourselves, you Greek fool.'

Attilius reached for the plans again. 'Which town has he come from?' He expected the slave to shout back Baiae or

Cumae. Puteoli at the very worst. Neapolis would be a disaster.

But the reply was like a punch in the stomach: 'Nola!'

The messenger was so rimed with dust he looked more ghost than man. And even as he told his story – of how the water had failed in Nola's reservoir at dawn and of how the failure had been preceded by a sharp smell of sulphur that had started in the middle of the night – a fresh sound of hooves was heard in the road outside and a second horse trotted into the yard.

The rider dismounted smartly and offered a rolled papyrus. A message from the city fathers at Neapolis. The Augusta had gone down there at noon.

Attilius read it carefully, managing to keep his face expressionless. There was quite a crowd in the yard by now. Two horses, a pair of riders, surrounded by the gang of aqueduct workers who had abandoned their evening meal to listen to what was happening. The commotion was beginning to attract the attention of passers-by in the street, as well as some of the local shopkeepers. 'Hey, waterman!' shouted the owner of the snack bar opposite. 'What's going on?'

It would not take much, thought Attilius – merely the slightest breath of wind – for panic to take hold like a hillside fire. He could feel a fresh spark of it within himself. He called to a couple of slaves to close the gates to the yard and told Polites to see to it that the two messengers were given food and drink. 'Musa, Becco – get hold of a cart and start loading it. Quicklime, puteolanum, tools – everything we might need to repair the matrix. As much as a couple of oxen can pull.'

The two men looked at one another. 'But we don't know

what the damage is,' objected Musa. 'One cartload may not be enough.'

'Then we'll pick up extra material as we pass through Nola.'

He strode towards the aqueduct's office, the messenger from Nola at his heels.

'But what am I to tell the aediles?' The rider was scarcely more than a boy. The hollows of his eyes were the only part of his face not caked with dirt, the soft pink discs emphasising his fearful look. 'The priests want to sacrifice to Neptune. They say the sulphur is a terrible omen.'

'Tell them we are aware of the problem.' Attilius gestured vaguely with the plans. 'Tell them we are organising repairs.'

He ducked through the low entrance into the small cubicle. Exomnius had left the Augusta's records in chaos. Bills of sale, receipts and invoices, promissory notes, legal stipulations and opinions, engineers' reports and storeroom inventories, letters from the department of the Curator Aquarum and orders from the naval commander in Misenum – some of them twenty or thirty years old – spilled out of chests, across a table and over the concrete floor. Attilius swept the table clear with his elbow and unrolled the plans.

Nola! How was this possible? Nola was a big town, thirty miles to the east of Misenum, and nowhere near the sulphur fields. He used his thumb to mark out the distances. With a cart and oxen it would take them the best part of two days merely to reach it. The map showed him as clearly as a painting how the calamity must have spread, the matrix emptying with mathematical precision. He traced it with his finger, his lips moving silently. Two and a half miles per hour! If Nola had gone down at dawn, then Acerrae and Atella would have followed in the middle of the morning. If Neapolis, twelve miles round the coast from Misenum, had lost its supply at noon, then Puteoli's must have gone at the eighth hour, Cumae's at the ninth, Baiae's at the tenth. And now, at last, inevitably, at the twelfth, it was their turn.

Eight towns down. Only Pompeii, a few miles upstream from Nola, so far unaccounted for. But even without it: more than two hundred thousand people without water.

He was aware of the entrance behind him darkening, of Corax coming up and leaning against the door frame, watching him.

He rolled up the map and tucked it under his arm. 'Give me the key to the sluices.'

'Why?'

'Isn't it obvious? I'm going to shut off the reservoir.'

'But that's the Navy's water. You can't do that. Not without the authority of the admiral.'

'Then why don't you get the authority of the admiral? I'm closing those sluices.' For the second time that day, their faces were barely a hand's breadth apart. 'Listen to me, Corax. The Piscina Mirabilis is a strategic reserve. Understand? That's what it's there for – to be shut off in an emergency – and every moment we waste arguing we lose more water. Now give me the key, or you'll answer for it in Rome.'

'Very well. Have it your way, pretty boy.' Without taking his eyes from Attilius's face, he removed the key from the ring on his belt. 'I'll go and see the admiral all right. I'll tell him what's been going on. And then we'll see who answers for what.'

Attilius grabbed the key and pushed sideways past him, out into the yard. He shouted to the nearest slave, 'Close the gates after me, Polites. No one is to be let in without my permission.'

'Yes, aquarius.'

There was still a crowd of curious onlookers in the street but they cleared a path to let him through. He took no notice of their questions. He turned left, then left again, down a steep flight of steps. The water organ was still piping away in the distance. Washing hung above his head, strung between the walls. People turned to stare at him as he jostled them out of his way. A girl prostitute in a saffron dress, ten years old at most, clutched at his arm and wouldn't let go until he dug into the pouch on his belt and gave her a couple of copper coins. He saw her dart through the crowd and hand them to a fat Cappadocian – her owner, obviously – and as he hurried on he cursed his gullibility.

The building that housed the sluice-gate was a small redbrick cube, barely taller than a man. A statue of Egeria, goddess of the water-spring, was set in a niche beside the door. At her feet lay a few stems of withered flowers and some mouldy lumps of bread and fruit – offerings left by pregnant women who believed that Egeria, consort of Numa, the Prince of Peace, would ease their delivery when their time came. Another worthless superstition. A waste of food.

He turned the key in the lock and tugged angrily at the heavy wooden door.

He was level now with the floor of the Piscina Mirabilis. Water from the reservoir poured under pressure down a tunnel in the wall, through a bronze grille, swirled in the open conduit at his feet, and then was channelled into three pipes that fanned out and disappeared under the flagstones behind him, carrying the supply down to the port and town of Misenum. The flow was controlled by a sluice-gate, set flush with the wall, worked by a wooden handle attached to an iron wheel. It was stiff from lack of use. He had to pound it with the heel of his hand to loosen it, but when he put his back into it, it began to turn. He wound the handle as fast as he could. The gate descended, rattling like a portcullis, gradually choking off the flow of water until at last it ceased altogether, leaving a smell of moist dust.

Only a puddle remained in the stone channel, evaporating so rapidly in the heat he could see it shrinking. He bent down and dabbed his fingers in the wet patch, then touched them to his tongue. No taste of sulphur.

He had done it now, he thought. Deprived the Navy of its water, in a drought, without authority, three days into his first command. Men had been stripped of their rank and sent to the treadmills for lesser crimes. It occurred to him that he had been a fool to let Corax be the first to get to the admiral. There was certain to be a court of inquiry. Even now the overseer would be making sure who got the blame.

Locking the door to the sluice chamber, he glanced up and down the busy street. Nobody was paying him any attention. They did not know what was about to happen. He felt himself to be in possession of some immense secret and the knowledge made him furtive. He headed down a narrow alley towards the harbour, keeping close to the wall, eyes on the gutter, avoiding people's gaze.

The admiral's villa was on the far side of Misenum and to reach it the engineer had to travel the best part of half a mile – walking, mostly, with occasional panicky bursts of running – across the narrow causeway and over the revolving wooden bridge which separated the two natural harbours of the naval base.

He had been warned about the admiral before he left Rome.

'The commander-in-chief is Gaius Plinius,' said the Curator Aquarum. 'Pliny. You'll come across him sooner or later. He thinks he knows everything about everything. Perhaps he does. He will need careful stroking. You should take a look at his latest book. The *Natural History*. Every known fact about Mother Nature in thirty-seven volumes.'

There was a copy in the public library at the Porticus of Octavia. The engineer had time to read no further than the table of contents.

'*The world, its shape, its motion. Eclipses, solar and lunar. Thunderbolts. Music from the stars. Sky portents, recorded instances. Sky-beams, sky-yawning, colours of the sky, sky-flames, sky-wreaths, sudden rings. Eclipses. Showers of stones . . .*'

There were other books by Pliny in the library. Six volumes on oratory. Eight on grammar. Twenty volumes on the war in Germany, in which he had commanded a cavalry unit. Thirty volumes on the recent history of the Empire, which he had served as procurator in Spain and Belgian Gaul. Attilius wondered how he managed to write so much and rise so high in the imperial administration at the same time. The Curator said, 'Because he doesn't have a wife.' He laughed at his own joke. 'And he doesn't sleep, either. You watch he doesn't catch you out.'

The sky was red with the setting sun and the large lagoon to his right, where the warships were built and repaired, was deserted for the evening; a few seabirds called mournfully among the reeds. To his left, in the outer harbour, a passenger ferry was approaching through the golden glow, her sails furled, a dozen oars on either side dipping slowly in unison as she steered between the anchored triremes of the imperial fleet. She was too late to be the nightly arrival from Ostia, which meant she was probably a local service. The weight of the passengers crammed on her open deck was pressing her low to the surface.

'Showers of milk, of blood, of flesh, of iron, of wool, of bricks. Portents. The earth at the centre of the world. Earthquakes. Chasms. Air-holes. Combined marvels of fire and water: mineral pitch; naptha; regions constantly glowing. Harmonic principle of the world . . .'

He was moving more quickly than the water pipes were emptying and when he passed through the triumphal arch that marked the entrance to the port he could see that the big public fountain at the crossroads was still flowing. Around it was grouped the usual twilight crowd – sailors dousing their befuddled heads, ragged children shrieking and splashing, a line of women and slaves with earthenware pots at their hips and on their shoulders, waiting to collect their water for the night. A marble statue of the Divine Augustus, carefully positioned beside the busy intersection to remind the citizens who was responsible for this blessing, gazed coldly above them, frozen in perpetual youth.

The overloaded ferry had come alongside the quay. Her gangplanks, fore and aft, had been thrown down and the timber was already bowing under the weight of passengers scrambling ashore. Luggage was tossed from hand to hand. A taxi owner, surprised by the speed of the exodus, was running around kicking his bearers to get them on their feet. Attilius called across the street to ask where the ferry was from, and the taxi owner shouted back over his shoulder, 'Neapolis, my friend – and before that, Pompeii.'

Pompeii.

Attilius, on the point of moving off, suddenly checked his

stride. Odd, he thought. Odd that they had heard no word from Pompeii, the first town on the matrix. He hesitated, swung round and stepped into the path of the oncoming crowd. 'Any of you from Pompeii?' He waved the rolled-up plans of the Augusta to attract attention. 'Was anyone in Pompeii this morning?' But nobody took any notice. They were thirsty after the voyage – and, of course, they would be, he realised, if they had come from Neapolis, where the water had failed at noon. Most passed to either side of him in their eagerness to reach the fountain, all except for one, an elderly holy man, with the conical cap and curved staff of an augur, who was walking slowly, scanning the sky.

'I was in Neapolis this afternoon,' he said, when Attilius stopped him, 'but this morning I was in Pompeii. Why? Is there something I can do to help you, my son?' His rheumy eyes took on a crafty look, his voice dropped. 'No need to be shy. I am practised in the interpretation of all the usual phenomena – thunderbolts, entrails, bird omens, unnatural manifestations. My rates are reasonable.'

'May I ask, holy father,' said the engineer, 'when you left Pompeii?'

'At first light.'

'And were the fountains playing? Was there water?'

So much rested on his answer, Attilius was almost afraid to hear it.

'Yes, there was water.' The augur frowned and raised his staff to the fading light. 'But when I arrived in Neapolis the streets were dry and in the baths I smelled sulphur. That is why I decided to return to the ferry and to come on here.' He squinted again at the sky, searching for birds. 'Sulphur is a terrible omen.'

'True enough,' agreed Attilius. 'But are you certain? And are you sure the water was running?'

'Yes, my son. I'm sure.'

There was a commotion around the fountain and both men turned to look. It was nothing much to start with, just some pushing and shoving, but quickly punches were being thrown. The crowd seemed to contract, to rush in on itself and become denser, and from the centre of the melee a large earthenware pot went sailing into the air, turned slowly and landed on the quayside, smashing into fragments. A woman screamed. Wriggling between the backs at the edge of the mob, a man in a Greek tunic emerged, clutching a waterskin tightly to his chest. Blood was pouring from a gash in his temple. He sprawled, picked himself up and stumbled forwards, disappearing into an alleyway.

And so it starts, thought the engineer. First this fountain, and then the others all around the port, and then the big basin in the forum. And then the public baths, and then the taps in the military school, and in the the big villas – nothing emerging from the empty pipes except the clank of shuddering lead and the whistle of rushing air –

The distant water organ had become stuck on a note and died with a long moan.

Someone was yelling that the bastard from Neapolis had pushed to the front and stolen the last of the water, and, like a beast with a single brain and impulse, the crowd turned and began to pour down the narrow lane in pursuit. And suddenly, as abruptly as it had begun, the riot was over, leaving behind a scene of smashed and abandoned pots, and a couple of women crouched in the dust, their hands pressed over their heads for protection, close to the edge of the silent fountain.

Vespera

[20:07 hours]

'Earthquakes may occur in swarms at areas of stress concentrations – such as nearby faults – and in the immediate vicinity of magma where pressure changes are occurring.'

Haraldur Sigurdsson (editor),
Encyclopaedia of Volcanoes

The admiral's official residence was set high on the hill-side overlooking the harbour and by the time Attilius reached it and was conducted on to the terrace it was dusk. All around the bay, in the seaside villas, torches, oil lamps and braziers were being lit, so that gradually a broken thread of yellow light had begun to emerge, wavering for mile after mile, picking out the curve of the coast, before vanishing in the purple haze towards Capri.

A marine centurion in full uniform of breastplate and crested helmet, with a sword swinging at his belt, was hurrying away as the engineer arrived. The remains of a large meal were being cleared from a stone table beneath a trellised pergola. At first he did not see the admiral, but the instant the slave announced him – 'Marcus Attilius Primus, aquarius of the Aqua Augusta!' – a stocky man in his middle fifties at the far end of the terrace turned on his heel and came waddling towards him,

trailed by what Attilius assumed were the guests of his abandoned dinner party: four men sweating in togas, at least one
of whom, judging by the purple stripe on his formal dress, was
a senator. Behind them – obsequious, malevolent, inescapable
– came Corax.

Attilius had for some reason imagined that the famous
scholar would be thin, but Pliny was fat, his belly protruding
sharply, like the ramming post of one of his warships. He was
dabbing at his forehead with his napkin.

'Shall I arrest you now, aquarius? I could, you know, that's
already clear enough.' He had a fat man's voice: a high-pitched
wheeze, which became even hoarser as he counted off the charges
on his pudgy fingers. 'Incompetence to start with – who can
doubt that? Negligence – where were you when the sulphur
infected the water? Insubordination – on what authority did you
shut off our supply? Treason – yes, I could make a charge of
treason stick. What about fomenting rebellion in the imperial
dockyards? I've had to order out a century of marines – fifty
to break some heads in the town and try to restore public order,
the other fifty to the reservoir, to guard whatever water's left.
Treason –'

He broke off, short of breath. With his puffed-out cheeks,
pursed lips and sparse grey curls plastered down with perspi-
ration, he had the appearance of an elderly, furious cherub,
fallen from some painted, peeling ceiling. The youngest of his
guests – a pimply lad in his late teens – stepped forward to
support his arm, but Pliny shrugged him away. At the back of
the group Corax grinned, showing a mouthful of dark teeth.
He had been even more effective at spreading poison than
Attilius had expected. What a politician. He could probably
show the senator a trick or two.

He noticed that a star had come out above Vesuvius. He had never really looked properly at the mountain before, certainly not from this angle. The sky was dark but the mountain was darker, almost black, rising massively above the bay to a pointed summit. And there was the source of the trouble, he thought. Somewhere there, on the mountain. Not on the seaward side, but round to landward, on the north-eastern slope.

'Who are you anyway?' Pliny eventually managed to rasp out. 'I don't know you. You're far too young. What's happened to the proper aquarius? What was his name?'

'Exomnius,' said Corax.

'Exomnius, precisely. Where's he? And what does Acilius Aviola think he's playing at, sending us boys to do men's work? Well? Speak up! What have you to say for yourself?'

Behind the admiral Vesuvius formed a perfect natural pyramid, with just that little crust of light from the waterfront villas running around its base. In a couple of places the line bulged slightly and those, the engineer guessed, must be towns. He recognised them from the map. The nearer would be Herculaneum; the more distant, Pompeii.

Attilius straightened his back. 'I need,' he said, 'to borrow a ship.'

He spread out his map on the table in Pliny's library, weighing down either side with a couple of pieces of magnetite which he took from a display cabinet. An elderly slave shuffled behind the admiral's back, lighting an elaborate bronze candelabrum. The walls were lined with cedarwood cabinets, packed with rolls of papyri stacked end-on, in dusty honeycombs, and even with the doors to the terrace pushed wide open, no breeze came off the sea to dispel the heat. The oily black strands of smoke from the candles rose undisturbed. Attilius could feel the sweat trickling down the sides of his belly, irritating him, like a crawling insect.

'Tell the ladies we shall rejoin them directly,' said the admiral. He turned away from the slave and nodded at the engineer. 'All right. Let's hear it.'

Attilius glanced around at the faces of his audience, intent in the candlelight. He had been told their names before they sat down and he wanted to make sure he remembered them: Pedius Cascus, a senior senator who, he dimly recalled, had been a consul years ago and who owned a big villa along the coast at Herculaneum; Pomponianus, an old Army comrade of Pliny, rowed over for dinner from his villa at Stabiae; and Antius, captain of the imperial flagship, the *Victoria*. The pimply youth was Pliny's nephew, Gaius Plinius Caecilius Secundus.

He put his finger on the map and they all leant forward, even Corax.

'This is where I thought originally that the break must be, admiral – here, in the burning fields around Cumae. That would explain the sulphur. But then we learnt that the supply had gone down in Nola as well – over here, to the east. That was at dawn. The timing is crucial, because according to a witness who was in Pompeii at first light, the fountains there were still running this morning. As you can see, Pompeii is some distance back up the matrix from Nola, so logically the Augusta should have failed there in the middle of the night. The fact that it didn't can only mean one thing. The break has to be here' – he circled the spot – 'somewhere here, on this five-mile stretch, where she runs close to Vesuvius.'

Pliny frowned at the map. 'And the ship? Where does that come in?'

'I believe we have two days' worth of water left. If we set off overland from Misenum to discover what's happened it will take us at least that long simply to find where the break has occurred. But if we go by sea to Pompeii – if we travel light and pick up most of what we need in the town – we should be able to start repairs tomorrow.'

In the ensuing silence, the engineer could hear the steady drip of the water clock beside the doors. Some of the gnats whirling around the candles had become encrusted in the wax.

Pliny said, 'How many men do you have?'

'Fifty altogether, but most of those are spread out along the length of the matrix, maintaining the settling tanks and the reservoirs in the towns. I have a dozen altogether in Misenum. I'd take half of those with me. Any other labour we need, I'd hire locally in Pompeii.'

'We could let him have a liburnian, admiral,' said Antius. 'If he left at first light he could be in Pompeii by the middle of the morning.'

Corax seemed to be panicked by the mere suggestion. 'But with respect, this is just more of his moonshine, admiral. I wouldn't pay much attention to any of this. For a start, I'd like to know how he's so sure the water's still running in Pompeii.'

'I met a man on the quayside, admiral, on my way here. An augur. The local ferry had just docked. He told me he was in Pompeii this morning.'

'An augur!' mocked Corax. 'Then it's a pity he didn't see this whole thing coming! But all right – let's say he's telling the truth. Let's say this is where the break is. I know this part of the matrix better than anyone – five miles long and every

foot of her underground. It will take us more than a day just
to find out where she's gone down.'

'That's not true,' objected Attilius. 'With that much water
escaping from the matrix, a blind man could find the break.'

'With that much water backed up in the tunnel, how do we
get inside it to make the repairs?'

'Listen,' said the engineer. 'When we get to Pompeii, we
split into three groups.' He had not really thought this through.
He was having to make it up as he went along. But he could
sense that Antius was with him and the admiral had yet to take
his eyes from the map. 'The first group goes out to the Augusta
– follows the spur from Pompeii to its junction with the matrix
and then works westwards. I can assure you, finding where
the break is will not be a great problem. The second group
stays in Pompeii and puts together enough men and materials
to carry out the repairs. A third group rides into the mountains, to the springs at Abellinum, with instructions to shut off
the Augusta.'

The senator looked up sharply. 'Can that be done? In Rome,
when an aqueduct has to be closed for repairs, it stays shut
down for weeks.'

'According to the drawings, senator, yes – it can be done.'
Attilius had only just noticed it himself, but he was inspired
now. The whole operation was taking shape in his mind even
as he described it. 'I have never seen the springs of the Serinus
myself, but it appears from this plan that they flow into a basin
with two channels. Most of the water comes west, to us. But a
smaller channel runs north, to feed Beneventum. If we send
all the water north, and let the western channel drain off, we
can get inside to repair it. The point is, we don't have to dam
it and build a temporary diversion, which is what we have to

do with the aqueducts of Rome, before we can even start on the maintenance. We can work much more quickly.'

The senator transferred his drooping eyes to Corax. 'Is this true, overseer?'

'Maybe,' conceded Corax grudgingly. He seemed to sense he was beaten, but he would not give up without a fight. 'However, I still maintain he's talking moonshine, admiral, if he thinks we can get all this done in a day or two. Like I said, I know this stretch. We had problems here nearly twenty years ago, at the time of the great earthquake. Exomnius was the aquarius, new in the job. He'd just arrived from Rome, his first command, and we worked on it together. All right – it didn't block the matrix completely, I grant you that – but it still took us weeks to render all the cracks in the tunnel.'

'What great earthquake?' Attilius had never heard mention of it.

'Actually, it was seventeen years ago.' Pliny's nephew piped up for the first time. 'The earthquake took place on the Nones of February, during the consulship of Regulus and Verginius. Emperor Nero was in Neapolis, performing on stage at the time. Seneca describes the incident. You must have read it, uncle? The relevant passage is in *Natural Questions*. Book six.'

'Yes, Gaius, thank you,' said the admiral sharply. 'I have read it, although obviously I'm obliged for the reference.' He stared at the map and puffed out his cheeks. 'I wonder –' he muttered. He shifted round in his chair and shouted at the slave. 'Dromo! Bring me my glass of wine. Quickly!'

'Are you ill, uncle?'

'No, no.' Pliny propped his chin on his fists and returned his attention to the map. 'So is this what has damaged the Augusta? An earthquake?'

'Then surely we would have felt it?' objected Antius. 'That last quake brought down a good part of Pompeii. They're still rebuilding. Half the town is a building site. We've had no reports of anything on that scale.'

'And yet,' continued Pliny, almost to himself, 'this is certainly earthquake weather. A flat sea. A sky so breathless the birds can scarcely fly. In normal times we would anticipate a storm. But when Saturn, Jupiter and Mars are in conjunction with the sun, instead of occurring in the air, the thunder is sometimes unleashed by Nature underground. That is the definition of an earthquake, in my opinion – a thunderbolt hurled from the interior of the world.'

The slave had shuffled up beside him, carrying a tray, in the centre of which stood a large goblet of clear glass, three-quarters full. Pliny grunted and lifted the wine to the candle-light.

'A Caecuban,' whispered Pomponianus, in awe. 'Forty years old and still drinking beautifully.' He ran his tongue round his fat lips. 'I wouldn't mind another glass myself, Pliny.'

'In a moment. Watch.' Pliny waved the wine back and forth in front of them. It was thick and syrupy, the colour of honey. Attilius caught the sweet mustiness of its scent as it passed beneath his nose. 'And now watch more closely.' He set the glass carefully on the table.

At first, the engineer did not see what point he was trying to make, but as he studied the glass more closely he saw that the surface of the wine was vibrating slightly. Tiny ripples radiated out from the centre, like the quivering of a plucked string. Pliny picked up the glass and the movement ceased; he replaced it and the motion resumed.

'I noticed it during dinner. I have trained myself to be alert to things in Nature, which other men might miss. The shaking is not continuous. See now – the wine is still.'

'That's really remarkable, Pliny,' said Pomponianus. 'I congratulate you. I'm afraid once I have a glass in my hand, I don't tend to put it down until it's empty.'

The senator was less impressed. He folded his arms and pushed himself back in the chair, as if he had somehow made himself look a fool by watching a childish trick. 'I don't know what's significant about that. So the table trembles? It could be anything. The wind –'

'There is no wind.'

'– heavy footsteps somewhere. Or perhaps Pomponianus, here, was stroking one of the ladies under the table.'

Laughter broke the tension. Only Pliny did not smile. 'We know that this world we stand on, which seems to us so still, is in fact revolving eternally, at an indescribable velocity. And it may be that this mass hurtling through space produces a sound of such volume that it is beyond the capacity of our human ears to detect. The stars out there, for example, might be tinkling like wind chimes, if only we could hear them. Could it be that the patterns in this wineglass are the physical expression of that same heavenly harmony?'

'Then why does it stop and start?'

'I have no answer, Cascus. Perhaps at one moment the earth glides silently, and at another it encounters resistance. There is a school which holds that winds are caused by the earth travelling in one direction and the stars in the other. Aquarius – what do you think?'

'I'm an engineer, admiral,' said Attilius tactfully, 'not a philosopher.' In his view, they were wasting time. He thought of mentioning the strange behaviour of the vapour on the hillside that morning, but decided against it. Tinkling stars! His foot was tapping with impatience. 'All I can tell you is that the matrix of an aqueduct is built to withstand the most extreme forces. Where the Augusta runs underground, which is most of the way, she's six feet high and three feet wide, and she rests on a base of concrete one and a half feet thick, with walls of the same dimensions. Whatever force breached that must have been powerful.'

'More powerful than the force which shakes my wine?' The admiral looked at the senator. 'Unless we are not dealing with a phenomenon of nature at all. In which case, what is it? A deliberate act of sabotage, perhaps, to strike at the fleet? But who would dare? We haven't had a foreign enemy set foot in this part of Italy since Hannibal.'

'And sabotage would hardly explain the presence of sulphur.'

'Sulphur,' said Pomponianus suddenly. 'That's the stuff in thunderbolts, isn't it? And who throws thunderbolts?' He looked around excitedly. 'Jupiter! We should sacrifice a white bull to Jupiter, as a deity of the upper air, and have the haruspices inspect the entrails. They'll tell us what to do.'

The engineer laughed.

'What's so funny about that?' demanded Pomponianus. 'It's not so funny as the idea that the world is flying through space – which, if I may say so, Pliny, rather begs the question of why we don't all fall off.'

'It's an excellent suggestion, my friend,' said Pliny soothingly. 'And, as admiral, I also happen to be the chief priest of Misenum, and I assure you, if I had a white bull to hand I would kill it on the spot. But for the time being, a more practical solution may be needed.' He sat back in his chair and wiped his napkin across his face, then unfolded and inspected it, as if it might contain some vital clue. 'Very well, aquarius. I shall give you your ship.' He turned to the captain. 'Antius — which is the fastest liburnian in the fleet?'

'That would be the *Minerva*, admiral. Torquatus's ship. Just back from Ravenna.'

'Have her made ready to sail at first light.'

'Yes, admiral.'

'And I want notices posted on every fountain telling the citizens that rationing is now in force. Water will only be allowed to flow twice each day, for one hour exactly, at dawn and dusk.'

Antius winced. 'Aren't you forgetting that tomorrow is a public holiday, admiral? It's Vulcanalia, if you recall?'

'I'm perfectly aware it's Vulcanalia.'

And so it is, thought Attilius. In the rush of leaving Rome and fretting about the aqueduct he had completely lost track of the calendar. The twenty-third of August, Vulcan's day, when live fish were thrown on to bonfires, as a sacrifice, to appease the god of fire.

'But what about the public baths?' persisted Antius.

'Closed until further notice.'

'They won't like that, admiral.'

'Well, it can't be helped. We've all grown far too soft, in any case.' He glanced briefly at Pomponianus. 'The Empire wasn't built by men who lazed around the baths all day. It will do some people good to have a taste of how life used to be. Gaius — draft a letter for me to sign to the aediles of Pompeii, asking them to provide whatever men and materials may be necessary for the repair of the aqueduct. You know the kind of thing. "In the name of the Emperor Titus Caesar Vespasianus Augustus, and in accordance with the power vested in me by the Senate and People of Rome, blah blah" – something to make them jump. Corax – it's clear that you know the terrain around Vesuvius better than anyone else. You should be the one to ride out and locate the fault, while the aquarius assembles the main expedition in Pompeii.'

The overseer's mouth flapped open in dismay.

'What's the matter? Do you disagree?'

'No, admiral.' Corax hid his anxiety quickly, but Attilius had noticed it. 'I don't mind looking for the break. Even so, would it not make more sense for one of us to remain at the reservoir to supervise the rationing –'

Pliny cut him off impatiently. 'Rationing will be the Navy's responsibility. It's primarily a question of public order.'

For a moment Corax looked as if he might be on the point of arguing, but then he bowed his head, frowning.

From the terrace came the sound of female voices and a peal of laughter.

He doesn't want me to go to Pompeii, thought Attilius, suddenly. This whole performance tonight – it's been to keep me away from Pompeii.

A woman's elaborately coiffeured head appeared at the doorway. She must have been about sixty. The pearls at her throat were the largest Attilius had ever seen. She crooked her finger at the senator. 'Cascus, darling, how much longer are you planning to keep us waiting?'

'Forgive us, Rectina,' said Pliny. 'We've almost finished. Does anyone have anything else to add?' He glanced at each of them in turn. 'No? In that case, I for one propose to finish my dinner.'

He pushed back his chair and everyone stood. The ballast

of his belly made it hard for him to rise. Gaius offered his arm, but the admiral waved him away. He had to rock forwards several times and the strain of finally pushing himself up on to his feet left him him breathless. With one hand he clutched at the table, with the other he reached for his glass, then stopped, his outstretched fingers hovering in mid-air.

The wine had resumed its barely perceptible trembling.

He blew out his cheeks. 'I think perhaps I shall sacrifice that white bull after all, Pomponianus. And you,' he said to Attilius, 'will give me back my water within two days.' He picked up the glass and took a sip. 'Or – believe me – we shall all have need of Jupiter's protection.'

Nocte intempesta

[23:22 hours]

'Magma movement may also disturb the local water table, and changes in flow and temperature of ground-water may be detected.'

Encyclopaedia of Volcanoes

T wo hours later – sleepless, naked, stretched out on his narrow wooden bed – the engineer lay waiting for the dawn. The familiar, hammering lullaby of the aqueduct had gone and in its place crowded all the tiny noises of the night – the creak of the sentries' boots in the street outside, the rustle of mice in the rafters, the hacking cough of one of the slaves downstairs in the barracks. He closed his eyes, only to open them again almost immediately. In the panic of the crisis he had managed to forget the sight of the corpse, dragged from the pool of eels, but in the darkness he found himself replaying the whole scene – the concentrated silence at the water's edge; the body hooked and dragged ashore; the blood; the screams of the woman; the anxious face and the pale white limbs of the girl.

Too exhausted to rest, he swung his bare feet on to the warm floor. A small oil lamp flickered on the nightstand. His uncompleted letter home lay beside it. There was no point now, he thought, in finishing it. Either he would repair the Augusta, in which case his mother and sister would hear from him on his return. Or they would hear *of* him, when he was shipped back to Rome, in disgrace, to face a court of inquiry – a dishonour to the family name.

He picked up the lamp and took it to the shelf at the foot of the bed, setting it down among the little shrine of figures that represented the spirits of his ancestors. Kneeling, he reached across and plucked out the effigy of his great-grandfather. Could the old man have been one of the original engineers on the Augusta? It was not impossible. The records of the Curator Aquarum showed that Agrippa had shipped in a workforce of forty thousand, slaves and legionaries, and had built her in eighteen months. That was six years after he built the Aqua Julia in Rome and seven years before he built the Virgo, and his great-grandfather had certainly worked on both of those. It pleased him to imagine that an earlier Attilius might have come south to this sweltering land – might even have sat on this very spot as the slaves dug out the Piscina Mirabilis. He felt his courage strengthening. Men had built the Augusta; men would fix her. *He* would fix her.

And then his father.

He replaced one figure and took up another, running his thumb tenderly over the smooth head.

Your father was a brave man; make sure you are, too.

He had been a baby when his father had finished the Aqua Claudia, but so often had he been told the story of the day of its dedication – of how, at four months old, he had been passed over the shoulders of the engineers in the great crowd on the Esquiline Hill – that it sometimes seemed to him he could remember it all at first hand: the elderly Claudius, twitching and stammering as he sacrificed to Neptune, and then the water appearing in the channel, as if by magic, at the exact moment that he raised his hands to the sky. But that had had nothing to do with the intervention of the gods, despite the gasps of those present. That was because his father had known the laws of engineering and had opened the sluices at the head of the aqueduct exactly eighteen hours before the ceremony was due to reach its climax, and had ridden back into the city faster than the water could chase him.

He contemplated the piece of clay in his palm.

And you, father? Did you ever come to Misenum? Did you know Exomnius? The aquarii of Rome were always a family – as close as a cohort, you used to say. Was Exomnius one of those engineers on the Esquiline on your day of triumph? Did he swing me in his arms with the rest?

He stared at the figure for a while, then kissed it and put it carefully with the others.

He sat back on his haunches.

First the aquarius disappears and then the water. The more he considered it, the more convinced he was that these must be connected. But how? He glanced around the roughly plastered walls. No clue here, that was for sure. No trace of any man's character left behind in this plain cell. And yet, according to Corax, Exomnius had run the Augusta for twenty years.

He retrieved the lamp and went out into the passage, shielding the flame with his hand. Drawing back the curtain opposite, he shone the light into the cubicle where Exomnius's possessions were stored. A couple of wooden chests, a pair of bronze candelabra, a cloak, sandals, a pisspot. It was not much to show for a lifetime. Neither of the chests was locked, he noticed.

He glanced towards the staircase, but the only sound

coming from below was snoring. Still holding the lamp, he lifted the lid of the nearest chest and began to rummage through it with his free hand. Clothes – old clothes mostly – which, as he disturbed them, released a strong smell of stale sweat. Two tunics, loincloths, a toga, neatly folded. He closed the lid quietly and raised the other. Not much in this chest, either. A skin scraper for removing oil in the baths. A jokey figure of Priapus with a vastly extended penis. A clay beaker for throwing dice, with more penises inlaid around its rim. The dice themselves. A few glass jars containing various herbs and unguents. A couple of plates. A small bronze goblet, badly tarnished.

He rolled the dice as gently as he could in the beaker and threw them. His luck was in. Four sixes – the Venus throw. He tried again and threw another Venus. The third Venus settled it. Loaded dice.

He put away the dice and picked up the goblet. Was it really bronze? Now he examined it more closely, he was not so sure. He weighed it in his hand, turned it over, breathed on it and rubbed the bottom with his thumb. A smear of gold appeared and part of an engraved letter *P.* He rubbed again, gradually increasing the radius of gleaming metal, until he could make out all the initials.

N. P. N. l. A.

The *l* stood for *libertus* and showed it to be the property of a freed slave.

A slave who had been freed by an owner whose family name began with a *P,* and who was rich enough, and vulgar enough, to drink his wine from a gold cup.

Her voice was suddenly as clear in his mind as if she had been standing beside him.

'My name is Corelia Ampliata, daughter of Numerius Popidius Ampliatus, owner of the Villa Hortensia . . .'

The moonlight shone on the smooth black stones of the narrow street and silhouetted the lines of the flat roofs. It felt almost as hot as it had been in the late afternoon; the moon as bright as the sun. As he mounted the steps between the shuttered, silent houses, he could picture her darting before him – the movement of her hips beneath the plain white dress.

'A few hundred paces – aye, but every one of them uphill!'

He came again to the level ground and to the high wall of the great villa. A grey cat ran along it and disappeared over the other side. The glinting metal dolphins leapt and kissed above the chained gate. He could hear the sea in the distance, moving against the shore, and the throb of the cicadas in the garden. He rattled the iron bars and pressed his face to the warm metal. The porter's room was shuttered and barred. There was not a light to be seen.

He was remembering Ampliatus's reaction when he turned up on the seashore: *'What's happened to Exomnius? But surely Exomnius is still the aquarius?'* There had been surprise in his voice and, now he came to think about it, possibly something more: alarm.

'Corelia!' He called her name softly. 'Corelia Ampliata!'

No response. And then a whisper in the darkness, so low he almost missed it: 'Gone.'

A woman's voice. It came from somewhere to his left. He stepped back from the gate and peered into the shadows. He could make out nothing except a small mound of rags piled in a drift against the wall. He moved closer and saw that the shreds of cloth were moving slightly. A skinny foot protruded, like a bone. It was the mother of the dead slave. He went down on one knee and cautiously touched the rough fabric of her dress. She shivered, then groaned and muttered something. He withdrew his hand. His fingers were sticky with blood.

'Can you stand?'

'Gone,' she repeated.

He lifted her carefully until she was sitting, propped against the wall. Her swollen head dropped forward and he saw that her matted hair had left a damp mark on the stone. She had been whipped and badly beaten, and thrown out of the household to die.

N. P. N. l. A: Numerius Popidius Numerii libertus Ampliatus. Granted his freedom by the family Popidii. It was a fact of life that there was no crueller master than an ex-slave.

He pressed his fingers lightly to her neck to make sure she was still alive. Then he threaded one arm under the crook of her knees and with the other grasped her round her shoulders. It cost him no effort to rise. She was mere rags and bones. Somewhere, in the streets close to the harbour, the night-watchman was calling the fifth division of the darkness: 'Media noctis inclinatio' – midnight.

The engineer straightened his back and set off down the hill as the day of Mars turned into the day of Mercury.

MERCURY

23 August

The day before the eruption

Diluculum

[06:00 hours]

'Prior to AD 79, a reservoir of magma had accumulated beneath the volcano. It is not possible to say when this magma chamber began to form, but it had a volume of at least 3.6 cubic kilometres, was about 3 km below the surface, and was compositionally stratified, with volatile-rich alkalic magma (55 percent SiO_2 and almost 10 per cent K_2O) overlying slightly denser, more mafic magma.'

Peter Francis, Volcanoes: A Planetary Perspective

A t the top of the great stone lighthouse, hidden beyond the ridge of the southern headland, the slaves were dousing the fires to greet the dawn. It was supposed to be a sacred place. According to Virgil, this was the spot where Misenus, the herald of the Trojans, slain by the sea god Triton, lay buried with his oars and trumpet.

Attilius watched the red glow fade beyond the tree-crested promontory, while in the harbour the outlines of the warships took shape against the pearl-grey sky.

He turned and walked back along the quay to where the others were waiting. He could make out their faces at last — Musa, Becco, Corvinus, Polites — they were becoming as familiar to him as family. No sign yet of Corax.

'Nine brothels!' Musa was saying. 'Believe me, if you want

to get laid, Pompeii's the place. Even Becco can give his hand a rest for a change. Hey, aquarius!' he shouted, as Attilius drew closer. 'Tell Becco he can get himself laid!'

The dockside stank of shit and gutted fish. Attilius could see a putrid melon and the bloated, whitened carcass of a rat lapping at his feet between the pillars of the wharf. So much for poets! He had a sudden yearning for one of those cold, northern seas he had heard about — the Atlantic, perhaps, or the Germanicum — a land where a deep tide daily swept the sand and rocks; some place healthier than this tepid Roman lake.

He said, 'As long as we fix the Augusta, Becco can screw every girl in Italy for all I care.'

'There you go, Becco. Your prick will soon be as long as your nose —'

The ship the admiral had promised was moored before them: the *Minerva*, named for the goddess of wisdom, with an owl, the symbol of her deity, carved into her prow. A liburnian. Smaller than the big triremes. Built for speed. Her high stern-post reared out behind her, then curled across her low deck like the sting of a scorpion preparing to strike. She was deserted.

'— Cuculla and Zmyrina. And then there's this red-haired Jewess, Martha. And a little Greek girl, if you like that kind of thing — her mother's barely twenty —'

'What use is a ship without a crew?' muttered Attilius. He was fretting already. He could not afford to waste an hour. 'Polites — run to the barracks, there's a good lad, and find out what's happening.'

'— Aegle and Maria —'

The young slave got to his feet.

'No need,' said Corvinus, and gestured with his head towards the entrance to the port. 'Here they come.'

Attilius said, 'Your ears must be sharper than mine –' but then he heard them, too. A hundred pairs of feet, doubling along the road from the military school. As the marchers crossed the wooden bridge of the causeway, the sharp rhythm became a continuous thunder of leather on wood, then a couple of torches appeared and the unit swung into the street leading to the harbour front. They came on, five abreast, three officers wearing body armour and crested helmets in the lead. At a first shout of command the column halted; at a second, it broke and the sailors moved towards the ship. None spoke. Attilius drew back to let them pass. In their sleeveless tunics, the misshapen shoulders and hugely muscled arms of the oarsmen appeared grotesquely out of proportion to their lower bodies.

'Look at them,' drawled the tallest of the officers. 'The cream of the Navy: human oxen.' He turned to Attilius and raised his fist in salute. 'Torquatus, captain of the *Minerva*.'

'Marcus Attilius. Engineer. Let's go.'

It did not take long to load the ship. Attilius had seen no point in dragging the heavy amphorae of quicklime and sacks of puteolanum down from the reservoir and ferrying them across the bay. If Pompeii was, as they described her, swarming with builders, he would use the admiral's letter to commandeer what he needed. Tools, though, were a different matter. A man should always use his own tools.

He arranged a chain to pass them on board, handing each in turn to Musa, who threw them on to Corvinus – axes, sledge-hammers, saws, picks and shovels, wooden trays to hold the fresh cement, hoes to mix it, and the heavy flat-irons they used to pound it into place – until eventually it had all reached Becco, standing on the deck of the *Minerva*. They worked swiftly, without exchanging a word, and by the time they had finished it was light and the ship was making ready to sail.

Attilius walked up the gangplank and jumped down to the deck. A line of marines with boathooks was waiting to push her away from the quay. From his platform beneath the stern-post, next to the helmsman, Torquatus shouted down, 'Are you ready, engineer?' and Attilius called back that he was. The sooner they left, the better.

'But Corax isn't here,' objected Becco.

To hell with him, thought Attilius. It was almost a relief. He would manage the job alone. 'That's Corax's look-out.'

The mooring ropes were cast off. The boathooks dropped like lances and connected with the dock. Beneath his feet, Attilius felt the deck shake as the oars were unshipped and the *Minerva* began to move. He looked back towards the shore. A crowd had gathered around the public fountain, waiting for the water to appear. He wondered if he should have stayed at the reservoir long enough to supervise the opening of the sluices. But he had left six slaves behind to run the Piscina and the building was ringed by Pliny's marines.

'There he is!' shouted Becco. 'Look! It's Corax!' He started waving his arms above his head. 'Corax! Over here!' He gave Attilius an accusing look. 'You see! You should have waited!'

The overseer had been slouching past the fountain, a bag across his shoulder, seemingly deep in thought. But now he looked up, saw them, and started to run. He moved fast for a man in his forties. The gap between the ship and the quay was widening quickly – three feet, four feet – and it seemed to Attilius impossible that he could make it, but when he reached the edge he threw his bag and then leapt after it, and a couple of the marines stretched out and caught his arms and hauled him aboard. He landed upright, close to the stern, glared at Attilius and jerked his middle finger at him. The engineer turned away.

The *Minerva* was swinging out from the harbour, prow first, and sprouting oars, two dozen on either side of her narrow hull. A drum sounded below deck, and the blades dipped. It sounded again and they splashed the surface, two men pulling on each shaft. The ship glided forwards – imperceptibly to begin with, but picking up speed as the tempo of the drum beats quickened. The pilot, leaning out above the ramming post and staring straight ahead, pointed to the right, Torquatus called out an order, and the helmsman swung hard on the huge oar that served as a rudder, steering a course between two anchored triremes. For the first time in four days, Attilius felt a slight breeze on his face.

'You have an audience, engineer!' shouted Torquatus, and gestured towards the hill above the port. Attilius recognised the long white terrace of the admiral's villa set amid the myrtle groves, and, leaning against the balustrade, the corpulent figure of Pliny himself. He wondered what was going through the old man's mind. Hesitantly, he raised his arm. A moment later Pliny responded. Then the *Minerva* passed between the two great warships, the *Concordia* and the *Neptune*, and when he looked again the terrace was deserted.

In the distance, behind Vesuvius, the sun was starting to appear.

Pliny watched the liburnian gather speed as she headed towards open water. Against the grey, her oars stroked vivid flashes of white, stirring somewhere a long-forgotten memory of the leaden Rhine at daybreak – at Vetera, this must have been, thirty years ago – and the troop-ferry of Legion V 'The Larks' taking his cavalry to the far bank. Such times! What he would not give to embark again on a voyage at first light, or better still to command the fleet in action, a thing he had never done in his two years as admiral. But the effort of simply coming out of his library and on to the terrace to see the *Minerva* go – of rising from his chair and taking a few short steps – had left him breathless, and when he lifted his arm to acknowledge the wave of the engineer he felt as if he were hoisting an exercise weight.

'Nature has granted man no better gift than the shortness of life. The senses grow dull, the limbs are numb, sight, hearing, gait, even the teeth and alimentary organs die before we do, and yet this period is reckoned a portion of life.'

Brave words. Easy to write when one was young and death was still skulking over a distant hill somewhere; less easy when one was fifty-six and the enemy was advancing in full view across the plain.

He leaned his fat belly against the balustrade, hoping that neither of his secretaries had noticed his weakness, then pushed himself away and shuffled back inside.

He had always had a fondness for young men of Attilius's kind. Not in the filthy Greek way, of course – he had never had time for any of that malarkey, although he had seen plenty of it in the Army – but rather spiritually, as the embodiment of the muscular Roman virtues. Senators might dream of empires; soldiers might conquer them; but it was the engineers, the fellows who laid down the roads and dug out the aqueducts, who actually *built* them, and who gave to Rome her global reach. He promised himself that when the aquarius returned he would summon him to dinner and pick his brains to discover exactly what had happened to the Augusta. And then together they would consult some of the texts in the admiral's library and he would teach him a few of the mysteries of Nature, whose surprises were never-ending. These intermittent, harmonic tremors, for example – what were these? He should record the phenomenon and include it in the next edition of the *Natural History*. Every month he discovered something new that required explanation.

His two Greek slaves stood waiting patiently beside the table – Alcman for reading aloud, Alexion for dictation. They had been in attendance since soon after midnight, for the admiral had long ago disciplined himself to function without much rest. 'To be awake is to be alive,' that was his motto. The only man he had ever known who could get by on less sleep was the late Emperor, Vespasian. They used to meet in Rome in the middle of the night to transact their official business. That was why Vespasian had put him in charge of the fleet: 'My ever-vigilant Pliny,' he had called him, in that country bumpkin's accent of his, and had pinched his cheek.

He glanced around the room at the treasures accumulated during his journeys across the Empire. One hundred and sixty notebooks, in which he had recorded every interesting fact he had ever read or heard (Larcius Licinius, the governor of Hispania Tarraconensis, had offered him four hundred thousand sesterces for the lot, but he had not been tempted). Two pieces of magnetite, mined in Dacia, and locked together by their mysterious magic. A lump of shiny grey rock from Macedonia, reputed to have fallen from the stars. Some German amber with an ancient mosquito imprisoned inside its translucent cell. A piece of concave glass, picked up in Africa, which gathered together the sun's rays and aimed them to a point of such concentrated heat it would cause the hardest wood to darken and smoulder. And his water clock, the most accurate in Rome, built according to the specifications of Ctesibius of Alexandria, inventor of the water organ, its apertures bored through gold and gems to prevent corrosion and plugging.

The clock was what he needed. It was said that clocks were like philosophers: you could never find two that agreed. But a clock by Ctesibius was the Plato of timepieces.

'Alcman, fetch me a bowl of water. No –' He changed his mind when the slave was halfway to the door, for had not the geographer, Strabo, described the luxurious Bay of Neapolis as 'the wine bowl'? 'On second thoughts, wine would be more appropriate. But something cheap. A Surrentum, perhaps.' He sat down heavily. 'All right, Alexion – where were we?'

'Drafting a signal to the Emperor, admiral.'

'Ah yes. Just so.'

Now that it was light, he would have to send a dispatch by flash to the new emperor, Titus, to alert him to the problem on the aqueduct. It would shoot, from signal tower to signal tower, all the way up to Rome, and be in the Emperor's hands by noon. And what would the new Master of the World make of that, he wondered?

'We shall signal the Emperor, and after we have done that, I think we shall start a new notebook, and record some scientific observations. Would that interest you?'

'Yes, admiral.' The slave picked up his stylus and wax tablet, struggling to suppress a yawn. Pliny pretended not to see it. He tapped his finger against his lips. He knew Titus well. They had served in Germania together. Charming, cultivated, clever – and completely ruthless. News that a quarter of a million people were without water could easily tip him over the edge into one of his lethal rages. This would require some careful phrasing.

'To His Most Eminent Highness, the Emperor Titus, from the Commander-in-Chief, Misenum,' he began. 'Greetings!'

The *Minerva* passed between the great concrete moles that protected the entrance to the harbour and out into the expanse of the bay. The lemony light of early morning glittered on the water. Beyond the thicket of poles that marked the oyster beds, where the seagulls swooped and cried, Attilius could see the fishery of the Villa Hortensia. He got to his feet for a better view, bracing himself against the motion of the boat. The terraces, the garden paths, the slope where Ampliatus had set up his chair to watch the execution, the ramps along the shoreline, the gantries between the fish-pens, the big eel pond set away from the rest – all deserted. The villa's crimson-and-gold cruiser was no longer moored at the end of the jetty.

It was exactly as Atia had said: they had gone.

The old woman had still not recovered her senses when he left the reservoir before dawn. He had lain her on a straw mattress in one of the rooms beside the kitchen, and had told the domestic slave, Phylo, to summon a doctor and to see that she was cared for. Phylo had made a face, but Attilius had told him gruffly to do as he was told. If she died – well, that might be a merciful release. If she recovered – then, as far as he was concerned, she could stay. He would have to buy another slave in any case, to look after his food and clothes. His needs were few; the work would be light. He had never paid much attention to such matters. Sabina had looked after the household when he was married; after she had gone, his mother had taken over.

The great villa looked dark and shuttered, as though for a funeral; the screams of the gulls were like the cries of mourners.

Musa said, 'I hear he paid ten million for it.'

Attilius acknowledged the remark with a grunt, without taking his eyes off the house. 'Well, he's not there now.'

'Ampliatus? Of course he's not. He never is. He has houses everywhere, that one. Mostly, he's in Pompeii.'

'Pompeii?'

Now the engineer looked round. Musa was sitting cross-legged, his back propped against the tools, eating a fig. He always seemed to be eating. His wife sent him to work each day with enough food to feed half a dozen. He stuffed the last of the fruit into his mouth and sucked his fingers. 'That's where he comes from. Pompeii's where he made his money.'

'And yet he was born a slave.'

'So it goes these days,' said Musa bitterly. 'Your slave dines off silver plate, while your honest, free-born citizen works from dawn till nightfall for a pittance.'

The other men were sitting towards the stern, gathered around Corax, who had his head hunched forwards and was talking quietly – telling some story that required a lot of emphatic hand gestures and much heavy shaking of his head. Attilius guessed he was describing the previous night's meeting with Pliny.

Musa uncorked his waterskin and took a swig then wiped the top and offered it up to Attilius. The engineer took it and squatted beside him. The water had a vaguely bitter taste.

Sulphur. He swallowed a little, more to be friendly than because he was thirsty, wiped it in return and handed it back.

'You're right, Musa,' he said carefully. 'How old is Ampliatus? Not even fifty. Yet he's gone from slave to master of the Villa Hortensia in the time it would take you or I to scrape together enough to buy some bug-infested apartment. How could any man do that honestly?'

'An honest millionaire? As rare as hen's teeth! The way I hear it,' said Musa, looking over his shoulder and lowering his voice, 'he really started coining it just after the earthquake. He'd been left his freedom in old man Popidius's will. He was a good-looking lad, Ampliatus, and there was nothing he wouldn't do for his master. The old man was a lecher – I don't think he'd leave the dog alone. And Ampliatus looked after his wife for him, too, if you know what I mean.' Musa winked. 'Anyway, Ampliatus got his freedom, and a bit of money from somewhere, and then Jupiter decided to shake things up a bit. This was back in Nero's time. It was a very bad quake – the worst anyone could remember. I was in Nola, and I thought my days were up, I can tell you.' He kissed his lucky amulet – a prick and balls, made of bronze, which hung from a leather thong around his neck. 'But you know what they say: one man's loss is another's gain. Pompeii caught it worst of all. But while everyone else was getting out, talking about the town being finished, Ampliatus was going round, buying up the ruins. Got hold of some of those big villas for next to nothing, fixed them up, divided them into three or four, then sold them off for a fortune.'

'Nothing illegal about that, though.'

'Maybe not. But did he really own them when he sold them? That's the thing.' Musa tapped the side of his nose. 'Owners dead. Owners missing. Legal heirs on the other side of the Empire. Half the town was rubble, don't forget. The Emperor sent a commissioner down from Rome to sort out who owned what. Suedius Clemens was his name.'

'And Ampliatus bribed him?'

'Let's just say Suedius left a richer man than he arrived. Or so they say.'

'And what about Exomnius? He was the aquarius at the time of the earthquake – he must have known Ampliatus.'

Attilius could see at once that he had made a mistake. The eager light of gossip was immediately extinguished in Musa's eyes. 'I don't know anything about that,' he muttered, and busied himself with his bag of food. 'He was a fine man, Exomnius. He was good to work for.'

Was, thought Attilius. *Was* a fine man. *Was* good to work for. He tried to make a joke of it. 'You mean he didn't keep dragging you out of bed before dawn?'

'No. I mean he was straight and would never try to trick an honest man into saying more than he ought.'

'Hey, Musa!' shouted Corax. 'What are you going on about over there? You gossip like a woman! Come and have a drink!'

Musa was on his feet at once, swaying down the deck to join the others. As Corax threw him the wineskin, Torquatus jumped down from the stern and made his way towards the centre of the deck, where the mast and sails were stowed.

'We'll have no need of those, I fear.' He was a big man. Arms akimbo he scanned the sky. The fresh, sharp sun glinted on his breastplate; already it was hot. 'Right, engineer. Let's see what my oxen can do.' He swung his feet on to the ladder and descended down the hatch to the lower deck. A moment later, the tempo of the drum increased and Attilius felt the ship lurch slightly. The oars flashed. The silent Villa Hortensia dwindled further in the distance behind them.

The *Minerva* pushed on steadily as the heat of the morning settled over the bay. For two hours the oarsmen kept up the same remorseless pace. Clouds of steam curled from the terraces of the open-air baths in Baiae. In the hills above Puteoli, the fires of the sulphur mines burned pale green.

The engineer sat apart, his hands clasped around his knees, his hat pulled low to shield his eyes, watching the coast slide by, searching the landscape for some clue as to what had happened on the Augusta.

Everything about this part of Italy was strange, he thought. Even the rust-red soil around Puteoli possessed some quality of magic, so that when it was mixed with lime and flung into the sea it turned to rock. This puteolanum, as they called it, in honour of its birthplace, was the discovery that had transformed Rome. And it had also given his family their profession, for what had once needed laborious construction in stone and brick could now be thrown up overnight. With shuttering and cement Agrippa had sunk the great wharves of Misenum, and had irrigated the Empire with aqueducts – the Augusta here in Campania, the Julia and the Virgo in Rome, the Nemausus in southern Gaul. The world had been remade.

But nowhere had this hydraulic cement been used to greater effect than in the land where it was discovered. Piers and jetties, terraces and embankments, breakwaters and fish-farms had transformed the Bay of Neapolis. Whole villas seemed to thrust themselves up from the waves and to float offshore. What had once been the realm of the super-rich – Caesar, Crassus, Pompey – had been flooded by a new class of millionaires, men like Ampliatus. Attilius wondered how many of the owners, relaxed and torpid as this sweltering August stretched and yawned and settled itself into its fourth week, would be aware by now of the failure of the aqueduct. Not many, he would guess. Water was something that was carried in by slaves, or which appeared miraculously from the nozzle of one of Sergius Orata's shower-baths. But they would know soon enough. They would know once they had to start drinking their swimming pools.

The further east they rowed, the more Vesuvius dominated the bay. Her lower slopes were a mosaic of cultivated fields and villas, but from her halfway point rose dark green, virgin forest. A few wisps of cloud hung motionless around her tapering peak. Torquatus declared that the hunting up there was excellent – boar, deer, hare. He had been out many times with his dogs and net, and also with his bow. But one had to look out for the wolves. In winter, the top was snow-capped.

Squatting next to Attilius he took off his helmet and wiped his forehead. 'Hard to imagine,' he said, 'snow in this heat.'

'And is she easy to climb?'

'Not too hard. Easier than she looks. The top's fairly flat when you get up there. Spartacus made it the camp for his rebel army. Some natural fortress that must have been. No wonder the scum were able to hold off the legions for so long. When the skies are clear you can see for fifty miles.'

They had passed the city of Neapolis and were parallel with a smaller town which Torquatus said was Herculaneum, although the coast was such a continuous ribbon of development – ochre walls and red roofs, occasionally pierced by the dark green spear-thrusts of cypresses – that it was not always possible to tell where one town ended and another began. Herculaneum looked stately and well-pleased with herself at the foot of the luxuriant mountain, her windows facing out to sea. Brightly coloured pleasure-craft, some shaped like sea-creatures, bobbed in the shallows. There were parasols on the beaches, people casting fishing lines from the jetties. Music, and the shouts of children playing ball, wafted across the placid water.

'Now that's the greatest villa on the Bay,' said Torquatus. He nodded towards an immense colonnaded property that sprawled along the shoreline and rose in terraces above the sea. 'That's the Villa Calpurnia. I had the honour to take the new Emperor there last month, on a visit to the former consul, Pedius Cascus.'

'Cascus?' Attilius pictured the lizard-like senator from the previous evening, swaddled in his purple-striped toga. 'I had no idea he was so rich.'

'Inherited through his wife, Rectina. She had some connection with the Piso clan. The admiral comes here often, to use the library. Do you see that group of figures, reading in the shade beside the pool? They are philosophers.' Torquatus found this very funny. 'Some men breed birds as a pastime, others have dogs. The senator keeps philosophers!'

'And what species are these philosophers?'

'Followers of Epicurus. According to Cascus, they hold that man is mortal, the gods are indifferent to his fate, and therefore the only thing to do in life is enjoy oneself.'

'I could have told him that for nothing.'

Torquatus laughed again then put on his helmet and tightened the chin-strap. 'Not long to Pompeii now, engineer. Another half-hour should do it.'

He walked back towards the stern.

Attilius shielded his eyes and contemplated the villa. He had never had much use for philosophy. Why one human being should inherit such a palace, and another be torn apart by eels, and a third break his back in the stifling darkness rowing a liburnian – a man could go mad trying to reason why the world was so arranged. Why had he had to watch his wife die in front of him when she was barely older than a girl? Show him the philosophers who could answer that and he would start to see the point of them.

She had always wanted to come on holiday to the Bay of Neapolis, and he had always put her off, saying he was too busy. And now it was too late. Grief at what he had lost and regret at what he had failed to do, his twin assailants, caught him unawares again, and hollowed him, as they always did. He felt a physical emptiness in the pit of his stomach. Looking at the coast he remembered the letter a friend had shown him on the day of Sabina's funeral; he had learnt it off by heart. The jurist, Servius Sulpicus, more than a century earlier, had been sailing back from Asia to Rome, lost in grief, when he found himself contemplating the Mediterranean shore. Afterwards he described his feelings to Cicero, who had also just lost his daughter: 'There behind me was Aegina, in front of me Megara, to the right Piraeus, to the left Corinth; once flourishing towns, now lying low in ruins before one's eyes, and I began to think to myself: "How can we complain if one of us dies or is killed, ephemeral creatures as we are, when the corpses of so many towns lie abandoned in a single spot. Check yourself, Servius, and remember that you were born a mortal man. Can you be so greatly moved by the loss of one poor little woman's frail spirit?"'

To which, for Attilius, the answer still remained, more than two years later: yes.

He let the warmth soak his body and face for a while, and despite himself he must have floated off to sleep, for when he next opened his eyes, the town had gone, and there was yet another huge villa slumbering beneath the shade of its giant umbrella pines, with slaves watering the lawn and scooping leaves from the surface of the swimming pool. He shook his head to clear his mind, and reached for the leather sack in which he carried what he needed – Pliny's letter to the aediles of Pompeii, a small bag of gold coins and the map of the Augusta.

Work was always his consolation. He unrolled the plan, resting it against his knees, and felt a sudden stir of anxiety. The proportions of the sketch, he realised, were not at all accurate. It failed to convey the immensity of Vesuvius, which still they had not passed, and which must surely, now he looked at it, be seven or eight miles across. What had seemed a mere thumb's-width on the map was in reality half a morning's dusty trek in the boiling heat of the sun. He reproached himself for his naivety – boasting to a client, in the comfort of his library, of what could be done, without first checking the actual lie of the land. The rookie's classic error.

He pushed himself to his feet and made his way over to the men, who were crouched in a circle, playing dice. Corax had his hand cupped over the beaker and was shaking it hard. He did not look up as Attilius's shadow fell across him. 'Come on, Fortuna, you old whore,' he muttered and rolled the dice. He threw all aces – a dog – and groaned. Becco gave a cry of joy and scooped up the pile of copper coins.

'My luck was good,' said Corax, 'until he appeared.' He jabbed his finger at Attilius. 'He's worse than a raven, lads. You mark my words – he'll lead us all to our deaths.'

'Not like Exomnius,' said the engineer, squatting beside them. 'I bet he always won.' He picked up the dice. 'Whose are these?'

'Mine,' said Musa.

'I'll tell you what. Let's play a different game. When we get to Pompeii, Corax is going out first to the far side of Vesuvius, to find the break on the Augusta. Someone must go with him. Why don't you throw for the privilege?'

'Whoever wins goes with Corax!' exclaimed Musa.

'No,' said Attilius. 'Whoever loses.'

Everyone laughed, except Corax.

'Whoever loses!' repeated Becco. 'That's a good one!'

They took it in turns to roll the dice, each man clasping his hands around the cup as he shook it, each whispering his own particular prayer for luck.

Musa went last, and threw a dog. He looked crestfallen.

'You lose!' chanted Becco. 'Musa the loser!'

'All right,' said Attilius, 'the dice settle it. Corax and Musa will locate the fault.'

'And what about the others?' grumbled Musa.

'Becco and Corvinus will ride to Abellinum and close the sluices.'

'I don't see why it takes two of them to go to Abellinum. And what's Polites going to do?'

'Polites stays with me in Pompeii and organises the tools and transport.'

'Oh, that's fair!' said Musa, bitterly. 'The free man sweats out his guts on the mountain, while the slave gets to screw the whores in Pompeii!' He snatched up his dice and hurled them into the sea. 'That's what I think of my luck!'

From the pilot at the front of the ship came a warning shout – 'Pompeii ahead!' – and six heads turned as one to face her.

She came into view slowly from behind a headland, and she was not at all what the engineer had expected – no sprawling resort like Baiae or Neapolis, strung out along the coastline of the bay, but a fortress-city, built to withstand a siege, set back a quarter of a mile from the sea, on higher ground, her port spread out beneath her.

It was only as they drew closer that Attilius saw that her walls were no longer continuous – that the long years of the Roman peace had persuaded the city fathers to drop their guard. Houses had been allowed to emerge above the ramparts, and to spill, in widening, palm-shaded terraces, down towards the docks. Dominating the line of flat roofs was a temple, looking out to sea. Gleaming marble pillars were surmounted by what at first appeared to be a frieze of ebony figures. But the frieze, he realised, was alive. Craftsmen, almost naked and blackened by the sun, were moving back and forth against the white stone – working, even though it was a public holiday. The ring of chisels on stone and the rasp of saws carried clear in the warm air.

Activity everywhere. People walking along the top of the wall and working in the gardens that looked out to sea. People swarming along the road in front of the town – on foot, on horseback, in chariots and on the backs of wagons – throwing up a haze of dust and clogging the steep paths that led up from the port to the two big city gates. As the *Minerva* turned into the narrow entrance of the harbour the din of the crowd grew louder – a holiday crowd, by the look of it, coming into town from the countryside to celebrate the festival of Vulcan. Attilius scanned the dockside for fountains but could see none.

The men were all silent, standing in line, each with his own thoughts.

He turned to Corax. 'Where does the water come into the town?'

'On the other side of the city,' said Corax, staring intently at the town. 'Beside the Vesuvius Gate. *If –*' he gave heavy emphasis to the word '– it's still flowing.'

That would be a joke, thought Attilius, if it turned out the water was not running after all and he had brought them all this way merely on the word of some old fool of an augur.

'Who works there?'

'Just some town slave. You won't find him much help.'

'Why not?'

Corax grinned and shook his head. He would not say. A private joke.

'All right. Then the Vesuvius Gate is where we'll start from.' Attilius clapped his hands. 'Come on, lads. You've seen a town before. The cruise is over.'

They were inside the harbour now. Warehouses and cranes crowded against the water's edge. Beyond them was a river – the Sarnus, according to Attilius's map – choked with barges waiting to be unloaded. Torquatus, shouting orders, strode down the length of the ship. The drumbeats slowed and ceased. The oars were shipped. The helmsman turned the rudder slightly and they glided alongside the wharf at walking-pace, no more than a foot of clear water between the deck and the quay. Two groups of sailors carrying mooring cables jumped ashore and wound them quickly around the stone posts. A moment later the ropes snapped taut and, with a jerk that almost knocked Attilius off his feet, the *Minerva* came to rest.

He saw it as he was recovering his balance. A big, plain stone plinth with a head of Neptune gushing water from his mouth into a bowl that was shaped like an oyster-shell, and the bowl *overflowing* – this was what he would never forget – cascading down to rinse the cobbles, and wash, unregarded, into the sea. Nobody was queuing to drink. Nobody was paying it any attention. Why should they? It was just an ordinary miracle. He vaulted over the low side of the warship and swayed towards it, feeling the strange solidity of the ground after the voyage across the bay. He dropped his sack and put his hands into the clear arc of water, cupped them, raised them to his lips. It tasted sweet and pure and he almost laughed aloud with pleasure and relief, then plunged his head beneath the pipe, and let the water run everywhere – into his mouth and nostrils, his ears, down the back of his neck – heedless of the people staring at him as if he had gone insane.

Hora quarta

[09:48 hours]

*'Isotope studies of Neapolitan volcanic magma show
signs of significant mixing with the surrounding rock,
suggesting that the reservoir isn't one continuous molten
body. Instead, the reservoir might look more like a
sponge, with the magma seeping through numerous
fractures in the rock. The massive magma layer may
feed into several smaller reservoirs that are closer to
the surface and too small to identify with seismic
techniques . . .'*

American Association for the Advancement of Science,
news bulletin, 'Massive Magma Layer feeds Mt. Vesuvius',
November 16 2001

A man could buy anything he needed in the harbour of
Pompeii. Indian parrots, Nubian slaves, nitrum salt
from the pools near Cairo, Chinese cinnamon, African
monkeys, Oriental slave-girls famed for their sexual tricks . . .
Horses were as easy to come by as flies. Half a dozen dealers
hung around outside the customs shed. The nearest sat on a
stool beneath a crudely drawn sign of the winged Pegasus,
bearing the slogan 'Baculus: Horses Swift Enough for the
Gods'.

'I need five,' Attilius told the dealer. 'And none of your

clapped-out nags. I want good, strong beasts, capable of working all day. And I need them now.'

'That's no problem, citizen.' Baculus was a small, bald man, with the brick-red face and glassy eyes of a heavy drinker. He wore an iron ring too large for his finger, which he twisted nervously, round and round. 'Nothing's a problem in Pompeii, provided you've the money. Mind you, I'll require a deposit. One of my horses was stolen the other week.'

'And I also want oxen. Two teams and two wagons.'

'On a public holiday?' He clicked his tongue. 'That, I think, will take longer.'

'How long?'

'Let me see.' Baculus squinted at the sun. The more difficult he made it sound, the more he could charge. 'Two hours. Maybe three.'

'Agreed.'

They haggled over the price, the dealer demanding an outrageous sum which Attilius immediately divided by ten. Even so, when eventually they shook hands, he was sure he had been swindled and it irritated him, as any kind of waste always did. But he had no time to seek out a better bargain. He told the dealer to bring round four of the horses immediately to the Vesuvius Gate and then pushed his way back through the traders towards the *Minerva*.

By now the crew had been allowed up on deck. Most had peeled off their sodden tunics and the stench of sweat from the sprawled bodies was strong enough to compete with the stink of the nearby fish-sauce factory, where liquefying offal was decomposing in vats in the sunshine. Corvinus and Becco were picking their way between the oarsmen, carrying the tools, throwing them over the side to Musa and Polites. Corax stood with his back to the boat, peering towards the town, occasionally rising on tiptoe to see over the heads of the crowd.

He noticed Attilius and stopped. 'So the water runs,' he said, and folded his arms. There was something almost heroic about his stubbornness, his unwillingness to concede he had been wrong. It was then that Attilius knew, beyond question, that once all this was over he would have to get rid of him.

'Yes, she runs,' he agreed. He waved to the others to stop what they were doing and to gather round. It was agreed that they would leave Polites to finish the unloading and to guard the tools on the dockside; Attilius would send word to him about where to meet up later. Then the remaining five set off towards the nearest gate, Corax trailing behind, and whenever Attilius looked back it seemed that he was searching for someone, his head craning from side to side.

The engineer led them up the ramp from the harbour towards the city wall, beneath the half-finished temple of Venus and into the dark tunnel of the gate. A customs official gave them a cursory glance to check they were not carrying anything they might sell, then nodded them into the town.

The street beyond the gate was not as steep as the ramp outside, or as slippery, but it was narrower, so that they were almost crushed by the weight of bodies surging into Pompeii. Attilius found himself borne along past shops and another big temple – this one dedicated to Apollo – and into the blinding open space and swarming activity of the forum.

It was imposing for a provincial town: basilica, covered market, more temples, a public library – all brilliantly coloured and shimmering in the sunlight; three or four dozen statues of emperors and local worthies high up on their pedestals. Not all of it was finished. A webwork of wooden scaffolding covered some of the large buildings. The high walls acted to trap the noise of the crowd and reflect it back at them – the flutes and drums of the buskers, the cries of the beggars and hawkers, the sizzle of cooking food. Fruit-sellers were offering green figs and pink slices of melon. Wine merchants crouched beside rows of red amphorae propped in nests of yellow straw. At the foot of a nearby statue a snake-charmer sat cross-legged, playing a pipe, a grey serpent rising groggily from the mat in front of him, another draped round his neck. Small pieces of fish were frying on an open range. Slaves, bowed under the weight of bundles of wood, were hurrying in relays to pile them on to the big bonfire being built in the centre of the forum for the evening sacrifice to Vulcan. A barber advertised himself as an expert in pulling teeth and had a foot-high pile of grey and black stumps to prove it.

The engineer took off his hat and wiped his forehead. Already there was something about the place he did not much like. A hustler's town, he thought. Full of people on the make. She would welcome a visitor for exactly as long as it took to fleece him. He beckoned to Corax to ask him where he would find the aediles – he had to cup his hand to the man's ear to make himself heard – and the overseer pointed towards a row of three small offices lining the southern edge of the square, all closed for the holiday. A long notice-board was covered in proclamations, evidence of a thriving bureaucracy. Attilius cursed to himself. Nothing was ever easy.

'You know the way to the Vesuvius Gate,' he shouted to Corax. 'You lead.'

Water was pumping through the city. As they fought their way towards the far end of the forum he could hear it washing clear the big public latrine beside the Temple of Jupiter and bubbling in the streets beyond. He kept in close behind Corax, and once or twice he found himself splashing through the little torrents that were running in the gutters, bearing away the dust and rubbish down the slope towards the sea. He counted seven fountains, all overflowing. The Augusta's loss was clearly Pompeii's gain. The whole force of the aqueduct had nowhere to run except here. So while the other towns around the bay were baking dry in the heat, the children of Pompeii paddled in the streets.

It was hard work, toiling up the hill. The press of people was mainly moving in the opposite direction, down towards the attractions of the forum, and by the time they reached the big northern gate Baculus was already waiting for them with their horses. He had hitched them to a post beside a small building that backed on to the city wall. Attilius said, 'The castellum aquae?' and Corax nodded.

The engineer took it in at a glance – the same redbrick construction as the Piscina Mirabilis, the same muffled sound of rushing water. It looked to be the highest point in the town and that made sense: invariably an aqueduct entered beneath a city's walls where the elevation was greatest. Gazing back down the hill he could see the water towers which regulated the pressure of the flow. He sent Musa inside the castellum to fetch out the water-slave while he turned his attention to the horses. They did not appear too bad. You would not want to enter them for a race at the Circus Maximus, but they would do the job. He counted out a small pile of gold coins and gave them to Baculus, who tested each one with his teeth. 'And the oxen?'

These, Baculus promised, with much solemn pressing of his hands to his heart and rolling of his eyes to heaven, would be ready by the seventh hour. He would attend to it immediately. He wished them all the blessings of Mercury on their journey, and took his leave – but only as far, Attilius noticed, as the bar across the street.

He assigned the horses on the basis of their strength. The best he gave to Becco and Corvinus, on the grounds that they would have the most riding to do, and he was still explaining his reasons to an aggrieved Corax when Musa reappeared to announce that the castellum aquae was deserted.

'What?' Attilius wheeled round. 'Nobody there at all?'

'It's Vulcanalia, remember?'

Corax said, 'I told you he'd be no help.'

'Public holidays!' Attilius could have punched the brick-work in frustration. 'Somewhere in this town there had better be people willing to work.' He regarded his puny expedition uneasily, and thought again how unwise he had been in the admiral's library, mistaking what was theoretically possible with what actually could be achieved. But there was nothing else for it now. He cleared his throat. 'All right. You all know what you have to do? Becco, Corvinus – have either of you ever been up to Abellinum before?'

'I have,' said Becco.

'What's the set-up?'

'The springs rise beneath a temple dedicated to the water-goddesses, and flow into a basin within the nymphaeum. The aquarius in charge is Probus, who also serves as priest.'

'An aquarius as priest!' Attilius laughed bitterly and shook his head. 'Well, you can tell this heavenly engineer, whoever he is, that the goddesses, in their celestial wisdom, require him to close his main sluice and divert all his water to Beneventum. Make sure it's done the moment you arrive. Becco – you are to remain behind in Abellinum and see it stays closed for twelve hours. Then you open it again. Twelve hours – as near exact as you can make it. Have you got that?'

Becco nodded.

'And if, by any remote chance, we can't make the repairs in twelve hours,' said Corax sarcastically, 'what then?'

'I've thought of that. As soon as the water is closed off, Corvinus leaves Becco at the basin and follows the course of the Augusta back down the mountains until he reaches the rest of us north-east of Vesuvius. By that time it will be clear how much work needs to be done. If we can't fix the problem in twelve hours, he can take word back to Becco to keep the sluice-gate closed until we've finished. That's a lot of riding, Corvinus. Are you up to it?'

'Yes, aquarius.'

'Good man.'

'Twelve hours!' repeated Corax, shaking his head. 'That's going to mean working through the night.'

'What's the matter, Corax? Scared of the dark?' Once again, he managed to coax a laugh from the other men. 'When you locate the problem, make an assessment of how much material we'll need for the repair job, and how much labour. You stay there and send Musa back with a report. I'll make sure I requisition enough torches along with everything else we need from the aediles. Once I've loaded up the wagons, I'll wait here at the castellum aquae to hear from you.'

'And what if I don't locate the problem?'

It occurred to Attilius that the overseer, in his bitterness, might even try to sabotage the entire mission. 'Then we'll set out anyway, and get to you before nightfall.' He smiled. 'So don't try to screw me around.'

'I'm sure there are plenty who'd like to screw you, pretty

boy, but I'm not one of them.' Corax leered back at him. 'You're a long way from home, young Marcus Attilius. Take my advice. In this town – watch your back. If you know what I mean.'

And he thrust his groin back and forth in the same obscene gesture he had made out on the hillside the previous day, when Attilius had been prospecting for the spring.

He saw them off from the pomoerium, the sacred boundary just beyond the Vesuvius Gate, kept clear of buildings in honour of the city's guardian deities.

The road ran around the town like a racetrack, passing beside a bronze works and through a big cemetery. As the men mounted their horses Attilius felt he ought to say something – some speech like Caesar's, on the eve of battle – but he could never find those kinds of words. 'When this is done, I'll buy wine for everyone. In the finest place in Pompeii,' he added lamely.

'And a woman,' said Musa, pointing at him. 'Don't forget the women, aquarius!'

'The women you can pay for yourself.'

'If he can find a whore who'll have him!'

'Screw you, Becco. See you later, cocksuckers!'

And before Attilius could think of anything else to say they were kicking their heels into the sides of their horses and wheeling away through the crowds thronging into the city – Corax and Musa to the left, to pick up the trail to Nola; Becco and Corvinus right, towards Nuceria and Abellinum. As they trotted into the necropolis, only Corax looked back – not at Attilius, but over his head, towards the walls of the city. His glance swept along the ramparts and watchtowers for a final time, then he planted himself more firmly in the saddle and turned in the direction of Vesuvius.

The engineer followed the progress of the riders as they disappeared behind the tombs, leaving only a blur of brown dust above the white sarcophagi to show where they had passed. He stood for a few moments – he barely knew them, yet so many of his hopes, so much of his future went with them! – then he retraced his steps towards the city gate.

It was only as he joined the line of pedestrians queuing at the gate that he noticed the slight hump in the ground where the tunnel of the aqueduct passed beneath the city wall. He stopped and swivelled, following the line of it towards the nearest manhole, and saw to his surprise that its course pointed directly at the summit of Vesuvius. Through the haze of dust and heat the mountain loomed even more massively over the countryside than it had above the sea, but less distinctly; more bluish-grey than green. It was impossible that the spur should actually run all the way on to Vesuvius itself. He guessed it must swerve off to the east at the edge of the lower slopes and travel inland to join up with the Augusta's main line. He wondered where exactly. He wished he knew the shape of the land, the quality of rock and soil. But Campania was a mystery to him.

He went back through the shadowy gate and into the glare of the small square, acutely aware suddenly of being alone in a strange town. What did Pompeii know or care of the crisis beyond its walls? The heedless activity of the place seemed deliberately to mock him. He walked around the side of the castellum aquae and along the short alley that led to its entrance. 'Is anyone there?'

No answer. He could hear the rush of the aqueduct much

more clearly here, and when he pushed open the low wooden door he was hit at once by the drenching spray and that sharp, coarse, sweet smell – the smell that had pursued him all his life – of fresh water on warm stone.

He went inside. Fingers of light from two small windows set high above his head pierced the cool darkness. But he did not need light to know how the castellum was arranged for he had seen dozens of them over the years – all identical, all laid out according to the principles of Vitruvius. The tunnel of the Pompeii spur was smaller than the Augusta's main matrix, but still big enough for a man to squeeze along it to make repairs. The water jetted from its mouth through a bronze mesh screen into a shallow concrete reservoir divided by wooden gates, which in turn fed a set of three big lead pipes. The central conduit would carry the supply for the drinking fountains; that to its left would be for private houses; that to its right for the public baths and theatres. What was unusual was the force of the flow. It was not only drenching the walls. It had also swept a mass of debris along the tunnel, trapping it against the metal screen. He could make out leaves and twigs and even a few small rocks. Slovenly maintenance. No wonder Corax had said the water-slave was useless.

He swung one leg over the concrete wall of the reservoir and then the other, and lowered himself into the swirling pool. The water came up almost to his waist. It was like stepping into warm silk. He waded the few paces to the grille and ran his hands underwater, around the edge of the mesh frame, feeling for its fastenings. When he found them, he unscrewed them. There were two more at the top. He undid those as well, lifted away the grille, and stood aside to let the rubbish swirl past him.

'Is somebody there?'

The voice startled him. A young man stood in the doorway. 'Of course there's somebody here, you fool. What does it look like?'

'What are you doing?'

'You're the water-slave? Then I'm doing your fucking job for you – that's what I'm doing. Wait there.' Attilius swung the grille back into place and refastened it, waded over to the side of the reservoir and hauled himself out. 'I'm Marcus Attilius. The new aquarius of the Augusta. And what do they call you, apart from a lazy idiot?'

'Tiro, aquarius.' The boy's eyes were open wide in alarm, his pupils darting from side to side. 'Forgive me.' He dropped to his knees. 'The public holiday, aquarius – I slept late – I –'

'All right. Never mind that.' The boy was only about sixteen – a scrap of humanity, as thin as a stray dog – and Attilius regretted his roughness. 'Come on. Get up off the floor. I need you to take me to the magistrates.' He held out his hand but the slave ignored it, his eyes still flickering wildly back and forth. Attilius waved his palm in front of Tiro's face. 'You're blind?'

'Yes, aquarius.'

A blind guide. No wonder Corax had smiled when Attilius had asked about him. A blind guide in an unfriendly city! 'But how do you perform your duties if you can't see?'

'I can hear better than any man.' Despite his nervousness, Tiro spoke with a trace of pride. 'I can tell by the sound of the water how well it flows and if it's obstructed. I can smell it. I can taste it for impurities.' He lifted his head, sniffing the air. 'This morning there's no need for me to adjust the gates. I've never heard the flow so strong.'

'That's true.' The engineer nodded: he had underestimated the boy. 'The main line is blocked somewhere between here and Nola. That's why I've come, to get help to repair it. You're the property of the town?' Tiro nodded. 'Who are the magistrates?'

'Marcus Holconius and Quintus Brittius,' said Tiro promptly. 'The aediles are Lucius Popidius and Gaius Cuspius.'

'Which is in charge of the water supply?'

'Popidius.'

'Where will I find him?'

'It's a holiday –'

'Where's his house then?'

'Straight down the hill, aquarius, towards the Stabian Gate. On the left. Just past the big crossroads.' Tiro scrambled to his feet eagerly. 'I can show you if you like.'

'Surely I can find it by myself?'

'No, no.' Tiro was already in the alley, anxious to prove himself. 'I can take you there. You'll see.'

They descended into the town together. It tumbled away below them, a jumble of terracotta roofs sloping down to a sparkling sea. Framing the view to the left was the blue ridge of the Surrentum peninsula; to the right was the tree-covered flank of Vesuvius. Attilius found it hard to imagine a more perfect spot in which to build a city, high enough above the bay to be wafted by the occasional breeze, close enough to the shore to enjoy the benefits of the Mediterranean trade. No wonder it had risen again so quickly after the earthquake.

The street was lined with houses, not the sprawling apartment blocks of Rome, but narrow-fronted, windowless dwellings that seemed to have turned their backs on the crowded traffic and to be looking inwards upon themselves. Open doors revealed an ocasional flash of what lay beyond – cool mosaic hallways, a sunny garden, a fountain – but apart from these glimpses, the only relief from the monotony of the drab walls were election slogans daubed in red paint.

'THE ENTIRE MASS HAVE APPROVED THE CANDIDACY OF CUSPIUS FOR THE OFFICE OF AEDILE.'

'THE FRUIT DEALERS TOGETHER WITH HELVIUS VESTALIS UNANIMOUSLY URGE THE ELECTION OF MARCUS HOLCONIUS PRISCUS AS MAGISTRATE WITH JUDICIAL POWER.'

'THE WORSHIPPERS OF ISIS UNANIMOUSLY URGE THE ELEC-TION OF LUCIUS POPIDIUS SECUNDUS AS AEDILE.'

'Your whole town appears to be obsessed with elections, Tiro. It's worse than Rome.'

'The free men vote for the new magistrates each March, aquarius.'

They were walking quickly, Tiro keeping a little ahead of Attilius, threading along the crowded pavement, occasionally stepping into the gutter to splash through the running stream. The engineer had to ask him to slow down. Tiro apologised. He had been blind from birth, he said cheerfully: had been dumped on the refuse tip outside the city walls and left to die. But someone had picked him up and he'd lived by running errands for the town since he was six years old. He knew his way by instinct.

'This aedile, Popidius,' said Attilius, as they passed his name for the third time, 'his must have been the family which once had Ampliatus as a slave.'

But Tiro, despite the keenness of his ears, seemed for once not to have heard.

They came to a big crossroads, dominated by an enormous triumphal arch, resting on four marble pillars. A team of four horses, frozen in stone, plunged and reared against the brilliant blue sky, hauling the figure of Victory in her golden chariot. The monument was dedicated to yet another Holconius – Marcus Holconius Rufus, dead these past sixty years – and Attilius paused long enough to read the inscription: military tribune, priest of Augustus, five times magistrate, patron of the town.

Always the same few names, he thought. Holconius, Popidius, Cuspius . . . The ordinary citizens might put on their togas every spring, turn out to listen to the speeches, throw their tablets into the urns and elect a new set of magistrates. But still the familiar faces came round again and again. The engineer had almost as little time for politicians as he had for the gods.

He was about to put his foot down to cross the street when he suddenly pulled it back. It appeared to him that the large stepping stones were rippling slightly. A great dry wave was passing through the town. An instant later he lurched, as he had done when the *Minerva* was moored, and he had to grab at Tiro's arm to stop himself falling. A few people screamed; a horse shied. On the opposite corner of the crossroads a tile slid down a steep-pitched roof and shattered on the pavement. For a few moments the centre of Pompeii was almost silent. And then, gradually, activity began again. Breath was exhaled. Conversations resumed. The driver flicked his whip over the back of his frantic horse and the cart jumped forwards.

Tiro took advantage of the lull in the traffic to dart across to the opposite side and, after a brief hesitation, Attilius followed, half-expecting the big raised stones to give way again beneath his leather soles. The sensation made him jumpier than he cared to admit. If you couldn't trust the ground you trod on, what could you trust?

The slave waited for him. His blank eyes, endlessly searching for what he could not see, gave him a look of constant unease. 'Don't worry, aquarius. It happens all the time this summer. Five times, ten times, even, in the past two days. The ground is complaining of the heat!'

He offered his hand but Attilius ignored it – he found it demeaning, the blind man reassuring the sighted – and mounted the high pavement unaided. He said irritably, 'Where's this bloody house?' and Tiro gestured vaguely to a doorway across the street, a little way down.

It did not look much. The usual blank walls. A bakery on one side, with a queue of customers waiting to enter a confectionery shop. A stink of urine from the laundry opposite, with pots left on the pavement for passers-by to piss in (nothing cleaned clothes as well as human piss). Next to the laundry, a theatre. Above the big door of the house was another of the ubiquitous, red-painted slogans: 'HIS NEIGHBOURS URGE THE ELECTION OF LUCIUS POPIDIUS SECUNDUS AS AEDILE. HE WILL PROVE WORTHY.' Attilius would never have found the place on his own.

'Aquarius, may I ask you something?'

'What?'

'Where is Exomnius?'

'Nobody knows, Tiro. He's vanished.'

The slave absorbed this, nodding slowly. 'Exomnius was like you. He could not get used to the shaking, either. He said it reminded him of the time before the big earthquake, many years ago. The year I was born.'

He seemed to be on the edge of tears. Attilius put a hand on his shoulder and studied him intently. 'Exomnius was in Pompeii recently?'

'Of course. He lived here.'

Attilius tightened his grip. 'He lived *here*? In Pompeii?'

He felt bewildered and yet he also grasped immediately that it must be true. It explained why Exomnius's quarters at Misenum had been so devoid of personal possessions, why Corax had not wanted him to come here, and why the over-seer had behaved so strangely in Pompeii – all that looking around, searching the crowds for a familiar face.

'He had rooms at Africanus's place,' said Tiro. 'He was not here all the time. But often.'

'And how long ago did you speak to him?'

'I can't remember.' The youth really was beginning to seem frightened now. He turned his head as though trying to look at Attilius's hand on his shoulder. The engineer quickly released him and patted his arm reassuringly.

'Try to remember, Tiro. It could be important.'

'I don't know.'

'After the Festival of Neptune or before?' Neptunalia was on the twenty-third day of July: the most sacred date in the calendar for the men of the aqueducts.

'After. Definitely. Perhaps two weeks ago.'

'Two weeks? Then you must have been one of the last to talk to him. And he was worried about the tremors?' Tiro nodded again. 'And Ampliatus? He was a great friend of Ampliatus, was he not? Were they often together?'

The slave gestured to his eyes. 'I cannot see –'

No, thought Attilius, but I bet you heard them: not much escapes those ears of yours. He glanced across the street at the house of Popidius. 'All right, Tiro. You can go back to the castellum. Do your day's work. I'm grateful for your help.'

'Thank you, aquarius.' Tiro gave a little bow and took Attilius's hand and kissed it. Then he turned and began climbing back up the hill towards the Vesuvius Gate, dancing from side to side through the holiday crowd.

Hora quinta

[11:07 hours]

'Injections of new magma can also trigger eruptions by upsetting the thermal, chemical, or mechanical equilibrium of older magma in a shallow reservoir. New magmas coming from deeper, hotter sources can suddenly raise the temperature of the cooler resident magma causing it to convect and vesiculate.'

Volcanology *(second edition)*

The house had a double door – heavy-studded, bronze-hinged, firmly closed. Attilius hammered on it a couple of times with his fist. The noise he made seemed too feeble to be heard above the racket of the street. But almost at once it opened slightly and the porter appeared – a Nubian, immensely tall and broad in a sleeveless crimson tunic. His thick black arms and neck, as solid as tree trunks, glistened with oil, like some polished African hardwood.

Attilius said lightly, 'A keeper worthy of his gate, I see.'

The porter did not smile. 'State your business.'

'Marcus Attilius, aquarius of the Aqua Augusta, wishes to present his compliments to Lucius Popidius Secundus.'

'It's a public holiday. He's not at home.'

Attilius put his foot against the door. 'He is now.' He opened his bag, and pulled out the admiral's letter. 'Do you

113

see this seal? Give it to him. Tell him it's from the commander-in-chief at Misenum. Tell him I need to see him on the Emperor's business.'

The porter looked down at Attilius's foot. If he had slammed the door he would have snapped it like a twig. A man's voice behind him cut in: 'The Emperor's business, did he just say, Massavo? You had better let him in.' The Nubian hesitated – Massavo: that was the right name for him, thought Attilius – then stepped backwards, and the engineer slipped quickly through the opening. The door was closed and locked behind him; the sounds of the city were extinguished.

The man who had spoken wore the same crimson uniform as the porter. He had a bunch of keys attached to his belt – the household steward, presumably. He took the letter and ran his thumb across the seal, checking to see if it was broken. Satisfied, he studied Attilius. 'Lucius Popidius is entertaining guests for Vulcanalia. But I shall see that he receives it.'

'No,' said Attilius. 'I shall give it to him myself. Immediately.'

He held out his hand. The steward tapped the cylinder of papyrus against his teeth, trying to decide what to do. 'Very well.' He gave Attilius the letter. 'Follow me.'

He led the way down the narrow corridor of the vestibule towards a sunlit atrium, and for the first time Attilius began to appreciate the immensity of the old house. The narrow façade was an illusion. He could see beyond the shoulder of the steward straight through into the interior, a hundred and fifty feet or more, successive vistas of light and colour – the shaded passageway with its black and white mosaic floor; the dazzling brilliance of the atrium with its marble fountain; a tablinum for receiving visitors, guarded by two bronze busts; and then a colonnaded swimming pool, its pillars wrapped with vines. He could hear finches chirruping in an aviary somewhere, and women's voices, laughing.

They came into the atrium and the steward said, brusquely, 'Wait here,' before disappearing to the left, behind a curtain that screened a narrow passageway. Attilius glanced around. Here was money, old money, used to buy absolute privacy in the middle of the busy town. The sun was almost directly overhead, shining through the square aperture in the atrium's roof, and the air was warm and sweet with the scent of roses. From this position he could see most of the swimming pool. Elaborate bronze statues decorated the steps at the nearest end – a wild boar, a lion, a snake rising from its coils, and Apollo playing the cithara. At the far end, four women reclined on couches, fanning themselves, each with her own maid standing behind her. They noticed Attilius staring and there was a little flutter of laughter from behind their fans. He felt himself redden with embarrassment and he quickly turned his back on them, just as the curtain parted and the steward reappeared, beckoning.

Attilius knew at once, by the humidity and by the smell of oil, that he was being shown into the house's private baths. And of course, he thought, it was bound to have its own suite, for with money such as this, why mix with the common herd? The steward took him into the changing room and told him to remove his shoes then they went back out into the passageway and into the tepidarium, where an immensely fat old man lay face down, naked, on a table, being worked on by a young masseur. His white buttocks vibrated as the masseur made chopping motions up and down his spine. He turned his head slightly as Attilius passed by, regarded him with a single, bloodshot grey eye, then closed it again.

The steward slid open a door, releasing a billow of fragrant vapour from the dim interior, then stood aside to let the engineer pass through.

It was hard at first to see very much in the caldarium. The only light came from a couple of torches mounted on the wall and from the glowing coals of a brazier, the source of the steam which filled the room. Gradually Attilius made out a large sunken bath with three dark heads of hair, seemingly disembodied, floating in the greyness. There was a ripple of water as one of the heads moved and a splash as a hand was raised and gently waved.

'Over here, aquarius,' said a languid voice. 'You have a message for me, I believe, from the Emperor? I don't know these Flavians. Descended from a tax-collector, I believe. But Nero was a great friend of mine.'

Another head was stirring. 'Fetch us a torch!' it commanded. 'Let us at least see who disturbs us on a feast day.'

A slave in the corner of the room, who Attilius had not noticed, took down one of the torches from the wall and held it close to the engineer's face so that he could be inspected. All three heads were now turned towards him. Attilius could feel the pores of his skin opening, the sweat running freely down his body. The mosaic floor was baking hot beneath his bare feet – a hypocaust, he realised. Luxury was certainly piled upon luxury in the house of the Popidii. He wondered if Ampliatus, in the days when he was a slave here, had ever been made to sweat over the furnace in midsummer.

The heat of the torch on his cheek was unbearable. 'This is no place to conduct the Emperor's business,' he said and pushed the slave's arm away. 'To whom am I speaking?'

'He's certainly a rude enough fellow,' declared the third head.

'I am Lucius Popidius,' said the languid voice, 'and these gentlemen are Gaius Cuspius and Marcus Holconius. And our esteemed friend in the tepidarium is Quintus Brittius. Now do you know who we are?'

'You're the four elected magistrates of Pompeii.'

'Correct,' said Popidius. 'And this is our town, aquarius, so guard your tongue.' •

Attilius knew how the system worked. As aediles, Popidius and Cuspius would hand out the licences for all the businesses, from the brothels to the baths; they were responsible for keeping the streets clean, the water flowing, the temples open. Holconius and Brittius were the duoviri – the commission of two men – who presided over the court in the basilica and dispensed the Emperor's justice: a flogging here, a crucifixion there, and no doubt a fine to fill the city's coffers whenever possible. He would not be able to accomplish much without them so he forced himself to stand quietly, waiting for them to speak. Time, he thought: I am losing so much time.

'Well,' said Popidius after a while. 'I suppose I have cooked for long enough.' He sighed and stood, a ghostly figure in the steam, and held out his hand for a towel. The slave replaced the torch in its holder, knelt before his master and wrapped a cloth around his waist. 'All right. Where's this letter?' He took it and padded into the adjoining room. Attilius followed.

Brittius was on his back and the young slave had obviously been giving him more than a massage for his penis was red and engorged and pointing hard against the fat slope of his belly. The old man batted away the slave's hands, and reached for a towel. His face was scarlet. He scowled at Attilius. 'Who's this then, Popi?'

'The new aquarius of the Augusta. Exomnius's replacement. He's come from Misenum.' Popidius broke open the seal and unrolled the letter. He was in his early forties, delicately handsome. The dark hair slicked back over his small ears emphasised his aquiline profile as he bent forwards to read; the skin of his body was white, smooth, hairless. He has had it plucked, thought Attilius with disgust.

The others were now coming in from the caldarium, curious to find out what was happening, slopping water over the black and white floor. Around the walls ran a fresco of a garden, enclosed inside a wooden fence. In an alcove, on a pedestal carved to resemble a water nymph, stood a circular marble basin.

Brittius propped himself up on his elbow. 'Read it out, Popi. What's it say?'

A frown creased Popidius's smooth skin. 'It's from Pliny. "In the name of the Emperor Titus Caesar Vespasianus Augustus, and in accordance with the power vested in me by the Senate and People of Rome —"'

'Skip the blather!' said Brittius. 'Get to the meat of it.' He rubbed his thumb and middle finger together, counting money. 'What's he after?'

'It seems the aqueduct has failed somewhere near Vesuvius. All the towns from Nola westwards are dry. He says he wants us — "orders" us, he says — to "provide immediately sufficient men and materials from the colony of Pompeii to effect repairs to the Aqua Augusta, under the command of Marcus Attilius Primus, engineer, of the Department of the Curator Aquarum, Rome".'

'Does he indeed? And who foots the bill, might I ask?'

'He doesn't say.'

Attilius cut in: 'Money is not an issue. I can assure your honours that the Curator Aquarum will reimburse any costs.'

'Really? You have the authority to make that promise, do you?'

Attilius hesitated. 'You have my word.'

'Your word? Your word won't put gold back in our treasury once it's gone.'

'And look at this,' said one of the other men. He was in his middle-twenties, well-muscled, but with a small head: Attilius guessed he must be the second junior magistrate, the aedile, Cuspius. He turned the tap above the circular basin and water gushed out. 'There's no drought here – d'you see? So I say this: what's it to do with us? You want men and materials? Go to one of these towns that has no water. Go to Nola. We're swimming in it! Look!' And to make his point he opened the tap wider and left it running.

'Besides,' said Brittius craftily, 'it's good for business. Anybody on the bay who wants a bath, or a drink for that matter – he has to come to Pompeii. And on a public holiday, too. What do you say, Holconius?'

The oldest magistrate adjusted his towel around him like a toga. 'It's offensive to the priests to see men working on a holy day,' he announced judiciously. 'People should do as we are doing – they should gather with their friends and families to observe the religious rites. I vote we tell this young fellow, with all due respect to Admiral Pliny, to fuck off out of here.'

Brittius roared with laughter, banging on the side of the table in approval. Popidius smiled and rolled up the papyrus. 'I think you have our answer, aquarius. Why don't you come back tomorrow and we'll see what we can do?'

He tried to hand the letter back but Attilius reached past

him and firmly closed the tap. What a picture they looked, the three of them, dripping with water – *his* water – and Brittius, with his puny hard-on, now lost in the flabby folds of his lap. The sickly scented heat was unbearable. He wiped his face on the sleeve of his tunic.

'Now listen to me, your honours. From midnight tonight, Pompeii will also lose her water. The whole supply is being diverted to Beneventum, so we can get inside the tunnel of the aqueduct to repair it. I've already sent my men into the mountains to close the sluices.' There was a mutter of anger. He held up his hand. 'Surely it's in the interests of all citizens on the bay to co-operate?' He looked at Cuspius. 'Yes, all right – I could go to Nola for assistance. But at the cost of at least a day. And that's an extra day you'll be without water, as well as they.'

'Yes, but with one difference,' said Cuspius. 'We'll have some notice. How about this for an idea, Popidius? We could issue a proclamation, telling our citizens to fill every container they possess and in that way ours will still be the only town on the bay with a reserve of water.'

'We could even sell it,' said Brittius. 'And the longer the drought goes on, the better the price we could get for it.'

'It's not yours to sell!' Attilius was finding it hard to keep his temper. 'If you refuse to help me, I swear that the first thing I'll do after the main line is repaired is to see to it that the spur to Pompeii is closed.' He had no authority to issue such a threat, but he swept on anyway, jabbing his finger in Cuspius's chest. 'And I'll send to Rome for a commissioner to come down and investigate the abuse of the imperial aqueduct. I'll make you pay for every extra cupful you've taken beyond your proper share!'

'Such insolence!' shouted Brittius.

'He touched me!' said Cuspius, outraged. 'You all saw that? This piece of scum actually laid his filthy hand on me!' He stuck out his chin and stepped up close to Attilius, ready for a fight, and the engineer might have retaliated, which would have been disastrous – for him, for his mission – if the curtain had not been swished aside to reveal another man, who had obviously been standing in the passageway listening to their conversation.

Attilius had only met him once, but he was not about to forget him in a hurry: Numerius Popidius Ampliatus.

What most astonished Attilius, once he had recovered from the shock of seeing him again, was how much they all deferred to him. Even Brittius swung his plump legs over the side of the table and straightened his back, as if it was somehow disrespectful to be caught lying down in the presence of this former slave. Ampliatus put a restraining hand on Cuspius's shoulder, whispered a few words in his ear, winked, tousled his hair, and all the while he kept his eyes on Attilius.

The engineer remembered the bloody remains of the slave in the eel pool, the lacerated back of the slave-woman.

'So what's all this, gentlemen?' Ampliatus suddenly grinned and pointed at Attilius. 'Arguing in the baths? On a religious festival? That's unseemly. Where were you all brought up?'

Popidius said, 'This is the new aquarius of the aqueduct.'

'I know Marcus Attilius. We've met, haven't we, aquarius? May I see that?' He took Pliny's letter from Popidius and scanned it quickly, then glanced at Attilius. He was wearing a tunic bordered in gold, his hair was glossy, and there was the same smell of expensive unguents that the engineer had noticed the previous day.

'What is your plan?'

'To follow the spur from Pompeii back to its junction with the Augusta, then to work my way along the main line towards Nola until I find the break.'

'And what is it you need?'

'I don't know yet exactly.' Attilius hesitated. The appearance of Ampliatus had disconcerted him. 'Quicklime. Puteolanum. Bricks. Timber. Torches. Men.'

'How much of each?'

'Perhaps six amphorae of lime to start with. A dozen baskets of puteolanum. Fifty paces of timber and five hundred bricks. As many torches as you can spare. Ten strong pairs of hands. I may need less, I may need more. It depends how badly the aqueduct is damaged.'

'How soon will you know?'

'One of my men will report back this afternoon.'

Ampliatus nodded. 'Well, if you want my opinion, your honours, I think we should do all in our power to help. Never let it be said that the ancient colony of Pompeii turned its back on an appeal from the Emperor. Besides, I have a fishery in Misenum that drinks water like Brittius here drinks wine. I want that aqueduct running again as soon as possible. What do you say?'

The magistrates exchanged uneasy glances. Eventually Popidius said, 'It may be that we were over-hasty.'

Only Cuspius risked a show of defiance. 'I still think this ought to be Nola's responsibility –'

Ampliatus cut him off. 'That's settled then. I can let you have all you need, Marcus Attilius, if you'll just be so good as to wait outside.' He shouted over his shoulder to the steward. 'Scutarius! Give the aquarius his shoes!'

None of the others spoke to Attilius or looked at him. They were like naughty schoolboys discovered fighting by their master.

The engineer collected his shoes and walked out of the tepidarium, into the gloomy passageway. The curtain was quickly drawn behind him. He leaned against the wall to pull on his shoes, trying to listen to what was being said, but he could make out nothing. From the direction of the atrium he heard a splash as someone dived into the swimming pool. This reminder that the house was busy for the holiday made up his mind for him. He dared not risk being caught eavesdropping. He opened the second curtain and stepped back out into the dazzling sunlight. Across the atrium, beyond the tablinum, the surface of the pool was rocking from the impact of the dive. The wives of the magistrates were still gossiping at the other end, where they had been joined by a dowdy middle-aged matron who sat demurely apart, her hands folded in her lap. A couple of slaves carrying trays laden with dishes passed behind them. There was a smell of cooking. A huge feast was clearly in preparation.

His eye was caught by a flash of darkness beneath the glittering water and an instant later the swimmer broke the surface.

'Corelia Ampliata!'

He said her name aloud, unintentionally. She did not hear him. She shook her head, and stroked her black hair away from her closed eyes, gathering it behind her with both hands. Her elbows were spread wide, her pale face tilted towards the sun, oblivious to his watching her.

'Corelia!' He whispered it, not wanting to attract the attention of the other women, and this time she turned. It took a moment for her to search him out against the glare of the atrium, but when she found him she began wading towards him. She was wearing a shift of thin material that came down almost to her knees and as her body emerged from the water she placed one dripping arm across her breasts and the other between her thighs, like some modest Venus arising from the waves. He stepped into the tablinum and walked towards the pool, past the funeral masks of the Popidii clan. Red ribbons linked the images of the dead, showing who was related to whom, in a criss-cross pattern of power stretching back for generations.

'Aquarius,' she hissed, 'you must leave this place!' She was standing on the circular steps that led out of the pool. 'Get out! Go! My father is here, and if he sees you –'

'Too late for that. We've met.' But he drew back slightly, so that he was hidden from the view of the women at the other end of the pool. I ought to look away, he thought. It would be the honourable thing to do. But he could not take his eyes off her. 'What are you doing here?'

'What am I doing here?' She regarded him as if he were an idiot and leaned toward him. 'Where else should I be? *My father owns this house.*'

At first he did not fully take in what she was saying. 'But I was told that Lucius Popidius lived here –'

'He does.'

He was still confused. 'Then – ?'

'We are to be married.' She said it flatly and shrugged, and there was something terrible in the gesture, an utter hopelessness, and suddenly all was clear to him – the reason for Ampliatus's unannounced appearance, Popidius's deference to him, the way the others had followed his lead. Somehow

Ampliatus had contrived to buy the roof from over Popidius's head and now he was going to extend his ownership completely, by marrying off his daughter to his former master. The thought of that ageing playboy, with his plucked and hairless body, sharing a bed with Corelia filled him with an unexpected anger, even though he told himself it was none of his business.

'But surely a man as old as Popidius is already married?'

'He was. He's been forced to divorce.'

'And what does Popidius think of such an arrangement?'

'He thinks it is contemptible, of course, to make a match so far beneath him – as you do, clearly.'

'Not at all, Corelia,' he said quickly. He saw that she had tears in her eyes. 'On the contrary. I should say you were worth a hundred Popidii. A thousand.'

'I hate him,' she said. But whether she meant Popidius or her father he could not tell.

From the passage came the sound of rapid footsteps and Ampliatus's voice, yelling, 'Aquarius!'

She shuddered. 'Please leave, I beg you. You were a good man to have tried to help me yesterday. But don't let him trap you, as he's trapped the rest of us.'

Attilius said stiffly, 'I am a freeborn Roman citizen, on the staff of the Curator Aquarum, in the service of the Emperor, here on official business to repair the imperial aqueduct – not some slave, to be fed to his eels. Or an elderly woman, for that matter, to be beaten half to death.'

It was her turn to be shocked. She put her hands to her mouth. 'Atia?'

'Atia, yes – is that her name? Last night I found her lying in the street and took her back to my quarters. She had been whipped senseless and left out to die like an old dog.'

'Monster!' Corelia stepped backwards, her hands still pressed to her face, and sank into the water.

'You take advantage of my good nature, aquarius!' said Ampliatus. He was advancing across the tablinum. 'I told you to wait for me, that was all.' He glared at Corelia – 'You should know better, after what I told you yesterday!' – then shouted across the pool – 'Celsia!' – and the mousy woman Attilius had noticed earlier jerked up in her chair. 'Get our daughter out of the pool! It's unseemly for her to show her tits in public!' He turned to Attilius. 'Look at them over there, like a lot of fat hens on their nests!' He flapped his arms at them, emitting a series of squawks – *cluuuuck, cluck-cluck-cluck!* – and the women raised their fans in distaste. 'They won't fly, though. Oh no. One thing I've learned about our Roman aristocrat – he'll go anywhere for a free meal. And his women are even worse.' He called out: 'I'll be back in an hour! Don't dish up without me!' And with a gesture to Attilius that he should fall in behind him, the new master of the House of the Popidii turned on his heel and strode towards the door.

As they passed through the atrium, Attilius glanced back at the pool where Corelia was still submerged, as if she thought that by completely immersing herself she could wash away what was happening.

Hora sexta

[12:00 hours]

'As magma rises from depth, it undergoes a large pressure decrease. At a 10-metre depth, for example, pressures are about 300 megapascals (MPa), or 3000 times the atmospheric pressure. Such a large pressure change has many consequences for the physical properties and flow of magma.'

Encyclopaedia of Volcanoes

Ampliatus had a litter and eight slaves waiting outside on the pavement, dressed in the same crimson livery as the porter and steward. They scrambled to attention as their master appeared but he walked straight past them, just as he ignored the small crowd of petitioners squatting in the shade of the wall across the street, despite the public holiday, who called out his name in a ragged chorus.

'We'll walk,' he said, and set off up the slope towards the crossroads, maintaining the same fast pace as he had in the house. Attilius followed at his shoulder. It was noon, the air scalding, the roads quiet. The few pedestrians who were about mostly hopped into the gutter as Ampliatus approached or drew back into the shop doorways. He hummed to himself as he walked, nodding an occasional greeting, and when the engineer looked back he saw that they were trailing a retinue that would have done credit to a senator – first, at a discreet distance, the slaves with the litter, and behind them the little straggle of supplicants: men with the dejected, exhausted look that came from dancing attendance on a great man since before dawn and knowing themselves doomed to disappointment.

About halfway up the hill to the Vesuvius Gate – the engineer counted three city blocks – Ampliatus turned right, crossed the street, and opened a little wooden door set into a wall. He put his hand on Attilius's shoulder to usher him inside and Attilius felt his flesh recoil at the millionaire's touch.

'Don't let him trap you, as he's trapped the rest of us.'

He eased himself clear of the grasping fingers. Ampliatus closed the door behind them and he found himself standing in a big, deserted space, a building site, occupying the best part of the entire block. To the left was a brick wall surmounted by a sloping, red-tiled roof – the back of a row of shops – with a pair of high wooden gates set into the middle; to the right, a complex of new buildings, very nearly finished, with large modern windows looking out across the expanse of scrub and rubble. A rectangular tank was being excavated directly beneath the windows.

Ampliatus had his hands on his hips and was studying the engineer's reaction. 'So then. What do you think I'm building? I'll give you one guess.'

'Baths.'

'That's it. What do you think?'

'It's impressive,' said Attilius. And it was, he thought. At least as good as anything he had seen under construction in Rome in the past ten years. The brickwork and the columns were beautifully finished. There was a sense of tranquillity – of space, and peace, and light. The high windows faced south-west to take advantage of the afternoon sun, which was just beginning to flood into the interior. 'I congratulate you.'

'We had to demolish almost the whole block to make way for it,' said Ampliatus, 'and that was unpopular. But it will be worth it. It will be the finest baths outside Rome. And more modern than anything you've got up there.' He looked around, proudly. 'We provincials, you know, when we put our minds to it, we can still show you big city men from Rome a thing or two.' He cupped his hands to his mouth and bellowed, 'Januarius!'

From the other side of the yard came an answering shout, and a tall man appeared at the top of a flight of stairs. He recognised his master and ran down the steps and across the yard, wiping his hands on his tunic, bobbing his head in a series of bows as he came closer.

'Januarius – this is my friend, the aquarius of the Augusta. He works for the Emperor!'

'Honoured,' said Januarius, and gave Attilius another bow.

'Januarius is one of my foremen. Where are the lads?'

'In the barracks, sir.' He looked terrified, as if he had been caught idling. 'It's the holiday –'

'Forget the holiday! We need them here now. Ten did you say you needed, aquarius? Better make it a dozen. Januarius, send for a dozen of the strongest men we have. Brebix's gang. Tell them they're to bring food and drink for a day. What else was it you needed?'

'Quicklime,' began Attilius, 'puteolanum –'

'That's it. All that stuff. Timber. Bricks. Torches – don't forget torches. He's to have everything he needs. And you'll require transport, won't you? A couple of teams of oxen?'

'I've already hired them.'

'But you'll have mine – I insist.'

'No.' Ampliatus's generosity was starting to make the engineer uneasy. First would come the gift, then the gift would turn out to be a loan, and then the loan would prove a debt impossible to pay back. That was no doubt how Popidius had ended up losing his house. *A hustler's town.* He glanced at the sky. 'It's noon. The oxen should be arriving down at the harbour by now. I have a slave waiting there with our tools.'

'Who did you hire from?'

'Baculus.'

'Baculus! That drunken thief! My oxen would be better. At least let me have a word with him. I'll get you a fat discount.'

Attilius shrugged. 'If you insist.'

'I do. Fetch the men from the barracks, Januarius, and send a boy to the docks to have the aquarius's wagons brought here for loading. I'll show you around while we're waiting, aquarius.' And again his hand fell upon the engineer's shoulder. 'Come.'

Baths were not a luxury. Baths were the foundation of civilisation. Baths were what raised even the meanest citizen of Rome above the level of the wealthiest hairy-arsed barbarian. Baths instilled the triple disciplines of cleanliness, healthfulness and strict routine. Was it not to feed the baths that the aqueducts had been invented in the first place? Had not the baths spread the Roman ethos across Europe, Africa and Asia as effectively as the legions, so that in whatever town in this far-flung empire a man might find himself, he could at least be sure of finding this one precious piece of home?

Such was the essence of Ampliatus's lecture as he conducted

Attilius around the empty shell of his dream. The rooms were unfurnished and smelled strongly of fresh paint and stucco and their footsteps echoed as they passed through the cubicles and exercise rooms into the main part of the building. Here, the frescoes were already in place. Views of the green Nile, studded with basking crocodiles, flowed into scenes from the lives of the gods. Triton swam beside the Argonauts and led them back to safety. Neptune transformed his son into a swan. Perseus saved Andromeda from the sea-monster sent to attack the Ethiopians. The pool in the caldarium was built to take twenty-eight paying customers at a time, and as the bathers lay on their backs they would gaze up at a sapphire ceiling, lit by five hundred lamps and swimming with every species of marine life, and believe themselves to be floating in an undersea grotto.

To attain the luxury he demanded, Ampliatus was employing the most modern techniques, the best materials, the most skilful craftsmen in Italy. There were Neapolitan glass windows in the dome of the laconium — the sweating-room — as thick as a man's finger. The floors and the walls and the ceilings were hollow, the furnace that heated the cavities so powerful that even if snow lay on the ground, the air inside would be sweltering enough to melt a man's flesh. It was built to withstand an earthquake. All the main fittings — pipes, drains, grills, vents, taps, stop-cocks, shower-nozzles, even the handles to flush the latrines — were of brass. The lavatory seats were Phrygian marble, with elbow rests carved in the shape of dolphins and chimeras. Hot and cold running water throughout. *Civilisation*.

Attilius had to admire the vision of the man. Ampliatus took so much pride in showing him everything it was almost as if he was soliciting an investment. And the truth was that if the engineer had had any money – if most of his salary had not already been sent back home to his mother and sister – he might well have given him every last coin, for he had never encountered a more persuasive salesman than Numerius Popidius Ampliatus.

'How soon before you're finished?'

'I should say a month. I need to bring in the carpenters. I want some shelves, a few cupboards. I thought of putting down sprung wood floors in the changing room. I was considering pine.'

'No,' said Attilius. 'Use alder.'

'Alder? Why?'

'It won't rot in contact with water. I'd use pine – or perhaps a cypress – for the shutters. But it would need to be something from the lowlands, where the sun shines. Don't touch pine from the mountains. Not for a building of this quality.'

'Any other advice?'

'Always use timber cut in the autumn, not the spring. Trees are pregnant in the spring and the wood is weaker. For clamping, use olive wood, scorched – it will last for a century. But you probably know all that.'

'Not at all. I've built a lot, it's true, but I've never understood much about wood and stone. It's money I understand. And the great thing about money is that it doesn't matter when you harvest it. It's an all-year crop.' He laughed at his own joke and turned to look at the engineer. There was something unnerving about the intensity of his gaze, which was not steady, but which shifted, as if he were constantly measuring different aspects of whomever he addressed, and Attilius thought, No, it's not money you understand, it's men – their strengths and their weaknesses; when to flatter, when to frighten. 'And you, aquarius?' Ampliatus said quietly. 'What is it that you know?'

'Water.'

'Well, that's an important thing to know. Water is at least as valuable as money.'

'Is it? Then why aren't I a rich man?'

'Perhaps you could be.' He made the remark lightly, left it floating for a moment beneath the massive dome, and then went on: 'Do you ever stop to think how curiously the world is ordered, aquarius? When this place is open, I shall make another fortune. And then I shall use that fortune to make another, and another. But without your aqueduct, I could not build my baths. That's a thought, is it not? Without Attilius: no Ampliatus.'

'Except that it's not my aqueduct. I didn't build it – the Emperor did.'

'True. And at a cost of two million a mile! "The late lamented Augustus" – was ever a man more justly proclaimed a deity? Give me the Divine Augustus over Jupiter any time. I say my prayers to him every day.' He sniffed the air. 'This wet paint makes my head ache. Let me show you my plans for the grounds.'

He led them back the way they had come. The sun was shining fully now through the large open windows. The gods on the opposite walls seemed alive with colour. Yet there was something haunted about the empty rooms – the drowsy stillness, the dust floating in the shafts of light, the cooing of the pigeons in the builders' yard. One bird must have flown into the laconium and become trapped. The sudden flapping of its wings against the dome made the engineer's heart jump.

Outside, the luminous air felt almost solid with the heat,

like melted glass, but Ampliatus did not appear to feel it. He climbed the open staircase easily and stepped on to the small sun deck. From here he had a commanding view of his little kingdom. That would be the exercise yard, he said. He would plant plane trees around it for shade. He was experimenting with a method of heating the water in the outdoor pool. He patted the stone parapet. 'This was the site of my first property. Seventeen years ago I bought it. If I told you how little I paid for it, you wouldn't believe me. Mark you, there was not much left of it after the earthquake. No roof, just the walls. I was twenty-eight. Never been so happy, before or since. Repaired it, rented it out, bought another, rented that. Some of these big old houses from the time of the Republic were huge. I split them up and fitted ten families into them. I've gone on doing it ever since. Here's a piece of advice for you, my friend: there's no safer investment than property in Pompeii.'

He swatted a fly on the back of his neck and inspected its pulpy corpse between his fingers. He flicked it away. Attilius could imagine him as a young man – brutal, energetic, remorseless. 'You had been freed by the Popidii by then?'

Ampliatus shot him a look. However hard he tries to be affable, thought Attilius, those eyes will always betray him.

'If that was meant as an insult, aquarius, forget it. Everyone knows Numerius Popidius Ampliatus was born a slave and he's not ashamed of it. Yes, I was free. I was manumitted in my master's will when I was twenty. Lucius, his son – the one you just met – made me his household steward. Then I did some debt-collecting for an old money-lender called Jucundus, and he taught me a lot. But I never would have been rich if it hadn't been for the earthquake.' He looked fondly towards Vesuvius.

His voice softened. 'It came down from the mountain one morning in February like a wind beneath the earth. I watched it coming, the trees bowing as it passed, and by the time it had finished this town was rubble. It didn't matter then who had been born a free man and who had been born a slave. The place was empty. You could walk the streets for an hour and meet no one except for the dead.'

'Who was in charge of rebuilding the town?'

'Nobody! That was the disgrace of it. All the richest families ran away to their country estates. They were all convinced there was going to be another earthquake.'

'Including Popidius?'

'Especially Popidius!' He wrung his hands, and whined, '"Oh, Ampliatus, the gods have forsaken us! Oh, Ampliatus, the gods are punishing us!" The gods! I ask you! As if the gods could care less who or what we fuck or how we live. As if earthquakes aren't as much a part of living in Campania as hot springs and summer droughts! They came creeping back, of course, once they saw it was safe, but by then things had started to change. *Salve lucrum!* "Hail profit!" That's the motto of the new Pompeii. You'll see it all over the town. *Lucrum gaudium!* "Profit is joy!" Not money, mark you – any fool can inherit money. Profit. That takes skill.' He spat over the low wall into the street below. 'Lucius Popidius! What skill does he have? He can drink in cold water and piss out hot, and that's about the limit of it. Whereas you –' and again Attilius felt himself being sized up '– you, I think, are a man of some ability. I see myself in you, when I was your age. I could use a fellow like you.'

'Use me?'

'Here, for a start. These baths could do with a man who

understands water. In return for your advice, I could cut you in. A share of the profits.'

Attilius shook his head, smiling. 'I don't think so.'

Ampliatus smiled back. 'Ah, you drive a hard bargain! I admire that in a man. Very well – a share of the ownership, too.'

'No. Thank you. I'm flattered. But my family has worked the imperial aqueducts for a century. I was born to be an engineer on the matrices, and I shall die doing it.'

'Why not do both?'

'What?'

'Run the aqueduct, and advise me as well. No one need ever know.'

Attilius looked at him closely, at his crafty, eager face. Beneath the money, the violence and the lust for power, he was really nothing bigger than a small-town crook. 'No,' he said coldly, 'that would be impossible.'

The contempt must have shown in his face because Ampliatus retreated at once. 'You're right,' he said, nodding. 'Forget I even mentioned it. I'm a rough fellow sometimes. I have these ideas without always thinking them through.'

'Like executing a slave before finding out if he's telling the truth?'

Ampliatus grinned and pointed at Attilius. 'Very good! That's right. But how can you expect a man like me to know how to behave? You can have all the money in the Empire but it doesn't make you a gentleman, right? You may think you're copying the aristocracy, showing a bit of class, but then it turns out you're a monster. Isn't that what Corelia called me? A monster?'

'And Exomnius?' Attilius blurted out the question. 'Did you

have an arrangement with him that nobody ever knew about?'

Ampliatus's smile did not waver. From down in the street came a rumble of heavy wooden wheels on stone. 'Listen – I think I can hear your wagons coming. We'd better go down and let them in.'

T he conversation might never have happened. Humming to himself again, Ampliatus dodged across the rubble-strewn yard. He swung open the heavy gates and as Polites led the first team of oxen into the site he made a formal bow. A man Attilius did not recognise was leading the second team; a couple more sat on the back of the empty cart, their legs dangling over the side. They jumped down immediately when they noticed Ampliatus and stood looking respectfully at the ground.

'Well done, lads,' said Ampliatus. 'I'll see you're rewarded for working a holiday. But it's an emergency and we've all got to rally round and help fix the aqueduct. For the common good – isn't that right, aquarius?' He pinched the cheek of the nearest man. 'You're under his command now. Serve him well. Aquarius: take as much as you want. It's all in the yard. Torches are inside in the storeroom. Is there anything more I can do for you?' He was obviously eager to go.

'I shall make an inventory of what we use,' said Attilius formally. 'You will be compensated.'

'There's no need. But as you wish. I wouldn't want to be accused of trying to corrupt you!' He laughed, and pointed again. 'I'd stay and help you load myself – nobody ever said that Numerius Popidius Ampliatus was afraid of getting his hands dirty! – but you know how it is. We're dining early because of the festival and I mustn't show my low birth by keeping all those fine gentlemen and their ladies waiting.' He held out his hand. 'So! I wish you luck, aquarius.'

Attilius took it. The grip was dry and firm; the palm and fingers, like his own, callused by hard work. He nodded. 'Thank you.'

Ampliatus grunted and turned away. Outside in the quiet street his litter was waiting for him and this time he clambered straight into it. The slaves ran around to take up their positions, four men on either side. Ampliatus clicked his fingers and they hoisted the bronze-capped poles — first to waist height, and then, grimacing with the strain, up on to their shoulders. Their master settled himself back on his cushions, staring straight ahead — unseeing, brooding. He reached behind his shoulder, unfastened the curtain and let it fall. Attilius stood in the gateway and watched him go, the crimson canopy swaying as it moved off down the hill, the little crowd of weary petitioners trudging after it.

He went back into the yard.

It was all there, as Ampliatus had promised, and for a while Attilius was able to lose himself in the simple effort of physical work. It was comforting to handle the materials of his craft again — the weighty, sharp-edged bricks, just big enough to fit a man's grasp, and their familiar brittle clink as they were stacked on the back of the cart; the baskets of powdery red puteolanum, always heavier and denser than you expected, sliding across the rough boards of the wagon; the feel of the timber, warm and smooth against his cheek as he carried it across the yard; and finally the quicklime, in its bulbous clay amphorae – difficult to grasp and heave up on to the cart.

He worked steadily with the other men and had a sense at last that he was making progress. Ampliatus was undeniably cruel and ruthless and the gods alone knew what else besides, but his stuff was good and in honest hands it would serve a better purpose. He had asked for six amphorae of lime but when it came to it he decided to take a dozen and increased the amount of puteolanum in proportion, to twenty baskets. He did not want to come back to Ampliatus to ask for more; what he did not use he could return.

He went into the bath-house to look for the torches and found them in the largest storeroom. Even these were of a superior sort – tightly wadded flax and resin impregnated with tar; good, solid wooden handles bound with rope. Next to them lay open wooden crates of oil lamps, mostly terracotta, but some of brass, and candles enough to light a temple. Quality, as Ampliatus said: you couldn't beat it. Clearly, this was going to be a most luxurious establishment.

'It will be the finest baths outside Rome . . .'

He was suddenly curious and with his arms full of torches he looked into some of the other storerooms. Piles of towels in one, jars of scented massage-oil in another, lead exercise weights, coils of rope and leather balls in a third. Everything ready and waiting for use; everything here except chattering, sweating humanity to bring it all to life. And water, of course. He peered through the open door into the succession of rooms. It would use a lot of water, this place. Four or five pools, showers, flush-latrines, a steam-room . . . Only public facilities, such as the fountains, were connected to the aqueduct free of charge, as the gift of the Emperor. But private baths like these would cost a small fortune in water-taxes. And if Ampliatus had made his money by buying big properties, subdividing them, and renting them out, then his overall consumption of water must be huge. He wondered how much he was paying for it. Presumably he could find out once he returned to Misenum and tried to bring some order to the chaos in which Exomnius had left the Augusta's records.

Perhaps he wasn't paying anything at all.

He stood there in the sunlight, in the echoing bath-house, listening to the cooing pigeons, turning the possibility over in his mind. The aqueducts had always been wide open to corruption. Farmers tapped into the main lines where they crossed their land. Citizens ran an extra pipe or two and paid the water inspectors to look the other way. Public work was awarded to private contractors and bills were paid for jobs that were never done. Materials went missing. Attilius suspected that the rottenness went right to the top – even Acilius Aviola, the Curator Aquarum himself, was rumoured to insist on a percentage of the take. The engineer had never had anything to do with it. But an honest man was a rare man in Rome; an honest man was a fool.

The weight of the torches was making his arms ache. He went outside and stacked them on one of the wagons, then leaned against it, thinking. More of Ampliatus's men had arrived. The loading had finished and they were sprawled in the shade, waiting for orders. The oxen stood placidly, flicking their tails, their heads in clouds of swarming flies.

If the Augusta's accounts, back at the Piscina Mirabilis, were in such a mess, might it be because they had been tampered with?

He glanced up at the cloudless sky. The sun had passed its zenith. Becco and Corvinus should have reached Abellinum by now. The sluice-gates might already be closed, the Augusta starting to drain dry. He felt the pressure of time again. Nevertheless, he made up his mind and beckoned to Polites. 'Go into the baths,' he ordered, 'and fetch another dozen torches, a dozen lamps and a jar of olive oil. And a coil of rope, while you're at it. But no more, mind. Then, when you've finished here, take the wagons and the men up to the castellum aquae, next to the Vesuvius Gate, and wait for me. Corax should be coming back soon. And while you're at it, see if you can buy some food for us.' He gave the slave his bag. 'There's money in there. Look after it for me. I shan't be long.'

He brushed the residue of brick dust and puteolanum from the front of his tunic and walked out of the open gate.

Hora septa

[14:10 hours]

> 'If magma is ready to be tapped in a high-level reservoir, even a small change of regional stress, usually associated with an earthquake, can disturb the stability of the system and bring about an eruption.'
>
> Volcanology *(second edition)*

Ampliatus's banquet was just entering its second hour, and of the twelve guests reclining around the table only one showed signs of truly enjoying it, and that was Ampliatus himself.

It was stiflingly hot for a start, even with one wall of the dining room entirely open to the air, and with three slaves in their crimson livery stationed around the table waving fans of peacock feathers. A harpist beside the swimming pool plucked mournfully at some formless tune.

And four diners to each couch! This was at least one too many, in the judgement of Lucius Popidius, who groaned to himself as each fresh course was set before them. He held to the rule of Varro, that the number of guests at a dinner party ought not to be less than that of the Graces (three), nor to exceed that of the Muses (nine). It meant that one was too close to one's fellow diners. Popidius, for example, reclined between Ampliatus's dreary wife, Celsia, and his own mother,

Taedia Secunda – close enough to feel the heat of their bodies. Disgusting. And when he propped himself on his left elbow and reached out with his right hand to take some food from the table, the back of his head would brush Celsia's shallow bosom and – worse – his ring occasionally become entangled with his mother's blonde hairpiece, shorn from the head of some German slave girl and now disguising the elderly lady's thin grey locks.

And the food! Did Ampliatus not understand that hot weather called for simple, cold dishes, and that all these sauces, all this elaboration, had gone out of fashion back in Claudius's time? The first of the hors d'oeuvres had not been too bad – oysters bred in Brundisium then shipped two hundred miles round the coast for fattening in the Lucrine Lake, so that the flavours of the two varieties could be tasted at once. Olives and sardines, and eggs seasoned with chopped anchovies – altogether acceptable. But then had come lobster, sea urchins and, finally, mice rolled in honey and poppy seeds. Popidius had felt obliged to swallow at least one mouse to please his host and the crunch of those tiny bones had made him break out in a sweat of nausea.

Sow's udder stuffed with kidneys, with the sow's vulva served as a side dish, grinning up toothlessly at the diners. Roast wild boar filled with live thrushes that flapped helplessly across the table as the belly was carved open, shitting as they went. (Ampliatus had clapped his hands and roared with laughter at that.) Then the delicacies: the tongues of storks and flamingos (not too bad), but the tongue of a talking parrot had always looked to Popidius like nothing so much as a maggot and it had indeed tasted much as he imagined a maggot might taste if it had been doused in vinegar. Then a stew of nightingales' livers . . .

He glanced around at the flushed faces of his fellow guests. Even fat Brittius, who once boasted that he had eaten the entire trunk of an elephant, and whose motto was Seneca's – 'eat to vomit, vomit to eat' – was starting to look green. He caught Popidius's eye and mouthed something at him. Popidius could not quite make it out. He cupped his ear and Brittius repeated it, shielding his mouth from Ampliatus with his napkin and emphasising every syllable: 'Tri-mal-chi-o.'

Popidius almost burst out laughing. Trimalchio! Very good! The freed slave of monstrous wealth in the satire by Titus Petronius, who subjects his guests to exactly such a meal and cannot see how vulgar and ridiculous he is showing himself. Ha ha! Trimalchio! For a moment, Popidius slipped back twenty years to his time as a young aristocrat at Nero's court, when Petronius, that arbiter of good taste, would keep the table amused for hours by his merciless lampooning of the nouveau riche.

He felt suddenly maudlin. Poor old Petronius. Too funny and stylish for his own good. In the end, Nero, suspecting his own imperial majesty was being subtly mocked, had eyed him for one last time through his emerald monocle and had ordered him to kill himself. But Petronius had succeeded in turning even that into a joke – opening his veins at the start of a dinner in his house at Cumae, then binding them to eat and to gossip with his friends, then opening them again, then binding them, and so on, as he gradually ebbed away. His last conscious act had been to break a fluorspar wine-dipper, worth three hundred thousand sesterces, which the Emperor had been expecting to inherit. *That* was style. *That* was taste.

And what would he have made of me, thought Popidius, bitterly. That I – a Popidius, who played and sang with the

Master of the World – should have come to this, at the age of forty-five: the prisoner of Trimalchio!

He looked across at his former slave, presiding at the head of the table. He was still not entirely sure how it had happened. There had been the earthquake, of course. And then, a few years later, the death of Nero. Then civil war, a mule-dealer as Emperor, and Popidius's world had turned upside-down. Suddenly Ampliatus was everywhere – rebuilding the town, erecting a temple, worming his infant son on to the town council, controlling the elections, even buying the house next door. Popidius had never had a head for figures, so when Ampliatus had told him he could make some money, too, he had signed the contracts without even reading them. And somehow the money had been lost, and then it turned out that the family house was surety, and his only escape from the humiliation of eviction was to marry Ampliatus's daughter. Imagine: his own ex-slave as his father-in-law! He thought the shame of it would kill his mother. She had barely spoken since, her face haggard with sleeplessness and worry.

Not that he would mind sharing a bed with Corelia. He watched her hungrily. She was stretched out with her back to Cuspius, whispering to her brother. He wouldn't mind screwing the boy, either. He felt his prick begin to stiffen. Perhaps he might suggest a threesome? No – she would never go for it. She was a cold bitch. But he would soon be warming her up. His gaze met Brittius's once more. What a funny fellow. He winked and gestured with his eyes to Ampliatus and mouthed in agreement, 'Trimalchio!'

'What's that you're saying, Popidius?'

Ampliatus's voice cut across the table like a whip. Popidius cringed.

'He was saying, "What a feast!"' Brittius raised his glass. 'That's what we're all saying, Ampliatus. What a magnificent feast.' A murmur of assent went round the table.

'And the best is yet to come,' said Ampliatus. He clapped his hands and one of the slaves hurried out of the dining room in the direction of the kitchen.

Popidius managed to force a smile. 'I for one have left room for dessert, Ampliatus.' In truth he felt like vomiting, and he would not have needed the usual cup of warm brine and mustard to do it, either. 'What is it to be then? A basket of plums from Mount Damascus? Or has that pastry chef of yours made a pie of Attican honey?' Ampliatus's cook was the great Gargilius, bought for a quarter of a million, recipe books and all. That was how it was along the Bay of Neapolis these days. The chefs were more celebrated than the people they fed. Prices had been pushed into the realms of insanity. The wrong sort of people had the money.

'Oh, it's not yet time for dessert, my dear Popidius. Or may I – if it's not too premature – call you "son"?' Ampliatus grinned and pointed and by a superhuman effort, Popidius succeeded in hiding his revulsion. O, Trimalchio, he thought, Trimalchio . . .

There was a sound of scuffling footsteps and then four slaves appeared, bearing on their shoulders a model trireme, as long as a man and cast in silver, surfing a sea of encrusted sapphires. The diners broke into applause. The slaves approached the table on their knees and with difficulty slid the trireme, prow first, across the table. It was entirely filled by an enormous eel. Its eyes had been removed and replaced by rubies. Its jaws were propped open and filled with ivory. Clipped to its dorsal fin was a thick gold ring.

Popidius was the first to speak. 'I say, Ampliatus – that's a whopper.'

'From my own fishery at Misenum,' said Ampliatus proudly. 'A moray. It must be thirty years old if it's a day. I had it caught last night. You see the ring? I do believe, Popidius, that this is the creature your friend Nero used to sing to.' He picked up a large silver knife. 'Now who will have the first slice? You, Corelia – I think you should try it first.'

Now that was a nice gesture, thought Popidius. Up till this point, her father had conspicuously ignored her, and he had begun to suspect ill-feeling between them, but here was a mark of favour. So it was with some astonishment that he saw the girl flash a look of undiluted hatred at her father, throw down her napkin, rise from her couch, and run sobbing from the table.

The first couple of pedestrians Attilius approached swore they had never heard of Africanus's place. But at the crowded bar of Hercules, a little further down the street, the man behind the counter gave him a shifty look and then provided directions in a quiet voice – walk down the hill for another block, turn right, then first left, then ask again: 'But be careful who you talk to, citizen.'

Attilius could guess what that meant and sure enough, from the moment he left the main road, the street curved and narrowed, the houses became meaner and more crowded. Carved in stone beside several of the squalid entrances was the sign of the prick and balls. The brightly coloured dresses of the prostitutes bloomed in the gloom like blue and yellow flowers. So this was where Exomnius had chosen to spend his time! Attilius's footsteps slowed. He wondered if he should turn back. Nothing could be allowed to jeopardise the main priority of the day. But then he thought again of his father, dying on his mattress in the corner of their little house – another honest fool, whose stubborn rectitude had left his widow poor – and he resumed his walk, but faster, angry now.

At the end of the street, a heavy first-floor balcony jutted over the pavement, reducing the road to scarcely more than a passageway. He shouldered his way past a group of loitering men, their faces flushed by heat and wine, through the nearest open door, and into a dingy vestibule. There was a sharp, almost feral stink of sweat and semen. Lupanars they called these places, after the howl of the lupa, the she-wolf, in heat. And lupa was the street-word for a harlot – a meretrix. The business sickened him. From upstairs came the sound of a flute, a thump on the floorboards, male laughter. On either side, from curtained cubicles, came the noises of the night – grunts, whispers, a child's whimper.

In the semi-darkness, a woman in a short green dress sat on a stool with her legs wide apart. She stood as she heard him enter and came towards him eagerly, arms outstretched in welcome, vermillion lips cracked into a smile. She had used antimony to blacken her eyebrows, stretching the lines so that they met across the bridge of her nose, a mark which some men prized as beauty, but which reminded Attilius of the death-masks of the Popidii. She was ageless – fifteen or fifty, he could not tell in the weak light.

He said, 'Africanus?'

'Who?' She had a thick accent. Cilician, perhaps. 'Not here,' she said quickly.

'What about Exomnius?' At the mention of his name her

painted mouth split wide. She tried to block his path, but he moved her out of his way, gently, his hands on her bare shoulders, and pulled back the curtain behind her. A naked man was squatting over an open latrine, his thighs bluish-white and bony in the darkness. He looked up, startled. 'Africanus?' asked Attilius. The man's expression was uncomprehending. 'Forgive me, citizen.' Attilius let the curtain fall and moved towards one of the cubicles on the opposite side of the vestibule, but the whore beat him to it, extending her arms to block his way.

'No,' she said. 'No trouble. He not here.'

'Where, then?'

She hesitated. 'Above.' She gestured with her chin towards the ceiling.

Attilius looked around. He could see no stairs.

'How do I get up there? Show me.'

She did not move so he lunged towards another curtain, but again she beat him to it. 'I show,' she said. 'This way.'

She ushered him towards a second door. From the cubicle beside it, a man cried out in ecstasy. Attilius stepped into the street. She followed. In the daylight he could see that her elaborately piled-up hair was streaked with grey. Rivulets of sweat had carved furrows down her sunken, powdered cheeks. She would be lucky to earn a living here much longer. Her owner would throw her out and then she'd be living in the necropolis beyond the Vesuvius Gate, spreading her legs for the beggars behind the tombs.

She put her hand to her turkey-throat, as if she had guessed what was in his mind, and pointed to the staircase a few paces further on, then hurried back inside. As he started to mount the stone steps he heard her give a low whistle. I am like Theseus in the labyrinth, he thought, but without the ball of thread from

Ariadne to guide me back to safety. If an attacker appeared above him and another blocked off his escape, he would not stand a chance. When he reached the top of the staircase he did not bother to knock but flung open the door.

His quarry was already halfway out of the window, presumably tipped off by the whistle from the elderly whore. But the engineer was across the room and had him by his belt before he could drop down to the flat roof below. He was light and scrawny and Attilius hauled him in as easily as an owner might drag a dog back by his collar. He deposited him on the carpet.

He had disturbed a party. Two men lay on couches. A negro boy was clutching a flute to his naked chest. An olive-skinned girl, no more than twelve or thirteen, and also naked, with silver-painted nipples, stood on a table, frozen in mid-dance. For a moment, nobody moved. Oil lamps flickered against crudely painted erotic scenes – a woman astride a man, a man mounting a woman from behind, two men lying with their fingers on one another's cocks. One of the reclining clients began trailing his hand slowly beneath the couch, patting the floor, feeling towards a knife which lay beside a plate of peeled fruit. Attilius planted his foot firmly in the middle of Africanus's back, Africanus groaned, and the man quickly withdrew his hand.

'Good.' Attilius nodded. He smiled. He bent and grabbed Africanus by his belt again and dragged him out of the door.

'Teenage girls!' said Ampliatus, as the sound of Corelia's footsteps died away. 'It's all just nerves before her wedding. Frankly, I'll be glad, Popidius, when she's your responsibility and not mine.' He saw his wife rise to follow her. 'No, woman! Leave her!' Celsia lay down meekly, smiling apologetically to the other guests. Ampliatus frowned at her. He wished she would not do that. Why should she defer to her so-called betters? He could buy and sell them all!

He stuck his knife into the side of the eel and twisted it then gestured irritably to the nearest slave to take over the carving. The fish stared up at him with blank red eyes. The Emperor's pet, he thought: a prince in its own little pond. Not any more.

He dunked his bread in a bowl of vinegar and sucked it, watching the dextrous hand of the slave as he piled their plates with lumps of bony grey meat. Nobody wanted to eat it yet nobody wanted to be the first to refuse. An atmosphere of dyspeptic dread descended, as heavy as the air around the table, hot and stale with the smell of food. Ampliatus allowed the silence to hang. Why should he set them at their ease? When he was a slave at table, he had been forbidden to speak in the dining room in the presence of guests.

He was served first but he waited until the others had all had their golden dishes set in front of them before reaching out and breaking off a piece of fish. He raised it to his lips, paused, and glanced around the table, until, one by one, beginning with Popidius, they reluctantly followed his example.

He had been anticipating this moment all day. Vedius Pollio had thrown his slaves to his eels not only to enjoy the novelty of seeing a man torn apart underwater rather than by beasts in the arena, but also because, as a gourmet, he maintained that human flesh gave the morays a more piquant flavour. Ampliatus chewed carefully yet he tasted nothing. The meat was bland

and leathery – inedible – and he felt the same sense of disappointment that he had experienced the previous afternoon by the seashore. Once again, he had reached out for the ultimate experience and once more he had grasped – nothing.

He scooped the fish out of his mouth with his fingers and threw it back on his plate in disgust. He tried to make light of it – 'So then! It seems that eels, like women, taste best when young!' – and grabbed for his wine to wash away the taste. But there was no disguising the fact that the pleasure had gone out of the afternoon. His guests were coughing politely into their napkins or picking the tiny bones out of their teeth and he knew they would all be laughing about him for days afterwards, just as soon as they could get away, especially Holconius and that fat pederast, Brittius.

'My dear fellow, have you heard the latest about Ampliatus? He thinks that fish, like wine, improves with age!'

He drank more wine, swilling it around in his mouth, and was just contemplating getting up to propose a toast – to the Emperor! to the Army! – when he noticed his steward approaching the dining room carrying a small box. Scutarius hesitated, clearly not wanting to disturb his master with a business matter during a meal, and Ampliatus would indeed have told him to go to blazes, but there was something about the man's expression . . .

He screwed up his napkin, got to his feet, nodded curtly to his guests, and beckoned to Scutarius to follow him into the tablinum. Once they were out of sight he flexed his fingers. 'What is it? Give it here.'

It was a *capsa*, a cheap beechwood document case, covered in rawhide, of the sort a schoolboy might use to carry his books around in. The lock had been broken. Ampliatus flipped open the lid. Inside were a dozen small rolls of papyri. He pulled out one at random. It was covered in columns of figures and for a moment Ampliatus squinted at it, baffled, but then the figures assumed a shape – he always did have a head for numbers – and he understood. 'Where is the man who brought this?'

'Waiting in the vestibule, master.'

'Take him into the old garden. Have the kitchen serve dessert and tell my guests I shall return shortly.'

Ampliatus took the back route, behind the dining room and up the wide steps into the courtyard of his old house. This was the place he had bought ten years earlier, deliberately settling himself next door to the ancestral home of the Popidii. What a pleasure it had been to live on an equal footing with his former masters and to bide his time, knowing even then that one day, somehow, he would punch a hole in the thick garden wall and swarm through to the other side, like an avenging army capturing an enemy city.

He sat himself on the circular stone bench in the centre of the garden, beneath the shade of a rose-covered pergola. This was where he liked to conduct his most private business. He could always talk here undisturbed. No one could approach him without being seen. He opened the box again and took out each of the papyri then glanced up at the wide uncorrupted sky. He could hear Corelia's goldfinches, chirruping in their rooftop aviary and, beyond them, the drone of the city coming back to life after the long siesta. The inns and the eating-houses would be coining it now as people poured into the streets ready for the sacrifice to Vulcan.

Salve lucrum!

Lucrum gaudium!

He did not look up as he heard his visitor approach.

'So,' he said, 'it seems we have a problem.'

Corelia had been given the finches not long after the family had moved into the house, on her tenth birthday. She had fed them with scrupulous attention, tended them when they were sick, watched them hatch, mate, flourish, die, and now, whenever she wanted to be alone, it was to the aviary that she came. It occupied half of the small balcony outside her room, above the cloistered garden. The top of the cage was sheeted as protection against the sun.

She was sitting, drawn up tightly in the shady corner, her arms clasped around her legs, her chin resting on her knees, when she heard someone come into the courtyard. She edged forward on her bottom and peered over the low balustrade. Her father had settled himself on to the circular stone bench, a box beside him, and was reading through some papers. He laid the last one aside and stared at the sky, turning in her direction. She ducked her head back quickly. People said she resembled him: 'Oh, she's the image of her father!' And, as he was a handsome man, it used to make her proud.

She heard him say, 'So, it seems we have a problem.'

She had discovered as a child that the cloisters played a peculiar trick. The walls and pillars seemed to capture the sound of voices and funnel them upwards, so that even whispers, barely audible at ground-level, were as distinct up here as speeches from the rostrum on election day. Naturally, this had only added to the magic of her secret place. Most of what she heard when she was growing up had meant nothing to her — contracts, boundaries, rates of interest — the thrill had simply been to have a private window on the adult world. She had never even told her brother what she knew, for it was only in the past few months that she had begun to decipher the mysterious language of her father's affairs. And it was here, a month ago, that she had heard her own future being bargained away by her father with Popidius: so much to be discounted on the announcement of the betrothal, the full debt to be discharged once the marriage was transacted, the property to revert in the event of a failure to produce issue, said issue to inherit fully on coming of age . . .

'My little Venus,' he had used to call her. 'My little brave Diana.'

. . . a premium payable on account of virginity, virginity attested by the surgeon, Pumponius Magonianus, payment waived on signing of contracts within the stipulated period . . .

'I always say,' her father had whispered, 'speaking man to man here, Popidius, and not to be too legal about it – you can't put a price on a good fuck.'

'*My little Venus . . .*'

'*It seems we have a problem . . .*'

A man's voice – harsh, not one she recognised – replied, 'Yes, we have a problem right enough.'

To which Ampliatus responded: 'And his name is Marcus Attilius . . .'

She leaned forward again so as not to miss a word.

Africanus wanted no trouble. Africanus was an honest man. Attilius marched him down the staircase, only half listening to his jabbering protests, glancing over his shoulder every few steps to make sure they were not being followed. 'I am an official here on the Emperor's business. I need to see where Exomnius lived. Quickly.' At the mention of the Emperor, Africanus launched into a fresh round of assurances of his good name. Attilius shook him. 'I haven't the time to listen to this. Take me to his room.'

'It's locked.'

'Where's the key?'

'Downstairs.'

'Get it.'

When they reached the street he pushed the brothel-keeper back into the gloomy hallway and stood guard as he fetched his cash-box from its hiding-place. The meretrix in the short green dress had returned to her stool: Zmyrina, Africanus called her – 'Zmyrina, which is the key to Exomnius's room?' – his hands shaking so much that when finally he managed to open the cash-box and take out the keys he dropped them and she had to stoop and retrieve them for him. She picked out a key from the bunch and held it up.

'What are you so scared about?' asked Attilius. 'Why try to run away at the mention of a name?'

'I don't want any trouble,' repeated Africanus. He took the key and led the way to the bar next door. It was a cheap place, little more than a rough stone counter with holes cut into it for the jars of wine. There was no room to sit. Most of the drinkers were outside on the pavement, propped against the wall. Attilius supposed this was where the lupanar's customers waited their turn for a girl and then came afterwards to refresh themselves and boast about their prowess. It had the same fetid smell as the brothel and he thought that Exomnius must have fallen a long way – the corruption must have really entered his soul – for him to have ended up down here.

Africanus was small and nimble, his arms and legs hairy, like a monkey's. Perhaps that was where he had got his name – from the African monkeys in the forum, performing tricks at the ends of their chains to earn a few coins for their owners. He scuttled through the bar and up the rickety wooden staircase to the landing. He paused with the key in his hand, and cocked his head to one side, looking at Attilius. 'Who are you?' he said.

'Open it.'

'Nothing's been touched. I give you my word.'

'That's valuable. Now open it.'

The whore-monger turned towards the door with the key outstretched and then gave a little cry of surprise. He gestured to the lock and when Attilius stepped up next to him he saw that it was broken. The interior of the room was dark, the air stuffy with trapped smells – bedding, leather, stale food. A thin grid of brilliant light on the opposite wall showed where the shutters were closed. Africanus went in first, stumbling against something in the blackness, and unfastened the window. The afternoon light flooded a shambles of strewn clothes and upended furniture. Africanus gazed around him in dismay. 'This was nothing to do with me – I swear it.'

Attilius took it all in at a glance. There had not been much in the room to start with – bed and thin mattress with a pillow and a coarse brown blanket, a washing-jug, a pisspot, a chest, a stool – but nothing had been left untouched. Even the mattress had been slashed; its stuffing of horsehair bulged out in tufts.

'I swear,' repeated Africanus.

'All right,' said Attilius. 'I believe you.' He did. Africanus would hardly have broken his own lock when he had a key, or left the room in such disorder. On a little three-legged table was a lump of white-green marble that turned out, on closer inspection, to be a half-eaten loaf of bread. A knife and a rotten apple lay beside it. There was a fresh smear of fingerprints in the dust. Attilius touched the surface of the table and inspected the blackened tip of his finger. This had been done recently, he thought. The dust had not had time to resettle. Perhaps it explained why Ampliatus had been so keen to show him every last detail of the new baths – to keep him occupied while the room was searched? What a fool he had been, holding forth about lowland pine and scorched olive wood! He said, 'How long had Exomnius rented this place?'

'Three years. Maybe four.'

'But he was not here all the time?'

'He came and went.'

Attilius realised he did not even know what Exomnius looked like. He was pursuing a phantom. 'He had no slave?'

'No.'

'When did you last see him?'

'Exomnius?' Africanus spread his hands. How was he supposed to remember? So many customers. So many faces.

'When did he pay his rent?'

'In advance. On the kalends of every month.'

'So he paid you at the beginning of August?' Africanus nodded. Then one thing was settled. Whatever else had happened to him, Exomnius had not planned to disappear. The man was obviously a miser. He would never have paid for a room he had no intention of using. 'Leave me,' he said. 'I'll straighten it up.'

Africanus seemed about to argue, but when Attilius took a step towards him he held up his hands in surrender and retreated to the landing. The engineer closed the broken door on him and listened to his footsteps descending to the bar.

He went around the room, reassembling it so that he could get an impression of how it had looked, as if by doing so he might conjure some clue as to what else it had held. He laid the eviscerated mattress back on the bed and placed the pillow – also slashed – at the head. He folded the thin blanket. He lay down. When he turned his head he noticed a pattern of small black marks on the wall and he saw that they were made by squashed insects. He imagined Exomnius lying here in the heat, killing bed bugs, and wondered why, if he was taking bribes from Ampliatus, he had chosen to live like a pauper. Perhaps he had spent all his money on whores? But that did not seem possible. A tumble with one of Africanus's girls could not have cost more than a couple of copper coins.

A floorboard creaked.

He sat up very slowly and turned to look at the door. The moving shadows of a pair of feet showed clearly beneath the cheap wood and for a moment he was sure it must be Exomnius, come to demand an explanation from this stranger who had taken his job and invaded his property and was now lying on his bed in his ransacked room. 'Who's there?' he called, and when the door opened slowly and he saw it was only Zmyrina, he felt oddly disappointed. 'Yes?' he said. 'What do you want? I told your master to leave me alone.'

She stood on the threshold. Her dress was split, to show her long legs. She had a fading purple bruise the size of a fist on her thigh. She gazed around the room and put her hands to her mouth in horror. 'Who done this?'

'You tell me.'

'He said he take care for me.'

159

'What?'

She came further into the room. 'He said when come back he take care for me.'

'Who?'

'Aelianus. He said.'

It took him a beat to work out who she meant – Exomnius. Exomnius Aelianus. She was the first person he had met who had used the aquarius's given, rather than his family, name. That just about summed him up. His only intimate – a whore. 'Well he isn't coming back,' he said roughly, 'to take care for you. Or for anyone else.'

She passed the back of her hand under her nose a couple of times and he realised that she was crying. 'He dead?'

'You tell me.' Attilius softened his tone. 'The truth is, no one knows.'

'Buy me from Africanus. He said. No whore everyone. Special him. Understand?' She touched her chest and gestured to Attilius, then touched herself again.

'Yes, I understand.'

He looked at Zmyrina with new interest. It was not uncommon, he knew, especially in this part of Italy. The foreign sailors, when they left the Navy after their twenty-five years' service and were granted Roman citizenship – the first thing most of them did with their demob money was head for the nearest slave-market and buy themselves a wife. The prostitute was kneeling now, picking up the scattered clothes and folding them, putting them away in the chest. And perhaps it was a point in Exomnius's favour, he thought, that he should have decided to choose her, rather than someone younger or prettier. Or, then again, perhaps he was just lying and never intended to come back for her. Either way, her future had more or less disappeared along with her principal client.

'He had the money, did he? Enough money to buy you? Only you wouldn't think it, to look at this place.'

'Not *here*.' She sat back on her heels and looked up at him with scorn. 'Not safe money *here*. Money hidden. Plenty money. Some place clever. Nobody find. He said. Nobody.'

'Somebody has tried —'

'Money not here.'

She was emphatic. No doubt she had searched it often enough when he wasn't around. 'Did he ever tell you where this place was?'

She stared at him, her vermillion mouth wide open, and suddenly she bent her head. Her shoulders were shaking. He thought at first she was crying again but when she turned he saw that the glint in her eyes was from tears of laughter. 'No!' She started rocking again. She looked almost girlish in her delight. She clapped her hands. It was the funniest thing she had ever heard, and he had to agree — the idea of Exomnius confiding in a whore of Africanus where he had hidden his money — it *was* funny. He began laughing himself, then swung his feet to the floor.

There was no point in wasting any more time here.

On the landing he glanced back at her, still kneeling on her haunches in her split dress, one of Exomnius's tunics pressed to her face.

Attilius hurried back the way he had come, along the shadowy side street. He thought, This must have been Exomnius's route from the brothel to the castellum aquae. This must have been what he saw whenever he came here – the whores and drunks, the puddles of piss and patches of vomit baked to crusts in the gutter, the graffiti on the walls, the little effigies of Priapus beside the doorways, with his enormous jutting cock dangling bells at its tip to ward off evil. So what was in his head as he walked this way for the final time? Zmyrina? Ampliatus? The safety of his hidden money?

He looked back over his shoulder but no one was paying him any attention. Still, he was glad to reach the wide central thoroughfare and the safety of its glaring light.

The town remained much quieter than it had been in the morning, the heat of the sun keeping most people off the road, and he made quick progress up the hill towards the Vesuvius Gate. As he approached the small square in front of the castellum aquae he could see the oxen and the carts, now fully laden with tools and materials. A small crowd of men sprawled in the dirt outside a bar, laughing at something. The horse he had hired was tethered to its post. And here was Polites – faithful Polites, the most trustworthy member of the work-gang – advancing to meet him.

'You were gone a long while, aquarius.'

Attilius ignored the tone of reproach. 'I'm here now. Where is Musa?'

'Still not here.'

'What?' He swore and cupped his hand to his eyes to check the position of the sun. It must be four hours – no, nearer five – since the others had ridden off. He had expected to receive some word by now. 'How many men do we have?'

'Twelve.' Polites rubbed his hands together uneasily.

'What's the matter with you?'

'They're a rough-looking lot, aquarius.'

'Are they? Their manners don't concern me. As long as they can work.'

'They've been drinking for an hour.'

'Then they'd better stop.'

Attilius crossed the square to the bar. Ampliatus had promised a dozen of his strongest slaves and once again he had more than kept his word. It looked as if he had supplied a troop of gladiators. A flagon of wine was being handed around, from one pair of tattooed arms to another, and to pass the time they had fetched Tiro from the castellum and were playing a game with him. One of them had snatched off the water-slave's felt cap and whenever he turned helplessly in the direction of whoever he thought was holding it, it would be tossed to someone else.

'Cut that out,' said the engineer. 'Leave the lad alone.' They ignored him. He spoke up more loudly. 'I am Marcus Attilius, aquarius of the Aqua Augusta, and you men are under my command now.' He snatched Tiro's cap and pressed it into his hand. 'Go back to the castellum, Tiro.' And then, to the slave gang: 'That's enough drinking. We're moving out.'

The man whose turn it was with the wine regarded Attilius with indifference. He raised the clay jar to his mouth, threw back his head and drank. Wine dribbled down his chin and on to his chest. There was an appreciative cheer and Attilius felt the anger ignite inside himself. To train so hard, to build and work, to pour so much skill and ingenuity into the aqueducts – and all to carry water to such brutes as these, and Africanus. They would be better left to wallow beside some mosquito-infested swamp. 'Who is the senior man among you?'

The drinker lowered the flagon. '"The senior man,"' he mocked. 'What is this? The fucking army?'

'You are drunk,' said Attilius quietly. 'But I am sober, and in a hurry. Now *move*.' He lashed out with his foot and caught the flagon, knocking it out of the drinker's hand. It spun away and landed on its side, where it lay, unbroken, emptying itself across the stones. For a moment, in the silence, the glug-glug of the wine was the only sound, and then there was a rush of activity – the men rising, shouting, the drinker lunging forward, with the apparent intention of sinking his teeth into Attilius's leg. Through all this commotion, one booming voice rang louder than the rest – 'Stop!' – and an enormous man, well over six feet tall, came running across the square and planted himself between Attilius and the others. He spread out his arms to keep them back.

'I am Brebix,' he said. 'A freed man.' He had a coarse red beard, trimmed, shovel-shaped. 'If anyone is senior, I am.'

'Brebix.' Attilius nodded. He would remember that name. This one, he saw, actually *was* a gladiator, or rather an ex-gladiator. He had the brand of his troop on his arm, a snake drawing back to strike. 'You should have been here an hour ago. Tell these men that if they have any complaints, they should take them to Ampliatus. Tell them that none has to come with me, but any who stay behind will have to answer for it to their master. Now get those wagons out through the gate. I'll meet you on the other side of the city wall.'

He turned, and the crowd of drinkers from the other bars, who had come thronging into the square in the hope of seeing a fight, stood aside to let him pass. He was trembling and he had to clench his fist in his palm to stop it showing. 'Polites!' he called.

'Yes?' The slave eased his way through the mob.

'Fetch me my horse. We've wasted long enough here.'

Polites looked anxiously towards Brebix, now leading the

reluctant work gang over to the wagons. 'These men, aquarius
— I don't trust them.'

'Neither do I. But what else can we do? Come on. Get my
horse. We'll meet up with Musa on the road.'

As Polites hurried away, Attilius glanced down the hill.
Pompeii was less like a seaside resort, more like a frontier
garrison: a boom town. Ampliatus was rebuilding her in his
own image. He would not be sorry if he never saw her again
— apart from Corelia. He wondered what she was doing, but
even as the image of her wading towards him through the glittering pool began to form in his mind he forced himself to
banish it. Get out of here, get to the Augusta, get the water
running, and then get back to Misenum and check the aqueduct's records for evidence of what Exomnius had been up to.
Those were his priorities. To think of anything else was foolish.

In the shadow of the castellum aquae Tiro crouched, and
Attilius was on the point of raising his hand in farewell, until
he saw those flickering, sightless eyes.

The public sundial showed it was well into the ninth hour
when Attilius passed on horseback beneath the long vault
of the Vesuvius Gate. The ring of hooves on stone echoed like
a small detachment of cavalry. The customs official poked his
head out of his booth to see what was happening, yawned and
turned away.

The engineer had never been a natural rider. For once,
though, he was glad to be mounted. It gave him height, and
he needed every advantage he could get. When he trotted over
to Brebix and the men they were obliged to squint up at him,
screwing their eyes against the glare of the sky.

'We follow the line of the aqueduct towards Vesuvius,' he said. The horse wheeled and he had to shout over his shoulder. 'And no dawdling. I want us in position before dark.'

'In position where?' asked Brebix.

'I don't know yet. It should be obvious when we see it.'

His vagueness provoked an uneasy stir among the men – and who could blame them? He would have liked to have known where he was going himself. Damn Musa! He brought his mount under control and turned it towards the open country. He raised himself from the saddle so that he could see the course of the road beyond the necropolis. It ran straight towards the mountain through neat, rectangular fields of olive trees and corn, separated by low stone walls and ditches – centuriated land, awarded to demobbed legionaries decades ago. There was not much traffic on the paved highway – a cart or two, a few pedestrians. No sign of any plume of dust that might be thrown up by a galloping horseman. Damn him, damn him . . .

Brebix said, 'Some of the lads aren't too keen on being out near Vesuvius after nightfall.'

'Why not?'

A man called out, 'The giants!'

'Giants?'

Brebix said, almost apologetically, 'Giants have been seen, aquarius, bigger than any man. Wandering over the earth by day and night. Sometimes journeying through the air. Their voices sound like claps of thunder.'

'Perhaps they *are* claps of thunder,' said Attilius. 'Have you considered that? There can be thunder without rain.'

'Aye, but this thunder is never in the air. It's on the ground. Or even under the ground.'

'So this is why you drink?' Attilius forced himself to laugh. 'Because you are scared to be outside the city walls after dark? And you were a gladiator, Brebix? I'm glad I never wagered money on you! Or did your troop only ever fight blind boys?' Brebix began to swear, but the engineer talked over his head, to the work gang. 'I asked your master to lend me men, not women! We've argued long enough! We have to go five miles before dark. Perhaps ten. Now drive those oxen forward, and follow me.'

He dug his heels into the flanks of his horse and it started off at a slow trot. He passed along the avenue between the tombs. Flowers and small offerings of food had been left on some, to mark the Festival of Vulcan. A few people were picnicking in the shade of the cypresses. Small black lizards scattered across the stone vaults like spreading cracks. He did not look back. The men would follow, he was sure. He had goaded them into it and they were scared of Ampliatus.

At the edge of the cemetery he drew on the reins and waited until he heard the creak of the wagons trundling over the stones. They were just crude farm carts – the axle turned with the wheels, which were no more than simple sections of tree-trunk, a foot thick. Their rumble could be heard a mile away. First the oxen passed him, heads down, each team led by a man with a stick, and then the lumbering carts, and finally the rest of the work gang. He counted them. They were all there, including Brebix. Beside the road, the marker-stones of the aqueduct, one every hundred paces, dwindled into the distance. Neatly spaced between them were the round stone inspection covers that provided access to the tunnel. The regularity and precision of it gave the engineer a fleeting sense of confidence. If nothing else, he knew how this worked.

He spurred his horse.

An hour later, with the afternoon sun dipping towards the bay, they were halfway across the plain – the parched and narrow fields and bone-dry ditches spread out all around them, the ochre-coloured walls and watchtowers of Pompeii dissolving into the dust at their backs, the line of the aqueduct leading them remorselessly onwards, towards the blue-grey pyramid of Vesuvius, looming ever more massively ahead.

Hora duodecima

[18:47 hours]

'While rocks are extremely strong in compression, they
are weak in tension (strengths of about 1.5×10^7 bars).
Thus, the strength of the rocks capping a cooling and
vesiculating magma body is easily exceeded long before
the magma is solid. Once this happens, an explosive erup-
tion occurs.'

Volcanoes: A Planetary Perspective

Pliny had been monitoring the frequency of the trembling throughout the day – or, more accurately, his secretary, Alexion, had been doing it for him, seated at the
table in the admiral's library, with the water clock on one side
and the wine bowl on the other.

The fact that it was a public holiday had made no difference to the admiral's routine. He worked whatever day it was.
He had broken off from his reading and dictation only once, in
the middle of the morning, to bid goodbye to his guests, and
had insisted on accompanying them down to the harbour to see
them aboard their boats. Lucius Pomponianus and Livia were
bound for Stabiae, on the far side of the bay, and it had been
arranged that they would take Rectina with them in their modest
cruiser, as far as the Villa Calpurnia in Herculaneum. Pedius
Cascus, without his wife, would take his own fully manned

liburnian to Rome for a council meeting with the Emperor. Old, dear friends! He had embraced them warmly. Pomponianus could play the fool, it was true, but his father, the great Pomponianus Secundus, had been Pliny's patron, and he felt a debt of honour to the family. And as for Pedius and Rectina – their generosity to him had been without limit. It would have been hard for him to finish the *Natural History*, living outside Rome, without the use of their library.

Just before he boarded his ship, Pedius had taken him by the arm. 'I didn't like to mention it earlier, Pliny, but are you sure you're quite well?'

'Too fat,' wheezed Pliny, 'that's all.'

'What do your doctors say?'

'Doctors? I won't let those Greek tricksters anywhere near me. Only doctors can murder a man with impunity.'

'But look at you, man – your heart –'

'"In cardiac disease the one hope of relief lies undoubtedly in wine." You should read my book. And that, my dear Pedius, is a medicine I can administer myself.'

The senator looked at him, then said grimly, 'The Emperor is concerned about you.'

That gave Pliny a twinge in his heart, right enough. He was a member of the imperial council himself. Why had he not been invited to this meeting, to which Pedius was hurrying? 'What are you implying? That he thinks I'm past it?'

Pedius said nothing – a nothing that said everything. He suddenly opened his arms and Pliny leaned forwards and hugged him, patting the senator's stiff back with his pudgy hand. 'Take care, old friend.'

'And you.'

To his shame, when Pliny pulled back from the embrace,

his cheek was wet. He stayed on the quayside, watching until the ships were out of sight. That was all he seemed to do these days: watch other people leave.

The conversation with Pedius had stayed with him all day, as he shuffled back and forth on the terrace, periodically wandering into the library to check Alexion's neat columns of figures. *'The Emperor is concerned about you.'* Like the pain in his side, it would not go away.

He took refuge, as always, in his observations. The number of *harmonic episodes,* as he had decided to call the tremors, had increased steadily. Five in the first hour, seven in the second, eight in the third, and so on. More striking still had been their lengthening duration. Too small to measure at the beginning of the day, as the afternoon went on, Alexion had been able to use the accuracy of the water clock to estimate them – first at one-tenth part of the hour, and then one-fifth, until finally, for the whole eleventh hour, he had recorded one tremor only. The vibration of the wine was continuous.

'We must change our nomenclature,' muttered Pliny, leaning over his shoulder. 'To call such movements an *episode* will no longer suffice.'

And increasing in proportion with the movement of the earth, as if Man and Nature were bound by some invisible link, came reports of agitation in the town – a fight at the public fountains when the first hour's discharge had ended and not everyone had filled their pots; a riot outside the public baths when they had failed to open at the seventh hour; a woman stabbed to death for the sake of two amphorae of water – water! – by a drunk outside the Temple of Augustus; now it was said that armed gangs were hanging round the fountains, waiting for a fight.

Pliny had never had any difficulty issuing orders. It was the essence of command. He decreed that the evening's sacrifice to Vulcan should be cancelled and that the bonfire in the forum must be dismantled at once. A large public gathering at night was a recipe for trouble. It was unsafe, in any case, to light a fire of such a size in the centre of the town when the pipes and fountains were dry and the drought had rendered the houses as flammable as kindling.

'The priests won't like that,' said Antius.

The flagship captain had joined Pliny in the library. The admiral's widowed sister, Julia, who kept house for him, was also in the room, holding a tray of oysters and a jug of wine for his supper.

'Tell the priests that we have no choice. I'm sure Vulcan in his mountain forge will forgive us, just this once.' Pliny massaged his arm irritably. It felt numb. 'Have all the men, apart from the sentry patrols, confined to their barracks from dusk. In fact, I want a curfew imposed across the whole of Misenum from vespera until dawn. Anyone found on the streets is to be imprisoned and fined. Understood?'

'Yes, admiral.'

'Have we opened the sluices in the reservoir yet?'

'It should be happening now, admiral.'

Pliny brooded. They could not afford another such day. Everything depended on how long the water would last. He made up his mind. 'I'm going to take a look.'

Julia came towards him anxiously with the tray. 'Is that wise, brother? You ought to eat and rest –'

'Don't nag, woman!' Her face crumpled and he regretted his tone at once. Life had knocked her about enough as it was – humiliated by her wastrel husband and his ghastly mistress, then left widowed with a boy to bring up. That gave him an idea. 'Gaius,' he said, in a gentler voice. 'Forgive me, Julia. I spoke too sharply. I'll take Gaius with me, if that will make you happier.'

On his way out, he called to his other secretary, Alcman, 'Have we had a signal back yet from Rome?'

'No, admiral.'

'The Emperor is concerned about you . . .'

He did not like this silence.

P liny had grown too fat for a litter. He travelled instead by carriage, a two-seater, with Gaius wedged in next to him. Beside his red and corpulent uncle he looked as pale and insubstantial as a wraith. The admiral squeezed his knee fondly. He had made the boy his heir and had fixed him up with the finest tutors in Rome – Quintilian for literature and history; the Smyrnan, Nicetes Sacerdos, for rhetoric. It was costing him a fortune but they told him the lad was brilliant. He would never make a soldier, though. It would be a lawyer's life for him.

An escort of helmeted marines trotted on foot on either side of the carriage, clearing a path for them through the narrow streets. A couple of people jeered. Someone spat.

'What about our water, then?'

'Look at that fat bastard! I bet you he's not going thirsty!'

Gaius said, 'Shall I close the curtains, uncle?'

'No, boy. Never let them see that you're afraid.'

He knew there would be a lot of angry people on the streets tonight. Not just here, but in Neapolis and Nola and all the other towns, especially on a public festival. Perhaps Mother Nature is punishing us, he thought, for our greed and selfishness. We torture her at all hours by iron and wood, fire and stone. We dig her up and dump her in the sea. We sink mineshafts into her and drag out her entrails – and all for a jewel to wear on a pretty finger. Who can blame her if she occasionally quivers with anger?'

They passed along the harbour front. An immense line of people had formed, queuing for the drinking-fountain. Each had been allowed to bring one receptacle only and it was obvious to Pliny that an hour was never going to be sufficient for them all to receive their measure. Those who had been at the head of the line already had their ration and were hurrying away, cradling their pots and pans as if they were carrying gold. 'We shall have to extend the flow tonight,' he said, 'and trust to that young aquarius to carry out the repairs as he promised.'

'And if he doesn't, uncle?'

'Then half this town will be on fire tomorrow.'

Once they were free of the crowd and on to the causeway the carriage picked up speed. It rattled over the wooden bridge then slowed again as they climbed the hill towards the Piscina Mirabilis. Jolting around in the back Pliny felt sure he was about to faint and perhaps he did. At any rate, he nodded off, and the next thing he knew they were drawing into the courtyard of the reservoir, past the flushed faces of half a dozen marines. He returned their salute and descended, unsteadily, on Gaius's arm. If the Emperor takes away my command, he thought, I shall die, as surely as if he orders one of his praetorian guard to strike my head from my shoulders. I shall never write another book. My life-force has gone. I am finished.

'Are you all right, uncle?'

'I am perfectly well, Gaius, thank you.'

Foolish man! he reproached himself. Stupid, trembling, credulous old man! One sentence from Pedius Cascus, one routine meeting of the imperial council to which you are not invited, and you fall to pieces. He insisted on going down the steps into the reservoir unaided. The light was fading and a slave went on ahead with a torch. It was years since he had last been down here. Then, the pillars had been mostly submerged, and the crashing of the Augusta had drowned out any attempt at conversation. Now it echoed like a tomb. The size of it was astonishing. The level of the water had fallen so far beneath his feet he could barely make it out, until the slave held his torch over the mirrored surface, and then he saw his own face staring back at him – querulous, broken. The reservoir was also vibrating slightly, he realised, just like the wine.

'How deep is it?'

'Fifteen feet, admiral,' said the slave.

Pliny contemplated his reflection. '"There has never been anything more remarkable in the whole world,"' he murmured.

'What was that, uncle?'

'"When we consider the abundant supplies of water in public buildings, baths, pools, open channels, private houses, gardens and country estates, and when we think of the distances traversed by the water before it arrives, the raising of arches, the tunnelling of mountains and the building of level routes across deep valleys, then we shall readily admit that there has never been anything more remarkable than our aqueducts in the whole world." I quote myself, I fear. As usual.' He pulled back his head. 'Allow half the water to drain away tonight. We shall let the rest go in the morning.'

'And then what?'

'And then, my dear Gaius? And then we must hope for a better day tomorrow.'

In Pompeii, the fire for Vulcan was to be lit as soon as it was dark. Before that, there was to be the usual entertainment in the forum, supposedly paid for by Popidius, but in reality funded by Ampliatus – a bullfight, three pairs of skirmishing gladiators, some boxers in the Greek style. Nothing too elaborate, just an hour or so of diversion for the voters while they waited for the night to arrive, the sort of spectacle an aedile was expected to lay on in return for the privilege of office.

Corelia feigned sickness.

She lay on her bed, watching the lines of light from the closed shutters creep slowly up the wall as the sun sank, thinking about the conversation she had overheard, and about the engineer, Attilius. She had noticed the way he looked at her, both in Misenum yesterday, and this morning, when she was bathing. Lover, avenger, rescuer, tragic victim – in her imagination she pictured him briefly in all these parts, but always the fantasy dissolved into the same brutal coupling of facts: she had brought him into the orbit of her father and now her father was planning to kill him. His death would be her fault.

She listened to the sounds of the others preparing to leave. She heard her mother calling for her, and then her footsteps on the stairs. Quickly she felt for the feather she had hidden under her pillow. She opened her mouth and tickled the back of her throat, vomited noisily, and when Celsia appeared she wiped her lips and gestured weakly to the contents of the bowl.

Her mother sat on the edge of the mattress and put her

hand on Corelia's brow. 'Oh my poor child. You feel hot. I should send for the doctor.'

'No, don't trouble him.' A visit from Pumponius Magonianus, with his potions and purges, was enough to make anyone ill. 'Sleep is all I need. It was that endless, awful meal. I ate too much.'

'But my dear, you hardly ate a thing!'

'That's not true –'

'Hush!' Her mother held up a warning finger. Someone else was mounting the steps, with a heavier tread, and Corelia braced herself for a confrontation with her father. He would not be so easy to fool. But it was only her brother, in his long white robes as a priest of Isis. She could smell the incense on him.

'Hurry up, Corelia. He's shouting for us.'

No need to say who *he* was.

'She's ill.'

'Is she? Even so, she must still come. He won't be happy.'

Ampliatus bellowed from downstairs and they both jumped. They glanced towards the door.

'Yes, can't you make an effort, Corelia?' said her mother. 'For his sake?'

Once, the three of them had formed an alliance: had laughed about him behind his back – his moods, his rages, his obsessions. But lately that had stopped. Their domestic triumvirate had broken apart under his relentless fury. Individual strategies for survival had been adopted. Corelia had observed her mother become the perfect Roman matron, with a shrine to Livia in her dressing room, while her brother had subsumed himself in his Egyptian cult. And she? What was she supposed to do? Marry Popidius and take a second master? Become more of a slave in the household than Ampliatus had ever been?

She was too much her father's daughter not to fight.

'Run along, both of you,' she said bitterly. 'Take my bowl of vomit and show it to him, if you like. But I'm not going to his stupid spectacle.' She rolled on to her side and faced the wall. Another roar came from below.

Her mother breathed her martyr's sigh. 'Oh, very well. I'll tell him.'

It was exactly as the engineer had suspected. Having led them almost directly north towards the summit for a couple of miles, the aqueduct spur suddenly swung eastwards, just as the ground began to rise towards Vesuvivus. The road turned with it and for the first time they had their backs to the sea and were pointing inland, towards the distant foothills of the Appenninus.

The Pompeii spur wandered away from the road more often now, hugging the line of the terrain, weaving back and forth across their path. Attilius relished this subtlety of aqueducts. The great Roman roads went crashing through Nature in a straight line, brooking no opposition. But the aqueducts, which had to drop the width of a finger every hundred yards – any more and the flow would rupture the walls; any less and the water would lie stagnant – they were obliged to follow the contours of the ground. Their greatest glories, such as the triple-tiered bridge in southern Gaul, the highest in the world, that carried the aqueduct of Nemausus, were frequently far from human view. Sometimes it was only the eagles, soaring in the hot air above some lonely mountainscape, who could appreciate the true majesty of what men had wrought.

They had passed through the gridwork of centuriated fields and were entering into the wine-growing country, owned by the big estates. The ramshackle huts of the smallholders on the plain, with their tethered goats and their half-dozen ragged hens pecking in the dust, had given way to handsome farmhouses with red-tile roofs that dotted the lower slopes of the mountain.

Surveying the vineyards from his horse, Attilius felt almost dazed by the vision of such abundance, such astonishing fertility, even in the midst of a drought. He was in the wrong business. He should give up water and go into wine. The vines had escaped from ordinary cultivation and had fastened themselves on to every available wall and tree, reaching to the top of the tallest branches, enveloping them in luxuriant cascades of green and purple. Small white faces of Bacchus, made of marble to ward off evil, with perforated eyes and mouths, hung motionless in the still air, peering from the foliage like ambushers ready to strike. It was harvest-time and the fields were full of slaves – slaves on ladders, slaves bent halfway to the ground by the weight of the baskets of grapes on their backs. But how, he wondered, could they possibly manage to gather it all in before it rotted?

They came to a large villa looking out across the plain to the bay and Brebix asked if they could stop for a rest.

'All right. But not for long.'

Attilius dismounted and stretched his legs. When he wiped his forehead the back of his hand came away grey with dust and when he tried to drink he found that his lips were caked. Polites had bought a couple of loaves and some greasy sausages and he ate hungrily. Astonishing, always, the effects of a bit of food in an empty stomach. He felt his spirits lift with each mouthful. This was always where he preferred to be – not in some filthy town, but out in the country, with the hidden veins of civilisation, beneath an honest sky. He noticed that Brebix was sitting alone and he went over and broke off half a loaf for him and held it out, along with a couple of sausages. A peace offering.

Brebix hesitated, nodded and took them. He was naked to the waist, his sweating torso criss-crossed with scars.

'What class of fighter were you?'

'Guess.'

It was a long time since Attilius had been to the games. 'Not a retiarius,' he said eventually. 'I don't see you dancing around with a net and a trident.'

'You're right there.'

'So, a thrax, then. Or a murmillo, perhaps.' A thrax carried a small shield and a short, curved sword; a murmillo was a heavier fighter, armed like an infantryman, with a gladius and a full rectangular shield. The muscles of Brebix's left arm – his shield arm, more likely than not – bulged as powerfully as his right. 'I'd say a murmillo.' Brebix nodded. 'How many fights?'

'Thirty.'

Attilius was impressed. Not many men survived thirty fights. That was eight or ten years of appearances in the arena. 'Whose troop were you with?'

'Alleius Nigidius. I fought all around the bay. Pompeii, mostly. Nuceria. Nola. After I won my freedom I went to Ampliatus.'

'You didn't turn trainer?'

Brebix said quietly, 'I've seen enough killing, aquarius. Thanks for the bread.' He got to his feet lightly, in a single, fluid motion, and went over to the others. It took no effort to imagine him in the dust of the amphitheatre. Attilius could guess the mistake his opponents had made. They would have thought he was massive, slow, clumsy. But he was as agile as a cat.

The engineer took another drink. He could see straight across the bay to the rocky islands off Misenum – little Prochyta and the high mountain of Aenaria – and for the first time he noticed that there was a swell on the water. Flecks of white foam had appeared among the tiny ships that were strewn like filings across the glaring, metallic sea. But none had hoisted a sail. And that was strange, he thought – that was odd – but it was a fact: *there was no wind*. Waves but no wind.

Another trick of nature for the admiral to ponder.

The sun was just beginning to dip behind Vesuvius. A hare eagle – small, black, powerful, famed for never emitting a cry – wheeled and soared in silence above the thick forest. They would soon be heading into shadow. Which was good, he thought, because it would be cooler, and also bad, because it meant there was not long till dusk.

He finished his water and called to the men to move on.

S ilence also in the great house.
    She could always tell when her father had gone. The whole place seemed to let out its breath. She slipped her cloak around her shoulders and listened again at the shutters before she opened them. Her room faced west. On the other side of the courtyard the sky was as red as the terracotta roof, the garden beneath her balcony in shadow. A sheet still lay across the top of the aviary and she pulled it back, to give the birds

some air, and then – on impulse: it had never occurred to her before that moment – she released the catch and opened the door at the side of the cage.

She drew back into the room.

The habits of captivity are hard to break. It took a while for the goldfinches to sense their opportunity. Eventually, one bird, bolder than the rest, edged along its perch and hopped on to the bottom of the door frame. It cocked its red-and-black-capped head at her and blinked one tiny bright eye then launched itself into the air. Its wings cracked. There was a flash of gold in the gloom. It swooped across the garden and came to rest on the ridge-tiles opposite. Another bird fluttered to the door and took off, and then another. She would have liked to stay and watch them all escape but instead she closed the shutters.

She had told her maid to go with the rest of the slaves to the forum. The passage outside her room was deserted, as were the stairs, as was the garden in which her father had held what he thought was his secret conversation. She crossed it quickly, keeping close to the pillars in case she encountered anyone. She passed through into the atrium of their old house and turned towards the tablinum. This was where her father still conducted his business affairs – rising to greet his clients at dawn, meeting them either singly or in groups until the law courts opened, whereupon he would sweep out into the street, followed by his usual anxious court of petitioners. It was a symbol of Ampliatus's power that the room contained not the usual one but three strong boxes, made of heavy wood bonded with brass, attached by iron rods to the stone floor.

Corelia knew where the keys were kept because in happier days – or was it simply a device to convince his associates of what a charming fellow he was? – she had been allowed to creep in and sit at his feet while he was working. She opened the drawer of the small desk, and there they were.

The document case was in the second strong box. She did not bother to unroll the small papyri, but simply stuffed them into the pockets of her cloak, then locked the safe and replaced the key. The riskiest part was over and she allowed herself to relax a little. She had a story ready in case she was stopped – that she was recovered now, and had decided to join the others in the forum after all – but nobody was about. She walked across the courtyard and down the staircase, past the swimming pool with its gently running fountain, and the dining room in which she had endured that terrible meal, moving swiftly around the colonnade towards the red-painted drawing room of the Popidii. Soon she would be the mistress of all this: a ghastly thought.

A slave was lighting one of the brass candelabra but drew back respectfully against the wall to let her pass. Through a curtain. Another, narrower flight of stairs. And suddenly she was in a different world – low ceilings, roughly plastered walls, a smell of sweat: the slaves' quarters. She could hear a couple of men talking somewhere and a clang of iron pots and then, to her relief, the whinny of a horse.

The stables were at the end of the corridor, and it was as she had thought – her father had decided to take his guests by litter to the forum, leaving all the horses behind. She stroked the nose of her favourite, a bay mare, and whispered to her. Saddling her was a job for the slaves but she had watched them often enough to know how to do it. As she fastened the leather harness beneath the belly the horse shifted slightly and knocked against the wooden stall. She held her breath but no one came.

She whispered again: 'Easy, girl, it's only me, it's all right.'

The stable door opened directly on to the side street. Every sound seemed absurdly loud to her – the bang of the iron bar as she lifted it, the creak of the hinges, the clatter of the mare's hooves as she led her out into the road. A man was hurrying along the pavement opposite and he turned to look at her but he didn't stop – he was late, presumably, and on his way to the sacrifice. From the direction of the forum came the noise of music and then a low roar, like the breaking of a wave.

She swung herself up on to the horse. No decorous, feminine sideways mount for her tonight. She opened her legs and sat astride it like a man. The sense of limitless freedom almost overwhelmed her. This street – this utterly ordinary street, with its cobblers' shops and dressmakers, along which she had walked so many times – had become the edge of the world. She knew that if she hesitated any longer the panic would seize her completely. She pressed her knees into the flanks of the horse and pulled hard left on the reins, heading away from the forum. At the first crossroads she turned left again. She stuck carefully to the empty back streets and only when she judged that she was far enough away from the house to be unlikely to meet anyone she knew did she join the main road. Another wave of applause carried from the forum.

Up the hill she went, past the deserted baths her father was building, past the castellum aquae and under the arch of the city gate. She bowed her head as she passed the customs post, pulling the hood of her cloak low, and then she was out of Pompeii and on the road to Vesuvius.

Vespera

[20:00 hours]

'The arrival of magma into the near-surface swells the reservoir and inflates the surface . . .'

Encyclopaedia of Volcanoes

Attilius and his expedition reached the matrix of the Aqua Augusta just as the day was ending. One moment the engineer was watching the sun vanish behind the great mountain, silhouetting it against a red sky, making the trees look as though they were on fire, and the next it had gone. Looking ahead, he saw, rising out of the darkening plain, what appeared to be gleaming heaps of pale sand. He squinted at them, then spurred his horse and galloped ahead of the wagons.

Four pyramids of gravel were grouped around a roofless, circular brick wall, about the height of a man's waist. It was a settling tank. He knew there would be at least a dozen of these along the length of the Augusta – one every three or four miles was Vitruvius's recommendation – places where the water was deliberately slowed to collect impurities as they sank to the bottom. Masses of tiny pebbles, worn perfectly round and smooth as they were washed along the matrix, had to be dug out every few weeks and piled beside the aqueduct, to be carted away and either dumped or used for road-building.

A settling tank had always been a favourite place from which to run off a secondary line and as Attilius dismounted and strode across to it he saw that this was indeed the case here. The ground beneath his feet was spongy, the vegetation greener and more luxuriant, the soil singing with saturation. Water was bubbling over the carapace of the tank at every point, washing the brickwork with a shimmering, translucent film. The final manhole of the Pompeii spur lay directly in front of the wall.

He rested his hands on the lip and peered over the side. The tank was twenty feet across and, he would guess, at least fifteen deep. With the sun gone it was too dark to see all the way to the gravel floor but he knew there would be three tunnel mouths down there – one where the Augusta flowed in, one where it flowed out, and a third connecting Pompeii to the system. Water surged between his fingers. He wondered when Corvinus and Becco had shut off the sluices at Abellinum. With luck, the flow should be starting to ease very soon.

He heard feet squelching over the ground behind him. Brebix and a couple of the other men were walking across from the wagons.

'So is this the place, aquarius?'

'No, Brebix. Not yet. But not far now. You see that? The way the water is gushing from below? That's because the main line is blocked somewhere further down its course.' He wiped his hands on his tunic. 'We need to get moving again.'

It was not a popular decision, and quickly became even less so when they discovered that the wagons were sinking up to their axles in the mud. There was an outbreak of cursing and it took all their strength – shoulders and backs applied first to one cart and then to the other – to heave them up on to firmer ground. Half a dozen of the men went sprawling and lay there refusing to move and Attilius had to go round offering his hand and pulling them up on to their feet. They were tired, superstitious, hungry – it was worse than driving a team of ill-tempered mules.

He hitched his horse to the back of one of the wagons and when Brebix asked him what he was doing he said, 'I'll walk with the rest of you.' He took the halter of the nearest ox and tugged it forwards. It was the same story as when they left Pompeii. At first nobody moved but then, grudgingly, they set off after him. The natural impulse of men is to follow, he thought, and whoever has the strongest sense of purpose will always dominate the rest. Ampliatus understood that better than anyone he'd met.

They were crossing a narrow plain between high ground. Vesuvius was to their left; to their right, the distant cliffs of the Appenninus rose like a wall. The road had once again parted company with the aqueduct and they were following a track, plodding along beside the Augusta – marker-stone, manhole, marker-stone, manhole, on and on – through ancient groves of olives and lemons, as pools of darkness began to gather beneath the trees. There was little to hear above the rumble of the wheels except the occasional sound of goats' bells in the dusk.

Attilius kept glancing off to the line of the aqueduct. Water was bubbling around the edges of some of the manholes, and that was ominous. The aqueduct tunnel was six feet high. If the force of the water was sufficient to dislodge the heavy inspection covers, then the pressure must be immense, which in turn suggested that the obstruction in the matrix must be equally massive, otherwise it would have been swept away. Where were Corax and Musa?

An immense crash, like a peal of thunder, came from the direction of Vesuvius. It seemed to go rolling past them and echoed off the rock-face of the Appenninus with a flat boom. The ground heaved and the oxen shied, turning instinctively from the noise, dragging him with them. He dug his heels into the track and had just about managed to bring them to a halt when one of the men shrieked and pointed. 'The giants!' Huge white creatures, ghostly in the twilight, seemed to be issuing from beneath the earth ahead of them, as if the roof of Hades had split apart and the spirits of the dead were flying into the sky. Even Attilius felt the hair stiffen on the back of his neck and it was Brebix in the end who laughed and said, 'They're only birds, you fools! Look!'

Birds – immense birds: flamingos, were they? – rose in their hundreds like some great white sheet that fluttered and dipped and then settled out of sight again. Flamingos, thought Attilius: water birds.

In the distance he saw two men, waving.

N ero himself, if he had spent a year on the task, could not have wished for a finer artificial lake than that which the Augusta had created in barely a day and a half. A shallow depression to the north of the matrix had filled to a depth of three or four feet. The surface was softly luminous in the dusk, broken here and there by clumpy islands formed by the dark foliage of half-submerged olive trees. Water-fowl scudded between them; flamingos lined the distant edge.

The men of Attilius's work-gang did not stop for permission. They tore off their tunics and ran naked towards it, their sun-burnt bodies and dancing, snow-white buttocks giving them the appearance of some exotic herd of antelope come down for an evening drink and a bathe. Whoops and splashes carried to where Attilius stood with Musa and Corvinus. He made no attempt to stop them. Let them enjoy it while they could. Besides, he had a fresh mystery to contend with.

Corax was missing.

According to Musa, he and the overseer had discovered the lake less than two hours after leaving Pompeii – around noon it must have been – and it was exactly as Attilius had predicted: how could anyone miss a flood of this size? After a brief inspection of the damage, Corax had remounted his horse and set off back to Pompeii to report on the scale of the problem, as agreed.

Attilius's jaw was set in anger. 'But that must have been seven or eight hours ago.' He did not believe it. 'Come on, Musa – what really happened?'

'I'm telling you the truth, aquarius. I swear it!' Musa's eyes were wide in apparently sincere alarm. 'I thought he would be coming back with you. Something must have happened to him!'

Beside the open manhole, Musa and Corvinus had lit a fire, not to keep themselves warm – the air was still sultry – but to ward off evil. The timber they had found was as dry as tinder, the flames bright in the darkness, spitting fountains of red sparks that rose whirling with the smoke. Huge white moths mingled with the flakes of ash.

'Perhaps we missed him on the road somehow.'

Attilius peered behind him into the encroaching gloom. But even as he said it he knew that it could not be right. And in any case, a man on horseback, even if he had taken a different route, would surely have had time to reach Pompeii, discover they had left and catch up with them. 'This makes no sense.

Besides, I thought I made it clear that you were to bring us the message, not Corax.'

'You did.'

'Well?'

'He insisted on going to fetch you.'

He has run away, thought Attilius. It had to be the likeliest explanation. He and his friend Exomnius together – they had fled.

'This place,' said Musa, looking around. 'I'll be honest with you, Marcus Attilius – it gives me the creeps. That noise just now – did you hear it?'

'Of course we heard it. They must have heard it in Neapolis.'

'And just you wait till you see what's happened to the matrix.'

Attilius went over to one of the wagons and collected a torch. He returned and thrust it into the flames. It ignited immediately. The three of them gathered around the opening in the earth and once again he caught the whiff of sulphur rising from the darkness. 'Fetch me some rope,' he said to Musa. 'It's with the tools.' He glanced at Corvinus. 'And how did it go with you? Did you close the sluices?'

'Yes, aquarius. We had to argue with the priest but Becco convinced him.'

'What time did you shut it off?'

'The seventh hour.'

Attilius massaged his temples, trying to work it out. The level of water in the flooded tunnel would start to drop in a couple of hours. But unless he sent Corvinus back to Abellinum almost immediately, Becco would follow his instruction, wait twelve hours, and reopen the sluices during the sixth watch of the night. It was all desperately tight. They would never manage it.

When Musa came back Attilius handed him the torch. He tied one end of the rope around his waist and sat on the edge of the open manhole. He muttered, 'Theseus in the labyrinth.'

'What?'

'Never mind. Just make sure you don't let go of the other end, there's a good fellow.'

Three feet of earth, thought Attilius, then two of masonry and then six of nothing from the top of the tunnel roof to the floor. Eleven feet in all. I had better land well. He turned and lowered himself into the narrow shaft, his fingers holding tight to the lip of the manhole, and hung there for a moment, suspended. How many times had he done this? And yet never in more than a decade had he lost the sense of panic at finding himself entombed beneath the earth. It was his secret dread, never confessed to anyone, not even to his father. Especially not to his father. He shut his eyes and let himself drop, bending his knees as he landed to absorb the shock. He crouched there for a moment, recovering his balance, the stink of sulphur in his nostrils, then cautiously felt outwards with his hands. The tunnel was only three feet wide. Dry cement beneath his fingers. Darkness when he opened his eyes – as dark as when they were closed. He stood, squeezed himself back a pace and shouted up to Musa, 'Throw down the torch!'

The flame guttered as it fell and for a moment he feared it had gone out, but when he bent to take the handle it flared again, lighting the walls. The lower part was encrusted with lime deposited by the water over the years. Its roughened, bulging surface looked more like the wall of a cave than anything man-made and he thought how quickly Nature seized back what She had yielded – brickwork was crumbled by rain and frost, roads were buried under green drifts of weeds, aqueducts were clogged by the very water they were built to carry. Civilisation was a relentless war which Man was doomed to lose eventually. He picked at the lime with his thumbnail. Here was another example of Exomnius's idleness. The lime was almost as thick as his finger. It ought to have been scraped back every couple of years. No maintenance work had been done on this stretch for at least a decade.

He turned awkwardly in the confined space, holding the torch in front of him, and strained his eyes into the darkness. He could see nothing. He began to walk, counting each pace, and when he reached eighteen he gave a murmur of surprise. It was not simply that the tunnel was entirely blocked – he had expected that – but rather it seemed as if the floor had been driven upwards, pushed from below by some irresistible force. The thick concrete bed on which the channel rested had been sheared and a section of it sloped towards the roof. He heard Musa's muffled shout behind him: 'Can you see it?'

'Yes, I see it!'

The tunnel narrowed dramatically. He had to get down on his knees and shuffle forwards. The fracturing of the base had, in turn, buckled the walls and collapsed the roof. Water was seeping through a compressed mass of bricks and earth and lumps of concrete. He scraped at it with his free hand, but the stench of sulphur was at its strongest here and the flames of his torch began to dwindle. He backed away quickly, reversing all the way to the shaft of the manhole. Looking up he could just make out the faces of Musa and Corvinus framed by the evening sky. He leaned his torch against the tunnel wall.

'Hold the rope fast. I'm coming out.' He untied it from around his waist and gave it a sharp pull. The faces of the men had vanished. 'Ready?'

'Yes!'

He tried not to think of what might happen if they let him fall. He grasped the rope with his right hand and hauled himself up, then grabbed it with his left and hauled again. The rope swung wildly. He got his head and shoulders into the inspection shaft and for a moment he thought his strength would let him down but another heave with each hand brought his knees into contact with the aperture and he was able to wedge his back against the side of the shaft. He decided it was easier to let go of the rope and to work himself up, pushing his body up with his knees and then with his back, until his arms were over the side of the manhole and he was able to eject himself into the fresh night air.

He lay on the ground, recovering his breath as Musa and Corvinus watched him. A full moon was rising.

'Well?' said Musa. 'What did you make of it?'

The engineer shook his head. 'I've never come across anything like it. I've seen roof falls and I've seen land slips on the sides of mountains. But this? This looks as though an entire section of the floor has just been shifted upwards. That's new to me.'

'Corax said exactly the same.'

Attilius got to his feet and peered down the shaft. His torch was still burning on the tunnel floor. 'This land,' he said bitterly. 'It looks solid enough. But it's no more firm than water.' He started walking, retracing his steps along the course of the Augusta. He counted off eighteen paces and stopped. Now that he studied the ground more closely he saw that it was bulging slightly. He scraped a mark with the edge of his foot and walked on, counting again. The swollen section did not seem very wide. Six yards, perhaps, or eight. It was difficult to be precise.

He made another mark. Away to his left, Ampliatus's men were still clowning around in the lake.

He experienced a sudden rush of optimism. Actually, it wasn't too big, this blockage. The more he pondered it, the less likely it seemed to him to have been the work of an earthquake, which could easily have shaken the roof down along an entire section – now *that* would have been a disaster. But this was much more localised: more as if the land, for some strange reason, had risen a yard or two along a narrow line.

He turned in a full circle. Yes, he could see it now. The ground had heaved. The matrix had been obstructed. At the same time the pressure of the movement had opened a crack in the tunnel wall. The water had escaped into the depression and formed a lake. But if they could clear the blockage and let the Augusta drain . . .

He decided at that moment that he would not send Corvinus back to Abellinum. He would try to fix the Augusta overnight. To confront the impossible: that was the Roman way! He cupped his hands to his mouth and shouted to the men. 'All right, gentlemen! The baths are closing! Let's get to work!'

Women did not often travel alone along the public highways of Campania and, as Corelia passed them, the peasants working in the dried-up, narrow fields turned to stare at her. Even some brawny farmer's wife, as broad as she was tall and armed with a stout hoe, might have hesitated to venture out unprotected at vespera. But an obviously rich young girl? On a fine-looking horse? How juicy a prize was that? Twice men stepped out into the road and attempted to block her path or grab at the reins, but each time she spurred her mount onwards and after a few hundred paces they gave up trying to chase her.

She knew the route the aquarius had taken from her eaves-dropping that afternoon. But what had sounded a simple enough journey in a sunlit garden – following the line of the Pompeii aqueduct to the point where it joined the Augusta – was a terrifying undertaking when actually attempted at dusk and by the time she reached the vineyards on the foothills of Vesuvius she was wishing she had never come. It was true what her father said of her – headstrong, disobedient, foolish, that she acted first and thought about it afterwards. These were the familiar charges he had flung at her the previous evening in Misenum, after the death of the slave, as they were embarking to return to Pompeii. But it was too late to turn back now.

Work was ending for the day and lines of exhausted, silent slaves, shackled together at the ankle, were shuffling beside the road in the twilight. The clank of their chains against the stones and the flick of the overseer's whip across their backs were the only sounds. She had heard about such wretches, crammed into the prison blocks attached to the larger farms and worked to death within a year or two: she had never actually seen them close up. Occasionally a slave found the energy to raise his eyes from the dirt and meet her glance; it was like staring through a hole into hell.

And yet she would not give in, even as nightfall emptied the road of traffic and the line of the aqueduct became harder to follow. The reassuring sight of the villas on the lower slopes of the mountain gradually dissolved, to be replaced by isolated points of torchlight and lamplight, winking in the darkness. Her horse slowed to a walk and she swayed in the saddle in time with its plodding motion.

It was hot. She was thirsty. (Naturally, she had forgotten

to bring any water: that was something the slaves always carried for her.) She was sore where her clothes chafed against her sweating skin. Only the thought of the aquarius and the danger he was in kept her moving. Perhaps she would be too late? Perhaps he had been murdered already? She was just beginning to wonder whether she would ever catch up with him when the heavy air seemed to turn solid and to hum around her, and an instant later, from deep inside the mountain to her left, came a loud crack. Her horse reared, pitching her backwards, and she was almost thrown, the reins snapping through her sweaty fingers, her damp legs failing to grip its heaving flanks. When it plunged forwards again and set off at a gallop she only saved herself by wrapping her fingers tightly in its thick mane and clinging for her life.

It must have charged for a mile or more and when at last it began to slow and she was able to raise her head she found that they had left the road and were cantering over open ground. She could hear water somewhere near and the horse must have heard it, too, or smelled it, because it turned and began walking towards the sound. Her cheek had been pressed close to the horse's neck, her eyes shut tight, but now, as she raised her head, she could make out white heaps of stone and a low brick wall that seemed to enclose an enormous well. The horse bent to drink. She whispered to it, and gently, so as not to alarm it, dismounted. She was trembling with shock.

Her feet sank into mud. Far in the distance she could see the lights of camp fires.

Attilius's first objective was to remove the debris from underground: no easy task. The tunnel was only wide enough for one man at a time to confront the obstruction, to swing a pick-axe and dig with a shovel, and once a basket was filled it had to be passed along the matrix from hand to hand until it reached the bottom of the inspection shaft, then attached to a rope and hauled to the surface, emptied, and sent back again, by which time a second basket had already been loaded and dispatched on its way.

Attilius, in his usual way, had taken the first turn with the pick. He tore a strip from his tunic and tied it round his mouth and nose to try to reduce the smell of the sulphur. Hacking away at the brick and earth and then shovelling it into the basket was bad enough. But trying to wield the axe in the cramped space and still find the force to smash the concrete into manageable lumps was a labour fit for Hercules. Some of the fragments took two men to carry and before long he had scraped his elbows raw against the walls of the tunnel. As for the heat, compounded by the sweltering night, the sweating bodies and the burning torches – that was worse than he imagined it could be even in the gold mines of Hispania. But still, Attilius had a sense of progress, and that gave him extra strength. He had found the spot where the Augusta was choked. All his problems would be overcome if could clear these few narrow yards.

After a while, Brebix tapped him on the shoulder and offered to take over. Attilius gratefully handed him the pick and watched in admiration as the big man, despite the fact that his bulk completely filled the tunnel, swung it as easily as if it were a toy. The engineer squeezed back along the line and the others shifted to make room for him. They were working as a team now, like a single body: the Roman way again. And whether it was the restorative effects of their bathe, or relief at having a specific task to occupy their thoughts, the mood of the men appeared transformed. He began to think that perhaps they were not such bad fellows after all. You could say what you liked about Ampliatus: at least he knew how to train a slave-gang. He took the heavy basket from the man beside him – the same man, he noticed, whose wine he had kicked away – turned and shuffled with it to the next in the line.

Gradually he lost track of time, his world restricted to this narrow few feet of tunnel, his sensations to the ache of his arms and back, the cuts on his hands from the sharp debris, the pain of his skinned elbows, the suffocating heat. He was so absorbed that at first he did not hear Brebix shouting to him.

'Aquarius! *Aquarius!*'

'Yes?' He flattened himself against the wall and edged past the men, aware for the first time that the water in the tunnel was up to his ankles. 'What is it?'

'Look for yourself.' Attilius took a torch from the man behind him and held it up close to the compacted mass of the blockage. At first glance it looked solid enough, but then he saw that it was seeping water everywhere. Tiny rivulets were running down the oozing bulk, as if it had broken into a sweat. 'See what I mean?' Brebix prodded it with the axe. 'If this lot goes, we'll be drowned like rats in a sewer.'

Attilius was aware of the silence behind him. The slaves had all stopped work and were listening. Looking back he saw that they had already cleared four or five yards of debris. So what was left to hold back the weight of the Augusta? A few feet? He did not want to stop. But he did not want to kill them all, either.

'All right,' he said, reluctantly. 'Clear the tunnel.'

They needed no second telling, leaning the torches up against the walls, dropping their tools and baskets and lining up for the rope. No sooner had one man climbed it, his feet disappearing into the inspection shaft, than another had it in his hands and was hauling himself to safety. Attilius followed Brebix up the tunnel and by the time they reached the manhole they were the only ones left below ground.

Brebix offered him the rope. Attilius refused it. 'No. You go. I'll stay down and see what else can be done.' He realised Brebix was looking at him as if he were mad. 'I'll fasten the rope around me for safety. When you get to the top, untie it from the wagon and pay out enough for me to reach the end of the tunnel. Keep a firm hold.'

Brebix shrugged. 'Your choice.'

As he turned to climb, Attilius caught his arm. 'You are strong enough to hold me, Brebix?'

The gladiator grinned briefly. 'You – and your fucking mother!'

Despite his weight, Brebix ascended the rope as nimbly as a monkey, and then Attilius was alone. As he knotted the rope around his waist for a second time he thought that perhaps he *was* mad, but there seemed no alternative, for until the tunnel was drained they could not repair it, and he did not have the time to wait for all the water to seep through the obstruction. He tugged on the rope. 'All right, Brebix?'

'Ready!'

He picked up his torch and began moving back along the tunnel, the water above his ankles now, sloshing around his shins as he stepped over the abandoned tools and baskets. He moved slowly, so that Brebix could pay out the rope, and by the time he reached the debris he was sweating, from nerves as much as from the heat. He could sense the weight of the Augusta behind it. He transferred the torch into his left hand

and with his right began pulling at the exposed end of a brick that was level with his face, working it up and down and from side to side. A small gap was what he needed: a controlled release of pressure from somewhere near the top. At first the brick wouldn't budge. Then water started to bubble around it and suddenly it shot through his fingers, propelled by a jet that fired it past his head, so close that it grazed his ear.

He cried out and backed away as the area around the leak bulged then sprang apart, peeling outwards and downwards in a V – all of this occurring in an instant, yet somehow slowly enough for him to register each individual stage of the collapse – before a wall of water descended over him, smashing him backwards, knocking the torch out of his hand and submerging him in darkness. He hurtled underwater very fast – on his back, head-first – swept along the tunnel, scrabbling for a purchase on the smooth cement render of the matrix, but there was nothing he could grip. The surging current rolled him, flipped him over on to his stomach, and he felt a flash of pain as the rope snapped tight beneath his ribs, folding him and jerking him upwards, grazing his back against the roof. For a moment he thought he was saved, only for the rope to go slack again and for him to plunge to the bottom of the tunnel, the current sweeping him on – on like a leaf in a gutter – on into the darkness.

Nocte concubia

*'Many observers have commented on the tendency for
eruptions to be initiated or become stronger at times of
full moon when the tidal stresses in the crust are
greatest.'*

Volcanology *(second edition)*

A mpliatus had never cared much for Vulcanalia. The
festival marked that point in the calendar when nights
fell noticeably earlier and mornings had to start by
candlelight: the end of the promise of summer and the start of
the long, melancholy decline into winter. And the ceremony
itself was distasteful. Vulcan dwelt in a cave beneath a mountain and spread devouring fire across the earth. All creatures
went in fear of him, except for fish, and so – on the principle
that gods, like humans, desire most that which is least attain-
able – he had to be appeased by a sacrifice of fish thrown alive
on to a burning pyre.

It was not that Ampliatus was entirely lacking in religious
feeling. He always liked to see a good-looking animal slaugh-
tered – the placid manner of a bull, say, as it plodded towards
the altar, and the way it stared at the priest so bemusedly; then
the stunning and unexpected blow from the assistant's hammer
and the flash of the knife as its throat was cut; the way it fell,

as stiff as a table, with its legs sticking out; the crimson gouts of blood congealing in the dust and the yellow sac of guts boiling from its slit belly for inspection by the haruspices. Now *that* was religious. But to see hundreds of small fish tossed into the flames by the superstitious citizenry as they filed past the sacred fire, to watch the silvery bodies writhing and springing in the heat: there was nothing noble in it as far as he was concerned.

And it was particularly tedious this year because of the record numbers who wished to offer a sacrifice. The endless drought, the failure of springs and the drying of wells, the shaking of the ground, the apparitions seen and heard on the mountain – all this was held to be the work of Vulcan, and there was much apprehension in the town. Ampliatus could see it in the reddened, sweating faces of the crowd as they shuffled around the edge of the forum, staring into the fire. The fear in the air was palpable.

He did not have a very good position. The rulers of the town, as tradition demanded, were gathered on the steps of the Temple of Jupiter – the magistrates and the priests at the front, the members of the Ordo, including his own son, grouped behind, whereas Ampliatus, as a freed slave, with no official recognition, was invariably banished by protocol to the back. Not that he minded. On the contrary. He relished the fact that power, *real* power, should be kept hidden: an invisible force that permitted the people these civic ceremonials while all the time jerking the participants as if they were marionettes. Besides, and this was what was truly exquisite, most people knew that it was actually he – that fellow standing third from the end in the tenth row – who really ran the town. Popidius and Cuspius, Holconius and Brittius – they knew it, and he felt that they squirmed, even as they acknowledged the tribute of the mob. And most of the mob knew it, too, and were all the more respectful towards him as a result. He could see them searching out his face, nudging and pointing.

'*That's Ampliatus,*' he imagined them saying, '*who rebuilt the town when the others ran away! Hail Ampliatus! Hail Ampliatus! Hail Ampliatus!*'

He slipped away before the end.

Once again, he decided he would walk rather than ride in his litter, passing down the steps of the temple between the ranks of the spectators – a nod bestowed here, an elbow squeezed there – along the shadowy side of the building, under the triumphal arch of Tiberius and into the empty street. His slaves carried his litter behind him, acting as a bodyguard, but he was not afraid of Pompeii after dark. He knew every stone of the town, every hump and hollow in the road, every storefront, every drain. The vast full moon and the occasional streetlight – another of his innovations – showed him the way home clearly enough. But it was not just Pompeii's buildings he knew. It was its people, and the mysterious workings of its soul, especially at elections: five neighbourhood wards – Forenses, Campanienses, Salinienses, Urbulanenses, Pagani – in each of which he had an agent; and all the craft guilds – the laundrymen, the bakers, the fishermen, the perfume-makers, the goldsmiths and the rest – again, he had them covered. He could even deliver half the worshippers of Isis, his temple, as a block vote. And in return for easing whichever booby he selected into power he received those licences and permits, planning permissions and favourable judgements in the Basilica which were the invisible currency of power.

He turned down the hill towards his house – his *houses*, he should say – and stopped for a moment to savour the night air. He loved this town. In the early morning the heat could feel oppressive, but usually, from the direction of Capri, a line of dark blue rippling waves would soon appear and by the fourth hour a sea breeze would be sweeping over the city, rustling the leaves, and for the rest of the day Pompeii would smell as sweet as spring. True, when it was hot and listless, as it was tonight, the grander people complained that the town stank. But he almost preferred it when the air was heavier – the dung of the horses in the streets, the urine in the laundries, the fish sauce factories down in the harbour, the sweat of twenty thousand human bodies crammed within the city walls. To Ampliatus this was the smell of life: of activity, money, profit.

He resumed his walk and when he reached his front door he stood beneath the lantern and knocked loudly. It was still a pleasure for him to come in through the entrance he had not been permitted to use as a slave and he rewarded the porter with a smile. He was in an excellent mood, so much so that he turned when he was halfway down the vestibule and said, 'Do you know the secret of a happy life, Massavo?'

The porter shook his immense head.

'To die.' Ampliatus gave him a playful punch in the stomach and winced; it was like striking wood. 'To die, and then to come back to life, and relish every day as a victory over the gods.'

He was afraid of nothing, no one. And the joke was, he was not nearly as rich as everyone assumed. The villa in Misenum – ten million sesterces, far too expensive, but he had simply had to have it! – that had only been bought by borrowing, chiefly on the strength of this house, which had itself been paid for through a mortgage on the baths, and they were not even finished. Yet Ampliatus kept it all running somehow by the force of his will, by cleverness and by public confidence, and if that fool Lucius Popidius thought he was getting his old family home back once he had married Corelia – well, sadly, he should have got himself a decent lawyer before he signed the settlement.

As he passed the swimming pool, lit by torches, he paused to study the fountain. The mist of the water mingled with the scent of the roses, but even as he watched it seemed to him that it was beginning to lose its strength, and he thought of the solemn young aquarius, out in the darkness somewhere, trying to repair the aqueduct. He would not be coming back. It was a pity. They might have done business together. But he was honest, and Ampliatus's motto was always 'May the gods protect us from an honest man'. He might even be dead by now.

The flaccidity of the fountain began to perturb him. He thought of the silvery fish, springing and sizzling in the flames, and tried to imagine the reaction of the townspeople when they discovered the aqueduct was failing. Of course, he realised, they would blame it all on Vulcan, the superstitious fools. He had not considered that. In which case tomorrow might be an appropriate moment finally to produce the prophecy of Biria Onomastia, the sibyl of Pompeii, which he had taken the precaution of commissioning earlier in the summer. She lived in a house near the amphitheatre and at night, amid swathes of smoke, she communed with the ancient god, Sabazios, to whom she sacrificed snakes – a disgusting procedure – on an altar supporting two magical bronze hands. The whole ceremony had given him the creeps, but the sibyl had predicted an amazing future for Pompeii, and it would be useful to let word of it spread. He decided he would summon the magistrates in the morning. For now, while the others were still in the forum, he had more urgent business to attend to.

His prick began to harden even as he climbed the steps to the private apartments of the Popidii, a path he had trodden so many times, so long ago, when the old master had used him like a dog. What secret, frantic couplings these walls had witnessed over the years, what slobbering endearments they had overheard as Ampliatus had submitted to the probing fingers and had spread himself for the head of the household. Far younger than Celsinus he had been, younger even than Corelia – who was she to complain about marriage in the absence of love? Mind you, the master had always whispered that he loved him, and perhaps he had – after all, he had left him his freedom in his will. Everything that Ampliatus had grown to be had had its origin in the hot seed spilled up here. He had never forgotten it.

The bedroom door was unlocked and he went in without knocking. An oil lamp burned low on the dressing table. Moonlight spilled through the open shutters, and by its soft glow he saw Taedia Secunda lying prone upon her bed, like a corpse upon its bier. She turned her head as he appeared. She was naked; sixty if she was a day. Her wig was laid out on a dummy's head beside the lamp, a sightless spectator to what was to come. In the old days it was she who had always issued the commands – here, there, *there* – but now the roles were reversed, and he was not sure if she didn't enjoy it more, although she never uttered a word. Silently she turned and raised herself on her hands and knees, offering him her bony haunches, blue-sheened by the moon, waiting, motionless, while her former slave – her master now – climbed up on to her bed.

* * *

T wice after the rope gave way Attilius managed to jam his knees and elbows against the narrow walls of the matrix in an effort to wedge himself fast and twice he succeeded only to be pummelled loose by the pressure of the water and propelled further along the tunnel. Limbs weakening, lungs bursting, he sensed he had one last chance and tried again, and this time he stuck, spread wide like a starfish. His head broke the surface and he choked and spluttered, gasping for breath.

In the darkness he had no idea where he was or how far he had been carried. He could see and hear nothing, feel nothing except the cement against his hands and knees and the pressure of the water up to his neck, hammering against his body. He had no idea how long he clung there but gradually he became aware that the pressure was slackening and that the level of the water was falling. When he felt the air on his shoulders he knew that the worst was over. Very soon after that his chest was clear of the surface. Cautiously he let go of the walls and stood. He swayed backward in the slow-moving current and then came upright, like a tree that had survived a flash-flood.

His mind was beginning to work again. The backed-up waters were draining away and because the sluices had been closed in Abellinum twelve hours earlier there was nothing left to replenish them. What remained was being tamed and reduced by the infinitesimal gradient of the aqueduct. He felt something tugging at his waist. The rope was streaming out behind him. He fumbled for it in the darkness and hauled it in, coiling it around his arm. When he reached the end he ran his fingers over it. Smooth. Not frayed or hacked. Brebix must simply have let go of it. Why? Suddenly he was panicking, frantic to escape. He leaned forward and began to wade but it was like a nightmare – his hands stretched out invisible in front him feeling along the walls into the infinite dark, his legs unable to move faster than an old man's shuffle. He felt himself doubly imprisoned, by the earth pressing in all around him, by the weight of the water ahead. His ribs ached. His shoulder felt as if it had been branded by fire.

He heard a splash and then in the distance a pin-prick of yellow light dropped like a falling star. He stopped wading and listened, breathing hard. More shouts, followed by a second splash, and then another torch appeared. They were searching for him. He heard a faint shout – 'Aquarius!' – and tried to decide whether he should reply. He was scaring himself with shadows, surely? The wall of debris had given way so abruptly and with such force that no normal man would have had the strength to hold him. But Brebix was not a man of normal strength and what had happened was not unexpected: the glad-iator was supposed to have been braced against it.

'Aquarius!'

He hesitated. There was no other way out of the tunnel, that was for certain. He would have to go on and face them. But his instinct told him to keep his suspicions to himself. He shouted back, 'I'm here!' and splashed on through the dwin-dling water towards the waving lights.

They greeted him with a mixture of wonder and respect – Brebix, Musa and young Polites all crowding forward to meet him – for it had seemed to them, they said, that nothing could have survived the flood. Brebix insisted that the rope had shot through his hands like a serpent and as proof he showed his palms. In the torchlight each was crossed by a vivid burn-mark. Perhaps he was telling the truth. He sounded contrite enough. But then any assassin would look shame-faced if his victim came back to life. 'As I recall it, Brebix, you said you could hold me and my mother.'

'Aye, well your mother's heavier than I thought.'

'You're favoured by the gods, aquarius,' declared Musa. 'They have some destiny in mind for you.'

'My destiny,' said Attilius, 'is to repair this fucking aqueduct and get back to Misenum.' He unfastened the rope from around his waist, took Polites's torch and edged past the men, shining the light along the tunnel.

How quickly the water was draining! It was already below his knees. He imagined the current swirling past him, on its way to Nola and the other towns. Eventually it would work its way all around the bay, across the arcades north of Neapolis and over the great arch at Cumae, down the spine of the peninsula to Misenum. Soon this section would be drained entirely. There would be nothing more than puddles on the floor. Whatever happened, he had fulfilled his promise to the admiral. He had cleared the matrix.

The point where the tunnel had been blocked was still a mess but the force of the flood had done most of their work for them. Now it was a matter of clearing out the rest of the earth and rubble, smoothing the floor and walls, putting down a bed of concrete and a fresh lining of bricks, then a render of cement – nothing fancy: just temporary repairs until they could get back to do a proper job in the autumn. It was still a lot of work to get through in a night, before the first tongues of fresh water reached them from Abellinum, after Becco had reopened the sluices. He told them what he wanted and Musa started adding his own suggestions. If they brought down the bricks now, he said, they could stack them along the wall and have them ready to use when the water cleared. They could make a start on mixing the cement above ground immediately. It was the first time he had shown any desire to co-operate since Attilius had taken charge of the aqueduct. He seemed awed by the engineer's survival. I should come back from the dead more often, Attilius thought.

Brebix said, 'At least that stink has gone.'

Attilius had not noticed it before. He sniffed the air. It was true. The pervasive stench of sulphur seemed to have been washed away. He wondered what that had all been about – where it had come from in the first place, why it should have evaporated – but he did not have time to consider it. He heard his name being called and he kicked his way back through the water to the inspection shaft. It was Corvinus's voice: 'Aquarius!'

'Yes?' The face of the slave was silhouetted by a red glow. 'What is it?'

'I think you ought to come and see.' His head disappeared abruptly.

Now what? Attilius took the rope and tested it carefully, then started climbing. In his bruised and exhausted state it was harder work than before. He ascended slowly – right hand, left hand, right hand, hauling himself into the narrow access shaft, working himself up, thrusting his arms over the lip of the manhole and levering himself out into the warm night.

In the time he had been underground the moon had risen – huge, full and red. It was like the stars in this part of the world – like everything, in fact – unnatural and overblown. There was quite an operation in progress on the surface by now: the heaps of spoil excavated from the tunnel, a couple of big bonfires spitting sparks at the harvest moon, torches planted in the ground to provide additional light, the wagons drawn up and mostly unloaded. He could see a thick rim of mud in the moonlight around the shallow lake, where it had already mostly drained. The slaves of Ampliatus's work-gang were leaning against the carts, waiting for orders. They watched him with curiosity as he hauled himself to his feet. He must look a sight, he realised, drenched and dirty. He shouted into the tunnel for Musa to come up and set them back to work, then looked around for Corvinus. He was about thirty paces away, close to the oxen, with his back to the manhole. Attilius shouted to him impatiently.

'Well?'

Corvinus turned and by way of explanation stepped aside, revealing behind him a figure in a hooded cloak. Attilius set off towards them. It was only as he came closer and the stranger pulled back the hood that he recognised her. He could not have been more startled if Egeria herself, the goddess of the water-spring, had suddenly materialised in the moonlight. His first instinct was that she must have come with her father and he looked around for other riders, other horses. But there was only one horse, chewing placidly on the thin grass. She was alone and as he reached her he raised his hands in astonishment.

'Corelia – what is this?'

'She wouldn't tell me what she wants,' interrupted Corvinus. 'She says she'll only talk to you.'

'Corelia?'

She nodded suspiciously towards Corvinus, put her finger to her lips and shook her head.

'See what I mean? The moment she turned up yesterday I knew she was trouble –'

'All right, Corvinus. That's enough. Get back to work.'

'But –'

'*Work!*'

As the slave slouched away he examined her more closely. Cheeks smudged, hair dishevelled, cloak and dress spattered with mud. But it was her eyes, unnaturally wide and bright, that were most disturbing. He took her hand. 'This is no place for you,' he said gently. 'What are you doing here?'

'I wanted to bring you these,' she whispered and from the folds of her cloak she began producing small cylinders of papyrus.

T he documents were of different ages and conditions. Six in total, small enough to fit into the cradle of one arm. Attilius took a torch and with Corelia beside him moved away from the activity around the aqueduct to a private spot behind one of the wagons, looking out over the flooded ground. Across what remained of the lake ran a wavering path of moonlight, as wide and straight as a Roman road. From the far side came the rustle of wings and the cries of the waterfowl.

He took her cloak from her shoulders and spread it out for her to sit on. Then he jammed the handle of the torch into the earth, squatted and unrolled the oldest of the documents. It was a plan of one section of the Augusta – this very section: Pompeii, Nola and Vesuvius were all marked in ink that had faded from black to pale grey. It was stamped with the imperial seal of the Divine Augustus as if it had been inspected and officially approved. A surveyor's drawing. Original. Drafted more than a century ago. Perhaps the great Marcus Agrippa himself had once held it in his hands? He turned it over. Such a document could only have come from one of two places, either the archive of the Curator Aquarum in Rome, or the Piscina Mirabilis in Misenum. He rolled it carefully.

The next three papyri consisted mostly of columns of numerals and it took him a while to make much sense of them. One was headed *Colonia Veneria Pompeianorum* and was divided into years – DCCCXIV, DCCCXV and so on – going back nearly two decades, with further subdivisions of notations, figures and totals. The quantities increased annually until, by the year that had ended last December – Rome's eight hundred and thirty-third – they had doubled. The second document seemed at first glance to be identical until he studied it more closely and then he saw that the figures throughout were roughly half as large as in the first. For example, for the last year, the grand total of three hundred and fifty-two thousand recorded in the first papyrus had been reduced in the second to one hundred and seventy-eight thousand.

The third document was less formal. It looked like the monthly record of a man's income. Again there were almost two decades' worth of figures and again the sums gradually mounted until they had almost doubled. And a good income it was – perhaps fifty thousand sesterces in the last year alone, maybe a third of a million overall.

Corelia was sitting with her knees drawn up, watching him. 'Well? What do they mean?'

He took his time answering. He felt tainted: the shame of one man, the shame of them all. And who could tell how high the rot had spread? But then he thought, No, it would not have gone right the way up to Rome, because if Rome had been a part of it, Aviola would never have sent him south to Misenum. 'These look like the actual figures for the amount of water consumed in Pompeii.' He showed her the first papyrus. 'Three hundred and fifty thousand quinariae last year – that would be about right for a town of Pompeii's size. And this second set of records I presume is the one that my predecessor, Exomnius, officially submitted to Rome. They wouldn't know the difference, especially after the earthquake, unless they sent an inspector down to check. And this' – he did not try to hide his contempt as he flourished the third document – 'is what your father paid him to keep his mouth shut.' She looked at him, bewildered. 'Water is expensive,' he explained, 'especially if you're rebuilding half a town. "At least as valuable as money" – that's what your father said to me.' No doubt it would have made the difference between profit and loss. *Salve lucrum!*

He rolled up the papyri. They must have been stolen from the squalid room above the bar. He wondered why Exomnius would have run the risk of keeping such an incriminating record so close to hand. But then he supposed that incrimination was precisely what Exomnius would have had in mind. They would have given him a powerful hold over Ampliatus: *Don't ever think of trying to move against me – of silencing me, or cutting me out of the deal, or threatening me with exposure – because if I am ruined, I can ruin you with me.*

Corelia said, 'What about those two?'

The final pair of documents were so different from the others it was as if they did not belong with them. They were much newer, for a start, and instead of figures they were covered in writing. The first was in Greek.

The summit itself is mostly flat, and entirely barren. The soil looks like ash, and there are cave-like pits of blackened rock, looking gnawed by fire. This area appears to have been on fire

in the past and to have had craters of flame which were subse-
quently extinguished by a lack of fuel. No doubt this is the
reason for the fertility of the surrounding area, as at Caetana,
where they say that soil filled with the ash thrown up by Etna's
flames makes the land particularly good for vines. The enriched
soil contains both material that burns and material that fosters
production. When it is over-charged with the enriching substance
it is ready to burn, as is the case with all sulphurous substances,
but when this has been exuded and the fire extinguished the soil
becomes ash-like and suitable for produce.

Attilius had to read it through twice, holding it to the torch-light, before he was sure he had the sense of it. He passed it to Corelia. *The summit?* The summit of what? Of Vesuvius, presumably – that was the only summit round here. But had Exomnius – lazy, ageing, hard-drinking, whore-loving Exomnius – really found the energy to climb all the way up to the top of Vesuvius, in a drought, to record his impressions in Greek? It defied belief. And the language – *'cave-like pits of blackened rock . . . fertility of the surrounding area'* – that didn't sound like the voice of an engineer. It was too literary, not at all the sort of phrases that would come naturally to a man like Exomnius, who was surely no more fluent in the tongue of the Hellenes than Attilius was himself. He must have copied it from somewhere. Or had it copied for him. By one of the scribes in that public library on Pompeii's forum, perhaps.

The final papyrus was longer, and in Latin. But the content was equally strange:

Lucilius, my good friend, I have just heard that Pompeii, the
famous city in Campania, has been laid low by an earthquake

which also disturbed all the adjacent districts. Also, part of the town of Herculaneum is in ruins and even the structures which are left standing are shaky. Neapolis also lost many private dwellings. To these calamities others were added: they say that a flock of hundreds of sheep were killed, statues were cracked, and some people were deranged and afterwards wandered about unable to help themselves.

I have said that a flock of hundreds of sheep were killed in the Pompeiian district. There is no reason you should think this happened to those sheep because of fear. For they say that a plague usually occurs after a great earthquake, and this is not surprising. For many death-carrying elements lie hidden in the depths. The very atmosphere there, which is stagnant either from some flaw in the earth or from inactivity and the eternal darkness, is harmful to those breathing it. I am not surprised that sheep have been infected — sheep which have a delicate constitution — the closer they carried their heads to the ground, since they received the afflatus of the tainted air near to the ground itself. If the air had come out in greater quantity it would have harmed people too; but the abundance of pure air extinguished it before it rose high enough to be breathed by people.

Again, the language seemed too flowery to be the work of Exomnius, the execution of the script too professional. In any case, why would Exomnius have claimed to have *just heard* about an earthquake which had happened seventeen years earlier? And who was Lucilius? Corelia had leaned across to read the document over his shoulder. He could smell her perfume, feel her breath on his cheek, her breast pressed against his arm. He said, 'And you are sure these were with the other papyri? They could not have come from somewhere else?'

'They were in the same box. What do they mean?'

'And you didn't see the man who brought the box to your father?'

Corelia shook her head. 'I could only hear him. They talked about you. It was what they said that made me decide to find you.' She shifted fractionally closer to him and lowered her voice. 'My father said he didn't want you to come back from this expedition alive.'

'Is that so?' He made an effort to laugh. 'And what did the other man say?'

'He said that it would not be a problem.'

Silence. He felt her hand touch his — her cool fingers on his raw cuts and scratches — and then she rested her head against his chest. She was exhausted. For a moment, for the first time in three years, he allowed himself to relish the sensation of a having a woman's body close to his.

So this was what it was like to be alive, he thought. He had forgotten.

After a while she fell asleep. Carefully, so as not to wake her, he disengaged his arm. He left her and walked back over to the aqueduct.

The repair work had reached a decisive point. The slaves had stopped bringing debris up out of the tunnel and had started lowering bricks down into it. Attilius nodded warily to Brebix and Musa who were standing talking together. Both men fell silent as he approached and glanced beyond him to the place where Corelia was lying, but he ignored their curiosity.

His mind was in a turmoil. That Exomnius was corrupt was no surprise — he had been resigned to that. And he had assumed his dishonesty explained his disappearance. But these other documents, this piece of Greek and this extract from a letter, these cast the mystery in a different light entirely. Now it seemed that Exomnius had been worried about the soil through which the Augusta passed – the sulphurous, tainted soil – at least three weeks before the aqueduct had been contaminated. Worried enough to look out a set of the original plans and to go researching in Pompeii's library.

Attilius stared distractedly down into the depths of the matrix. He was remembering his exchange with Corax in the Piscina Mirabilis the previous afternoon: Corax's sneer – *'He knew this water better than any man alive. He would have seen this coming'* – and his own, unthinking retort – *'Perhaps he did, and that was why he ran away.'* For the first time he had a presentiment of something terrible. He could not define it. But too much was happening that was out of the ordinary – the failure of the matrix, the trembling of the ground, springs running backwards into the earth, sulphur poisoning . . . Exomnius had sensed it, too.

The fire of the torches glowed in the tunnel.

'Musa?'

'Yes, aquarius?'

'Where was Exomnius from? Originally?'

'Sicily, aquarius.'

'Yes, yes, I know Sicily. Which part exactly?'

'I think the east.' Musa frowned. 'Caetana. Why?'

But the engineer, gazing across the narrow moonlit plain towards the shadowy mass of Vesuvius, did not reply.

JUPITER

24 August

The day of the eruption

Hora prima

[06:20 hours]

'At some point, hot magma interacted with ground-water seeping downwards through the volcano, initiating the first event, the minor phreato-magmatic eruption which showered fine-grained grey tephra over the eastern flanks of the volcano. This probably took place during the night or on the morning of 24 August.'

Volcanoes: A Planetary Perspective

H e kept his increasing anxiety to himself all through the sweltering night, as they worked by torchlight to repair the matrix.

He helped Corvinus and Polites on the surface mix the wooden troughs of cement, pouring in the quicklime and the powdery puteolanum and a tiny amount of water – no more than a cupful, mind, because that was the first secret of making a good cement: the drier the mixture, the stronger it set – and then he helped the slaves carry it down in baskets into the matrix and spread it out to form a new base for the conduit. He helped Brebix smash up the rubble they had dug out earlier and they added a couple of layers of that into the base, for strength. He helped saw the planks they used to shutter the walls and to crawl along over the wet cement. He passed bricks to Musa as he laid them. Finally he stood shoulder-to-shoulder with Corvinus to apply the thin coat of render. (And here was the second secret of perfect cement: to pound it as hard as possible, 'hew it as you would hew wood', to squeeze out every last bubble of water or air which might later be a source of weakness.)

By the time the sky above the manhole was turning grey he knew that they had probably done enough to bring the Augusta back into service. He would have to return to repair her properly. But for now, with a bit of luck, she would hold. He walked with his torch to the end of the patched-up section, inspecting every foot. The waterproof render would be setting even as the aqueduct started to flow again. By the end of the first day it would be hard; by the end of the third it would be stronger than rock.

If being stronger than rock means anything any more. But he kept the thought to himself.

'Cement that dries underwater,' he said to Musa when he came back. 'Now *that* is a miracle.'

He let the others climb up ahead of him. The breaking day showed that they had pitched their camp in rough pasture, littered with large stones, flanked by mountains. To the east were the steep cliffs of the Appenninus, with a town – Nola, presumably – just becoming visible in the dawn light about five or six miles away. But the shock was to discover how close they were to Vesuvius. It lay directly to the west and the land started to rise almost immediately, within a few hundred paces of the aqueduct, steepening to a point so high the engineer had to tilt his head back to see the summit. And what was most unsettling, now that the shadows were lifting, were the streaks of greyish-white beginning to appear across one of its flanks. They stood out clearly against the surrounding forest, shaped like arrow-heads, pointing towards the summit. If it had not been August he would have sworn that they were made of snow. The others had noticed them as well.

'Ice?' said Brebix, gawping at the mountain. 'Ice in August?'

'Did you ever see such a thing, aquarius?' asked Musa.

Attilius shook his head. He was thinking of the description in the Greek papyri: *'the ash thrown up by Etna's flames makes the land particularly good for vines'*.

'Could it,' he said hesitantly, almost to himself, 'could it perhaps be *ash*?'

'But how can there be ash without fire?' objected Musa. 'And if there had been a fire that size in the darkness we would have seen it.'

'That's true.' Attilius glanced around at their exhausted, fearful faces. The evidence of their work was everywhere – heaps of rubble, empty amphorae, dead torches, scorched patches where the night's fires had been allowed to burn themselves out. The lake had gone, and with it, he noticed, the birds. He had not heard them leave. Along the mountain ridge opposite Vesuvius the sun was beginning to appear. There was a strange stillness in the air. No birdsong of any sort, he realised. No dawn chorus. That would send the augurs into a frenzy. 'And you're sure it was not there yesterday, when you arrived with Corax?'

'Yes.' Musa was staring at Vesuvius transfixed. He wiped his hands uneasily on his filthy tunic. 'It must have happened last night. That crash which shook the ground, remember? That must have been it. The mountain has cracked and spewed.'

There was a general muttering of uneasiness among the men and someone cried out, 'That can only be the giants!'

Attilius wiped the sweat from his eyes. It was starting to feel hot already. Another scorching day in prospect. And something more than heat – a tautness, like a drumskin stretched too far. Was it his mind playing tricks, or did the ground seem to be vibrating slightly? A prickle of fear stirred the hair on the back of his scalp. Etna and Vesuvius – he was beginning to sense the same terrible connection that Exomnius must have recognised.

'All right,' he said briskly. 'Let's get away from this place.' He set off towards Corelia. 'Bring everything up out of the matrix,' he called over his shoulder. 'And look sharp about it. We've finished here.'

She was still asleep, or at least he thought she was. She was lying beside the more distant of the two wagons, curled up on her side, her legs drawn up, her hands raised in front of her face and balled into fists. He stood looking down at her for a moment, marvelling at the incongruity of her beauty in this desolate spot – Egeria among the humdrum tools of his profession.

'I've been awake for hours.' She rolled on to her back and opened her eyes. 'Is the work finished?'

'Finished enough.' He knelt and began collecting together the papyri. 'The men are going back to Pompeii. I want you to go on ahead of them. I'll send an escort with you.'

She sat up quickly. 'No!'

He knew how she would react. He had spent half the night thinking about it. But what other choice did he have? He spoke quickly. 'You must return those documents to where you found them. If you set off now you should be back in Pompeii well before midday. With luck, he need never know you took them, or brought them out here to me.'

'But they are the proof of his corruption –'

'No.' He held up his hand to quiet her. 'No, they're not.

On their own, they mean nothing. Proof would be Exomnius giving testimony before a magistrate. But I don't have him. I don't have the money your father paid him or even a single piece of evidence that he spent any of it. He's been very careful. As far as the world is concerned, Exomnius was as honest as Cato. Besides, this isn't as important as getting you away from here. Something's happening to the mountain. I'm not sure what. Exomnius suspected it weeks ago. It's as if —' He broke off. He didn't know how to put it into words. 'It's as if it's — *coming alive*. You'll be safer in Pompeii.'

She was shaking her head. 'And what will you do?'

'Return to Misenum. Report to the admiral. If anyone can make sense of what is happening, he can.'

'Once you're alone they'll try to kill you.'

'I don't think so. If they'd wanted to do that, they had plenty of chances last night. If anything, I'll be safer. I have a horse. They're on foot. They couldn't catch me even if they tried.'

'I also have a horse. Take me with you.'

'That's impossible.'

'Why? I can ride.'

For a moment he played with the image of the two of them turning up in Misenum together. The daughter of the owner of the Villa Hortensia sharing his cramped quarters at the Piscina Mirabilis. Hiding her when Ampliatus came looking for her. How long would they get away with it? A day or two. And then what? The laws of society were as inflexible as the laws of engineering.

'Corelia, listen.' He took her hands. 'If I could do anything to help you, in return for what you've done for me, I would. But this is madness, to defy your father.'

'You don't understand.' Her grip on his fingers was ferocious. 'I can't go back. Don't make me go back. I can't bear to see him again, or to marry that man –'

'But you know the law. When it comes to marriage, you're as much your father's property as any one of those slaves over there.' What could he say? He hated the words even as he uttered them. 'It may not turn out to be as bad as you fear.' She groaned, pulled away her hands and buried her face. He blundered on. 'We can't escape our destiny. And, believe me, there are worse ones than marrying a rich man. You could be working in the fields and dead at twenty. Or a whore in the back streets of Pompeii. Accept what has to happen. Live with it. You'll survive. You'll see.'

She gave him a long, slow look – contempt, was it, or hatred? 'I swear to you, I sooner would be a whore.'

'And I swear you would not.' He spoke more sharply. 'You're young. What do you know of how people live?'

'I know I cannot be married to someone I despise. Could you?' She glared at him. 'Perhaps you could.'

He turned away. 'No, Corelia.'

'Are you married?'

'No.'

'But you *were* married?'

'Yes,' he said quietly, 'I was married. My wife is dead.'

That shut her up for a moment. 'And did you despise her?'

'Of course not.'

'Did she despise you?'

'Perhaps she did.'

She was briefly silent again. 'How did she die?'

He did not ever talk of it. He did not even think of it. And if, as sometimes happened, especially in the wakeful hours before dawn, his mind ever started off down that miserable road, he had trained himself to haul it back and set it on a different course. But now — there was something about her: she had got under his skin. To his astonishment, he found himself telling her.

'She looked something like you. And she had a temper, too, like yours.' He laughed briefly, remembering. 'We were married three years.' It was madness; he could not stop himself. 'She was in childbirth. But it came from the womb feet first, like Agrippa. That's what the name means – Agrippa – aegre partus – "born with difficulty" – did you know that? I thought at first it was a fine omen for a future aquarius, to be born like the great Agrippa. I was sure it was a boy. But the day went on – it was June in Rome, and hot: almost as hot as down here – and even with a doctor and two women in attendance, the baby would not move. And then she began to bleed.' He closed his eyes. 'They came to me before nightfall. "Marcus Attilius, choose between your wife and your child!" I said that I chose both. But they told me that was not to be, so I said – of course I said – "My wife." I went into the room to be with her. She was very weak, but she disagreed. Arguing with me, even then! They had a pair of shears, you know – the sort that a gardener might use? And a knife. And a hook. They cut off one foot, and then the other, and used the knife to quarter the body, and then the hook to draw out the skull. But Sabina's bleeding didn't stop, and the next morning she also died. So I don't know. Perhaps at the end she did despise me.'

He sent her back to Pompeii with Polites. Not because the Greek slave was the strongest escort available, or the best horseman, but because he was the only one Attilius trusted. He gave him Corvinus's mount and told him not to let her out of his sight until she was safely home.

She went meekly in the end, with barely another word, and he felt ashamed of what he had said. He had silenced her well enough, but in a coward's way – unmanly and self-pitying. Had ever an unctuous lawyer in Rome used a cheaper trick of rhetoric to sway a court than this ghastly parading of the ghosts of a dead wife and child? She swept her cloak around her and then flung her head back, flicking her long dark hair over her collar, and there was something impressive in the gesture: she would do as he asked but she would not accept that he was right. Never a glance in his direction as she swung herself easily into the saddle. She made a clicking sound with her tongue and tugged the reins and set off down the track behind Polites.

It took all his self-control not to run after her. A poor reward, he thought, for all the risks she ran for me. But what else did she expect of him? And as for fate – the subject of his pious little lecture – he *did* believe in fate. One was shackled to it from birth as to a moving wagon. The destination of the journey could not be altered, only the manner in which one approached it – whether one chose to walk erect or to be dragged complaining through the dust.

Still, he felt sick as he watched her go, the sun brightening the landscape as the distance between them increased, so that he was able to watch her for a long time, until at last the horses passed behind a clump of olive trees, and she was gone.

I n Misenum, the admiral was lying on his mattress in his windowless bedroom, remembering.

He was remembering the flat, muddy forests of Upper Germany, and the great oak trees that grew along the shore of the northern sea – if one could speak of a shore in a place where the sea and the land barely knew a boundary – and the rain and the wind, and the way that in a storm the trees, with a terrible splintering, would sometimes detach themselves from the bank, vast islands of soil trapped within their roots, and drift upright, their foliage spread like rigging, bearing down on the fragile Roman galleys. He could still see in his mind the sheet lightning and the dark sky and the pale faces of the Chauci warriors amid the trees, the smell of the mud and the rain, the terror of the trees crashing into the ships at anchor, his men drowning in that filthy barbarian sea –

He shuddered and opened his eyes to the dim light, hauled himself up, and demanded to know where he was. His secretary, sitting beside the couch next to a candle, his stylus poised, looked down at his wax tablet.

'We were with Domitius Corbulo, admiral,' said Alexion, 'when you were in the cavalry, fighting the Chauci.'

'Ah yes. Just so. The Chauci. I remember –'

But what did he remember? The admiral had been trying for months to write his memoirs – his final book, he was sure – and it was a welcome distraction from the crisis on the aqueduct to return to it. But what he had seen and done and what he had read or been told seemed nowadays to run together, in a kind of seamless dream. Such things he had witnessed! The empresses – Lollia Paulina, Caligula's wife, sparkling like a fountain in the candlelight at her betrothal banquet, cascading with forty million sesterces' worth of pearls and emeralds. And the Empress Agrippina, married to the drooling Claudius: he had seen her pass by in a cloak made entirely out of gold. And gold-mining he had watched, of course, when he was procurator in northern Spain – the miners cutting away at the mountainside, suspended by ropes, so that they looked, from a distance, like a species of giant bird pecking at the rockface. Such work, such danger – and to what end? Poor Agrippina, murdered here, in this very town, by Ancietus, his predecessor as admiral of the Misene Fleet, on the orders of her son, the Emperor Nero, who put his mother to sea in a boat that collapsed and then had her stabbed to death by sailors when she somehow struggled ashore. Stories! This was his problem. He had too many stories to fit into one book.

'The Chauci –' How old was he then? Twenty-four? It was his first campaign. He began again. 'The Chauci, I remember, dwelt on high wooden platforms to escape the treacherous tides of that region. They gathered mud with their bare hands, which they dried in the freezing north wind, and burnt for fuel. To drink they consumed only rainwater, which they collected in tanks at the front of their houses – a sure sign of their lack of civilisation. Miserable bloody bastards, the Chauci.' He paused. 'Leave that last bit out.'

The door opened briefly, admitting a shaft of brilliant white light. He heard the rustling of the Mediterranean, the hammering of the shipyards. So it was morning already. He must have been awake for hours. The door closed again. A slave tip-toed across to the secretary and whispered into his ear. Pliny rolled his fat body over on to one side to get a better view. 'What time is it?'

'The end of the first hour, admiral.'

'Have the sluices been opened at the reservoir?'

'Yes, admiral. We have a message that the last of the water has drained away.'

Pliny groaned and flopped back on to his pillow.

'And it seems, sir, that a most remarkable discovery has just been made.'

The work-gang had left about a half-hour after Corelia. There were no elaborate farewells: the contagion of fear had spread throughout the men to infect Musa and Corvinus and all were eager to get back to the safety of Pompeii. Even Brebix, the former gladiator, the undefeated hero of thirty fights, kept turning his small, dark eyes nervously towards Vesuvius. They cleared the matrix and flung the tools, the unused bricks and the empty amphorae on to the backs of the wagons. Finally, a couple of the slaves shovelled earth across the remains of the night's fires and buried the grey scars left by the cement. By the time this was finished it was as if they had never been there.

Attilius stood warily beside the inspection shaft with his arms folded and watched them prepare to leave. This was his moment of greatest danger, now that the work was done. It would be typical of Ampliatus to make sure he extracted a final measure of use out of the engineer before dispensing with him. He was ready to fight, to sell himself dearly if he had to.

Musa had the only other horse and once he was in the saddle he called down to Attilius. 'Are you coming?'

'Not yet. I'll catch you up later.'

'Why not come now?'

'Because I'm going to go up on to the mountain.'

Musa looked at him, astonished. 'Why?'

A good question. *Because the answer to what has been happening down here must lie up there. Because it's my job to keep the water running. Because I am afraid.* The engineer shrugged. 'Curiosity. Don't worry. I haven't forgotten my promise, if that's what's bothering you. Here.' He threw Musa his leather purse. 'You've done well. Buy the men some food and wine.'

Musa opened the purse and inspected its contents. 'There's plenty here, aquarius. Enough for a woman as well.'

Attilius laughed. 'Go safely, Musa. I'll see you soon. Either in Pompeii or Misenum.'

Musa gave him a second glance and seemed about to say something, but changed his mind. He wheeled away and set off after the carts and Attilius was alone.

Again, he was struck by the peculiar stillness of the day, as if Nature were holding Her breath. The noise of the heavy wooden wheels slowly faded into the distance and all he could hear was the occasional tinkle of a goat's bell and the ubiquitous chafing of the cicadas. The sun was quite high now. He glanced around at the empty countryside, then lay on his stomach and peered into the matrix. The heat pressed heavily on his back and shoulders. He thought of Sabina and of Corelia and of the terrible image of his dead son. He wept. He did not try to stop himself but for once surrendered to it, choking and shaking with grief, gulping the tunnel air, inhaling the cold and bitter odour of the wet cement. He felt oddly apart from himself, as if he had divided into two people, one crying and the other watching him cry.

After a while he stopped and raised himself to wipe his face on the sleeve of his tunic and it was only when he looked down again that his eye was caught by something – by a glint of reflected light in the darkness. He drew his head back slightly to let the sun shine directly along the shaft and he saw very faintly that the floor of the aqueduct was glistening.

He rubbed his eyes and looked again. Even as he watched the quality of the light seemed to change and become more substantial, rippling and widening as the tunnel began to fill with water.

He whispered to himself, 'She runs!'

When he was satisfied that he was not mistaken and that the Augusta had indeed begun to flow again, he rolled the heavy manhole cover across to the shaft. He slowly lowered it, pulling his fingers back at the last instant to let it drop the final few inches. With a thud the tunnel was sealed.

He untethered his horse and climbed into the saddle. In the shimmering heat, the marker-stones of the aqueduct dwindled into the distance like a line of submerged rocks. He pulled on the reins and turned away from the Augusta to face Vesuvius. He spurred the horse and they moved off along the track that led towards the mountain, walking at first but quickening to a trot as the ground began to rise.

At the Piscina Mirabilis the last of the water had drained away and the great reservoir was empty – a rare sight. It had last been allowed to happen a decade ago and that had been for maintenance, so that the slaves could shovel out the sediment and check the walls for signs of cracking. The admiral listened attentively as the slave explained the workings of the system. He was always interested in technical matters.

'And how often is this supposed to be done?'

'Every ten years would be customary, admiral.'

'So this was going to be done again soon?'

'Yes, admiral.'

They were standing on the steps of the reservoir, about

halfway down – Pliny, his nephew Gaius, his secretary Alexion, and the water-slave, Dromo. Pliny had issued orders that nothing was to be disturbed until he arrived and a marine guard had been posted at the door to prevent unauthorised access. Word of the discovery had got out, however, and there was the usual curious crowd in the courtyard.

The floor of the Piscina looked like a muddy beach after the tide had gone out. There were little pools here and there, where the sediment was slightly hollowed, and a litter of objects – rusted tools, stones, shoes – that had fallen into the water over the years and had sunk to the bottom, some of them entirely shrouded so that they appeared as nothing more than small humps on the smooth surface. The rowing boat was grounded. Several sets of footprints led out from the bottom of the steps towards the centre of the reservoir, where a larger object lay, and then returned. Dromo asked if the admiral would like him to fetch it.

'No,' said Pliny, 'I want to see it where it lies for myself. Oblige me, would you, Gaius.' He pointed to his shoes and his nephew knelt and unbuckled them while the admiral leaned on Alexion for support. He felt an almost childish anticipation and the sensation intensified as he descended the last of the steps and cautiously lowered his feet into the sediment. Black slime oozed between his toes, deliciously cool, and immediately he was a boy again, back at the family home in Comum, in Transpadane Italy, playing on the shores of the lake, and the intervening years – nearly half a century of them – were as insubstantial as a dream. How many times did this occur each day? It never used to happen. But lately almost anything could set it off – a touch, a smell, a sound, a colour glimpsed – and immediately memories he did not know he still possessed came flooding back, as if there was was nothing left of him any more but a breathless sack of remembered impressions.

He hoisted the folds of his toga and began stepping gingerly across the surface, his feet sinking deep into the mud, which then made a delightful sucking noise each time he lifted them. He heard Gaius shout behind him, 'Be careful, uncle!' but he shook his head, laughing. He kept away from the tracks the others had made: it was more enjoyable to rupture the crust of mud where it was still fresh and just beginning to harden in the warm air. The others followed at a respectful distance.

What an extraordinary construction it was, he thought, this underground vault, with its pillars each ten times higher than a man! What imagination had first envisioned it, what will and strength had driven it through to construction – and all to store water that had already been carried for sixty miles! He had never had any objection to deifying emperors. 'God is man helping man,' that was his philosophy. The Divine Augustus deserved his place in the pantheon simply for commissioning the Campanian aqueduct and the Piscina Mirabilis. By the time he reached the centre of the reservoir he was breathless with the effort of repeatedly hoisting his feet out of the clinging sediment. He propped himself against a pillar as Gaius came up beside him. But he was glad that he had made the effort. The water-slave had been wise to send for him. This was some-thing to see, right enough: a mystery of Nature had become also a mystery of Man.

The object in the mud was an amphora used for storing quicklime. It was wedged almost upright, the bottom part buried in the soft bed of the reservoir. A long, thin rope had been attached to its handles and this lay in a tangle around it. The lid, which had been sealed with wax, had been prised off. Scattered, gleaming in the mud, were perhaps a hundred small silver coins.

'Nothing has been removed, admiral,' said Dromo anxiously. 'I told them to leave it exactly as they found it.'

Pliny blew out his cheeks. 'How much is in there, Gaius, would you say?'

His nephew buried both hands into the amphora, cupped them, and showed them to the admiral. They brimmed with silver denarii. 'A fortune, uncle.'

'And an illegal one, we may be sure. It corrupts the honest mud.' Neither the earthenware vessel nor the rope had much of a coating of sediment, which meant, thought Pliny, that it could not have lain on the reservoir floor for long – a month at most. He glanced up towards the vaulted ceiling. 'Someone must have rowed out,' he said, 'and lowered it over the side.'

'And then let go of the rope?' Gaius looked at him in wonder. 'But who would have done such a thing? How could he have hoped to retrieve it? No diver could swim down this deep!'

'True.' Pliny dipped his own hand into the coins and examined them in his plump palm, stroking them apart with his thumb. Vespasian's familiar, scowling profile decorated one side, the sacred implements of the augur occupied the other. The inscription round the edge – IMP CAES VESP AVG COS III – showed that they had been minted during the Emperor's third consulship, eight years earlier. 'Then we must assume that their owner didn't plan to retrieve them by diving, Gaius, but by draining the reservoir. And the only man with the authority to empty the piscina whenever he desired was our missing aquarius, Exomnius.'

Hora quarta

[10:37 hours]

'Average magma ascent rates obtained in recent studies suggest that magma in the chamber beneath Vesuvius may have started rising at a velocity of > 0.2 metres per second into the conduit of the volcano some four hours before the eruption – that is, at approximately 9 a.m. on the morning of 24 August.'

Burkhard Müller-Ullrich (editor), Dynamics of Volcanism

The quattuorviri – the Board of Four: the elected magistrates of Pompeii – were meeting in emergency session in the drawing room of Lucius Popidius. The slaves had carried in a chair for each of them, and a small table, around which they sat, mostly silent, arms folded, waiting. Ampliatus, out of deference to the fact that he was not a magistrate, reclined on a couch in the corner, eating a fig, watching them. Through the open door he could see the swimming pool and its silent fountain, and also, in a corner of the tiled garden, a cat playing with a little bird. This ritual of extended death intrigued him. The Egyptians held the cat to be a sacred animal: of all creatures the nearest in intelligence to Man. And in the whole of Nature, only cats and men – that he could think of – derived an obvious pleasure from cruelty. Did that mean that cruelty and intelligence were inevitably entwined? Interesting.

He ate another fig. The noise of his slurping made Popidius wince. 'I must say, you seem supremely confident, Ampliatus.' There was an edge of irritation in his voice.

'I am supremely confident. You should relax.'

'That's easy enough for you to say. Your name is not on fifty notices spread around the city assuring everyone that the water will be flowing again by midday.'

'Public responsibility – the price of elected office, my dear Popidius.' He clicked his juicy fingers and a slave carried over a small silver bowl. He dunked his hands and dried them on the slave's tunic. 'Have faith in Roman engineering, your honours. All will be well.'

It was four hours since Pompeii had woken to another hot and cloudless day and to the discovery of the failure of its water supply. Ampliatus's instinct for what would happen next had proved correct. Coming on the morning after most of the town had turned out to sacrifice to Vulcan it was hard, even for the least superstitious, not to see this as further evidence of the god's displeasure. Nervous groups had started forming on the street corners soon after dawn. Placards, signed by L. Popidius Secundus, posted in the forum and on the larger fountains, announced that repairs were being carried out on the aqueduct and that the supply would resume by the seventh hour. But it was not much reassurance for those who remembered the terrible earthquake of seventeen years ago – the water had failed on that occasion, too – and all morning there had been uneasiness across the town. Some shops had failed to open. A few people had left, with their possessions piled on carts, loudly proclaiming that Vulcan was about to destroy Pompeii for a second time. And now word had got out that the quattuorviri were meeting at the House of Popidius. A crowd had gathered in the street outside.

Occasionally, in the comfortable drawing room, the noise of the mob could be heard: a growl, like the sound of the beasts in their cages in the tunnels of the amphitheatre, immediately before they were let loose to fight the gladiators.

Brittius shivered. 'I told you we should never have agreed to help that engineer.'

'That's right,' agreed Cuspius. 'I said so right at the start. Now look where it's got us.'

You could learn so much from a man's face, thought Ampliatus. How much he indulged himself in food and drink, what manner of work he did, his pride, his cowardice, his strength. Popidius, now: he was handsome and weak; Cuspius, like his father, brave, brutal, stupid; Brittius sagged with self-indulgence; Holconius vinegary-sharp and shrewd – too many anchovies and too much garum sauce in *that* diet.

'Balls,' said Ampliatus amiably. 'Think about it. If we hadn't helped him, he would simply have gone to Nola for assistance and we would still have lost our water, only a day later – and how would that have looked when Rome got to hear of it? Besides, this way we know where he is. He's in our power.'

The others did not notice, but old Holconius turned round at once. 'And why is it so important that we know where he is?'

Ampliatus was momentarily lost for an answer. He laughed it off. 'Come on, Holconius! Isn't it always useful to know as much as possible? That's worth the price of lending him a few slaves and some wood and lime. Once a man is in your debt, isn't it easier to control him?'

'That's certainly true,' said Holconius drily and glanced across the table at Popidius.

Even Popidius was not stupid enough to miss the insult. He

flushed scarlet. 'Meaning?' he demanded. He pushed back his chair.

'Listen!' commanded Ampliatus. He wanted to stop this conversation before it went any further. 'I want to tell you about a prophecy I commissioned in the summer, when the tremors started.'

'A prophecy?' Popidius sat down again. He was immediately interested. He loved all that stuff, Ampliatus knew: old Biria with her two magical bronze hands, covered in mystic symbols, her cage full of snakes, her milky-white eyes that couldn't see a man's face but could stare into the future. 'You've consulted the sibyl? What did she say?'

Ampliatus arranged his features in a suitably solemn expression. 'She sacrificed serpents to Sabazius, and skinned them for their meaning. I was present throughout.' He remembered the flames on the altar, the smoke, the glittering hands, the incense, the sibyl's wavering voice: high-pitched, barely human – like the curse of that old woman whose son he had fed to the eels. He had been awed by the whole performance, despite himself. 'She saw a town – our town – many years from now. A thousand years distant, maybe more.' He let his voice fall to a whisper. 'She saw a city famed throughout the world. Our temples, our amphitheatre, our streets – thronging with people of every tongue. That was what she saw in the guts of the snakes. Long after the Caesars are dust and the Empire has passed away, what we have built here will endure.'

He sat back. He had half convinced himself. Popidius let out his breath. 'Biria Onomastia,' he said, 'is never wrong.'

'And she will repeat all this?' asked Holconius sceptically. 'She will let us use the prophecy?'

'She will,' Ampliatus affirmed. 'She'd better. I paid her

plenty for it.' He thought he heard something. He rose from the couch and walked out into the sunshine of the garden. The fountain that fed the swimming pool was in the form of a nymph tipping a jug. As he came closer he heard it again, a faint gurgling, and then water began to trickle from the vessel's lip. The flow stuttered, spurted, seemed to stop, but then it began to run more strongly. He felt suddenly overwhelmed by the mystic forces he had unleashed. He beckoned to the others to come and look. 'You see. I told you. The prophecy is correct!'

Amid the exclamations of pleasure and relief, even Holconius managed a thin smile. 'That's good.'

'Scutarius!' Ampliatus shouted to the steward. 'Bring the quattuorviri our best wine – the Caecuban, why not? Now, Popidius, shall I give the mob the news or will you?'

'You tell them, Ampliatus. I need a drink.'

Ampliatus swept across the atrium towards the great front door. He gestured to Massavo to open it and stepped out on to the threshold. Perhaps a hundred people – *his* people was how he liked to think of them – were crowded into the street. He held up his arms for silence. 'You all know who I am,' he shouted, when the murmur of voices had died away, 'and you all know you can trust me!'

'Why should we?' someone shouted from the back.

Ampliatus ignored him. 'The water is running again! If you don't believe me – like that insolent fellow there – go and look at the fountains and see for yourselves. The aqueduct is repaired! And later today, a wonderful prophecy, by the sibyl, Biria Onomastia, will be made public. It will take more than a few trembles in the ground and one hot summer to frighten the colony of Pompeii!'

A few people cheered. Ampliatus beamed and waved.

'Good day to you all, citizens! Let's get back to business. *Salve lucrum! Lucrum gaudium!*' He ducked back into the vestibule. 'Throw them some money, Scutarius,' he hissed, still smiling at the mob. 'Not too much, mind you. Enough for some wine for them all.'

He lingered long enough to hear the effects of his largesse, as the crowd struggled for the coins, then headed back towards the atrium, rubbing his hands with delight. The disappearance of Exomnius had jolted his equanimity, he would not deny it, but in less than a day he had dealt with the problem, the fountain looked to be running strongly, and if that young aquarius was not dead yet he would be soon. A cause for celebration! From the drawing room came the sound of laughter and the clink of crystal glass. He was about to walk around the pool to join them when, at his feet, he noticed the body of the bird he had watched being killed. He prodded it with his toe then stopped to pick it up. Its tiny body was still warm. A red cap, white cheeks, black and yellow wings. There was a bead of blood in its eye.

A goldfinch. Nothing to it but fluff and feathers. He weighed it in his hand for a moment, some dark thought moving in the back of his mind, then let it drop and quickly mounted the steps into the pillared garden of his old house. The cat saw him coming and darted out of sight behind a bush but Ampliatus was not interested in pursuing it. His eyes were fixed on the empty cage on Corelia's balcony and the darkened, shuttered windows of her room. He bellowed, 'Celsia!' and his wife came running. 'Where's Corelia?'

'She was ill. I let her sleep —'

'Get her! Now!' He shoved her in the direction of the staircase, turned, and hurried towards his study.

It was not possible —

She would not dare —

He knew there was something wrong the moment he picked up the lamp and took it over to his desk. It was an old trick, learned from his former master — a hair in the drawer to tell him if a curious hand had been meddling in his affairs — but it worked well enough, and he had let it be understood that he would crucify the slave who could not be trusted.

There was no hair. And when he opened the strong box and took out the document case there were no papyri, either. He stood there like a fool, tipping up the empty *capsa* and shaking it like a magician who had forgotten the rest of his trick, then hurled it across the room where it splintered against the wall. He ran out to the courtyard. His wife had opened Corelia's shutters and was standing on the balcony, her hands pressed to her face.

Corelia had her back to the mountain as she came through the Vesuvius Gate and into the square beside the castellum aquae. The fountains had started to run again, but the flow was still weak and from this high vantage point it was possible to see that a dusty pall had formed over Pompeii, thrown up by the traffic in the waterless streets. The noise of activity rose as a general hum above the red roofs.

She had taken her time on the journey home, never once spurring her horse above walking pace as she skirted Vesuvius and crossed the plain. She saw no reason to speed up now. As she descended the hill towards the big crossroads, Polites plodding faithfully behind her, the blank walls of the houses seemed to rise on either side to enclose her like a prison. Places she had relished since childhood – the hidden pools and the scented flower gardens, the shops with their trinkets and fabrics, the theatres and the noisy bath-houses – were as dead to her now as ash. She noticed the angry, frustrated faces of the people at the fountains, jostling to jam their pots beneath the dribble of water, and she thought again of the aquarius. She wondered where he was and what he was doing. His story of his wife and child had haunted her all the way back to Pompeii.

She knew that he was right. Her fate was inescapable. She felt neither angry nor afraid any more as she neared her father's house, merely dead to it all – exhausted, filthy, thirsty. Perhaps this would be her life from now on, her body going through the routine motions of existence and her soul elsewhere, watchful and separate? She could see a crowd in the street up ahead, bigger than the usual collection of hangers-on who waited for hours for a word with her father. As she watched they seemed to break into some outlandish, ritualistic dance, leaping into the air with their arms outstretched then dropping to their knees to scrabble on the stones. It took her a moment to realise that they were having money thrown to them. That was typical of her father, she thought – the provincial Caesar, trying to buy the affection of the mob, believing himself to be acting like an aristocrat, never recognising his own puffed-up vulgarity.

Her contempt was suddenly greater than her hatred and it strengthened her courage. She led the way round to the back of the house, towards the stables, and at the sound of the hooves on the cobbles an elderly groom came out. He looked wide-eyed with surprise at her dishevelled appearance, but she took no notice. She jumped down from the saddle and handed him the reins. 'Thank you,' she said to Polites and then, to the groom, 'See that this man is given food and drink.'

She passed quickly out of the glare of the street and into the gloom of the house, climbing the stairs from the slaves' quarters. As she walked she drew the rolls of papyri from beneath her cloak. Marcus Attilius had told her to replace them in her father's study and hope their removal had not been noticed. But she would not do that. She would give them to him herself. Even better, she would tell him where she had been. He would know that she had discovered the truth and then he could do to her what he pleased. She did not care. What could be worse than the fate he had already planned? You cannot punish the dead.

It was with the exhilaration of rebellion that she emerged through the curtain into the House of Popidius and walked towards the swimming pool that formed the heart of the villa. She heard voices to her right and saw in the drawing room her future husband and the magistrates of Pompeii. They turned to look at her at exactly the moment that her father, with her mother and brother behind him, appeared on the steps leading to their old home. Ampliatus saw what she was carrying and for one glorious instant she saw the panic in his face. He shouted at her – 'Corelia!' – and started towards her but she swerved away and ran into the drawing room, scattering his secrets across the table and over the carpet before he had a chance to stop her.

It seemed to the engineer that Vesuvius was playing a game with him, never coming any closer however hard he rode towards her. Only occasionally, when he looked back, shielding his eyes against the sun, did he realise how high he was climbing. Soon he had a clear view of Nola. The irrigated fields around it were like a clear green square, no larger than a doll's handkerchief lying unfolded on the brown Campanian plain. And Nola itself, an old Samnite fortress, appeared no more formidable than a scattering of tiny children's bricks dropped off the edge of the distant mountain range. The citizens would have their water running by now. The thought gave him fresh confidence.

He had deliberately aimed for the edge of the nearest white-grey streak and he reached it soon after the middle of the morning, at the point where the pastureland on the lower slopes ended and the forest began. He passed no living creature, neither man nor animal. The occasional farmhouse beside the track was deserted. He guessed everyone must have fled, either in the night when they heard the explosion or at first light, when they woke to this ghostly shrouding of ash. It lay across the ground, like a powdery snow, quite still, for there was not a breath of wind to disturb it. When he jumped down from his horse he raised a cloud that clung to his sweating legs. He scooped up a handful. It was odourless, fine-grained, warm from the sun. In the distant trees it covered the foliage exactly as would a light fall of snow.

He put a little in his pocket, to take back to show the admiral, and drank some water, swilling the dry taste of the dust from his mouth. Looking down the slope he could see another rider, perhaps a mile away, also making steady progress towards this same spot, presumably led by a similar curiosity to discover what had happened. Attilius considered waiting for him, to exchange opinions, but decided against it. He wanted to press on. He spat out the water, remounted, and rode back across the flank of the mountain, away from the ash, to rejoin the track that led into the forest.

Once he was among the trees the woodland closed around him and quickly he lost all sense of his position. There was nothing for it but to follow the hunters' track as it wound through the trees, over the dried-up beds of streams, meandering from side to side but always leading him higher. He dismounted to take a piss. Lizards rustled away among the dead leaves. He saw small red spiders and their fragile webs, hairy caterpillars the size of his forefinger. There were clumps of crimson berries that tasted sweet on his tongue. The vegetation was commonplace – alder, brambles, ivy. Torquatus, the captain of the liburnian, had been right, he thought: Vesuvius was easier to ascend than she looked, and when the streams were full there would be enough up here to eat and drink to sustain an army. He could readily imagine the Thracian gladiator, Spartacus, leading his followers along this very trail a century and a half before, climbing towards the sanctuary of the summit.

It took him perhaps another hour to pass through the forest. He had little sense of time. The sun was mostly hidden by the trees, falling in shafts through the thick canopy of leaves. The sky, broken into fragments by the foliage, formed a brilliant, shifting pattern of blue. The air was hot, fragrant with the scent of dried pine and herbs. Butterflies flitted among the trees. There was no noise except the occasional soft hooting of wood pigeons. Swaying in the saddle in the heat he felt drowsy. His head nodded. Once he thought he heard a larger animal moving along the track behind him but when he stopped to listen the sound had gone. Soon afterwards the forest began to thin. He came to a clearing.

And now it was as if Vesuvius had decided to play a different game. Having for hours never seemed to come any closer, suddenly the peak rose directly in front of him – a few hundred feet high, a steeper incline, mostly of rock, without sufficient soil to support much in the way of vegetation except for straggly bushes and plants with small yellow flowers. And it was exactly as the Greek writer had described: a black cap, long ago scorched by fire. In places, the rock bulged outwards, almost as if it were being pushed up from beneath, sending small flurries of stones rattling down the slope. Further along the ridge, larger landslips had occurred. Huge boulders, the size of a man, had been sent crashing into the trees – and recently, by the look of them. Attilius remembered the reluctance of the men to leave Pompeii. *'Giants have journeyed through the air, their voices like claps of thunder . . .'* The sound must have carried for miles.

It was too steep a climb for his horse. He dismounted and found a shady spot where he could tie its reins to a tree. He scouted around for a stick and selected one about half as thick as his wrist – smooth, grey, long-dead – and with that to support his weight he set out to begin his final ascent.

The sun up here was merciless, the sky so bright it was almost white. He moved from rock to cindery rock in the suffocating heat and the air itself seemed to burn his lungs, a dry heat, like a blade withdrawn from a fire. No lizards underfoot here, no birds overhead – it was a climb directly into the sun. He could feel the heat through the soles of his shoes. He forced himself to press on, without looking back, until the ground ceased to rise and what was ahead of him was no longer black rock but blue sky. He clambered over the ridge and peered across the roof of the world.

The summit of Vesuvius was not the sharp peak that it had appeared from the base but a rough and circular plain, perhaps two hundred paces in diameter, a wilderness of black rock, with a few brownish patches of sickly vegetation that merely emphasised its deadness. Not only did it look to have been on fire in the past, as the Greek papyri had said, but to be burning now. In at least three places thin columns of grey vapour were rising, fluttering and hissing in the silence. There was the same sour stench of sulphur that there had been in the pipes of the Villa Hortensia. This is the place, thought Attilius. This is the heart of the evil. He could sense something huge and malevolent. One could call it Vulcan or give it whatever name one liked. One could worship it as a god. But it was a tangible presence. He shuddered.

He kept close to the edge of the summit and began working his way around it, mesmerised to begin with by the sulphurous clouds that were whispering from the ground and then by the astonishing panoramas beyond the rim. Away to his right the bare rock ran down to the edge of the forest, and then there was nothing but an undulating green blanket. Torquatus had said that you could see for fifty miles, but to Attilius it seemed that the whole of Italy was spread beneath him. As he moved from north to west the Bay of Neapolis came into his vision. He could easily make out the promontory of Misenum and the islands off its point, and the imperial retreat of Capri, and beyond them, as sharp as a razor-cut, the fine line where the deep blue of the sea met the paler blue of the sky. The water was still flecked by the waves he had noticed the night before – scudding waves on a windless sea – although now he thought about it perhaps there *was* a breeze beginning to get up. He could feel it on his cheek: the one they called Caurus, blowing from the north-west, towards Pompeii, which appeared at his feet as no more than a sandy smudge set back from the coast.

He imagined Corelia arriving there, utterly unreachable now, a dot within a dot, lost to him forever.

It made him feel light-headed simply to look at it, as if he were himself nothing but a speck of pollen that might be lifted at any moment by the hot air and blown into the blueness. He felt an overwhelming impulse to surrender to it – a yearning for that perfect blue oblivion so strong that he had to force himself to turn away. Shaken, he began to pick his way directly across the summit towards the other side, back to where he had started, keeping clear of the plumes of sulphur which seemed to be multiplying all around him. The ground was shaking, bulging. He wanted to get away now, as fast as he could. But the terrain was rough, with deep depressions on either side of his path – 'cave-like pits of blackened rock', as the Greek writer had said – and he had to watch where he put his feet. And it was because of this – because he had his head down – that he smelled the body before he saw it.

It stopped him in his tracks – a sweet and cloying stink that entered his mouth and nostrils and coated them with a greasy film. The stench was emanating from the large dust bowl straight ahead of him. It was perhaps six feet deep and thirty across, simmering like a cauldron in the haze of heat, and what was most awful, when he peered over the side, was that everything in it was dead: not just the man, who wore a white tunic and whose limbs were so purplish-black Attilius thought at first he was a Nubian, but other creatures – a snake, a large bird, a litter of small animals – all scattered in this pit of death. Even the vegetation was bleached and poisoned.

The corpse was lying at the bottom, on its side, with its arms flung out, a water-gourd and a straw hat just beyond its reach, as if it had died straining for them. It must have lain out here for at least two weeks, putrefying in the heat. Yet the wonder was how much of it remained. It had not been attacked by insects, or picked to the bone by birds and animals. No clouds of blow-flies swarmed across its half-baked meat. Rather, its burnt flesh appeared to have poisoned anything that had tried to feast on it.

He swallowed hard to keep back his vomit. He knew at once that it had to be Exomnius. He had been gone two weeks or more, and who else would have ventured up here in August? But how could he be sure? He had never met the man. Yet he was reluctant to venture down on to that carpet of death. He forced himself to squat close to the lip of the pit and squinted at the blackened face. He saw a row of grinning teeth, like pips in a burst fruit; a dull eye, half-closed, sighting along the length of the grasping arm. There was no sign of any wound. But then the whole body was a wound, bruised and suppurating. What could have killed him? Perhaps he had succumbed to the heat. Perhaps his heart had given out. Attilius leaned down further and tried to poke at it with his stick and immediately he felt himself begin to faint. Bright lights wove and danced before him and he almost toppled forwards. He scrabbled with his hands in the dust and just managed to push himself back, gasping for breath.

'The afflatus of the tainted air near to the ground itself . . .'

His head was pounding. He threw up – bitter, vile-tasting fluid – and was still coughing and spitting mucus when he heard, in front of him, the crack of dry vegetation being broken by a step. He looked up groggily. On the other side of the pit, no more than fifty paces away, a man was moving across the summit towards him. He thought at first it must be part of the visions induced by the *tainted air* and he stood with an effort, swaying drunkenly, blinking the sweat out of his eyes, trying to focus, but still the figure came on, framed by the hissing jets of sulphur, with the glint in his hand of a knife.

It was Corax.

Attilius was in no condition to fight. He would have run. But he could barely raise his feet.

The overseer approached the pit cautiously – crouched low, his arms spread wide, shifting lightly from foot to foot, reluctant to take his eyes off the engineer, as if he suspected a trick. He darted a quick glance at the body, frowned at Attilius, then looked back down again. He said softly, 'So what's all this then, pretty boy?' He sounded almost offended. He had planned his assault carefully, had travelled a long way to carry it out, had waited in the darkness for daylight and had followed his quarry at a distance – he must have been the horseman I saw behind me, thought Attilius – all the time relishing the prospect of revenge, only to have his plans thrown awry at the last moment. It was not fair, his expression said – another in the long series of obstacles that life had thrown in the way of Gavius Corax. 'I asked you: what's all this?'

Attilius tried to speak. His voice was thick and slurred. He wanted to say that Exomnius had not been wrong, that there was terrible danger here, but he could not pronounce the words. Corax was scowling at the corpse and shaking his head. 'The stupid old bastard, climbing up here at his age! Worrying about the mountain. And for what? For nothing! Nothing – except landing us with you.' He returned his attention to Attilius. 'Some clever young cunt from Rome, come to teach us all our jobs. Still fancy your chances, pretty boy? Nothing to say now, I notice. Well, why don't I cut you another mouth and we'll see what comes out of that?'

He hunched forwards, tossing his knife from hand to hand, his face set and ready for the kill. He began to circle the pit and it was all Attilius could do to stumble in the opposite direction. When the overseer stopped, Attilius stopped, and when he reversed his steps and started prowling the other way, Attilius followed suit. This went on for a while, but the tactic obviously enraged Corax – 'Fuck this,' he yelled, 'I'm not playing your stupid games!' – and suddenly he made a rush at his prey. Red-faced, panting for breath in the heat, he ran down the side of the hollow and across it and had just reached the other slope when he stopped. He glanced down at his legs in surprise. With a terrible slowness he tried to wade forwards, opening and shutting his mouth like a landed fish. He dropped his knife and sank to his knees, batting feebly at the air in front of him, then he crashed forwards on to his face.

There was nothing that Attilius could do except to watch him drown in the dry heat. Corax made a couple of feeble attempts to move, each time seeming to stretch for something beyond his reach as Exomnius must have done. Then he gave up and quietly lay on his side. His breathing became more shallow then stopped, but long before it ceased altogether Attilius had left him – stumbling across the bulging, trembling summit of the mountain, through the thickening plumes of sulphur, now flattened by the gathering breeze and pointing in the direction of Pompeii.

Down in the town, the light wind, arriving during the hottest part of the day, had come as a welcome relief. The Caurus raised tiny swirls of dust along the streets as they emptied for the siesta, fluttering the coloured awnings of the bars and snack-houses, stirring the foliage of the big plane trees close to the amphitheatre. In the House of Popidius it ruffled the surface of the swimming pool. The little masks of dancing fauns and bacchantes hanging between the pillars stirred and chimed. One of the papyri lying on the carpet was caught by the gust and rolled towards the table. Holconius put out his foot to stop it.

'What's going on?' he asked.

Ampliatus was tempted to strike Corelia there and then but checked himself, sensing that it would somehow be her victory if he was to be seen beating her in public. His mind moved quickly. He knew all there was to know about power. He knew that there were times when it was wisest to keep your secrets close: to possess your knowledge privately, like a favourite lover, to be shared with no one. He also knew that there were times when secrets, carefully revealed, could act like hoops of steel, binding others to you. In a flash of inspiration he saw that this was one of those occasions.

'Read them,' he said. 'I have nothing to hide from my friends.' He stooped and collected the papyri and piled them on the table.

'We should go,' said Brittius. He drained his glass of wine and began to rise to his feet.

'Read them!' commanded Ampliatus. The magistrate sat down sharply. 'Forgive me. Please. I insist.' He smiled. 'They come from the room of Exomnius. It's time you knew. Help yourself to more wine. I shall only be a moment. Corelia, you will come with me.' He seized her by the elbow and steered her towards the steps. She dragged her feet but he was too strong for her. He was vaguely aware of his wife and son following. When they were out of sight, around the corner, in the pillared garden of their old house, he twisted her flesh between his fingers. 'Did you really think,' he hissed, 'that you could hurt me – a feeble girl like you?'

'No,' she said, wincing and wriggling to escape. 'But at least I thought I could try.'

Her composure disconcerted him. 'Oh?' He pulled her close to him. 'And how did you propose to do that?'

'By showing the documents to the aquarius. By showing them to everyone. So that they could all see you for what you are.'

'And what is that?' Her face was very close to his.

'A thief. A murderer. Lower than a *slave*.'

She spat out the last word and he drew back his hand and this time he would certainly have hit her but Celsinus grabbed his wrist from behind.

'No, father,' he said. 'We'll have no more of that.'

For a moment, Ampliatus was too astonished to speak. 'You?' he said. 'You as well?' He shook his hand free and glared at his son. 'Don't you have some religious rite to go to? And you?' He wheeled on his wife. 'Shouldn't you be praying to the holy matron, Livia, for guidance? Ach,' he spat, 'get out of my way, the pair of you.' He dragged Corelia along the path towards the staircase. The other two did not move. He turned and pushed her up the steps, along the passage, and into her room. She fell backwards on to her bed. 'Treacherous, ungrateful child!'

He looked around for something with which to punish her but all he could see were feeble, feminine possessions, neatly arranged – an ivory comb, a silk shawl, a parasol, strings of beads – and a few old toys which had been saved to be offered to Venus before her wedding. Propped in a corner was a wooden doll with movable limbs he had bought her for her birthday years ago and the sight of it jolted him. What had happened to her? He had loved her so much – his little girl! – how had it come to hatred? He was suddenly baffled. Had he not done everything, built all of this, raised himself out of the muck, for the sake of her and her brother? He stood panting, defeated, as she glared at him from the bed. He did not know what to say. 'You'll stay in here,' he finished lamely, 'until I have decided what should be done with you.' He went out, locking the door behind him.

His wife and son had left the garden. Typical, feeble rebels, he thought, melting away when his back was turned. Corelia had always had more balls than the rest of them put together. His little girl! In the drawing room the magistrates were leaning forward across the table, muttering. They fell silent as he approached and turned to watch him as he headed towards the sideboard and poured himself some wine. The lip of the decanter rattled against the glass. Was his hand shaking? He examined it, front and back. This was not like him: it looked steady enough. He felt better after draining the glass. He poured himself another, fixed a smile and faced the magistrates.

'Well?'

It was Holconius who spoke first. 'Where did you get these?'

'Corax, the overseer on the Augusta, brought them round to me yesterday afternoon. He found them in Exomnius's room.'

'You mean he stole them?'

'Found, stole –' Ampliatus fluttered his hand.

'This should have been brought to our attention immediately.'

'And why's that, your honours?'

'Isn't it obvious?' cut in Popidius excitedly. 'Exomnius believed there was about to be another great earthquake!'

'Calm yourself, Popidius. You've been whining about earthquakes for seventeen years. I wouldn't take all that stuff seriously.'

'Exomnius took it seriously.'

'Exomnius!' Ampliatus looked at him with contempt. 'Exomnius always was a bag of nerves.'

'Maybe so. But why was he having documents copied? This in particular. What do you think he wanted with this?' He waved one of the papyri.

Ampliatus glanced at it and took another gulp of wine. 'It's in Greek. I don't read Greek. You forget, Popidius: I haven't had the benefit of your education.'

'Well I do read Greek, and I believe I recognise this. I think this is the work of Strabo, the geographer, who travelled these parts in the time of the Divine Augustus. He writes here of a summit that is flat and barren and has been on fire in the past. Surely that must be Vesuvius? He says the fertile soil around Pompeii reminds him of Caetana, where the land is covered with ash thrown up by the flames of Etna.'

'So what?'

'Wasn't Exomnius a Sicilian?' demanded Holconius. 'What town was he from?'

Ampliatus waved his glass dismissively. 'I believe Caetana. But what of it?' He must learn the rudiments of Greek, he thought. If a fool like Popidius could master it, anyone could.

'As for this Latin document – this I certainly recognise,' continued Popidius. 'It's part of a book, and I know both the man who wrote it and the man to whom the passage is addressed. It's by Annaeus Seneca – Nero's mentor. Surely even *you* must have heard of him?'

Ampliatus flushed. 'My business is building, not books.' Why were they going on about all this stuff?

'The Lucilius to whom he refers is Lucilius Junior, a native of this very city. He had a house near the theatre. He was a procurator overseas – in Sicily, as I remember it. Seneca is describing the great Campanian earthquake. It's from his book, *Natural Questions*. I believe there is even a copy in our own library on the forum. It lays out the foundations of the Stoic philosophy.'

'"The Stoic philosophy!"' mocked Ampliatus. 'And what would old Exomnius have been doing with "the Stoic philosophy"?'

'Again,' repeated Popidius, with mounting exasperation, 'isn't it obvious?' He laid the two documents side by side. 'Exomnius believed there was a link, you see?' He gestured from one to the other. 'Etna and Vesuvius. The fertility of the land around Caetana and the land around Pompeii. The terrible omens of seventeen years ago – the poisoning of the sheep – and the omens all around us this summer. He was from Siciliy. He saw signs of danger. *And now he's disappeared.*'

Nobody spoke for a while. The effigies around the pool tinkled in the breeze.

Brittius said, 'I think these documents ought to be considered by a full meeting of the Ordo. As soon as possible.'

'No,' said Ampliatus.

'But the Ordo is the ruling council of the town! They have a right to be informed –'

'No!' Ampliatus was emphatic. 'How many citizens are members of the Ordo?'

'Eighty-five,' said Holconius.

'There you are. It will be all over the town within an hour. Do you want to start a panic, just as we're starting to get back on our feet? When we've got the prophecy of the sibyl to give them, to keep them sweet? Remember who voted for you, your honours – the traders. They won't thank you for scaring their business away. You saw what happened this morning, simply because the fountains stopped for a few hours. Besides, what does this add up to? So Exomnius was worried about earth tremors? So Campania has ashy soil like Sicily, and stinking fumaroles? So what? Fumaroles have been part of life on the bay since the days of Romulus.' He could see his words were striking home. 'Besides, this isn't the real problem.'

Holconius said, 'And what is the real problem?'

'The other documents – the ones that show how much Exomnius was paid to give this town cheap water.'

Holconius said quickly, 'Have a care, Ampliatus. Your little arrangements are no concern of ours.'

'*My* little arrangements!' Ampliatus laughed. 'That's a good one!' He set down his glass and lifted the decanter to pour himself another drink. Again, the heavy crystal rattled. He was becoming light-headed but he didn't care. 'Come now, your honours, don't pretend you didn't know! How do you think this town revived so quickly after the earthquake? I've saved you a fortune by my "little arrangements". Yes, and helped make myself one into the bargain – I don't deny it. But you wouldn't be here without me! Your precious baths, Popidius – where Brittius here likes to be wanked off by his little boys – how much do you pay for them? Nothing! And you, Cuspius, with your fountains. And you, Holconius, with your pool. And all the private baths and the watered gardens and the big public pool in the palaestra and the pipes in the new apartments! This town has been kept afloat for more than a decade by my "little arrangement" with Exomnius. And now some nosy bastard of an aquarius from Rome has got to hear about it. *That's* the real problem.'

'An outrage!' said Brittius, his voice quivering. 'An outrage – to be spoken to in such a way by this jumped-up slave.'

'Jumped up, am I? I wasn't so jumped up when I paid for the games that secured your election, Brittius. "Cold steel, no quarter, and the slaughterhouse right in the middle where all the stands can see it" – that's what you asked for, and that was what I gave.'

Holconius raised his hands. 'All right, gentlemen. Let's keep ourselves calm.'

Cuspius said, 'But surely we can just cut a deal with this new aquarius, like the one you had with the other fellow?'

'It seems not. I dropped a hint yesterday but all he did was look at me as if I'd just put my hand on his cock. I felt insulted for my generosity. No, I'm afraid I recognise his type. He'll take this up in Rome, they'll check the accounts and we'll have an imperial commission down here before the year's end.'

'Then what are we to do?' said Popidius. 'If this comes out, it will look bad for all of us.'

Ampliatus smiled at him over the rim of his glass. 'Don't worry. I've sorted it out.'

'How?'

'Popidius!' cautioned Holconius quickly. 'Take care.'

Ampliatus paused. They did not want to know. They were the magistrates of the town, after all. The innocence of ignorance – that was what they craved. But why should they have peace of mind? He would dip their hands in the blood along with his own.

'He'll go to meet his ancestors.' He looked around. 'Before he gets back to Misenum. An accident out in the countryside. Does anyone disagree? Speak up if you do. Popidius? Holconius? Brittius? Cuspius?' He waited. It was all a charade. The aquarius would be dead by now, whatever they said: Corax had been itching to slit his throat. 'I'll take that as agreement. Shall we drink to it?'

He reached for the decanter but stopped, his hand poised in mid-air. The heavy crystal glass was not merely shaking now: it was moving sideways along the polished wooden surface. He frowned at it stupidly. That could not be right. Even so, it reached the end of the sideboard and crashed to the floor. He glanced at the tiles. There was a vibration beneath his feet. It gradually built in strength and then a gust of hot air passed through the house, powerful enough to bang the shutters. An instant later, far away – but very distinctly, unlike anything he, or anyone else, had ever heard – came the sound of a double boom.

Hora sexta

[12:57 hours]

'The surface of the volcano ruptured shortly after noon allowing explosive decompression of the main magma body . . . The exit velocity of the magma was approximately 1,440 km. per hour (Mach 1). Convection carried incandescant gas and pumice clasts to a height of 28 km.

Overall, the thermal energy liberated during the course of the entire eruption may be calculated using the following formula:

$$Eth = V \cdot d \cdot T \cdot K$$

where Eth is in joules, V is the volume in cubic km., d is specific gravity (1.0), T is the temperature of the ejecta (500 degrees centigrade), and K a constant including the specific heat of the magma and the mechanical equivalent of heat (8.37 × 10^{14}).

Thus the thermal energy released during the A.D. 79 eruption would have been roughly 2 × 10^{18} joules – or about 100,000 times that of the Hiroshima atomic bomb.'

Dynamics of Volcanism

A fterwards, whenever they compared their stories, the survivors would always wonder at how differently the moment had sounded to each of them. A hundred and twenty miles away in Rome it was heard as a thud, as if a heavy statue or a tree had toppled. Those who escaped from Pompeii, which was five miles downwind, always swore they had heard two sharp bangs, whereas in Capua, some twenty miles distant, the noise from the start was a continuous, tearing crack of thunder. But in Misenum, which was closer than Capua, there was no sound at all, only the sudden appearance of a narrow column of brown debris fountaining silently into the cloudless sky.

For Attilius, it was like a great, dry wave which came crashing over his head. He was roughly two miles clear of the summit, following an old hunting trail through the forest, descending fast on horseback along the mountain's western flank. The effects of the poisoning had shrunk to a small fist of pain hammering behind his eyes and in place of the drowsiness everything seemed oddly sharpened and heightened. He had no doubt of what was coming. His plan was to pick up the coastal road at Herculaneum and ride directly to Misenum to warn the admiral. He reckoned he would be there by mid-afternoon. The bay sparkled in the sunlight between the trees, close enough for him to be able to make out individual lines of surf. He was noticing the glistening pattern of the spiders' webs hanging loosely in the foliage and a particular cloud of midges, swirling beneath a branch ahead of him, when suddenly they disappeared.

The shock of the blast struck him from behind and knocked him forward. Hot air, like the opening of a furnace door. Then something seemed to pop in his ears and the world became a soundless place of bending trees and whirling leaves. His horse stumbled and almost fell and he clung to its neck as they plunged down the path, both of them riding the crest of the scalding wave, and then abruptly it was gone. The trees sprang upright, the debris settled, the air became breathable again. He tried to talk to the horse but he had no voice and when he looked back towards the top of the mountain he saw that it had vanished and in its place a boiling stem of rock and earth was shooting upward.

From Pompeii it looked as if a sturdy brown arm had punched through the peak and was aiming to smash a hole in the roof of the sky – bang, bang: that double crack – and then a hard-edged rumble, unlike any other sound in Nature, that came rolling across the plain. Ampliatus ran outside with the magistrates. From the bakery next door and all the way up the street people were emerging to stare at Vesuvius, shielding their eyes, their faces turned towards this new dark sun rising in the north on its thundering plinth of rock. There were a couple of screams but no general panic. It was still too early, the thing was too awesome – too strange and remote – for it to be perceived as an immediate threat.

It would stop at any moment, Ampliatus thought. He willed it to do so. *Let it subside now, and the situation will still be controllable.* He had the nerve, the force of character; it was all a question of presentation. He could handle even this: 'The gods have given us a sign, citizens! Let us heed their instruction! Let us build a great column, in imitation of this celestial inspiration! We live in a favoured spot!' But the thing did not stop. Up and up it went. A thousand heads tilted backward as one to follow its trajectory and gradually the isolated screams became more widespread. The pillar, narrow at its base, was broadening as it rose, its apex flattening out across the sky.

Someone shouted that the wind was carrying it their way.

That was the moment at which he knew he would lose them. The mob had a few simple instincts – greed, lust, cruelty – he could play them like the strings of a harp because he was of the mob and the mob was him. But shrill fear drowned out every other note. Still, he tried. He stepped into the centre of the street and held his arms out wide. 'Wait!' he shouted. 'Cuspius, Brittius – all of you – link hands with me! Set them an example!'

The cowards did not even look at him. Holconius broke first, jamming his bony elbows into the press of bodies to force his way down the hill. Brittius followed, and then Cuspius. Popidius turned tail and darted back inside the house. Up ahead, the crowd had become a solid mass as people streamed from the sidestreets to join it. Its back was to the mountain now, its face was to the sea, its single impulse: flight. Ampliatus had a final glimpse of his wife's white face in the doorway and then he was engulfed by the stampeding crowd, spun like one of the revolving wooden models they used for practice in the gladiatorial school. He was thrown sideways, winded, and would have disappeared beneath their feet if Massavo had not seen him fall and scooped him up to safety on the step. He saw a mother drop her baby and heard its screams as it was trampled, saw an elderly matron slammed head first against the opposite wall then slip, unconscious, out of sight, as the mob swept on regardless. Some screamed. Some sobbed. Most were tight-mouthed, intent on saving their strength for the battle at the bottom of the hill, where they would have to fight their way through the Stabian Gate.

Ampliatus, leaning against the door-jamb, was aware of a wetness on his face and when he dabbed the back of his hand to his nose it came away smeared in blood. He looked above the heads of the crowd towards the mountain but already it had disappeared. A vast black wall of cloud was advancing towards the city, as dark as a storm. But it was not a storm, he realised, and it was not a cloud; it was a thundering waterfall of rock. He looked quickly in the other direction. He still had his gold-and-crimson cruiser moored down in the harbour. They could put to sea, try to head to the villa in Misenum, seek shelter there. But the cram of bodies in the street leading to the gate was beginning to stretch back up the hill. He would never reach the port. And even if he did, the crew would be scrambling to save themselves.

His decision was made for him. And so be it, he thought. This was exactly how it had been seventeen years ago. The cowards had fled, he had stayed, and then they had all come crawling back again! He felt his old energy and confidence returning. Once more the former slave would give his masters a lesson in Roman courage. The sibyl was never wrong. He gave a final, contemptuous glance to the river of panic streaming past him, stepped back and ordered Massavo to close the door. Close it and bolt it. They would stay, and they would endure.

In Misenum it looked like smoke. Pliny's sister, Julia, strolling on the terrace with her parasol, picking the last roses of summer for the dinner table, assumed it must be another of the hillside fires that had plagued the bay all summer. But the height of the cloud, its bulk and the speed of its ascent were like nothing she had ever seen. She decided she had better wake her brother, who was dozing over his books in the garden below.

Even in the heavy shade of the tree his face was as scarlet as the flowers in her basket. She hesitated to disturb him, because of course he would immediately start to get excited. He reminded her of how their father had been in the days before his death – the same corpulence, the same shortness of breath, the same uncharacteristic irritability. But if she let him sleep he would no doubt be even more furious to have missed the peculiar smoke, so she stroked his hair and whispered, 'Brother, wake up. There is something you will want to see.'

He opened his eyes at once. 'The water – is it flowing?'

'No. Not the water. It looks like a great fire on the bay, coming from Vesuvius.'

'Vesuvius?' He blinked at her then shouted to a nearby slave. 'My shoes! Quickly!'

'Now, brother, don't exert yourself too much –'

He did not even wait for his shoes. Instead, for the second time that day, he set off barefoot, lumbering across the dry grass towards the terrace. By the time he reached it most of the household slaves were lining the balustrade, looking east across the bay towards what looked like a gigantic umbrella pine made of smoke growing over the coast. A thick brown trunk, with black and white blotches, was rolling miles into the air, sprouting at its crown a clump of feathery branches. These broad leaves seemed in turn to be dissolving along their lower edges, beginning to rain a fine, sand-coloured mist back down to earth.

It was an axiom of the admiral's, one which he was fond of repeating, that the more he observed Nature, the less prone he was to consider any statement about Her to be impossible. But surely this *was* impossible. Nothing he had read of – and he had read everything – came close to matching this spectacle.

Perhaps Nature was granting him the privilege of witnessing something never before recorded in history? Those long years of accumulating facts, the prayer with which he had ended the *Natural History* – 'Hail Nature, mother of all creation, and mindful that I alone of the men of Rome have praised thee in all thy manifestations, be gracious towards me' – was it all being rewarded at last? If he had not been so fat he would have fallen to his knees. 'Thank you,' he whispered. 'Thank you.'

He must start work at once. *Umbrella pine . . . tall stem . . . feathery branches . . .* He needed to get all this down for posterity, while the images were still fresh in his head. He shouted to Alexion to collect pen and paper and to Julia to fetch Gaius.

'He's inside, working on the translation you set him.'

'Well, tell him to come out here at once. He won't want to miss this.' It could not be smoke, he thought. It was too thick. Besides, there was no sign of any fire at the base. But if not smoke, what? 'Be quiet, damn you!' He waved at the slaves to stop their jabbering. Listening hard, it was just possible to make out a low and ceaseless rumble carrying across the bay. If that was how it sounded at a distance of fifteen miles, what must it be like close to?

He beckoned to Alcman. 'Send a runner down to the naval school to find the flagship captain. Tell him I want a liburnian made ready and put at my disposal.'

'Brother – no!'

'Julia!' He held up his hand. 'You mean well, I know, but save your breath. This phenomenon, whatever it is, is a sign from Nature. This is *mine*.'

*   *   *

Corelia had thrown open her shutters and was standing on the balcony. To her right, above the flat roof of the atrium, a gigantic cloud was advancing, as black as ink, like a heavy curtain being drawn across the sky. The air was shaking with thunder. She could hear screams from the street. In the courtyard garden slaves ran back and forth, to no apparent purpose. They reminded her of dormice in a jar, before they were fished out for cooking. She felt somehow detached from the scene – a spectator in a box at the back of the theatre, watching an elaborate production. At any moment, a god would be lowered from the wings to whisk her off to safety. She shouted down – 'What's happening?' – but nobody paid her any attention. She tried again and realised she was forgotten.

The drumming of the cloud was getting louder. She ran to the door and tried to open it but the lock was too strong to break. She ran back on to the balcony but it was too high to jump. Below, and to the left, she saw Popidius coming up the steps from his part of the house, shepherding his elderly mother, Taedia Secunda, before him. A couple of their slaves, laden with bags, were following behind. She screamed at him – 'Popidius!' – and at the sound of his name he stopped and glanced around. She waved to him. 'Help me! He's locked me in!'

He shook his head in despair. 'He's trying to lock us all in! He's gone mad!'

'Please – come up and open the door!'

He hesitated. He wanted to help her. And he would have done so. But even as he took half a pace towards her something hit the tiled roof behind him and bounced off into the garden. A light stone, the size of a child's fist. He saw it land. Another struck the pergola. And suddenly it was dusk and the air was full of missiles. He was being hit repeatedly on the head and shoulders. Frothy rocks, they looked to be: a whitish, petrified sponge. They weren't heavy but they stung. It was like being caught in a sudden hailstorm – a warm, dark, dry hailstorm, if such a thing were imaginable. He ran for the cover of the atrium, ignoring Corelia's cries, pushing his mother in front of him. The door ahead – Ampliatus's old entrance – was hanging open and he stumbled out into the street.

Corelia did not see him go. She ducked back into her room to escape the bombardment. She had one last impression of the world outside, shadowy in the dust, and then all light was extinguished and there was nothing in the pitch darkness, not even a scream, only the roaring waterfall of rock.

I n Herculaneum life was peculiarly normal. The sun was shining, the sky and sea were a brilliant blue. As Attilius reached the coastal road he could even see fishermen out in their boats casting their nets. It was like some trick of the summer weather by which half of the bay was lost from view in a violent storm whilst the other half blessed its good fortune and continued to enjoy the day. Even the noise from the mountain seemed unthreatening – a background rumble, drifting with the veil of debris towards the peninsula of Surrentum.

Outside the town gates of Herculaneum a small crowd had gathered to watch the proceedings, and a couple of enterprising traders were setting up stalls to sell pastries and wine. A line of dusty travellers was already plodding down the road, mostly on foot and carrying luggage, some with carts piled high with their belongings. Children ran along behind them, enjoying the adventure, but the faces of their parents were rigid with fear.

Attilius felt as if he were in a dream. A fat man, his mouth full of cake, sitting on a milestone, called out cheerfully to ask what it was like back there.

'As black as midnight in Oplontis,' someone replied, 'and Pompeii must be even worse.'

'Pompeii?' said Attilius sharply. That woke him up. 'What's happening in Pompeii?'

The traveller shook his head, drawing his finger across his throat, and Attilius recoiled, remembering Corelia. When he had forced her to leave the aqueduct he had thought he was sending her out of harm's way. But now, as his eye followed the curve of the road towards Pompeii, to the point where it disappeared into the murk, he realised he had done the opposite. The outpouring of Vesuvius, caught by the wind, was blowing directly over the town.

'Don't go that way, citizen,' warned the man, 'there's no way through.'

But Attilius was already turning his horse to face the stream of refugees.

The further he went the more clogged the road became, and the more pitiful the state of the fleeing population. Most were coated in a thick grey dust, their hair frosted, their faces like death masks, spattered with blood. Some carried torches, still lit: a defeated army of whitened old men, of ghosts, trudging away from a calamitous defeat, unable even to speak. Their animals – oxen, asses, horses, dogs and cats – resembled alabaster figures come creakingly to life. Behind them on the highway they left a trail of ashy wheelmarks and footprints.

On one side of him, isolated crashes came from the olive

groves. On the other, the sea seemed to be coming to the boil in a myriad of tiny fountains. There was a clatter of stones on the road ahead. His horse stopped, lowered its head, refused to move. Suddenly the edge of the cloud, which had seemed to be almost half a mile away, appeared to come rushing towards them. The sky was dark and whirling with tiny projectiles and in an instant the day passed from afternoon sun to twilight and he was under a bombardment. Not hard stones but white clinker, small clumps of solidified ash, falling from some tremendous height. They bounced off his head and shoulders. People and wagons loomed out of the half-light. Women screamed. Torches dimmed in the darkness. His horse shied and turned. Attilius ceased to be a rescuer and became just another part of the panicking stream of refugees, frantically trying to outrun the storm of debris. His horse slipped down the side of the road into the ditch and cantered along it. Then the air lightened, became brownish, and they burst back into the sunshine.

Everyone was hurrying now, galvanised by the threat at their backs. Not only was the road to Pompeii impassable, Attilius realised, but a slight shift in the wind was spreading the danger westwards around the bay. An elderly couple sat weeping beside the road, too exhausted to run any further. A cart had overturned and a man was desperately trying to right it, while his wife soothed a baby and a little girl clung to her skirts. The fleeing column streamed around them and Attilius was carried in the flow, borne back along the road towards Herculaneum.

The shifting position of the wall of falling rock had been noticed at the city gates and by the time he reached them the traders were hastily packing away their goods. The crowd was breaking up, some heading for shelter in the town, others pouring out of it to join the exodus on the road. And still, amid all this, Attilius could see across the red-tiled roofs the normality of the fishermen on the bay and, further out, the big grain ships from Egypt steering towards the docks at Puteoli. *The sea*, he thought: if he could somehow launch a boat, it might just be possible to skirt the downpour of stones and approach Pompeii from the south – *by sea*. He guessed it would be useless to try to fight his way down to the waterfront in Herculaneum, but the great villa just outside it – the home of the senator, Pedius Cascus, with his troop of philosophers – perhaps they might have a vessel he could use.

He rode a little further along the crowded highway until he came to a high pair of gateposts, which he judged must belong to the Villa Calpurnia. He tied his horse to a railing in the courtyard and looked around for any sign of life but the enormous palace seemed to be deserted. He walked through the open door into the grand atrium, and then along the side of an enclosed garden. He could hear shouts, footsteps running along the marble corridors, and then a slave appeared around a corner pushing a wheelbarrow stacked high with rolls of papyri. He ignored Attilius's shout and headed through a wide doorway into the brilliant afternoon light, as another slave, also pushing a wheelbarrow – this one empty – hurried through the entrance and into the house. The engineer blocked his path.

'Where's the senator?'

'He's in Rome.' The slave was young, terrified, sweating.

'Your mistress?'

'Beside the pool. Please – let me past.'

Attilius moved aside to let him go and ran out into the sun. Beneath the terrace was the huge pool he had seen from the liburnian on his voyage to Pompeii and all around it people: dozens of slaves and white-robed scholars hurrying back and forth ferrying armfuls of papyri, stacking them into boxes at the water's edge, while a group of women stood to one side, staring along the coast towards the distant storm, which looked from here like an immense brown sea-fog. The craft offshore from Herculaneum were mere twigs against it. The fishing had stopped. The waves were getting up. Attilius could hear them crashing against the shore in quick succession; no sooner had one broken than another came in on top of it. Some of the women were wailing, but the elderly matron in the centre of the group, in a dark blue dress, seemed calm as he approached her. He remembered her – the woman with the necklace of giant pearls.

'Are you the wife of Pedius Cascus?'

She nodded.

'Marcus Attilius. Imperial engineer. I met your husband two nights ago, at the admiral's villa.'

She looked at him eagerly. 'Has Pliny sent you?'

'No. I came to beg a favour. To ask for a boat.'

Her face fell. 'Do you think if I had a boat I would be standing here? My husband took it yesterday to Rome.'

Attilius looked around the vast palace, at its statues and gardens, at the art treasures and books being piled up on the lawns. He turned to go.

'Wait!' She called after him. 'You must help us.'

'There's nothing I can do. You'll have to take your chance on the road with the rest.'

'I'm not afraid for myself. But the library – we must rescue the library. There are too many books to move by road.'

'My concern is for people, not books.'

'People perish. Books are immortal.'

'Then if books are immortal, they will survive without my assistance.'

He began climbing the path back up towards the house.

'Wait!' She gathered her skirts and ran after him. 'Where are you going?'

'To find a boat.'

'Pliny has boats. Pliny has the greatest fleet in the world at his command.'

'Pliny is on the other side of the bay.'

'Look across the sea! An entire mountain is threatening to descend on us! Do you think one man in one little boat can do anything? We need a fleet. Come with me!'

He would say this for her: she had the willpower of any man. He followed her around the pillared walkway surrounding the pool, up a flight of steps and into a library. Most of the compartments had been stripped bare. A couple of slaves were loading what remained into a wheelbarrow. Marble heads of ancient philosophers looked down, dumbstruck at what was happening.

'This is where we keep the volumes which my ancestors brought back from Greece. One hundred and twenty plays by Sophocles alone. All the works of Aristotle, some in his own hand. They are irreplaceable. We have never allowed them to be copied.' She gripped his arm. 'Men are born and die by the thousand every hour. What do we matter? These great works are all that will be left of us. Pliny will understand.' She sat at the small table, took up a pen and dipped it in an ornate brass inkstand. A red candle flickered beside her. 'Take him this letter. He knows this library. Tell him Rectina pleads with him for rescue.'

Behind her, across the terrace, Attilius could see the ominous darkness moving steadily around the bay, like the shadow on a sundial. He had thought it might diminish but if anything the force of it was intensifying. She was right. It would take big ships – warships – to make any impression against an enemy on this scale. She rolled the letter and sealed it with the dripping candle, pressing her ring into the soft wax. 'You have a horse?'

'I'd go faster with a fresh one.'

'You'll have it.' She called to one of the slaves. 'Take Marcus Attilius to the stables and saddle the swiftest horse we have.' She gave him the letter and, as he took it, clasped her dry and bony fingers around his wrist. 'Don't fail me, engineer.'

He pulled his hand free and ran after the slave.

Hora nona

[15:32 hours]

*'The effect of the sudden release of huge volumes of
magma can alter the geometry of the plumbing system,
destabilize the shallow reservoir, and induce structural
collapse. Such a situation frequently increases the eruption
intensity, inducing contact between phreatic fluids and
magma, as well as explosive decompression of the
hydrothermal system associated with the shallow reservoir.'*

Encyclopedia of Volcanoes

I t took Attilius just under two hours of hard riding to
reach Misenum. The road wound along the coastline,
sometimes running directly beside the water's edge,
sometimes climbing higher inland, past the immense villas of
the Roman elite. All the way along it he passed small groups
of spectators gathered at the edge of the highway to watch the
distant phenomenon. He mostly had his back to the mountain,
but when he rounded the northern edge of the bay and began
to descend towards Neapolis, he could see it again, away to his
left – a thing of extraordinary beauty now. A delicate veil of
white mist had draped itself around the central column, rising
for mile after mile in a perfect translucent cylinder, reaching
up to brush the lower edge of the mushroom-shaped cloud that
was toppling over the bay.

There was no sense of panic in Neapolis, a sleepy place at the best of times. He had far outpaced the weary, laden refugees emerging from beneath the hail of rock and no word of the catastrophe enveloping Pompeii had yet reached the city. The Greek-style temples and theatres facing out to sea gleamed white in the afternoon sun. Tourists strolled in the gardens. In the hills behind the town he could see the redbrick arcade of the Aqua Augusta where she ran above the surface. He wondered if the water was flowing yet but he did not dare stop to find out. In truth, he did not care. What had earlier seemed the most vital matter in the world had dwindled in importance to nothing. What were Exomnius and Corax now but dust? Not even dust; barely even a memory. He wondered what had happened to the other men. But the image of which he could not rid himself was Corelia – the way she had swept back her hair as she mounted her horse, and the way she had dwindled into the distance, following the road he had set for her – to the fate that he, and not Destiny, had decreed.

He passed through Neapolis and out into the open country again, into the immense road-tunnel that Agrippa had carved beneath the promontory of Pausilypon – in which the torches of the highway slaves, as Seneca had observed, did not so much pierce the darkness as reveal it – past the immense concrete grain-wharfs of the Puteoli harbour – another of Agrippa's projects – past the outskirts of Cumae – where the Sibyl was said to hang in her bottle and wish for death – past the vast oyster beds of Lake Avernus, past the great terraced baths of Baiae, past the drunks on the beaches and the souvenir shops with their brightly painted glassware, the children flying kites, the fishermen repairing their flaxen nets on the quaysides, the men playing bones in the shade of the oleanders, past the century of marines in full kit running at the double down to the naval base – past all the teeming life of the Roman super-power, while on the opposite side of the bay Vesuvius emitted a second, rolling boom, turning the fountain of rock from grey to black and pushing it even higher.

Pliny's greatest concern was that it might all be over before he got there. Every so often he would come waddling out of his library to check on the progress of the column. Each time he was reassured. Indeed, if anything, it seemed to be growing. An accurate estimation of its height was impossible. Posidonius held that mists, winds and clouds rose no more than five miles above the earth, but most experts – and Pliny, on balance, took the majority view – put the figure at one hundred and eleven miles. Whatever the truth, the thing – the column – 'the manifestation', as he had decided to call it – was enormous.

In order to make his observations as accurate as possible he had ordered that his water clock should be carried down to the harbour and set up on the poop deck of the liburnian. While this was being done and the ship made ready he searched his library for references to Vesuvius. He had never before paid much attention to the mountain. It was so huge, so obvious, so inescapably *there*, that he had preferred to concentrate on Nature's more esoteric aspects. But the first work he consulted, Strabo's *Geography*, brought him up short. *'This area appears to have been on fire in the past and to have had craters of flame . . .'* Why had he never noticed it? He called in Gaius to take a look.

'You see here? He compares the mountain to Etna. Yet how can that be? Etna has a crater two miles across. I have seen it with my own eyes, glowing across the sea at night. And all those islands that belch flames – Strongyle, ruled by Aeolus, god of wind, Lipari, and Holy Island, where Vulcan is said to live – you can see them all burning. No one has ever reported embers on Vesuvius.'

'He says the craters of flame *"were subsequently extinguished by a lack of fuel"*,' his nephew pointed out. 'Perhaps that means some fresh source of fuel has now been tapped by the mountain, and has brought it back to life.' Gaius looked up excitedly. 'Could that explain the arrival of the sulphur in the water of the aqueduct?'

Pliny regarded him with fresh respect. Yes. The lad was right. That must be it. Sulphur was the universal fuel of all these phenomena – the coil of flame at Comphantium in Bactria, the blazing fishpool on the Babylonian Plain, the field of stars near Mount Hesperius in Ethiopia. But the implications of that were awful: Lipari and Holy Island had once burned in mid-sea for days on end, until a deputation from the Senate had sailed out to perform a propitiatory ceremony. A similar explosive fire on the Italian mainland, in the middle of a crowded population, could be a disaster.

He pushed himself to his feet. 'I must get down to my ship. Alexion!' He shouted for his slave. 'Gaius, why don't you come with me? Leave your translation.' He held out his hand and smiled. 'I release you from your lesson.'

'Do you really, uncle?' Gaius stared across the bay, and chewed his lip. Clearly he, too, had realised the potential consequences of a second Etna on the bay. 'That's kind of you, but to be honest I have actually reached rather a tricky passage. Of course, if you insist –'

Pliny could see he was afraid, and who could blame him?

He felt a flutter of apprehension in his own stomach and he was an old soldier. It crossed his mind to order the boy to come – no Roman should ever succumb to fear: what had happened to the stern values of his youth? – but then he thought of Julia. Was it fair to expose her only son to needless danger? 'No, no,' he said, with forced cheerfulness. 'I won't insist. The sea looks rough. It will make you sick. You stay here and look after your mother.' He pinched his nephew's spotty cheek and ruffled his greasy hair. 'You'll make a good lawyer, Gaius Plinius. Perhaps a great one. I can see you in the Senate one day. You'll be my heir. My books will be yours. The name of Pliny will live through you –' He stopped. It was beginning to sound too much like a valedictory. He said gruffly, 'Return to your studies. Tell your mother I'll be back by nightfall.'

Leaning on the arm of his secretary, and without a backward glance, the admiral shuffled out of his library.

Attilius had ridden past the Piscina Mirabilis, over the causeway into the port, and was beginning his ascent of the steep road to the admiral's villa, when he saw a detachment of marines ahead clearing a path for Pliny's carriage. He just had time to dismount and step into the street before the procession reached him.

'Admiral!'

Pliny, staring fixedly ahead, turned vaguely in his direction. He saw a figure he did not recognise, covered in dust, his tunic torn, his face, arms and legs streaked with dried blood. The apparition spoke again. 'Admiral! It's Marcus Attilius!'

'Engineer?' Pliny signalled for the carriage to stop. 'What's happened to you?'

'It's a catastrophe, admiral. The mountain is exploding – raining rocks –' Attilius licked his cracked lips. 'Hundreds of people are fleeing east along the coastal road. Oplontis and Pompeii are being buried. I've ridden from Herculaneum. I have a message for you –' he searched in his pocket ' – from the wife of Pedius Cascus.'

'Rectina?' Pliny took the letter from his hands and broke the seal. He read it twice, his expression clouding, and suddenly he looked ill – ill and overwhelmed. He leaned over the side of the carriage and showed the hasty scrawl to Attilius: *Pliny, my dearest friend, the library is in peril. I am alone. I beg you to come for us by sea – at once – if you still love these old books and your faithful old Rectina.*' 'This is really true?' he asked. 'The Villa Calpurnia is threatened?'

'The entire coast is threatened, admiral.' What was wrong with the old man? Had drink and age entirely dulled his wits? Or did he think it was all just a show – some spectacular in the amphitheatre, laid on for his interest? 'The danger follows the wind. It swings like a weathervane. Even Misenum might not be safe.'

'Even Misenum might not be safe,' repeated Pliny. 'And Rectina is alone.' His eyes were watering. He rolled up the letter and beckoned to his secretary who had been running with the marines beside the carriage. 'Where is Antius?'

'At the quayside, admiral.'

'We need to move quickly. Climb in next to me, Attilius.' He rapped his ring on the side of the carriage. 'Forward!' Attilius squeezed in beside him as the carriage lurched down the hill. 'Now tell me everything you've seen.'

Attilius tried to order his thoughts, but it was hard to speak coherently. Still, he tried to convey the power of what he had witnessed when the roof of the mountain lifted off. And the blasting of the summit, he said, was merely the culmination of a host of other phenomena — the sulphur in the soil, the pools of noxious gas, the earth tremors, the swelling of the land which had severed the matrix of the aqueduct, the disappearance of the local springs. All these things were interconnected.

'And none of us recognised it,' said Pliny, with a shake of his head. 'We were as blind as old Pomponianus, who thought it was the work of Jupiter.'

'That's not quite true, admiral. One man recognised it — a native of the land near Etna: my predecessor, Exomnius.'

'Exomnius?' said Pliny, sharply. 'Who hid a quarter of a million sesterces at the bottom of his own reservoir?' He noticed the bafflement on the engineer's face. 'It was discovered this morning when the last of the water had drained away. Why? Do you know how he came by it?'

They were entering the docks. Attilius could see a familiar sight — the *Minerva* lying alongside the quay, her main mast raised and ready to sail — and he thought how odd it was, the chain of events and circumstances that had brought him to this place, at this time. If Exomnius had not been born a Sicilian, he would never have ventured on to Vesuvius and would never have disappeared, Attilius would never have been dispatched from Rome, would never have set foot in Pompeii, would never have known of Corelia or Ampliatus or Corax. For a brief moment, he glimpsed the extraordinary, perfect logic of it all, from poisoned fish to hidden silver, and he tried to think how best he could describe it to the admiral. But he had barely started before Pliny waved him to stop.

'The pettiness and avarice of man!' he said impatiently.

'It would make a book in itself. What does any of it matter now? Put it in a report and have it ready on my return. And the aqueduct?'

'Repaired, admiral. Or at any rate she was when I left her this morning.'

'Then you have done good work, engineer. And it will be made known in Rome, I promise you. Now go back to your quarters and rest.'

The wind was flapping the cables against the *Minerva*'s mast. Torquatus stood by the aft gangplank talking to the flagship commander, Antius, and a group of seven officers. They came to attention as Pliny's carriage approached.

'Admiral, with your permission, I would rather sail with you.'

Pliny looked at him in surprise, then grinned and clapped his pudgy hand on Attilius's knee. 'A scientist! You're just like me! I knew it the moment I saw you! We shall do great things this day, Marcus Attilius.' He was wheezing out his orders even as his secretary helped him from the carriage. 'Torquatus – we sail immediately. The engineer will join us. Antius – sound the general alarm. Have a signal flashed to Rome in my name: "Vesuvius exploded just before the seventh hour. The population of the bay is threatened. I am putting the entire fleet to sea to evacuate survivors."'

Antius stared at him. 'The *entire* fleet, admiral?'

'Everything that floats. What have you got out there?' Pliny peered short-sightedly towards the outer harbour where the warships rode at anchor, rocking in the gathering swell. 'The *Concordia* I can see, is that? The *Libertas*. *Justitia*. And what's that one – the *Pietas*? The *Europa*.' He waved his hand. 'All of them. And everything in the inner harbour that isn't in dry dock. Come on, Antius! You were complaining the other night

284

that we had the mightiest fleet in the world but it never saw action. Well, here is action for you.'

'But action requires an enemy, admiral.'

'There's your enemy.' He pointed to the dark pall spreading in the distance. 'A greater enemy than any force Caesar ever faced.'

For a moment Antius did not move and Attilius wondered if he might even be considering disobeying, but then a gleam came into his eyes and he turned to the officers. 'You heard your orders. Signal the Emperor and sound the general muster. And let it be known that I'll cut the balls off any captain who isn't at sea within half an hour.'

It was at the mid-point of the ninth hour, according to the admiral's water clock, that the *Minerva* was pushed away from the quayside and slowly began to swivel round to face the open sea. Attilius took up his old position against the rail and nodded to Torquatus. The captain responded with a slight shake of his head, as if to say he thought the venture madness.

'Note the time,' commanded Pliny and Alexion, squatting beside him, dipped his pen into his ink and scratched down a numeral.

A comfortable chair with armrests and a high back had been set up for the admiral on the small deck and from this elevated position he surveyed the scene as it swung before him. It had been a dream of his over the past two years to command the fleet in battle – to draw this immense sword from its scabbard – even though he knew Vespasian had only appointed him as a peacetime administrator, to keep the blade from rusting. But enough of drills. Now at last he could see what battle-stations really looked like: the piercing notes of the trumpets drawing men from every corner of Misenum, the rowing boats ferrying the first of the sailors out to the huge quadriremes, the advance guard already boarding the warships and swarming over the decks, the high masts being raised, the oars readied. Antius had promised him he would have twenty ships operational immediately. That was four thousand men – a legion!

When the *Minerva* was pointing directly eastwards the double bank of oars dipped, the drums began to beat below decks and she was stroked forwards. He could hear his personal standard, emblazoned with the imperial eagle, catching the wind from the stern-post behind him. The breeze was on his face. He felt a tightening of anticipation in his stomach. The whole of the town had turned out to watch. He could see them lining the streets, leaning out of the windows, standing on the flat roofs. A thin cheer carried across the harbour. He searched the hillside for his own villa, saw Gaius and Julia outside the library, and raised his hand. Another cheer greeted the gesture.

'You see the fickleness of the mob?' he called happily to Attilius. 'Last night I was spat at in the street. Today I am a hero. All they live for is a show!' He waved again.

'Yes – and see what they do tomorrow,' muttered Torquatus, 'if half their men are lost.'

Attilius was taken aback by his anxiety. He said quietly, 'You think we are in that much danger?'

'These ships look strong, engineer, but they are held together by rope. I'll happily fight against any mortal enemy. But only a fool sails into combat with Nature.'

The pilot at the prow shouted a warning and the helmsman, standing behind the admiral, heaved on the tiller. The *Minerva* threaded between the anchored warships, close enough for Attilius to see the faces of the sailors on the decks, and then she swung again, passing along the natural rock wall of the harbour, which seemed to open slowly, like the wheeled door of a great temple. For the first time they had a clear view of what was happening across the bay.

Pliny gripped the arms of his chair, too overcome to speak. But then he remembered his duty to science. 'Beyond the promontory of Pausilypon,' he dictated hesitantly, 'the whole of Vesuvius and the surrounding coast are masked by a drifting cloud, whitish-grey in colour, and streaked with black.' But that was too bland, he thought: he needed to convey some sense of awe. 'Thrusting above this, bulging and uncoiling, as if the hot entrails of the earth are being drawn out and dragged towards the heavens, rises the central column of the manifestation.' That was better. 'It grows,' he continued, 'as if supported by a continual blast. But at its uppermost reaches, the weight of the exuded material becomes too great, and in pressing down spreads sideways. Wouldn't you agree, engineer?' he called. 'It is the weight that is spreading it sideways?'

'The weight, admiral,' Attilius shouted back. 'Or the wind.'

'Yes, a good point. Add that to the record, Alexion. The wind appears stronger at the higher altitude, and accordingly topples the manifestation to the south-east.' He gestured to Torquatus. 'We should take advantage of this wind, captain! Make full sail!'

'Madness,' said Torquatus to Attilius, under his breath. 'What sort of commander seeks out a storm?' But he shouted to his officers: 'Raise the main sail!'

The tranverse pole which supported the sail was lifted from its resting place in the centre of the hull and Attilius had to scramble towards the stern as the sailors on either side seized the cables and began to haul it up the mast. The sail was still furled and when it reached its position beneath the carchesium – 'the drinking-cup', as they called the observation platform – a young lad of no more than ten shinned up the mast to release it. He scampered along the yard-arm, untying the fastenings, and when the last was loosened the heavy linen sail dropped and filled immediately, tautening with the force of the wind. The *Minerva* creaked and picked up speed, scudding through the waves, raising curls of white foam on either side of her sharp prow, like a chisel slicing through soft wood.

Pliny felt his spirits fill with the sail. He pointed to the left. 'There's our destination, captain. Herculaneum! Steer straight towards the shore – to the Villa Calpurnia!'

'Yes, admiral! Helmsman – take us east!'

The sail cracked and the ship banked. A wave of spray drenched Attilius – a glorious sensation. He rubbed the dust from his face and ran his hands through his filthy hair. Below decks, the drums had increased to a frantic tempo, and the oars became a blur in the crashing waves and spray. Pliny's secretary had to lay his arms across his papers to prevent them blowing away. Attilius looked up at the admiral. Pliny was leaning forwards in his chair, his plump cheeks glistening with sea-spray, eyes alight with excitement, grinning wide, all trace of his former exhaustion gone. He was a cavalryman on his horse again, pounding across the German plain, javelin in hand, to wreak havoc on the barbarians.

'We shall rescue Rectina and the library and carry them to safety, then join Antius and the rest of the fleet in evacuating people further along the coast – how does that sound to you, captain?'

'As the admiral wishes,' responded Torquatus stiffly. 'May I ask what time your clock shows?'

'The start of the tenth hour,' said Alexion.

The captain raised his eyebrows. 'So, then – just three hours of full daylight left.'

He left the implication hanging in the air, but the admiral waved it away. 'Look at the speed we're making, captain! We'll soon be at the coast.'

'Yes, and the wind which drives us forwards will make it all the harder for us to put to sea again.'

'Sailors!' mocked the admiral above the sound of the waves. 'Are you listening, engineer? I swear, they're worse than farmers when it comes to the weather. They moan when there isn't a wind, and then complain even louder when there is!'

'Admiral!' Torquatus saluted. 'If you will excuse me?' He turned away, his jaw clamped tight, and made his way, swaying, towards the prow.

'Observations at the tenth hour,' said Pliny. 'Are you ready, Alexion?' He placed his fingertips together and frowned. It was a considerable technical challenge to describe a phenomenon for which the language had not yet been invented. After a while, the various metaphors – columns, tree trunks, fountains and the like – seemed to obscure rather than illuminate, failing to capture the sublime power of what he was witnessing. He should have brought a poet with him – he would have been more use than this cautious captain. 'Drawing closer,' he began, 'the manifestation appears as a gigantic, heavy rain cloud, increasingly black. As with a storm viewed from a distance of several miles, it is possible to see individual plumes of rain, drifting like smoke across the dark surface. And yet, according to the engineer, Marcus Attilius, these are falls not of rain but of rock.' He pointed to the poop deck beside him. 'Come up here, engineer. Describe to us again what you saw. For the record.'

Attilius climbed the short ladder to the platform. There was something utterly incongruous about the way in which the admiral had arranged himself – with his slave, his portable desk, his throne-like chair and his water clock – when set against the fury into which they were sailing. Even though the wind was at his back, he could hear the roar from the mountain now, and the towering cascade of rock was suddenly much nearer, their ship as fragile as a leaf at the base of a waterfall. He started to give his account once more and then a bolt of lightning arced across the roiling mass of cloud – not white, but a brilliant, jagged streak of red. It hung in the air, like a vivid vein of blood, and Alexion started to cluck his tongue, which was how the superstitious worshipped lightning.

'Add that to the list of phenomena,' commanded Pliny. 'Lightning: a grievous portent.'

Torquatus shouted, 'We're sailing too close!'

Beyond the admiral's shoulder, Attilius could see the quadriremes of the Misene fleet, still in sunlight, streaming out of harbour in a V-formation, like a squadron of flying geese. But then he became aware that the sky was darkening. A barrage of falling stones was exploding on the surface of the sea to their right, creeping rapidly closer. The prows and sails of the quadriremes blurred, dissolved to ghost-ships, as the air was filled with whirling rock.

In the pandemonium, Torquatus was everywhere, bellowing orders. Men ran along the deck in the half-light. The ropes supporting the yard-arm were unhitched and the sail lowered. The helmsman swung hard left. An instant later a ball of lightning came hurtling from the sky, touched the top of the mast, travelled down it and then along the yard-arm. In the brilliance of its glare Attilius saw the admiral with his head ducked and his hands pressed to the back of his neck, and his secretary leaning forwards to protect his papers. The fireball shot off the edge of the pole and plunged into the sea, trailing fumes of sulphur. It died with a violent hiss, taking its light with it. He closed his eyes. If the sail had not been lowered it would surely have gone up in flames. He could feel the drumming of the stones on his shoulders, hear them rattling across the deck. The *Minerva* must be brushing along the edge of the cloud, he realised, and Torquatus was trying to row them out from beneath it — and abruptly he succeeded. There was a final lash of missiles and they burst back out into the sunshine.

He heard Pliny coughing and opened his eyes to see the admiral standing, brushing the debris from the folds of his toga. He had held on to a handful of stones and as he flopped back into his chair he examined them in his palm. All along the length of the ship, men were shaking their clothes and feeling their flesh for cuts. The *Minerva* was still steering directly towards Herculaneum, now less than a mile distant and clearly visible, but the wind was getting up, and the sea with it, the helmsman straining to keep them to their course as the waves crashed against the left side of the ship.

'Encounter with the manifestation,' said Pliny, calmly. He stopped to wipe his face on his sleeve and coughed again. 'Are you taking this down? What time is it?'

Alexion tipped the stones from his papers and blew away the dust. He leaned towards the clock. 'The mechanism is broken, admiral.' His voice was trembling. He was almost in tears.

'Well, no matter. Let's say the eleventh hour.' Pliny held up one of the stones and peered at it closely. 'The material is a frothy, bubbled pumice. Greyish-white. As light as ash, which falls in fragments no larger than a man's thumb.' He paused, and added gently: 'Take up your pen, Alexion. If there's one thing I can't abide it's cowardice.'

The secretary's hand was shaking. It was hard for him to write as the liburnian pitched and rolled. His pen slipped across the surface of the papyri in an illegible scrawl. The admiral's chair slid across the deck and Attilius grabbed it. He said, 'You ought to move below deck,' as Torquatus stumbled towards them, bare-headed.

'Take my helmet, admiral.'

'Thank you, captain, but this old skull of mine provides quite adequate protection.'

'Admiral – I beg you – this wind will run us straight into the storm – we must turn back!'

Pliny ignored him. 'The pumice is less like rock, than airy fragments of a frozen cloud.' He craned his neck to stare over the side of the ship. 'It floats on the surface of the sea like lumps of ice. Do you see? Extraordinary!'

Attilius had not noticed it before. The water was covered in a carpet of stone. The oars brushed it aside with every stroke but more floated in immediately to replace it. Torquatus ran to the low wall of the deck. They were surrounded.

A wave of pumice broke over the front of the ship.

'Admiral –'

'Fortune favours the brave, Torquatus. Steer towards the shore!'

For a short while longer they managed to plough on, but the pace of the oars was weakening, defeated not by the wind or the waves but by the clogging weight of pumice on the water. It deepened as they neared the coast, two or three feet thick – a broad expanse of rustling dry surf. The blades of the oars flailed helplessly across it, unable to bring any pressure to bear, and the ship began to drift with the wind towards the waterfall of rock. The Villa Calpurnia was tantalisingly close. Attilius recognised the spot where he had stood with Rectina. He could see figures running along the shore, the piles of books, the fluttering white robes of the Epicurean philosophers.

Pliny had stopped dictating and, with Attilius's assistance, had pulled himself up on to his feet. All around the timber was creaking as the pressure of the pumice squeezed the hull. The engineer felt him sag slightly as, for the first time, he seemed to appreciate that they were defeated. He stretched out his hand towards the shore. 'Rectina,' he murmured.

The rest of the fleet was beginning to scatter, the V-formation disintegrating as the ships battled to save themselves. And then it was dusk again and the familiar thunder of pumice hammering drowned out every other sound. Torquatus shouted, 'We've lost control of the ship! Everybody – below decks. Engineer – help me lift him down from here.'

'My records!' protested Pliny.

'Alexion has your records, admiral.' Attilius had him by one arm and the captain by the other. He was immensely heavy. He stumbled on the last step and nearly fell full-length but they managed to retrieve him and lugged him along the deck towards the open trapdoor that led down to the rowing stations as the air turned to rock. 'Make way for the admiral!' panted Torquatus and then they almost threw him down the ladder. Alexion went next with the precious papers, treading on the admiral's shoulders, then Attilius jumped down in a shower of pumice, and finally Torquatus, slamming the trap behind them.

Vespera

[20:02 hours]

'During [the first] phase the vent radius was probably of
the order of 100 metres. As the eruption continued,
inevitable widening of the vent permitted still higher
mass eruption rates. By the evening of the 24th, the
column height had increased. Progressively deeper levels
within the magma chamber were tapped, until after about
seven hours the more mafic grey pumice was reached.
This was ejected at about 1.5 million tonnes per second,
and carried by convection to maximum heights of around
33 kilometres.'

Volcanoes: A Planetary Perspective

In the stifling heat and the near-darkness beneath the
Minerva's decks they crouched and listened to the drumming of the stones above them. The air was rank with
the sweat and breath of two hundred sailors. Occasionally, a
foreign voice would cry out in some unrecognisable tongue
only to be silenced by a harsh shout from one of the officers.
A man near Attilius moaned repeatedly in Latin that it was the
end of the world — and that, indeed, was what it felt like to the
engineer. Nature had reversed herself so that they were
drowning beneath rock in the middle of the sea, drifting in the
depths of night during the bright hours of the day. The ship

was rocking violently but none of the oars was moving. There was no purpose to any activity for they had no idea of the direction in which they were pointing. There was nothing to do but endure, each man huddled in his own thoughts.

How long this went on, Attilius could not calculate. Perhaps one hour; perhaps two. He was not even sure where he was below decks. He knew that he was clinging to a narrow wooden gantry that seemed to run the length of the ship, with the double-banks of sailors crammed on benches on either side. He could hear Pliny wheezing somewhere close, Alexion snuffling like a child. Torquatus was entirely silent. The incessant hammering of the pumice fall, sharp to begin with as it rattled on the timber of the deck, gradually became more muffled, as pumice fell on pumice, sealing them off from the world. And that, for him, was the worst thing – the sense of this mass slowly pressing down on them, burying them alive. As time passed he began to wonder how long the joists of the deck would hold, or whether the sheer weight of what was above them would push them beneath the waves. He tried to console himself with the thought that pumice was light: the engineers in Rome, when they were constructing a great dome, sometimes mixed it into the cement in place of rock and fragments of brick. Nevertheless he gradually became aware that the ship was starting to list and very soon after that a cry of panic went up from some of the sailors to his right that water was pouring through the oar-holes.

Torquatus shouted at them roughly to be quiet then called down the gantry to Pliny that he needed to take a party of men above decks to try to shovel off the rock-fall.

'Do what you have to do, captain,' replied the admiral. His voice was calm. 'This is Pliny!' he suddenly bellowed above the roar of the storm. 'I expect every man to bear himself like a Roman soldier! And when we return to Misenum, you will all be rewarded, I promise you!'

There was some jeering from the darkness.

'If we return, more like!'

'It was you who got us into the mess!'

'Silence!' yelled Torquatus. 'Engineer, will you help me?' He had mounted the short ladder to the trapdoor and was trying to push it open but the weight of the pumice made it hard to lift. Attilius groped his way along the gantry and joined him on the ladder, holding on to it with one hand, heaving with the other at the wooden panel above his head. Together they raised it slowly, releasing a cascade of debris that bounced off their heads and clattered on to the timbers below. 'I need twenty men!' ordered Torquatus. 'You five banks of oars – follow me.'

Attilius climbed out after him into the whirl of flying pumice. There was a strange almost brownish light, as in a sandstorm, and as he straightened Torquatus grabbed his arm and pointed. It took Attilius a moment to see what he meant, but then he glimpsed it too – a row of winking yellow lights, showing faintly through the murk. Pompeii, he thought – Corelia!

'We've drifted beneath the worst of it and come in close to the coast!' shouted the captain. 'The gods alone know where! We'll try to run her aground! Help me at the helm!' He turned and pushed the nearest of the oarsmen back towards the trapdoor. 'Get back below and tell the others to row – to row for their lives! The rest of you – hoist the sail!'

He ran along the side of the ship towards the stern and Attilius followed, his head lowered, his feet sinking into the heavy blanket of white pumice that covered the deck like snow. They were so low in the water he felt he could almost have stepped down on to the carpet of rock and walked ashore. He clambered up on to the poop deck and with Torquatus he seized the great oar that steered the liburnian. But even with two men swinging on it the blade wouldn't move against the floating mass.

Dimly, he could see the shape of the sail beginning to rise before them. He heard the crack as it started to fill, and at the same time there was a ripple of movement along the banks of oars. The helm shuddered slightly beneath his hands. Torquatus pushed and he heaved, his feet scrabbling for a purchase in the loose stone, and slowly he felt the wooden shaft begin to move. For a while the liburnian seemed to list, motionless, and then a gust of wind propelled them forwards. He heard the drum beating again below, the oars settling into a steady rhythm, and from the gloom ahead the shape of the coast began to emerge – a breakwater, a sandy beach, a row of villas with torches lit along the terraces, people moving at the edge of the sea, where waves were pounding the shore, lifting the boats in the shallows and flinging them back on land. Whatever place this was, he realised with disappointment, it was not Pompeii.

Suddenly the rudder jumped and moved so freely he thought it must have snapped and Torquatus swung it hard, aiming them towards the beach. They had broken clear of the clinging pumice and were into the rolling waves, the force of the sea and the wind propelling them directly at the shore. He saw the crowd of people on the beach, all trying to load their possessions into the boats, turn to look at them in astonishment, saw them break and scatter as the liburnian bore down upon them. Torquatus cried out, 'Brace yourselves!' and an instant later the hull scraped rock and Attilius went flying down on to the main deck, his landing cushioned by the foot-thick mattress of stone.

He lay there for a moment, winded, his cheek pressed to

the warm, dry pumice, as the ship rolled beneath him. He heard the shouts of the sailors coming up from below decks, and the splashes as they jumped into the surf. He raised himself and saw the sail being lowered, the anchor flung over the side. Men with ropes were running up the beach, trying to find places to secure the ship. It was twilight – not the twilight thrown out by the eruption, which they seemed to have sailed straight through, but the natural dusk of early evening. The shower of stones was light and intermittent and the noise as they scattered over the deck and plopped into the sea was lost in the boom of the surf and the roar of the wind. Pliny had emerged from the trapdoor and was stepping carefully through the pumice, supported by Alexion – a solid and dignified figure in the midst of the panic all around him. If he felt any fear he did not show it and as Attilius approached he raised his arm almost cheerfully.

'Well, this is a piece of good fortune, engineer. Do you see where we are? I know this place well. This is Stabiae – a most pleasant town in which to spend an evening. Torquatus!' He beckoned to the captain. 'I suggest we stay here for the night.'

Torquatus regarded him with incredulity. 'We have no choice about it, admiral. No ship can be launched against this wind. The question is: how soon will it carry that wall of rock upon us?'

'Perhaps it won't,' said Pliny. He gazed across the surf at the lights of the little town, rising into the low hillside. It was separated from the beach by the coastal road that ran all around the bay. The highway was clogged with the same weary traffic of refugees that Attilius had encountered earlier at Herculaneum. On the shore itself, perhaps a hundred people had congregated with their possessions, hoping to escape by sea, but unable to do more than gaze hopelessly at the crashing waves. One fat and elderly man stood apart, surrounded by his household, occasionally throwing up his hands in lamentation, and Attilius felt a stir of recognition. Pliny had noticed him, too. 'That's my friend, Pomponianus. The poor old fool,' he said, sadly. 'A nervous fellow at the best of times. He'll need our comfort. We must wear our bravest faces. Assist me to the shore.'

Attilius jumped down into the sea, followed by Torquatus. The water was up to their waists at one moment, at the next it was swirling around their necks. It was no easy task to take off a man of the admiral's weight and condition. With Alexion's help Pliny finally got down on to his backside and shuffled forwards and as they took his arms he slipped into the water. They managed to keep his head above the surface, and then, in an impressive show of self-control, he shrugged off their support and waded ashore unaided.

'A stubborn old fool,' said Torquatus, as they watched him march up the beach and embrace Pomponianus. 'A magnificent, courageous, stubborn old fool. He's almost killed us twice and I swear he'll try again before he's finished.'

Attilius glanced along the coast towards Vesuvius but he could not see much in the gathering darkness except for the luminous white lines of the waves running in to batter the coast, and beyond them the inky black of the falling rock. Another line of red lightning split the sky. He said, 'How far are we from Pompeii?'

'Three miles,' answered Torquatus. 'Perhaps less. It looks like they're taking the worst of it, poor wretches. This wind – the men had better seek some shelter.'

He began wading towards the shore leaving Attilius alone. If Stabiae was three miles downwind of Pompeii, and

Vesuvius lay five miles the other side of the city, then this monstrous cloud must be eight miles long. Eight miles long, and – what? – at least five miles wide, given how far it reached out into the sea. Unless Corelia had fled very early she would have had no chance of escape.

He stood there for a while, buffeted by the sea, until at length he heard the admiral calling his name. Helplessly he turned and made his way through the restless shallows, up on to the beach to join the rest.

Pomponianus had a villa on the sea-front only a short walk along the road and Pliny was suggesting they should all return to it. Attilius could hear them arguing as he approached. Pomponianus, panicky, was objecting in his high voice that if they left the beach they would lose their chance of a place in a boat. But Pliny waved that away. 'No sense in waiting here,' he said. His voice was urgent. 'Besides, you can always sail with us, when the wind and sea are more favourable. Come, Livia – take my arm.' And with Pomponianus's wife on one side and Alexion on the other, and with the household slaves strung out behind them – lugging marble busts, carpets, chests and candelabra – he led them up on to the road.

He was hurrying as fast as he could, his cheeks puffed out, and Attilius thought, he knows – he knows from his observations what is about to happen. Sure enough they had just reached the gates of the villa when it came on them again like a summer storm – first a few heavy drops, as a warning, and then the air exploded over the myrtle bushes and the cobbled courtyard. Attilius could feel someone's body pressing into his from behind, he pushed into the man in front and together they tumbled through the door and into the darkened, deserted villa. People were wailing, knocking blindly into the furniture. He heard a woman's scream and a crash. The disembodied face of a slave appeared, illuminated from below by an oil lamp, and then the face vanished and he heard the familiar *wumph* as a torch was lit. They huddled in the comfort of the light, masters and slaves alike, as the pumice clattered on to the terracotta roof of the villa and smashed into the ornamental gardens outside. Someone went off with the oil lamp to fetch more torches and some candles, and the slaves went on lighting them long after there was sufficient light, as if somehow the brighter the scene, the more safe they would be. The crowded hall soon had an almost festive feel to it, and that was when Pliny, with his arm draped round the quivering shoulders of Pomponianus, declared that he would like to eat.

The admiral had no belief in an afterlife: 'Neither body nor mind has any more sensation after death than it had before birth.' Nevertheless, he put on a display of bravery over the next few hours which none who survived the evening would after-wards forget. He had long ago resolved that when death came for him he would endeavour to meet it in the spirit of Marcus Sergius, whom he had crowned in the *Natural History* as the most courageous man who had ever lived – wounded twenty-three times in the course of his campaigns, left crippled, twice captured by Hannibal and held in chains every day for twenty months; Sergius had ridden into his final battle with a right hand made of iron, a substitute for the one he had lost. He was not as successful as Scipio or Caesar, but what did that matter? 'All other victors truly have conquered men,' Pliny had written, 'but Sergius vanquished fortune also.'

'To vanquish fortune' – that was what a man should strive to do. Accordingly, as the slaves prepared his dinner, he told an astonished Pomponianus that he would first like to take a bath and he waddled off, escorted by Alexion, to soak in a cold tub. He removed his filthy clothes and clambered into the clear water, submerging his head completely into a silent world. Surfacing, he announced that he wished to dictate a few more observations – like the engineer, he reckoned the dimensions of the manifestation at roughly eight miles by six – then allowed himself to be patted dry by one of Pomponianus's body-slaves, anointed in saffron-oil, and dressed in one of his friend's clean togas.

Five of them sat down to dinner – Pliny, Pomponianus, Livia, Torquatus and Attilius – not an ideal number from the point of etiquette, and the din of the pumice on the roof made conversation difficult. Still, at least it meant that he had a couch to himself and space to stretch out. The table and the couches had been carried in from the dining room and set up in the sparkling hall. And if the food was not up to much – the fires were out and the best the kitchens could come up with were cold cuts of meat, fowl and fish – then Pomponianus, at Pliny's gentle prompting, had made up for it with the wine. He produced a Falernian, two hundred years old, a vintage from the consulship of Lucius Opimius. It was his final jar ('Not much point in hanging on to it now,' he observed gloomily).

The liquid in the candlelight was the colour of rough honey and after it was decanted but before it was mixed with a younger wine – for it was too bitter to be drunk undiluted – Pliny took it from the slave and inhaled it, catching in its musty aroma the whiff of the old Republic: of men of the stamp of Cato and Sergius; of a city fighting to become an empire; of the dust of the Campus Martius; of trial by iron and fire.

The admiral did most of the talking and he tried to keep it light, avoiding all mention, for example, of Rectina and the precious library of the Villa Calpurnia, or the fate of the fleet, which he supposed must be broken up by now and scattered all along the coast. (That alone might be enough to force his suicide, he realised: he had put to sea without waiting for imperial authority; Titus might not be forgiving.) Instead he chose to talk about the wine. He knew a lot about wine. Julia called him 'a wine bore'. But what did he care? To bore was the privilege of age and rank. If it had not been for wine his heart would have packed in years ago.

'The records tell us that the summer in the consulship of Opimius was very much like this one. Long hot days filled with endless sunshine – "ripe", as the vintners call it.' He swirled the wine in his glass and sniffed it. 'Who knows? Perhaps, two centuries from now, men will be drinking the vintage from this year of ours, and wondering what we were like. Our skill. Our courage.' The thunder of the barrage seemed to be increasing. Somewhere wood splintered. There was a crash of breaking tiles. Pliny looked around the table at his fellow diners – at Pomponianus, who was wincing at the roof and clinging to the hand of his wife; at Livia, who managed to give him a small, tight smile (she always had been twice the man her husband was); at Torquatus, who was frowning at the floor; and finally at the engineer, who had not said a word throughout the meal. He felt warmly towards the aquarius – a man of science, after his own heart, who had sailed in search of knowledge.

'Let us drink a toast,' he suggested, 'to the genius of Roman engineering – to the Aqua Augusta, which gave us warning of what was to happen, if only we had had the wit to heed it!' He raised his glass towards Attilius. 'The Aqua Augusta!'

'The Aqua Augusta!'

They drank, with varying degrees of enthusiasm. And it was a good wine, thought the admiral, smacking his lips. A perfect blend of the old and the young. Like himself and the engineer. And if it proved to be his last? Well then: it was an appropriate wine to end on.

When he announced that he was going to bed he could see that they assumed he must be joking. But no, he assured them, he was serious. He had trained himself to fall asleep at will – even upright, in a saddle, in a freezing German forest. This? This was nothing! 'Your arm, engineer, if you will be so kind.' He wished them all good night.

Attilius held a torch aloft in one hand and with the other he supported the admiral. Together they went out into the central courtyard. Pliny had stayed here often over the years. It was a favourite spot of his: the dappled light on the pink stone, the smell of the flowers, the cooing from the dovecote set in the wall above the veranda. But now the garden was in pitch darkness, trembling with the roar of falling stone. Pumice was strewn across the covered walkway and the clouds of dust from the dry and brittle rock set off his wheezing. He stopped outside the door of his usual room and waited for Attilius to clear a space so that he could pull it open. He wondered what had happened to the birds. Had they flown away just before the manifestation started, thus offering a portent, if an augur had been on hand to divine it? Or were they out there some-where in the black night, battered and huddled? 'Are you fright-ened, Marcus Attilius?'

'Yes.'

'That's good. To be brave, by definition, one has first to be afraid.' He rested his hand on the engineer's shoulder as he kicked off his shoes. 'Nature is a merciful deity,' he said. 'Her anger never lasts forever. The fire dies. The storm blows itself out. The flood recedes. And this will end as well. You'll see. Get some rest.'

He shuffled into the windowless room leaving Attilius to close the door behind him.

T he engineer stayed where he was, leaning against the wall, watching the rain of pumice. After a while he heard loud snores emanating from the bedroom. Extraordinary, he thought. Either the admiral was pretending to be asleep – which he doubted – or the old man really had nodded off. He glanced at the sky. Presumably Pliny was right, and the 'manifestation', as he still insisted on calling it, would begin to weaken. But that was not happening yet. If anything, the force of the storm was intensifying. He detected a different, harsher sound to the dropping rock, and the ground beneath his feet was trembling, as it had in Pompeii. He ventured out a cautious pace from beneath the canopy, holding his torch towards the ground, and immediately he was struck hard on his arm. He almost dropped the torch. He grabbed a lump of the freshly fallen rock. Pressing himself against the wall he examined it in the light.

It was greyer than the earlier pumice – denser, larger, as if several pieces had been welded together – and it was hitting the ground with greater force. The shower of frothy white rock had been unpleasant and frightening but not especially painful. To be struck by a piece of this would be enough to knock a man unconscious. How long had this been going on?

He carried it into the hall and gave it to Torquatus. 'It's getting worse,' he said. 'While we've been eating, the stones have been getting heavier.' And then, to Pomponianus, 'What sort of roofs do you have here, sir? Flat or pitched?'

'Flat,' said Pomponianus. 'They form terraces. You know – for the views across the bay.'

Ah yes, thought Attilius – the famous views. Perhaps if they had spent a little less time gazing out to sea and rather more looking over their shoulders at the mountain behind them, they might have been better prepared. 'And how old is the house?'

'It's been in my family for generations,' said Pomponianus proudly. 'Why?'

'It isn't safe. With that weight of rock falling on it – and on old timber, too – sooner or later the joists will give way. We need to go outside.'

Torquatus hefted the rock in his hand. 'Outside? Into this?'

For a moment nobody spoke. Then Pomponianus started to wail that they were finished, that they should have sacrificed to Jupiter as he had suggested right at the beginning, but that nobody ever listened to him –

'Shut up,' said his wife. 'We have cushions, don't we? And pillows and sheets? We can protect ourselves from rocks.'

Torquatus said, 'Where's the admiral?'

'Asleep.'

'He's resigned himself to death, hasn't he? All that nonsense about wine! But I'm not ready to die, are you?'

'No.' Attilius was surprised by the firmness of his answer. After Sabina had died, he had gone on numbly, and if he had been told his existence was about to end, he would not have cared much one way or the other. He did not feel that way now.

'Then let's return to the beach.'

Livia was shouting to the slaves to fetch pillows and linen as Attilius hurried back into the courtyard. He could still hear Pliny's snores. He banged on the door and tried to open it but even in the short time he had been away the path had filled again with debris. He had to kneel to clear it, then dragged open the door and ran in with his torch. He shook the admiral's fleshy shoulder and the old man groaned and blinked in the light.

'Let me be.'

He tried to roll back on his side. Attilius did not argue with him. He hooked his elbow under Pliny's armpit and hauled him to his feet. Staggering under the weight he pushed the protesting admiral towards the door and they were barely across the threshold when he heard one of the ceiling beams crack behind them and part of the roof came crashing to the floor.

They put the pillows on their heads crossways, so that the ends covered their ears, and tied them in place with strips torn from the sheets, knotting them tightly under their chins. Their bulging white heads gave them the look of blind, subterranean insects. Then each collected a torch or a lamp and with one hand on the shoulder of the person in front – apart from Torquatus, who took the lead and who was wearing his helmet rather than a pillow – they set off to walk the gauntlet down to the beach.

All around them was a fury of noise – the heaving sea, the blizzard of rock, the boom of roofs giving way. Occasionally Attilius felt the muffled thump of a missile striking his skull and his ears rang as they had not done since he had been beaten by his teachers as a child. It was like being stoned by a mob – as if the deities had voted Vulcan a triumph and this painful procession, stripped of all human dignity, was how he chose to humiliate his captives. They edged forwards slowly, sinking up to their knees in the loose pumice, unable to move any faster than the admiral, whose coughing and wheezing seemed to worsen each time he stumbled forwards. He was holding on to Alexion and being held on to by Attilius; behind the engineer came Livia and, behind her, Pomponianus, with the slaves forming a line of torches at the back.

The force of the bombardment had cleared the road of refugees but down on the beach there was a light and it was towards this that Torquatus led them. A few of the citizens of Stabiae and some of the men of the *Minerva* had broken up one of the useless ships and set it on fire. With ropes, the heavy sail from the liburnian and a dozen oars they had built themselves a large shelter beside the blaze. People who had been fleeing along the coast had come down from the road, begging for protection, and a crowd of several hundred was jostling for cover. They did not want to let the repulsive-looking newcomers share their makeshift tent and there was some jeering and scuffling around the entrance until Torquatus shouted that he had Admiral Pliny with him and would crucify any marine who refused to obey his orders.

Grudgingly, room was made, and Alexion and Attilius lowered Pliny to the sand just inside the entrance. He asked weakly for some water and Alexion took a gourd from a slave and held it to his lips. He swallowed a little, coughed and lay down on his side. Alexion gently untied the pillow and placed it under his head. He glanced up at Attilius. The engineer shrugged. He did not know what to say. It seemed to him unlikely that the old man could survive much more of this.

He turned away and peered into the interior of the shelter. People were wedged together, barely able to move. The weight of the pumice was causing the roof to dip and from time to time a couple of the sailors cleared it by lifting it with the ends of their oars, tipping the stones away. Children were crying. One boy sobbed for his mother. Otherwise nobody spoke or shouted. Attilius tried to work out what time it was – he assumed it must be the middle of the night but then again it would be impossible to tell even if it was dawn – and he wondered how long they could endure. Sooner or later, hunger or thirst, or the pressure of the pumice rising on either side of their tent, would force them to abandon the beach. And then what? Slow suffocation by rock? A death more drawn-out and ingenious than anything Man had ever devised in the arena? So much for Pliny's belief that Nature was a merciful deity!

He tugged the pillow from his sweating head and it was as his face was uncovered that he heard someone croaking his name. In the crowded near-darkness he could not make out who it was at first, and even when the man thrust his way towards him he did not recognise him for he seemed to be made of stone, his face chalk-white with dust, his hair raised in spikes, like Medusa's. Only when he spoke his name – 'It's me, Lucius Popidius' – did he realise that it was one of the aediles of Pompeii.

Attilius seized his arm. 'Corelia? Is she with you?'

'My mother – she collapsed on the road.' Popidius was weeping. 'I couldn't carry her any longer. I had to leave her.'

Attilius shook him. 'Where's Corelia?'

Popidius's eyes were blank holes in the mask of his face. He looked like one of the ancestral effigies on the wall of his house. He swallowed hard.

'You coward,' said Attilius.

'I tried to bring her,' whined Popidius. 'But that madman had locked her in her room.'

'So you abandoned her?'

'What else could I do? He wanted to imprison us all!' He clutched at Attilius's tunic. 'Take me with you. That's Pliny over there, isn't it? You've got a ship? For pity's sake – I can't go on alone –'

Attilius pushed him away and stumbled towards the entrance of the tent. The bonfire had been crushed to extinction by the rain of rocks and now that it had gone out the darkness on the beach was not even the darkness of night but of a closed room. He strained his eyes towards Pompeii. Who was to say that the whole world was not in the process of being destroyed? That the very force which held the universe together – the *logos*, as the philosophers called it – was not disintegrating? He dropped to his knees and dug his hands into the sand and he knew at that moment, even as the grains squeezed through his fingers, that everything would be annihilated – himself, and Pliny, Corelia, the library at Herculaneum, the fleet, the cities around the bay, the aqueduct, Rome, Caesar, everything that had ever lived or ever been built: everything would eventually be reduced to a shoal of rock and an endlessly pounding sea. None of them would leave so much as a footprint behind them; they would not even leave a memory. He would die here on the beach with the rest and their bones would be crushed to powder.

But the mountain had not done with them yet. He heard a woman scream and raised his eyes. Faint and miraculous, far in the distance and yet growing in intensity, he saw a corona of fire in the sky.

VENUS

25 August

The final day of the eruption

Inclinatio

[00:12 hours]

'There comes a point when so much magma is being erupted so quickly that the eruption column density becomes too great for stable convection to persist. When this condition prevails, column collapse takes place, generating pyroclastic flows and surges, which are far more lethal than tephra fall.'

Volcanoes: A Planetary Perspective

The light travelled slowly downwards from right to left. A sickle of luminous cloud – that was how Pliny described it – *a sickle of luminous cloud* sweeping down the western slope of Vesuvius leaving in its wake a patchwork of fires. Some were winking, isolated pinpricks – farmhouses and villas that had been set alight. But elsewhere whole swathes of the forest were blazing. Vivid, leaping sheets of red and orange flame tore jagged holes in the darkness. The scythe moved on, implacably, for at least as long as it would have taken to count to a hundred, flared briefly, and vanished.

'The manifestation,' dictated Pliny, 'has moved into a different phase.'

To Attilius, there was something indefinably sinister about that silent, moving crest – its mysterious appearance, its enigmatic death. Born in the ruptured summit of the mountain it must have rolled away to drown itself in the sea. He remembered the fertile vineyards, the heavy clumps of grapes, the manacled slaves. There would be no vintage this year, ripe or otherwise.

'It's hard to tell from here,' Torquatus said, 'but judging by its position, I reckon that cloud of flame may just have passed over Herculaneum.'

'And yet it doesn't seem to be on fire,' replied Attilius. 'That part of the coast looks entirely dark. It's as if the town has vanished —'

They looked towards the base of the burning mountain, searching for some point of light, but there was nothing.

The effect on the beach at Stabiae was to shift the balance of terror, first one way and then the other. They could soon smell the fires on the wind, a pungent, acrid taste of sulphur and cinders. Someone screamed that they would all be burned alive. People sobbed, none louder than Lucius Popidius, who was calling for his mother, and then someone else — it was one of the sailors who had been prodding the roof with his oar — exclaimed that the heavy linen was no longer sagging. That quietened the panic.

Attilius cautiously stretched out his arm beyond the shelter of the tent, his palm held upwards, as if checking for rain. The marine was right. The air was still full of small missiles but the storm was not as violent as before. It was as if the mountain had found a different outlet for its malevolent energy, in the rushing avalanche of fire rather than in the steady bombardment of rock. In that moment he made up his mind. Better to die doing something — better to fall beside the coastal highway and lie in some unmarked grave — than to cower beneath this flimsy shelter, filled with fearful imaginings, a spectator waiting for the end. He reached for his discarded pillow and planted it firmly on his head then felt around in the sand for the strip of sheet. Torquatus asked him quietly what he was doing.

'Leaving.'

'Leaving?' Pliny, reclining on the sand, his notes spread around him and weighed down with piles of pumice, looked up sharply. 'You'll do no such thing. I absolutely refuse you permission to go.'

'With the greatest respect, admiral, I take my orders from Rome, not from you.' He was surprised some of the slaves had not also made a run for it. Why not? Habit, he supposed. Habit, and the lack of anywhere to run to.

'But I need you here.' There was a wheedling note in Pliny's hoarse voice. 'What if something should happen to me? Someone must make sure my observations are not lost to posterity.'

'There are others who can do that, admiral. I prefer to take my chance on the road.'

'But you're a man of science, engineer. I can tell it. That's why you came. You're much more valuable to me here. Torquatus – stop him.'

The captain hesitated, then unfastened his chin-strap and took off his helmet. 'Take this,' he said. 'Metal is better protection than feathers.' Attilius started to protest but Torquatus thrust it into his hands. 'Take it – and good luck.'

'Thank you.' Attilius grasped his hand. 'May luck go with you, too.'

It fitted him well enough. He had never worn a helmet before. He stood and picked up a torch. He felt like a gladiator about to enter the arena.

'But where will you go?' protested Pliny.

Attilius stepped into the storm. The light stones pinged off the helmet. It was utterly dark apart from the few torches planted into the sand around the perimeter of the shelter and the distant, glowing pyre of Vesuvius.

'Pompeii.'

T orquatus had estimated the distance between Stabiae and Pompeii at three miles – an hour's walk along a good road on a fine day. But the mountain had changed the laws of time and space and for a long while Attilius seemed to make no progress at all.

He managed to get up off the beach and on to the road without too much difficulty and he was lucky that the view of Vesuvius was uninterrupted because the fires gave him an aiming-point. He knew that as long as he walked straight towards them he must come to Pompeii eventually. But he was pushing into the wind, so that even though he kept his head hunched, shrinking his world to his pale legs and the little patch of stone in which he waded, the rain of pumice stung his face and clogged his mouth and nostrils with dust. With each step he sank up to his knees in pumice and the effect was like trying to climb a hill of gravel, or a barn full of grain – an endless, featureless slope which rubbed his skin and tore at the muscles at the top of his thighs. Every few hundred paces he swayed to a stop and somehow, holding the torch, he had to drag first one foot and then the other out of the clinging pumice and pick the stones out of his shoes.

The temptation to lie down and rest was overwhelming and yet it had to be resisted, he knew, because sometimes he stumbled into the bodies of those who had given up already. His torch showed soft forms, mere outlines of humanity, with occasionally a protruding foot, or a hand clawing at the air. And it was not only people who had died on the road. He blundered into a team of oxen that had become stuck in the drifts and a horse that had collapsed between the shafts of an abandoned wagon, its burden too heavy to pull: a stone horse pulling a stone cart. All these things appeared as brief apparitions in the flickering circle of light he carried. There must have been much more that mercifully he could not see. Sometimes the living as well as the dead emerged fleetingly out of the darkness – a man carrying a cat; a young woman, naked and deranged; another couple carrying a long brass candelabrum slung across their shoulders, the man at the front and the woman at the back. They were heading in the opposite direction to him. From either side came isolated, barely human cries and moans, such as he imagined might be heard on a battlefield after the fighting was done. He did not stop, apart from once, when he heard a child crying out for its parents. He stopped, listening, and stumbled around for a while, trying to find the source of the voice, calling out in response, but the child went quiet, perhaps out of fear at the sound of a stranger, and eventually he gave up the search.

All this lasted for several hours.

At some point the crescent of light appeared again at the summit of Vesuvius, sweeping down, following more or less the same trajectory as before. The glow was brighter and when it reached the shore, or what he guessed was the shore, it did not die at once but rolled on out to sea before tapering away into the darkness. It was followed by the same easing in the fall of rock. But this time on the slopes of the mountain it seemed to extinguish the fires rather than rekindle them. Soon afterward his torch began to stutter. Most of the pitch had burned away. He pushed on with a renewed energy born of fear because he knew that when it died he would be left help-less in the darkness. And when that moment came it was indeed terrible – more horrible than he had feared. His legs had vanished and he could see nothing, not even if he brought his hand right up to his eyes.

The fires on the side of Vesuvius had also dwindled to an occasional tiny fountain of orange sparks. More red lightning gave a pinkish glow to the underside of the black cloud. He was no longer sure in which direction he was facing. He was disembodied, utterly alone, buried almost up to his thighs in stone, the earth whirling and thundering around him. He flung away his extinguished torch and let himself sink forwards. He stretched out his hands and lay there, feeling the mantle of pumice slowly accumulating around his shoulders, and it was peculiarly comforting, like being tucked up in bed at night as a child. He laid his cheek to the warm rock and felt himself relax. A great sense of tranquillity suffused him. If this was death then it was not too bad: he could accept this – welcome it, even, as one might a well-earned rest at the end of a hard day's work out on the arcades of the aqueducts.

In his dreams the ground was melting and he was drop-ping, tumbling, in a cascade of rocks, towards the centre of the earth.

He was woken by heat, and by the smell of burning. He did not know how long he had slept. Long enough to be almost entirely buried. He was in his grave. Panicking, he pushed with his forearms and slowly he felt the weight on his shoulders yield and split, heard the rustle of stones as they tumbled off him. He raised himself and shook his head, spitting the dust from his mouth, blinking his eyes, still buried below the waist.

The rain of pumice had mostly stopped – the familiar warning-sign – and in the distance, immediately before him, low in the sky, he saw again the familiar scythe of glowing cloud. Except that this time, instead of moving like a comet from right to left, it was descending fast and spreading laterally, coming his way. Immediately behind it was an interval of darkness which sprang into fire a few moments later as the heat found fresh fuel on the southern flank of the mountain; before it, carried on the furnace-wind, came a rolling boom of noise, such that if he had been Pliny he would have varied his metaphor and described it not as a cloud but as a wave – a boiling wave of red-hot vapour that scorched his cheeks and watered his eyes. He could smell his hair singeing.

He writhed to free himself from the grip of the pumice as the sulphurous dawn raced across the sky towards him. Something dark was growing in the centre of it, rising out of the ground, and he realised that the crimson light was silhouetting a town less than half a mile away. The vision brightened. He picked out city walls and watchtowers, the pillars of a roofless temple, a row of blasted, sightless windows – and *people*, the shadows of *people*, running in panic along the lines of the ramparts. The spectacle was sharp for only a little while, just long enough for him to recognise it as Pompeii, and then the glow behind it slowly faded, taking the city with it, back into the darkness.

Diluculum

[06:00 hours]

'It is dangerous to assume that the worst is over after the initial explosive phase. Predicting an eruption's end is even more difficult than predicting its beginning.'

Encyclopaedia of Volcanoes

He pulled off his helmet and used it as a bucket, digging the lip of the metal into the pumice and emptying it over his shoulder. Gradually as he worked he became aware of the pale white shapes of his arms. He stopped and raised them in wonder. Such a trivial matter, to be able to see one's hands, and yet he could have cried with relief. The morning was coming. A new day was struggling to be born. He was still alive.

He finished digging, wrestled his legs loose and hauled himself up on to his feet. The freshly ignited crop of fires high up on Vesuvius had restored his sense of direction. Perhaps it was his imagination but he even thought he could see the shadow of the city. Vague in the darkness, the plain of pumice spread out around him, a ghostly, gently undulating landscape. He set off towards Pompeii, wading up to his knees again, sweating, thirsty, dirty, with the acrid stench of burning in his nose and throat. He assumed, by the nearness of the city walls, that he must be almost inside the port, in which case there ought to be a river somewhere. But the pumice had submerged the Sarnus into the desert of stones. Through the dust he had a vague impression of low walls on either side of him and as he stumbled forward he realised that these weren't fences but buildings, buried buildings, and that he was labouring along a street at roof level. The pumice must be seven or eight feet deep at least.

Impossible to believe that people could have lived through such a bombardment. And yet they had. Not only had he seen them moving on the city's ramparts, he could see them now, emerging from holes in the ground, from beneath the tombs of their houses – individuals, couples supporting one another, whole familes, even a mother holding a baby. They stood around in the grainy brown half-light, brushing the dust from their clothes, gazing at the sky. Apart from an occasional scattering of missiles the fall of rock had ceased. But it would come again, Attilius was certain. There was a pattern. The greater the surge of burning air down the slopes of the mountain, the more energy it seemed to suck from the storm and the longer the lull before it started anew. There was no doubt, either, that the surges were growing in strength. The first appeared to have hit Herculaneum; the second to have travelled beyond it, out to sea; the third to have reached almost as far as Pompeii itself. The next might easily sweep across the entire town. He ploughed on.

The harbour had entirely vanished. A few masts poking out of the sea of pumice, a broken sternpost and the shrouded outline of a hull were the only clues that it had ever existed. He could hear the sea, but it sounded a long way off. The shape of the coast had altered. Occasionally, the ground shook and then would come the distant crash of walls and timbers giving way, roofs collapsing. A ball of lightning fizzed across the landscape and struck the distant columns of the temple of Venus. A fire started. It became harder to make progress. He sensed that he was wading up a slope and he tried to visualise how the port had looked, the ramped roads leading up from the wharfs and quaysides to the city gates. Torches loomed out of the smoky air and passed him. He had expected to encounter crowds of survivors seizing the opportunity to escape from the town but the traffic was all the other way. People were going back into Pompeii. Why? To search for those they had lost, he supposed. To see what they could retrieve from their homes. To loot. He wanted to tell them to run for it while they had the chance but he hadn't the breath. A man pushed him out of the way and overtook him, jerking from side to side like a marionette as he scrambled through the drifts.

Attilius reached the top of the ramp. He groped through the dusty twilight until he found a corner of heavy masonry and felt his way around it, into the low tunnel which was all that remained of the great entrance to the town. He could have reached up and touched the vaulted roof. Someone lumbered up to him from behind and seized his arm. 'Have you seen my wife?'

He was holding a small oil lamp, with his hand cupped around the flame – a young man, handsome, and incongruously immaculate, as if he had been out for a stroll before breakfast. Attilius saw that the fingers encircling the lamp were manicured.

'I'm sorry –'

'Julia Felix? You must know her. Everyone knows her.' His voice was trembling. He called out, 'Has anyone here seen Julia Felix?'

There was a stir of movement and Attilius realised there were a dozen or more people, crammed together, sheltering in the passageway of the gate.

'She's not been this way,' someone muttered.

The young man groaned and staggered towards the town. 'Julia! Julia!' His voice grew fainter as his wavering lamp disappeared into the darkness. 'Julia!'

Attilius said loudly, 'Which gate is this?'

He was answered by the same man. 'The Stabian.'

'So this is the road which leads up to the Gate of Vesuvius?'

'Don't tell him!' hissed a voice. 'He's just a stranger, come to rob us!'

Other men with torches were forcing their way up the ramp.

'Thieves!' shrieked a woman. 'Our properties are all unguarded! Thieves!'

A punch was thrown, someone swore and suddenly the narrow entrance was a tangle of shadows and waving torches. The engineer kept his hand on the wall and stumbled forward, treading on bodies. A man cursed and fingers closed around his ankle. Attilius jerked his leg free. He reached the end of the gate and glanced behind him just in time to see a torch jammed into a woman's face and her hair catch fire. Her screams pursued him as he turned and tried to run, desperate to escape the brawl, which now seemed to be sucking in people from the side alleys, men and women emerging from the darkness, shadows out of shadows, slipping and sliding down the slope to join the fight.

Madness: an entire town driven mad.

He waded on up the hill trying to find his bearings. He was sure this was the way to the Vesuvius Gate — he could see the orange fringes of fire working their way across the mountain far ahead – which meant he could not be far from the House of the Popidii, it should be on this very street. Off to his left was a big building, its roof gone, a fire burning somewhere inside it, lighting behind the windows the giant, bearded face of the god Bacchus – a theatre, was it? To his right were the stumpy shapes of houses, like a row of ground-down teeth, only a few feet of wall left visible. He swayed towards them. Torches were moving. A few fires had been lit. People were digging frantically, some with planks of wood, a few with their bare hands. Others were calling out names, dragging out boxes, carpets, pieces of broken furniture. An old woman screaming hysterically. Two men fighting over something – he could not see what – another trying to run with a marble bust cradled in his arms.

He saw a team of horses, frozen in mid-gallop, swooping out of the gloom above his head, and he stared at them stupidly for a moment until he realised it was the equestrian monument at the big crossroads. He went back down the hill again, past what he remembered was a bakery and at last, very faintly on a wall, at knee-height, he found an inscription: 'HIS NEIGHBOURS URGE THE ELECTION OF LUCIUS POPIDIUS SECUNDUS AS AEDILE. HE WILL PROVE WORTHY.'

He managed to squeeze through a window on one of the side streets and picked his way among the rubble, calling her name. There was no sign of life.

It was still possible to work out the arrangement of the two houses by the walls of the upper stories. The roof of the atrium had collapsed, but the flat space next to it must have been where the swimming pool was and over there must have been a second courtyard. He poked his head into some of the rooms of what had once been the upper floor. Dimly he could make out broken pieces of furniture, smashed crockery, scraps of hanging drapery. Even where the roofs had been sloping they had given way under the onslaught of stone. Drifts of pumice were mixed with terracotta tiles, bricks, splintered beams. He found an empty bird cage on what must have been a balcony and stepped through into an abandoned bedroom, open to the sky. Obviously it had been a young woman's room: abandoned jewellery, a comb, a broken mirror. In the filthy half-light, a doll, partly buried in the remains of the roof, looked grotesquely like a dead child. He lifted what he thought was a blanket from the bed and saw that it was a cloak. He tried the door – locked – then sat on the bed and examined the cloak more closely.

He had never had much of an eye for what women wore. Sabina used to say that she could have dressed in rags and he would never have noticed. But this, he was sure, was Corelia's. Popidius had said she had been locked in her room and this was a woman's bedroom. There was no sign of a body, either here or outside. For the first time he dared to hope she had escaped. But when? And to where?

He turned the cloak over in his hands and tried to think what Ampliatus would have done. *'He wanted to imprison us all'* – Popidius's phrase. Presumably he had blocked all the exits and ordered everyone to sit it out. But there must have come a moment, towards evening, as the roofs began to collapse, when even Ampliatus would have recognised that the old house was a death-trap. He was not the type to wait around and die without a fight. He would not have fled the city, though: that would not have been in character, and besides, by then it would have been impossible to travel very far. No: he would have tried to lead his family to a safe location.

Attilius raised Corelia's cloak to his face and inhaled her scent. Perhaps she would have tried to get away from her father. She hated him enough. But he would never have let her go. He imagined they must have organised a procession, very like the one from Pomponianus's villa at Stabiae. Pillows or blankets tied around their heads. Torches to provide a little light. Out into the hail of rock. And then – where? Where was safe? He tried to think as an engineer. What kind of roof was strong enough to withstand the stresses imposed by eight feet of pumice? Nothing flat, that was for sure. Something built with modern methods. A dome would be ideal. But where was there a modern dome in Pompeii?

He dropped the cloak and stumbled back on to the balcony.

Hundreds of people were out in the streets now, milling around at roof-level in the semi-darkness, like ants whose nest had been kicked to pieces. Some were aimless – lost, bewildered, demented with grief. He saw a man calmly removing his clothes and folding them as if preparing for a swim. Others appeared purposeful, pursuing their own private schemes of search or escape. Thieves – or perhaps they were the rightful owners: who could tell any more? – darted into the alleyways with whatever they could carry. Worst of all were the names called plaintively in the darkness. Had anyone seen Felicio or Pherusa, or Verus, or Appuleia – the wife of Narcissus? – or Specula or the lawyer Terentius Neo? Parents had become separated from their children. Children stood screaming outside the ruins of houses. Torches flared towards Attilius in the hope that he might be someone else – a father, a husband, a brother. He waved them away, shrugging off their questions, intent on counting off the city blocks as he passed them, climbing the hill north towards the Vesuvius Gate – one, two, three: each seemed to take an age to come to an end and all he could hope was that his memory had not let him down.

At least a hundred fires were burning on the south side of the mountain, spread out in a complex constellation, hanging low in the sky. Attilius had learned to distinguish between Vesuvius's flames. These ones were safe: the after-effects of a trauma that had passed. It was the prospect of another incandescent cloud appearing above them on the crest of the mountain that filled him with dread and made him push his aching legs beyond the point of exhaustion as he waded through the shattered city.

At the corner of the fourth block he found the row of shops, three-quarters buried, and scrambled up the slope of pumice on to the low roof. He crouched just behind the ridge. Its outline was sharp. There must be fires beyond it. Slowly he raised his head. Across the flat surface of the buried builder's yard were the nine high windows of Ampliatus's baths, each one brilliantly – defiantly – lit by torches and by scores of oil-lamps. He could see some of the painted gods on the far walls and the figures of men moving in front of them. All that was lacking was music: then it would have looked as though a party were in progress.

Attilius slithered down into the enclosed space and set off across it. Such was the intensity of the illumination he cast a shadow. As he came closer he saw that the figures were slaves and that they were clearing the drifts of pumice where they had been blown into the three big chambers – the changing room, the tepidarium and the caldarium – digging it out like snow with wooden shovels where it was deepest, or elsewhere merely sweeping it away with brooms. Patrolling behind them was Ampliatus, shouting that they should work harder, occasionally grabbing a shovel or a brush himself and showing how it should be done, before resuming his obsessive pacing. Attilius stood watching for a few moments, hidden in the darkness, and then cautiously began to climb towards the middle room – the tepidarium – at the back of which he could see the entrance to the domed sweating-chamber.

There was no chance he could enter without being seen so in the end he simply walked in – waded across the surface of the pumice, straight through the open window, his feet crunching on the tiled floor, the slaves staring at him in amazement. He was halfway to the sweating room when Ampliatus saw him – 'Aquarius!' – and hurried to intercept him. He was smiling, his palms spread wide. 'Aquarius! I've been expecting you!'

He had a cut in his temple and the hair on the left side of his scalp was stiff with blood. His cheeks were scratched and more blood had seeped through the coating of dust, carving red furrows in the white. The mouth was turned up at the corners: a mask of comedy. The dazzling light was reflected in his eyes, which were open very wide. Before Attilius could say anything he started talking again. 'We must get the aqueduct running immediately. Everything is ready, you see. Nothing is damaged. We could open for business tomorrow, if only we could connect the water.' He was talking very quickly, the words tumbling out of him, barely finishing one sentence before he went on to the next. So much in his head to express! He could see it all! 'People will need one place in the town that works. They'll need to bathe – it'll be dirty work, getting everything back in order. But it's not just that. It'll be a symbol to gather round. If they see the baths are working, it will give them confidence. Confidence is the key to everything. The key to confidence is water. Water is everything, d'you see? I need you, aquarius. Fifty-fifty. What do you say?'

'Where's Corelia?'

'Corelia?' Ampliatus's eyes were still alert for a potential deal. 'You want Corelia? In exchange for the water?'

'Perhaps.'

'A marriage? I'm willing to consider it.' He jerked his thumb. 'She's in there. But I'll want my lawyers to draw up terms.'

Attilius turned away and strode through the narrow entrance into the laconium. Seated on the stone benches around the small domed sweating room, lit by the torches in their iron holders on the wall, were Corelia, her mother and her brother. Opposite them were the steward, Scutarius, and the giant gatekeeper, Massavo. A second exit led to the caldarium. As the engineer came in, Corelia looked up.

'We need to leave,' he said. 'Hurry. Everyone.'

Ampliatus, at his back, blocked the door. 'Oh no,' he said. 'Nobody leaves. We've endured the worst. This isn't the time to run. Remember the prophecy of the sibyl.'

Attilius ignored him, directing his words to Corelia. She seemed paralysed with shock. 'Listen. The falling rock is not the main danger. It's when the fall stops that winds of fire travel down the mountain. I've seen them. Everything in their path is destroyed.'

'No, no. We're safer here than anywhere,' insisted Ampliatus. 'Believe me. The walls are three feet thick.'

'Safe from heat in a sweating room?' Attilius appealed to them all. 'Don't listen to him. If the hot cloud comes, this place will cook you like an oven. Corelia.' He held out his hand to her. She glanced quickly towards Massavo. They were under guard, Attilius realised: the laconium was their prison cell.

'Nobody is leaving,' repeated Ampliatus. 'Massavo!'

Attilius seized Corelia's wrist and tried to drag her towards the caldarium before Massavo had time to stop him, but the big man was too fast. He sprang to cover the exit and when Attilius attempted to shoulder him aside Massavo grabbed him by the throat with his forearm and dragged him back into the room. Attilius let go of Corelia and struggled to prise away the grip from his windpipe. Normally he could look after himself in a fight but not against an opponent of this size, not when his body was exhausted. He heard Ampliatus order Massavo to break his neck – 'Break it like the chicken he is!' – and then there was a whoosh of flame close to his ear and a scream of pain from Massavo. The arm released him. He saw Corelia with a torch clenched in both hands and Massavo on his knees. Ampliatus called her name, and there was something almost pleading in the way he said it, stretching out his hands to her. She whirled round, the fire streaking, and hurled the torch at her father, and then she was through the door and into the caldarium, shouting to Attilius to follow.

He blundered after her, down the tunnel and into the brightness of the hot room, across the immaculately cleaned floor, past the slaves, out through the window, into the darkness, sinking into the stones. When they were halfway across the yard he looked back and he thought perhaps that her father had given up – he could see no signs of pursuit at first – but of course, in his madness, Ampliatus had not: he never would.

330

The unmistakable bulk of Massavo appeared in the window with his master beside him and the light of the window quickly fragmented as torches were passed out to the slaves. A dozen men armed with brooms and shovels jumped out of the caldarium and began fanning out across the ground.

It seemed to take an age of slipping and sliding to clamber back up on to the perimeter roof and drop down into the street. For an instant they must have been dimly visible on the roof – long enough, at least, for one of the slaves to see them and shout a warning. Attilius felt a sharp pain in his ankle as he landed. He took Corelia's arm and limped a little way further up the hill and then they both drew back into the shadow of the wall as the torches of Ampliatus's men appeared in the road behind them. Their line of escape to the Stabian Gate was cut off.

He thought then that it was hopeless. They were trapped between two sets of fire – the flames of the torches and the flames on Vesuvius – and even as he looked wildly from one to the other he detected a faint gleam beginning to form in the same place high up on the mountain as before, where the surges had been born. An idea came to him in his desperation – absurd: he dismissed it – but it would not go away, and suddenly he wondered if it had not been in the back of his mind all along. What had he done, after all, except head towards Vesuvius while everyone else had either stayed put or run away – first along the coastal road from Stabiae to Pompeii, and then up the hill from the south of the city towards the north? Perhaps it had been waiting for him from the start: his destiny.

He peered towards the mountain. No doubt about it. The worm of light was growing. He whispered to Corelia, 'Can you run?'

'Yes.'

'Then run as you've never run before.'

They edged out from the cover of the wall. Ampliatus's men had their backs to them and were staring into the murk towards the Stabian Gate. He heard Ampliatus issuing more orders – 'You two take the side-street, you three down the hill' – and then there was nothing for it but to start thrashing their way through the pumice again. He had to grind his teeth against the agony in his leg and she was quicker than he was, as she had been when she had darted up the hill in Misenum, her skirts all gathered in one hand around her thighs, her long pale legs flashing in the dark. He stumbled after her, aware of fresh shouting from Ampliatus – 'There they go! Follow me!' – but when they reached the end of the block and he risked a glance over his shoulder he could only see one torch swaying after them. 'Cowards!' Ampliatus was shrieking. 'What are you afraid of?'

But it was obvious what had made them mutiny. The wave of fire was unmistakably sweeping down Vesuvius, growing by the instant, not in height but in breadth – roiling, gaseous, hotter than flame: white hot – only a madman would run towards it. Even Massavo would not follow his master now. People were abandoning their futile attempts to dig out their belongings and staggering down the hillside to escape it. Attilius felt the heat on his face. The scorching wind raised whirls of ash and debris. Corelia looked back at him but he urged her forward – against all instinct, against all sense, towards the mountain. They had passed another city block. There was only one to go. Ahead the glowing sky outlined the Vesuvius Gate.

'Wait!' Ampliatus shouted. 'Corelia!' But his voice was fainter, he was falling behind.

Attilius reached the corner of the castellum aquae with his head lowered into the stinging wind, half-blinded by the dust, and pulled Corelia after him, down the narrow alley. Pumice had almost completely buried the door. Only a narrow triangle of wood was showing. He kicked it, hard, and at the third attempt, the lock gave way and pumice poured through the opening. He pushed her in and slid down after her into the pitch darkness. He could hear the water, groped towards it, felt the edge of the tank and clambered over it, up to his waist in water, pulled her after him, and fumbled around the edges of the mesh screen for the fastenings, found them, lifted away the grille. He steered Corelia into the mouth of the tunnel and squeezed in after her.

'Move. As far up as you can go.'

A roaring, like an avalanche. She could not have heard him. He could not hear himself. But she scrambled forward instinctively. He followed, putting his hands on her waist and squeezing hard, pressing her down to her knees, so that as much of her body should be immersed as possible. He threw himself upon her. They clung to one another in the water. And then there was only scalding heat and the stench of sulphur in the darkness of the aqueduct, directly beneath the city walls.

Hora altera

'The human body cannot survive being in temperatures over 200 degrees centigrade for more than a few moments, especially in the fast moving current of a surge. Trying to breathe in the dense cloud of hot ash in the absence of oxygen would lead to unconsciousness in a few breaths, as well as causing severe burns to the respiratory tract . . . On the other hand, survival is possible in the more distal parts of a surge if there is adequate shelter to protect against the surge flow and its high temperature, as well as the missiles (rocks, building materials) entrained in the moving cloud of material.'

Encylopaedia of Volcanoes

An incandescent sandstorm raced down the hill towards Ampliatus. Exposed walls sheared, roofs exploded, tiles and bricks, beams and stones and bodies flew at him and yet so slowly, as it seemed to him in that long moment before his death, that he could see them turning against the brilliance. And then the blast hit him, burst his ear drums, ignited his hair, blew his clothes and shoes off, and whirled him upside down, slamming him against the side of a building.

He died in the instant it took the surge to reach the baths and shoot through the open windows, choking his wife who, obeying orders to the last, had remained in her place in the sweating room. It caught his son, who had broken free and was trying to reach the Temple of Isis. It lifted him off his feet, and then it overwhelmed the steward and the porter, Massavo, who were running down the street towards the Stabian Gate. It passed over the brothel, where the owner, Africanus, had returned to retrieve his takings, and where Zmyrina was hiding under Exomnius's bed. It killed Brebix, who had gone to the gladiators' school at the start of the eruption to be with his former comrades, and Musa and Corvinus, who had decided to stay with him, trusting to his local knowledge for protection. It even killed the faithful Polites, who had been sheltering in the harbour and who went back into the town to see if he could help Corelia. It killed more than two thousand in less than half a minute and it left their bodies arranged in a series of grotesque tableaux for posterity to gawp at.

For although their hair and clothes burned briefly, these fires were quickly snuffed out by the lack of oxygen, and instead a muffling, six-foot tide of fine ash, travelling in the wake of the surge, flowed over the city, shrouding the landscape and moulding every detail of its fallen victims. This ash hardened. More pumice fell. In their snug cavities the bodies rotted, and with them, as the centuries passed, the memory that there had even been a city on this spot. Pompeii became a town of perfectly shaped hollow citizens – huddled together or lonely, their clothes blown off or lifted over their heads, grasping hopelessly for their favourite possessions or clutching nothing – vacuums suspended in mid-air at the level of their roofs.

*　*　*

At Stabiae, the wind from the surge caught the makeshift shelter of the *Minerva*'s sail and lifted it clear of the beach. The people, exposed, could see the glowing cloud rolling over Pompeii and heading straight towards them.

Everyone ran, Pomponianus and Popidius in the lead.

They would have taken Pliny with them. Torquatus and Alexion had him by the arms and had raised him to his feet. But the admiral was finished with moving and when he told them, brusquely, to leave him and to save themselves, they knew he meant it. Alexion gathered up his notes and repeated his promise to deliver them to the old man's nephew. Torquatus saluted. And then Pliny was alone.

He had done all he could. He had timed the manifestation in all its stages. He had described its phases – column, cloud, storm, fire – and had exhausted his vocabulary in the process. He had lived a long life, had seen many things and now Nature had granted him this last insight into Her power. In these closing moments of his existence he continued to observe as keenly as he had when young – and what greater blessing could a man ask for than that?

The line of light was very bright and yet filled with flickering shadows. What did they mean? He was still curious.

Men mistook measurement for understanding. And they always had to put themselves at the centre of everything. That was their greatest conceit. The earth is becoming warmer – it must be our fault! The mountain is destroying us – we have not propitiated the gods! It rains too much, it rains too little – a comfort to think that these things are somehow connected to our behaviour, that if only we lived a little better, a little more frugally, our virtue would be rewarded. But here was Nature, sweeping toward him – unknowable, all-conquering, indifferent – and he saw in Her fires the futility of human pretensions.

It was hard to breathe, or even to stand in the wind. The air was full of ash and grit and a terrible brilliance. He was choking, the pain across his chest was an iron band. He staggered backward.

Face it, don't give in.

Face it, like a Roman.

The tide engulfed him.

For the rest of the day, the eruption continued, with fresh surges and loud explosions that rocked the ground. Towards the evening its force subsided and it started to rain. The water put out the fires and washed the ash from the air and drenched the drifting grey landscape of low dunes and hollows that had obliterated the fertile Pompeiian plain and the beautiful coast from Herculaneum to Stabiae. It filled the wells and replenished the springs and created the lines of new streams, meandering down towards the sea. The River Sarnus took a different course entirely.

As the air cleared, Vesuvius reappeared, but its shape was completely altered. It no longer rose to a peak but to a hollow, as if a giant bite had been taken from its summit. A huge moon, reddened by dust, rose over an altered world.

Pliny's body was recovered from the beach – 'he looked more asleep than dead', according to his nephew – and carried back to Misenum, along with his observations. These subsequently proved so accurate that a new word entered the language of science: 'Plinian', to describe 'a volcanic eruption in which a narrow blast of gas is ejected with great violence from a central vent to a height of several miles before it expands sideways'.

The Aqua Augusta continued to flow, as she would for centuries to come.

People who had fled from their homes on the eastern edges of the mountain began to make a cautious return before nightfall and many were the stories and rumours that circulated in the days that followed. A woman was said to have given birth to a baby made entirely of stone, and it was also observed that rocks had come to life and assumed human form. A plantation of trees that had been on one side of the road to Nola crossed to the other and bore a crop of mysterious green fruit which was said to cure every affliction, from worms to baldness.

Miraculous, too, were the tales of survival. A blind slave was said to have found his way out of Pompeii and to have buried himself inside the belly of a dead horse on the highway to Stabiae, in that way escaping the heat and the rocks. Two beautiful, blond children – twins – were found wandering, unharmed, in robes of gold, without a graze on their bodies, and yet unable to speak: they were sent to Rome and taken into the household of the Emperor.

Most persistent of all was the legend of a man and a woman who had emerged out of the earth itself at dusk on the day the eruption ended. They had tunnelled underground like moles, it was said, for several miles, all the way from Pompeii, and had come up where the ground was clear, drenched in the life-giving waters of a subterranean river, whch had given them its sacred protection. They were reported to have been seen walking together in the direction of the coast, even as the sun fell over the shattered outline of Vesuvius and the familiar evening breeze from Capri stirred the rolling dunes of ash.

But this particular story was generally considered far-fetched and was dismissed as a superstition by all sensible people.

Acknowledgements

*'I have prefaced these volumes with the names of my
authorities. I have done so because it is, in my opinion, a
pleasant thing and one that shows an honourable
modesty, to own up to those who were the means of one's
achievements . . .'*

Pliny, Natural History, *Preface.*

I 'm afraid I cannot claim, as Pliny did, to have consulted
2,000 volumes in the course of my researches.
Nevertheless, this novel could not have been written
without the scholarship of many others and, like Pliny, I believe
it would be 'a pleasant thing' – for me, at least, if not necessarily for them – to list some of my sources.

In addition to those works on volcanology cited in the
text, I would like to acknowledge my debt to Jean-Pierre
Adam *(Roman Building)*, Carlin A. Barton *(Roman Honor)*,
Mary Beagon *(Roman Nature)*, Marcel Brion *(Pompeii and
Herculaneum)*, Lionel Casson *(The Ancient Mariners)*, John
D'Arms *(Romans on the Bay of Naples)*, Joseph Jay Deiss
(Herculaneum), George Hauck *(The Aqueduct of Nemausus)*,
John F. Healy *(Pliny the Elder on Science and Technology)*,
James Higginbotham *(Piscinae)*, A. Trevor Hodge *(Roman
Aqueducts & Water Supply)*, Wilhelmina Feemster Jashemski

(The Gardens of Pompeii), Willem Jongman *(The Economy and Society of Pompeii)*, Ray Laurence *(Roman Pompeii)*, Amedeo Maiuri *(Pompeii)*, August Mau *(Pompeii: Its Life and Art)*, David Moore *(The Roman Pantheon)*, Salvatore Nappo *(Pompeii: Guide to the Lost City)*, L. Richardson, Jr *(Pompeii: An Architectural History)*, Chester G. Starr *(The Roman Imperial Navy)*, Antonio Varone *(Pompei, i misteri di una città sepolta)*, Andrew Wallace-Hadrill *(Houses and Society in Pompeii and Herculaneum)* and Paul Zanker *(Pompeii: Public and Private Life)*.

The translations of Pliny, Seneca and Strabo are mostly drawn from the editions of their work published by the Loeb Classical Library. I made much use of the edition of Vitruvius's *Ten Books on Architecture* edited by Ingrid D. Rowland and Thomas Noble Howe. The *Barrington Atlas of the Greek and Roman World*, edited by Richard J. A. Talbert, helped bring Campania to life. The volcanological analysis of the eruption by Haraldur Sigurdsson, Stanford Cashdollar and Stephen R. J. Sparks in *The American Journal of Archaeology* (86: 39–51) was invaluable.

I had the great pleasure of discussing the Romans on the Bay of Naples with John D'Arms, over dinner with his family in a suitably sweltering English garden, just before his death; I shall always remember his kindness and encouragement. Professor A. Trevor Hodge, whose pioneering work on the Roman aqueducts was crucial in visualising the Aqua Augusta, helpfully answered my inquiries. Professor Jasper Griffin's support enabled me to use the library of the Ashmolean Museum in Oxford. Dr Mary Beard, Fellow of Newnham College, Cambridge, read the manuscript before publication, and made many invaluable suggestions.

To all these scholars, I offer my thanks, and also the protection offered by that familiar rubric: the errors, misinterpretations and sheer liberties with the facts contained in the text are solely the responsibility of the author.

Robert Harris,
Kintbury, June 2003